'George Monteith.' The other held out his hand. 'Welcome to Seileach,' he said pleasantly. 'Will you be staying here long?'

'That depends a bit on whether the landlord can let me have a room for a few days,' said Jack cautiously. He wanted to create the impression that he had come upon the place by chance and had no definite plans.

'Delighted to have you,' said Martin. 'As soon as I've dealt with His Lordship's order, I'll call my wife and get her to show you the rooms.'

Jack made no sign that he had registered the reference to the Marquis's status. So this was the man who owned most of the property that Milton was interested in acquiring. When Ruth Crane appeared a few moments later, Jack thanked his new friends for their helpful suggestions, ordered a fresh glass of beer for Baldy and followed the landlady's comfortably rounded figure into the main body of the hotel.

Also by Mary Withall

Beacon On The Shore
The Gorse In Bloom
Where the Wild Thyme Grows
Fields of Heather
The Poppy Orchard

The Flight of the Cormorants

Mary Withall

CORONET BOOKS

Hodder & Stoughton

First published in Great Britain in 2000
by Hodder and Stoughton
First published in paperback in 2001
by Hodder and Stoughton
A division of Hodder Headline

A Coronet Paperback

10 9 8 7 6 5 4 3 2 1

ISBN 0 340 74872 9

Printed and bound in Great Britain by
Mackays of Chatham PLC, Chatham, Kent

Hodder and Stoughton
A division of Hodder Headline
338 Euston Road
London NW1 3BH

To John Campbell QC, Mike Baldock and the team of expert witnesses who fought and won the battle which inspired this novel. The characters and the circumstances portrayed are fictitious but the sentiments expressed mirror the opinions of the majority of those who have forsaken the conventional for a simpler but more satisfying, way of life.

ACKNOWLEDGEMENTS

My thanks are due to Dr George Hannah BSc, MB, ChB, MRCGP for a clear insight into the trials and tribulations of present day rural medical practice, my agent David Grossman and the editors and publishers who have steered me through the production of this and all my previous books.

Chapter One

The helicopter flew in low over the island, shattering the peace of a quiet August afternoon. Slicing through still air, it created its own whirlwinds, flattening ocean waves, and tearing up the heathers and grasses which clung doggedly to a two-hundred-foot high ridge of volcanic rock. It topped the ridge and slid down towards more level ground on the far side, the shadows of its rotor blades casting dark moving patterns across the weathered slates and neatly mown lawns of a conservation village. Identical white cottages arranged in orderly rows surrounded a harbour in which boats rode at anchor or lay upturned on the turf alongside a substantial wall of slate rocks.

'Eisdalsa Island,' the pilot announced. 'Used to be a source of roofing slates . . . the cottages were built to house the quarrymen and their families. Those great lakes were the quarries, disused now of course and filled with a combination of seawater and rainwater.' He indicated a number of these, two to the south and several more around the north-western shore of the island.

The pilot caused his machine to swerve up and away to

the south-east and once again they were over the sea, blinded by the sun reflected from the wave tops. To every side islands similar to the one they had just crossed rose out of the water, their triangular outlines fringed by waves breaking along the shores.

Milton T. Humbert sighed with pleasure. He loved islands; delighted in a landscape which fell into the sea skirted by a froth of white foam along a rocky shore; rejoiced to see a swathe of white beach dividing greensward from blue ocean.

'Gee, that is a sight to gladden the heart of any man!' he declared and the pilot nodded in agreement.

'You've certainly arrived on the right day, sir. Last week it was nothing like this.'

Milton had been surprised at the smooth Oxford English accent of the pilot. He had somehow expected everyone he encountered on arriving at Glasgow airport to have the broad Scottish tones of those men he had met around the globe, many of who had originated here in Argyll. He refrained from expressing his disappointment, however. Time enough to wallow in the Scottishness of the place once he had settled in at the castle.

Milton was not a snob but he enjoyed the little luxuries in life. A whole month in the shooting season on a Scottish estate was something he had promised himself for many a long year. On several occasions in the past he had planned just such a trip as this, only to be prevented by urgent business at the last moment. Now he had established his interests around the globe to such an extent that he had been compelled to delegate responsibility to others. To a team, in fact, of eager young men and women, only too happy to work twenty-six hours a day and eight days a week on his behalf. At last he felt free to indulge himself in his childhood passion for hunting.

His boyhood had been spent in the Appalachian Mountains where he had been taught to hunt squirrel, hare, rabbit and chipmunk and later bear and moose, by a full-blooded North American Indian. He had been a good shot even when his only weapon was a small air rifle. Absently he patted the leather case propped beside him. Inside it rested the Purdeys which had been his first major indulgence once his fortunes had taken a turn for the better in the 1960s. They had cost a king's ransom even in those days and were now worth a fortune. Although the guns had accompanied him on his travels all around the world, and although he had taken the opportunity to practise with them occasionally, he had until now never allowed himself the pleasure of using them in earnest.

Maggie had found the castle for him. She was good at that sort of thing.

> Situated on the island of Seileach in Argyll, Seileachan Castle has been the seat of the Marquises of Stirling since 1367. The castle offers exclusive accommodation, fishing and shooting in season during the months of August and September. Excellent, privately maintained grouse moors. Licensed to take a small quota of wild deer and goats. Game fishing along a three-mile stretch of private water.

Next to shooting, Milton's great passion was fishing. In his youth and under the tutorship of old Sam Twofeathers, he had graduated from the coarse fishing of his boyhood to fishing for trout and salmon in the fast-flowing mountain streams of his home state.

He stroked the case of rods stretched along the floor of the cabin and hummed softly to himself as the machine lost height, and hovered above an ugly granite structure of monstrous proportions. Seileachan Castle appeared to have been added to at different periods in history, each extension bearing little or no relationship to that which had gone before. Square towers and cone-shaped turrets hovered above crenellated battlements and sweeps of steeply angled, slated roof. The main building had over the centuries been extended to enclose a green expanse of lawn and it was upon this that the helicopter finally came to rest.

The rotors swung slowly to a stop and the pilot climbed down to assist his portly passenger. As Milton levered his 240-pound bulk through the undersized doorway, he glanced up to see a tractor approaching, towing a trailer. It was driven by a healthily bronzed young fellow clad only in a pair of twill shorts, the muscles of his well-developed torso rippling impressively as he leaped off and began manhandling luggage as it was pulled from the compartment by the pilot. His bushy flame-red hair merged at eye level with an equally ill-groomed beard. Milton could well believe the man to be a gillie (wasn't that what they called them?) and visualised him striding across the heather in kilt and plaid, his sporran banging against his knees.

The young fellow gave Milton a friendly nod in passing.

4

'Ye'll be looking for a fair amount of sport, I'm thinking,' he observed as he lifted the case of Purdeys with evident admiration. He placed the fishing rods carefully on top of the pile of cases and drew his vehicle out of range of the rotors before turning off the engine and returning to exchange a few words words with the pilot. In a few moments the latter returned to his seat in the helicopter and within seconds the engine roared into life again. Milton was obliged to step away to avoid the spinning blades.

With a cheerful wave, the pilot manoeuvred his machine into the air. He cleared the battlements and flew off. In the silence which followed his departure, the young man on the tractor restarted his two-stroke engine and with a friendly gesture towards the visitor, let in the gear.

'Just a moment,' Milton shouted to make himself heard above the noise of the motor. 'Where do I go?'

'Main door . . . over there.' The fellow waved vaguely in the direction of the west side of the quadrangle. 'Ye canna miss it!'

Further conversation was drowned by the loud puttering of the tractor's engine. The fellow drove off, leaving Milton sweating profusely under the noonday sun and regretting his decision to arrive for his initial encounter with Scottish aristocracy in the Harris tweed suit and flannel shirt which, so he had been advised by his London tailor, was the accepted uniform of the hunting fraternity.

As the portly American puffed and panted his way towards the main entrance to the castle, a young woman appeared from behind a border of flowering shrubs. She wiped her hands on her green cotton slacks and slipped the flower basket she was carrying into her left hand as she approached him.

'Mr Humbert, welcome to Seileachan Castle. I'm Cissy, George's wife.'

'George?' Milton was confused as well as hot and tired. He must have sounded a trifle querulous for instantly the woman changed her approach to something more formal.

'I'm so sorry, Lord George Monteith, Marquis of Stirling . . . your host . . .' she tailed off, hoping that the penny had finally dropped.

'Oh . . . how do you do . . . your ladyship?'

The poor man floundered, all the protocol he had been studying suddenly blown to the winds.

'To be absolutely correct,' she told him politely, 'you should address me as Lady Christina and George as my lord or Lord George, but I do assure you that "Cissy" and "George" will be more than adequate!'

'Well, in that case, my L— Cissy, you must call me Milton.'

Relieved that the sticky protocol had been resolved so easily, he set down his crocodile briefcase and mopped his brow with a red, spotted handkerchief.

'My goodness, you do look hot,' Cissy exclaimed. 'Shall we go inside and find something cool to drink?'

As they moved towards the main door, Milton relieved her of her flower basket, acutely aware that for the first time in many years he was enjoying playing the gallant to a charming woman.

'I think if you don't mind,' he told her, 'I will go and get into something more appropriate.' He gestured towards his tweeds and grinned sheepishly. 'Will my bags have been brought up to my room yet?'

'I'm sure they will be . . . by the time you have had a wash and so on.' She led him into the entrance hall, her metal-studded working boots ringing on the marble floor.

In the middle of the hall Milton stood stock still and gazed about him, awestruck. Stone pillars supported a fan-vaulted roof which soared above their heads to the full height of the building. Rich red and blue and green lights fell across the white marble from the Gothic stained glass windows to either side. A wide staircase swept to the upper floor, its stone treads covered by what must once have been a richly patterned Persian carpet, now threadbare and faded to a nondescript grey-blue.

Cissy took the basket from him and placed it on a side table.

'I'll take you straight up,' she said, leading the way.

On the first floor a well-proportioned gallery fronted the building. From the walls a row of steely-eyed, grim-faced gentlemen stared down at them.

'My husband's ancestors,' she explained. 'They all look very stern, don't they . . . all except this one. He's my favourite.'

She paused before the portrait of a portly, red-headed gentleman in the dress of the late-nineteenth century: stiff white collar, black cravat, frock coat and stove pipe trousers. In his hand he grasped a book, indicating, no doubt, a certain intellectual prowess. The face was pleas-ant, eyes lively, lips parted in a half-smile. Milton was sure he had seen these features somewhere recently but could not quite remember where. Behind the eyes there lurked a hint of sadness as though the artist had caught his subject in an unguarded moment when his outwardly cheerful countenance had betrayed his deeper feelings.

'Many say he was the noblest of all the Marquises,' Cissy told Milton. 'He was a great land owner with vast estates not only in Scotland but also in North America. He cared for the land despite his exploitation of its mineral resources, and treated his workforce in such a way that he was often accused, by less benevolent employers, of spoiling them.'

Milton examined the portrait with interest but made no comment. He was no judge of paintings and portraits generally left him cold. Being too polite to express this opinion, he remained silent. The painting was well executed and was pleasing enough, he supposed.

'The Fourth Marquis had a very tragic life,' Cissy continued. 'His wife died in childbirth and his only son died three years later after contracting measles.'

'Measles?' Milton tried to show some interest although the thought of a cool shower and a change of clothing was becoming pressing.

'A killer in those days,' Cissy explained. 'The local doctor was a clever man but even he was unable to save the child. The Marquis died a widower without any direct heir. His estate passed to a cousin who had little concern for either the land or the workers and allowed things to slip . . .'

This dull collection of long-dead aristocrats was enlivened by one single jewel of a painting. At the far end of the gallery hung a full-length portrait of a young woman, little more than a child. She was dressed in white silk and carried a bridal bouquet of white roses and heather.

'That is Jane, wife of the Fourth Marquis . . . the one who died so young. She has about her a look of eternal youth, don't you think? As though she was never meant to grow old.'

Milton felt it politic to appear affected both by the portrait itself and by the tragic story of the young Marchioness but fearing some terrible gaffe if he made any comment, he merely nodded silently and followed his hostess into the narrow corridor beyond. From this a number of doors opened into what were undoubtedly guest bedrooms. Cissy opened the second door on the right and ushered him in. The room was adequate, he supposed. He had been warned not to expect the standard of one of the plush suites offered by modern international hotels, but he could not disguise his dismay at the worn and faded appearance of the contents. The room was furnished in the grand style of the late-nineteenth century with heavy mahogany furniture and a large bed piled high with feather mattresses and bolsters. Milton was a stickler for the correct hardness in a mattress and his face fell when he saw it.

'I do hope you'll be comfortable here,' said his hostess, smiling disarmingly. He was powerless to deny it.

'I'll have your bags sent up right away,' Cissy told him, 'and that cold drink. Will lemonade do or would you prefer something stronger?'

'Lemonade will be fine, thank you.'

'Good. Luncheon will be served at one o'clock. You'll hear the gong.'

She was gone.

Left alone to investigate his surroundings he opened a heavy door to one side of the bed and found himself in a walk-in closet neatly fitted with drawers and hanging space. The Victorians obviously knew how to look after their clothes.

A similar door on the far side of the bed opened into a bathroom of quite outrageous proportions. The bath stood on a pedestal in the middle of the room, its feet ornately gilded lion's paws. Heavy brass taps and fittings completed the ensemble although, to his dismay, he could see no sign of a shower. Behind an elaborately carved wooden screen he discovered a WC whose porcelain bowl was decorated in the Chinese style of the 1880s. A wash hand basin, similarly decorated, stood alongside.

Milton let out a long, low whistle. He had attended a fair number of auction sales in recent years and he was well aware of the value of each of these fittings. Coupled with the paintings in the gallery, and Milton had recognised the names of some distinguished artists on those little brass plaques beneath them, he had to assume that the present Marquis was a very rich man. This being the case, how was it that he did not invest a little of his capital in repairs to the building?

Milton's business was real estate. In the early days he had bought and sold houses. Now he negotiated the purchase of large areas of land for development all around the globe. In the late-eighties he had been one of the first to realise the potential for providing holiday venues in obscure places where his company catered for every last need of the holidaymaker, so that there was no need for them to move outside the confines of the resort and little incentive to do so. He was quick to capitalise on the need for third-world countries to become involved in tourism, and bought land while it was cheap on the promise of employing local people and encouraging native crafts-men. It took most of these countries some years before they realised that, apart from a certain amount of employ-ment of nationals in the more menial tasks, the majority of the work was done by European and American staff.

But for Milton, the excitement and adventure had gone out of his business dealings during the 1980s when Elizabeth, his partner of twenty-five years, died of breast cancer. His daughters had taken up the reins on his behalf, both marrying shrewdly and profitably. Brought up in an atmosphere where money was paramount, they had seen nothing wrong in marrying with an eye to busi-ness. Their matches had been loudly applauded by Milton himself and even after all these years he still found it hard to understand why Elizabeth had been so disappointed in their choice of husbands.

But the construction business had been his first love and he still retained that old instinct for a structure in need of care and attention. He had a habit of making an assessment of any building the moment he entered it, and a natural instinct for detecting neglect. The moment he'd stepped into that magnificent entrance hall down below, he had realised that there was a deal of work to be done here. Crumbling cornices, tell-tale heaps of wood dust in corners where beetle had been active, split door panels, chipped paintwork, all cried out for attention.

He returned to the main bedroom and crossed to the window. His room faced away from the quadrangle so that he had sweeping views across green parkland to the gorse and heather-covered hills beyond. To his left was the inlet dividing the island of Seileach from the mainland, the seaway which had guided the helicopter pilot to his landing pad. Milton's gaze followed the narrow ribbon of water westwards to where it opened into a wide bay, a natural harbour for the vessels of every kind anchored there.

A sharp tap on the door caused him to turn around as the red-headed tractor driver, a shirt now covering his tanned torso, placed Milton's luggage, one piece after another, inside the door. When he had finished, he wiped his hands on his shorts and stepped forward, hand outstretched.

'Sorry our first meeting was a bit informal,' he said. 'I was rather pushed, d'ye see, with m'man being away an' all.'

'I'm sorry, I don't . . .' Milton was unaccustomed to being addressed thus by bell hops or any other kind of servant for that matter and did not know how to respond.

'I'm George Monteith . . . you met Cissy, my wife, earlier.'

He shook Milton vigorously by the hand. The American responded automatically while at the same time wearing a look of such utter bewilderment that George Monteith laughed heartily.

'Why, mon, d'ye no' recognise a Scottish peer when y'meet one!'

'Excuse me, my lord!' said Milton, recovering his senses sufficiently to remember the correct form of address.

'What did ye expect, man?' demanded the other. 'A crimson robe and a coronet?'

'Well, no, not exactly . . .'

For once in his life Milton T. Humbert was lost for words.

'Look, let's forget the title and all that,' said George good-naturedly, tiring of the joke at last. 'Just call me George and, with your permission, I'll address you as Milton, if that's OK?'

He nodded, observing that, now the game was over, George's manner of speech shared the same polished tones as the helicopter pilot had used.

'That's fine by me, George.'

Milton allowed the handful of coins he had been fingering to slip back into his pocket. He had been prepared to give the bell hop a tip. Thank God he had not gone so far as to offer anything to his lordship!

'I wondered if any of you might like to experience a touch of local colour?' George offered, as his guests passed the vintage port between them for the third time. Not only could these well-heeled gentlemen eat like gannets, they insisted on accompanying Cissy's excellent food with only the very best which the castle's cellars could supply. The Marquis smiled to himself to think what his dear old father would have thought of the exorbitant prices he now charged for wines laid down for his own personal use. They had been a major investment in the 1950s when George was christened and he was gratified to think that he had profited so hugely from his father's far-sighted gift.

'If you will excuse me,' the little Swiss banker felt in his top pocket for his mobile phone, 'I have some important calls to make this evening . . . another time, perhaps.' He rose to go and was instantly joined by the two Germans who, having eaten and drunk liberally, were bound for the lounge and a long, leisurely cigar before bed. Only Milton and the French Canadian fellow, Pierre d' Orsay, took up George's offer.

'We'll take the four-wheel drive,' His Lordship decided. 'It looked like rain earlier and the farm track gets quite boggy in the wet.'

Despite the lateness of the hour, it was still light when the Range Rover pulled across a cattle grid and mounted the steep slope to the hotel car park. The two visitors jumped out. Already, after only three days of walking and climbing across the rocky hillsides, Milton was feeling fitter and more lithe than he had for years. He landed on the gravel path with a springy step and wondered what Maggie would say if she could see him do so. D'Orsay came and stood beside him to take in the scene. The Canadian was a quiet person with little to say but when he did speak his words hit the mark, every time.

'*C'est magnifique!*' he breathed, and took a deep breath of the salt-laden air.

The sun was descending in the western sky like a huge ball of fire, its rays catching the formation of stratocirrus which streaked red and yellow across the vault of the heavens. This richness of colour was emphasised by

14

the lightest of blue skies and deep purple-black shadows on the undersides of the clouds. In the distance a jagged black line of mountains marked the southern extremity of the Isle of Mull while the waters between were dotted with islands. Some of these were no more than a piece of angled rock pointing upward from the ocean bed, others were larger, some even showing evidence of ancient habitation, but all displayed the same triangular silhouette against the evening sky. In the foreground, perhaps five hundred yards offshore, lay another island, larger than the rest, but much of it little more than a few feet above sea level. A single hillock, some two hundred feet at its highest point, stretched from end to end like the spine of a giant lizard. At first sight the island seemed deserted, but in the fading light cottages grouped about a narrow inlet began to spring into life as one after another their lights were switched on.

'What name has that island?' demanded d'Orsay when they had been joined by the Marquis.

'We call it Eisdalsa Island, but don't ask me to explain what the name means.'

'We flew over it the day I arrived,' Milton recalled. 'Didn't they mine slate from there or something?'

'These islands were first visited and presumably named by the Vikings,' George explained. 'They came here for the slate rock a thousand years ago and people have been quarrying it ever since. That hill over there is a granite dyke which was intruded into the slate beds during a period of volcanic activity on Mull. The slate has mostly been removed now and only the granite remains.'

'They took the whole top off the island?' Milton demanded, incredulously.

'Just about, but in more recent times the men quarried down below sea level . . . there are huge pits over there. Some go down a hundred and eighty feet. They're all filled with water now, of course, like large lakes. When the quarries were being worked pumps were kept operating day and night. It must have been pretty noisy in those days.'

Pierre, to whom the silence was a balm, shivered at the thought of its being broken by the constant sounds of machinery and sent up a small prayer that the place might remain as still and quiet as it was at this moment.

The bar was full, the air blue with tobacco smoke and loud conversation. The appearance of George Monteith brought forth a variety of greetings, cheerful, respectful or ribald according to the age and standing in the district of those present. The older men, born and bred in the parish, remembered the days when the old Marquis would ride through the village on horseback, his retrievers trotting alongside, and men stepped aside and doffed their caps in greeting as he passed. Those days were now long gone, and a good thing too in the eyes of most people. Incomers to the village, whose past histories remained a mystery until they chose to reveal them, assumed a status on a par with their aristocratic neighbour and paid him only that level of deference due to any other respected member of the community. So far as George was concerned, that was how he preferred it.

His companions stood back as he advanced to the bar

and ordered himself a pint. 'What'll it be, Milton?' he
enquired. 'Will you try one of our exclusive malt
whiskies or the McEwan's? There's not a great choice of
beer, I'm afraid . . . not on draught anyway.'

Milton, for whom beer always came out of stone-cold
bottles or cans, had no idea what he was talking about.
'I'll take some of that,' he pointed to a bottle of
Bruichladdich on the optic, 'on the rocks!'

There was a sudden hush as all eyes turned on him.

'Hey, did I say something wrong?' he enquired
jovially.

'You do not take ice with the Islay malt,' said a softly
spoken Highland voice from somewhere behind his right
shoulder.

'I take ice with anything I like, bud,' Milton's assertive
response was automatic. 'On the rocks, landlord,' he
repeated.

Conversation resumed all about them but Milton was
aware of the vacuum he had created about himself by his
remark. The landlord, a canny Yorkshireman, filled a tall
glass with ice and covered it with a double measure of the
whisky. He served many Americans in his bar and knew
their tastes. Fortunately they usually called in at
lunchtimes or, in the evenings, ordered their drinks in the
hotel lounge so that the locals need not be offended by
their Philistine ways.

'Pierre?' George, ignoring his companion's gaff, now
turned to the Canadian.

'A beer would be good. Thank you.' Pierre was not a
great drinker and would have preferred wine any time to
warm beer but it would be sacrilege to follow George's

offerings of earlier in the evening with last year's vintage plonk, which was all that was available across the bar.

He received his drink and quickly fell into conversation with his neighbour whom George had introduced as Ewan McWorter, the local doctor. In his discussion with Ewan, Pierre discovered that they had a common interest in fly fishing. By the end of the evening he had arranged a private expedition to a favoured stream outside the parish and was very satisfied with his encounter.

Milton, brushing off his earlier faux-pas, turned now to the scruffy little man who occupied the stool at the end of the bar. He looked like a permanent fixture and must surely be a fount of local knowledge.

'This is an out of the way kind of place,' Milton observed, loudly. 'What on earth do all these guys do for a living around here?'

Baldy McGillivray stared into the bottom of his empty glass before answering. 'Well, now,' he drawled, 'I could give you a quick rundown on the people hereabouts but trying to speak against all this noise gives a man a dry throat . . .'

'Here, let me.' Milton took the empty glass and called for a refill.

'Ah, that's better.' Baldy took a long draught and wiped the froth from around his lips. 'Now then . . . where shall we start?'

'How about with yourself?'

'Me? Oh, I'm semi-retired,' he replied. 'Have been for a few years now.'

'Baldy here is the best drystone wall builder in the district,' George chipped in. 'You want a pit dug or a dyke built . . . he's your man!'

McGillivray did not deny it.

Taking up the recital from his noble companion he explained, 'Robbie there . . . he's master of the puffer and Jamie is skipper of the *Lass of Lunga*, the wee fishing boat down in the harbour.'

'Puffer?'

'A flat-bottomed cargo boat,' George explained, 'used for carrying coal and such things as timber and other building materials to the smaller isles. She has a flat bottom and can be grounded on the beach at low tide to discharge cargo. When the tide rises she floats off. It's a fine ship for places where there is no jetty.'

'It's a tragedy she has to be laid up after all these years.' A balding elderly gentleman, smartly turned out in tweeds and smoking a pipe, leaned forward and tapped burned ash into the ash tray in front of Milton. The American, with the distaste of one who has given up the weed after a lifetime of heavy smoking, waved his hand to dispel offensive fumes and turned to survey the speaker.

'Why should she be laid up?' he enquired.

'No further Government subsidy,' the older man explained. 'The islanders cannot afford to pay the increased freight charges which now have to be charged.'

'How do they get their supplies?'

'In the same way their fathers did, of course. They row a boat or sail across to the nearest island which has a jetty and receives regular visits from a McArdle's ferry.'

'So McArdle's have the monopoly, do they?'

19

'They do now!' The old man applied a match to the tobacco he had been packing in as he spoke. 'More's the pity. A little competition never did anyone any harm.'

Milton nodded in agreement and Baldy, anxious not to be excluded from the conversation, chipped in with, 'Bill there is a carpenter from England. He does general building work and makes stools for sale in his spare time. And Percy, well, he's a general handyman . . . if you want any odd jobs done around your house – grass cutting, painting – he's your man.'

'In a beautiful place like this I would have expected more people to be engaged in tourism,' observed Milton, warming to his favourite topic.

'Oh, we have our fair share of those,' declared Baldy. 'Mary McCulloch has a couple staying in her place just now and two cottages on the island have visitors living in them for the whole of August.'

'Most people around here do bed and breakfast in the summer months,' George added, 'and several of the cottages locally are let throughout the season.'

'How long does that last?'

'From April to October.'

'And that's the sum total of the local tourist industry, is it?' Milton could feel a familiar stirring of intense excitement as he weighed the obvious potential of this idyllic location against the difficulties of realising it.

'There's a couple of gift shops in the village and a tea room and bar on the island. The Post Office has a wee grocery shoppie attached and sometimes there's a chippy opens as well,' Baldy proudly listed the local amenities.

'So what happens for the rest of the year?'

'People live their own lives and do their own thing, I suppose,' replied George for whom the inquisition was becoming a trifle irritating. 'Excuse me a moment,' he said now, seeing a familiar face on the far side of the room. He left Milton to continue his conversation with Baldy.

George joined the group around the dartboard and elbowed his way through to join a handsome woman in her late-thirties or early-forties, who watched the process of the match avidly and cheered every good throw.

'Evening, Kirsty. May I buy you a drink?' he offered.

'Thanks, George,' she replied cheerfully, 'but this'll do me for the rest of the evening.' She pushed a straggling lock of chestnut-coloured hair out of her eyes and waved a half-full pint pot at him. 'Cissy not with you this evening?' she enquired.

'No . . . castle's full of house guests. She's been at it all day. I suggested she had an early night. They'll be up at dawn tomorrow champing on their bacon and eggs.'

'Eat well, do they?' she laughed.

'Voraciously. They blame the air here but I suspect it's just habit. It's like feeding the Circean swine! Milton – he's the American over by the bar – arrived with a list of unacceptable dishes as long as your arm, but when it comes to the crunch he can't refuse anything Cissy puts before him!'

'She should try cooking badly for a change,' Kirsty laughed.

'That would be asking the impossible. Anyway . . . it was the house guests I wanted to talk to you about.' He turned away from the observant drinkers surrounding

21

them and led her to a corner seat at the edge of the crowd.

'They'll have had their fill of the outdoor life, out on the moors from dawn to dusk, and then eating and drinking the evenings away up at the castle. I wondered if between us we could set up something by way of entertainment on the island towards the end of their stay? A *ceilidh* would be the thing . . . something that looks spontaneous, if you know what I mean. Perhaps one or two of the boys would turn out in their kilts and we could find a piper from somewhere? A few lines of Rabbie Burns and an eightsome reel should do the trick! I think my fat American friend was expecting me to be wearing the kilt and sporran when he arrived the other day. The reality was not nearly so impressive.'

'Why, what were you wearing?' Kirsty asked, eyes glinting and her mouth twisted into a wicked grin.

'A pair of filthy shorts and not much else!' he replied. She laughed so loudly that those around them turned to look.

'How would it be if I offered them a meal of Scotch broth and haggis with all the trimmings?' she suggested. 'Then we can rustle up a few of the islanders for the *ceilidh* afterwards. There's a late ferry Saturday . . . we might even get Angus to delay it if we get him involved. We haven't had a good shindig for a week or two, it's about time we had a party.'

George had known he could rely on Kirsty Brown to help him out. Since she had taken over the licence for the Eisdalsa Island bar there had been many a good evening and some quite profitable events. Because she was such an obliging woman herself, others responded to her ideas wholeheartedly. She was a good person to have on your side when you were planning any changes and George Monteith knew that there would have to be a few of those in the near future. If things did not improve soon, he was going to have to make some serious decisions about the future of the estate. There would be opposition, he knew, but change was inevitable and people would have to accept that.

Kirsty squeezed his hand affectionately. George had been good to her in the early days. When she had first arrived on the island, recently divorced and seeking an entirely new way of life, he had made her leasing of the pub a relatively painless procedure. He had waited patiently for her money when her house sale in Edinburgh had fallen through and had tackled the work she needed doing before she could move in at his own expense. If he needed help now, she was only too willing to go halfway to meet him.

'We'll make it a night for your rich clients to remember,' she promised.

He kissed her lightly on the cheek. 'Cissy suggested I should ask you,' he told her, 'she was sure you would help.' He had already spotted another person with whom he must have a word and darted away into the crowd. Kirsty turned back to the noisy group around the dartboard. Her team was winning and soon her shouts of encouragement to the island lads could clearly be heard above the general hubbub.

The darts match had reached a crucial point it seemed for suddenly the entire bar fell silent and even Baldy could not be persuaded to talk. Every eye was on the players at the board. One . . . two . . . three . . . the darts struck home to a roar of approval. The leg had been a victory to the visiting side and before the home team could wreak its revenge everyone must recharge their glasses. It was some minutes before the noise level reduced sufficiently for Milton to resume his enquiries.

'Doesn't anyone use the sea as a tourist attraction?' he demanded. 'Surely boating must be a major activity in a place like this?'

'Yes, you might think so.' Baldy pondered the question before answering. 'Well, you see', he began at last, 'the men hereabouts have been born and bred to it. They know what they are doing with the tides and so on. Strangers easily get into difficulties by taking boats out when the conditions aren't right. There are many boats tied up in the harbour that go out to sea no more than once or twice a year because their owners are unwilling to take a chance with the weather.'

'All the more reason for the local experts to cash in on the situation and offer pleasure trips.' Milton found such lack of enterprise extraordinary. The whole place needed a good shaking up.

'Most people find the wee ferry ride to the island exciting enough,' observed the elderly pipe smoker. 'Especially when the wind is in the north-west!'

'Know something about the sea, do you?' demanded Milton, who kept a yacht in the marina at Cannes and a second on Hamilton Island on the Great Barrier Reef.

'Just a bit.' Bill Douglas downed his third whisky of the night and removed his hat and cane from the rack. 'Goodnight to you, sir,' he said to Milton, 'I hope you enjoy the rest of your stay.' With a friendly nod to Baldy and a cheerful goodnight for the barman, he stepped out into the night. At that moment there was a roar of approval from the group around the dartboard as the final darts struck home and the party began to break up. Suddenly the bar emptied of all but a few stragglers. Milton looked to Baldy for an explanation.

'Where have they all gone so suddenly?' he demanded. He knew that in England there were licensing laws which demanded the pubs be closed at eleven but he had been given to understand that things were different here in Scotland.

'The visiting team was from over on the island this evening,' Baldy explained. 'The last ferry leaves at eleven . . . if they don't go now they'll have to swim home!'

'What if the game hadn't finished in time?' Milton asked.

'It always does,' was the reply, 'one way or another.'

'Surely someone could take them over in another boat?'

'Oh, yes, but it's safer to use the ferry, d'you see, when one has been having more than a few drinks of an evening.'

Even Milton was forced to accept the logic of that argument but he still could not understand people allowing their lives to be organised around the sailing times of a small boat. Why didn't they pay the ferryman extra to fetch them when they were ready?

On their drive back to the castle he expressed his opinion on the laid-back attitude of the local inhabitants.

'There seems to be a distinct lack of drive . . . an unwillingness to see the possibilities of the place. I'm surprised someone hasn't taken the entire area and turned it into a proper holiday haven. It's got everything . . . and nothing.'

'Maybe some people prefer it as it is,' observed Pierre, quietly. 'Not everyone appreciates an over-developed holiday resort.'

'Oh, come now,' Milton protested, 'tell that to the thousands upon thousands of people who take advantage of my holiday resorts around the world.'

'Maybe those who come here are looking for something different. They are forced to make an effort to reach the place. There must be something special that attracts them here.'

'Everyone likes a few creature comforts,' Milton insisted. 'It wouldn't take much to turn this into a great little resort.'

George, who had been only half concentrating on the conversation, was brought up short by his next remark.

'I reckon a good developer could take this place and make it into the best little money spinner on the coast.'

Chapter Two

Jack walked into the lift in the wake of the family from Toowoomba he had seen registering moments before at the reception desk.

'Oh, God, I can't look,' cried the woman, as the transparent, cigar-shaped elevator rose rapidly to the fourteenth floor. She turned her back on the panorama falling away beneath her feet but the children, two small boys of perhaps six or seven, squealed with delight as they pointed out miniature motor boats and sailing craft darting across a sparkling blue sea and mingling with the grander pleasure cruisers plying between the islands. Paragliders, their colourful canopies soaring above the waves, dotted the expanse of ocean with rainbow colours while water skiers cut a white swathe across the path of an incoming ferry.

The neat complex of buildings constituting the Kookaburra Resort was spread out on the lower slopes before the hotel tower and around the hillsides to the rear. It had the appearance of a town built from a box of children's building bricks. Pink, blue and green tiles had been chosen to cap the uniformly white buildings. To the uninformed eye the choice of colours was random but to Jack each roof defined the purpose of the building it covered and made his job of directing new staff around the complex, much easier.

Tiny vehicles, uniformly white, darted to and fro along tree-shaded white concrete roads, while the occasional Lilliputian holiday maker, on foot and scantily clad, made his way towards the beach in defiance of the searing noonday heat.

At this hour it would already be crowded with those who rose early to procure the chaise-longues and the picnic tables in the best positions. No matter how many of these were provided, there were always squabbles amongst the guests. Jack had almost convinced himself that the troop of wild kangaroos who loped around the gardens of the resort in the early morning and at dusk, helped themselves to the loungers and spirited them away to their own kangaroo resort in the hills.

The lift came to a halt and, as the doors opened, Jack placed one suitcase across the magic eye so that the father could extricate family and baggage before they closed on him.

'Good on yer, mate,' he said as he lifted the last of the cases and the doors closed.

'My pleasure.' Jack's reply was lost as the doors snapped to and the lift continued skywards. 'No trouble,' he told the empty air. Similar phrases tripped off his lips a hundred times a day.

On the twenty-second floor the doors opened again and he stepped out on to a vast carpeted concourse divided by transparent panels into a series of work stations. As he passed hurriedly between desks where a dozen computer screens flickered blue against the soft grey tones of carpet and matching furniture, heads turned and nodded, disembodied voices called out in greeting.

'What delights confront us this afternoon, Maggie?' he demanded as he took his seat behind the largest of all the desks, removed the colourful kookaburra tie which distinguished staff from guests and undid the first three buttons on his shirt to allow the cool breeze from the air conditioner to do its work.

'One rejected credit card, two complaints of rowdy behaviour in 2869 . . . again, and a party stranded on the island without a ferry. No one told them that Starline don't run a service on Sunday. By the time they had sorted something out about a passage on the Wombat Island cat', she'd already sailed.'

'What did Clancy do?'

'Sent them across by Cessna . . . they were so thrilled they paid half the fare themselves without complaint.'

'Whose fault was it?'

'Ours. The staff on the desk didn't spot the mistake and actually ordered a taxi to take them to a ferry that didn't exist!'

'We should have paid the lot.'

'No doubt . . . But we saved a hundred and seventy-five dollars this way.'

'If the travel agents get to hear about it, it could lose us clients,' Jack exclaimed fiercely. 'Next time we pay the lot, understand?'

'Yes, sir!' Maggie replied emphatically. The title sounded like an insult.

Maggie Turner had been working for the company since Milton Humbert had set up his first resort on the beach in Miami. She had seen a dozen Jack McDougals come and go over the years and the theory was that she ate Milton's young executives for breakfast!

She had only consented to come here to Queensland because she had never seen the Great Barrier Reef and was looking for a change from all the demanding, arrogant and overweight US citizens at play. Not only was she to discover that Australians, although often more good-natured, could be just as rowdy and self-indulgent as her fellow countrymen, but that Japanese holiday makers when outside their home territory appeared to shed their native reserve as a snake sloughs its skin, creating more havoc than all the Australians and Americans put together! A good example was the party in room 2869 who had kept up their celebrations until the early hours and were ordering fresh supplies of food and drinks at four o'clock in the morning. It was people like these who deprived her of her best staff.

'Lord knows, it's difficult enough to recruit suitable people who are willing to work out here as it is,' she frequently complained to Jack. 'Not many youngsters want to be isolated ten miles off shore in a pseudo world where everyone but themselves is having a good time. They work twelve hours a day for a pittance. Why should they tolerate such behaviour from the clients?'

'Because the clients are the ones paying the money,' Jack would remind her. 'They're always right!'

Since it was left to Maggie to scour the countryside for suitable chamber maids, waiters and pool attendants, she found it difficult to go along with his reasoning. At this time of the year, staff from her personnel department were travelling around the university towns in several States, seeking out disenchanted, unemployed graduates. They enticed an endless stream of bright young people with promises of permanent jobs and the opportunity to train for management but few remained more than a week or two. When they discovered the kind of work they were expected to do and the conditions under which they had to live, most were quickly disillusioned. They soon discovered that what glamour the job entailed, ended behind the doors marked STAFF ONLY.

Maggie was forced to concede that Milton had chosen an idyllic setting for the first of his Australian ventures, but in truth, it might just as easily have been built almost anywhere in the world.

She had been struck by the similarity of the Kookaburra Resort to the others which Milton had set up in Florida, the Dominican Republic and Sri Lanka. The truth was that if the weather was right and the sea blue enough, you could stick one of these places just about anywhere and people would flock to it. She often wondered how long it would take their clients to realise that they might just as well visit the resort which was in their own back yard and save the expense of an air fare to some farflung part of the world.

Little or no provision was made for visitors to experience the country they were visiting outside the resort nor were they encouraged to meet local people. Indeed, the company made a conscious effort to avoid such contact by providing for the client's every need within the resort.

Pools, restaurants, souvenir shops and entertainment of every kind abounded, so that guests had no incentive to move beyond the boundaries of the resort. In this case, Milton had purchased the entire island. Every facility which was available to the guests was either provided by MTH Enterprises or franchised out to the small number of long-standing island inhabitants who were willing and able to make some kind of a living from Milton's venture. There were times, in moments of particular disenchantment, when Maggie likened the situation to a luxurious prison camp in which the clients were happy to pay for the privilege of being incarcerated. Privately she wondered at the gullibility of those who appeared to enjoy what they were getting for their money but then, who was she to attempt to disillusion anyone? They were contributing to her pension, weren't they? This close to retirement, she was not about to start making waves.

Jack's latest bad-tempered remark had been totally out of character and Maggie wondered if he too was losing his enthusiasm for the job. She had seen so many like him come and go during the years she herself had stuck loyally to her post. She, amongst all his associates, was the most tolerant of Milton's violent mood swings. She had known and admired his wife of twenty-five years and had grieved with him at her abrupt and untimely passing. She had understood his need to throw himself into work and had supported his more ambitious projects despite the misgivings of her fellow workers. In time her loyalty had been recognised and Milton had come to value her opinion. Plans for any new enterprise were brought first to her, for approval and refinement. He listened to her advice and, more often than not, took it.

It had been at Maggie's insistence that he had finally taken this long-anticipated vacation in Scotland.

She had gone to great lengths to find him just the right place. Somewhere which would offer him the excitement of the chase but would also provide the luxurious living to which he had become accustomed. Only by careful research amongst the shooting and fishing fraternity in the United Kingdom had she found what she was looking for in Seileachan Castle. Now it seemed that, far from finding a chance to relax and leave behind his business dealings for a time, he had dreamed up some new project there.

'I give up!' she said to herself, resolving never to become involved in Milton's private arrangements again.

'There's a message from MTH,' she said casually. 'You might want to respond to it later on . . . eight o'clock tonight will be about the right time. It will have to be a phone call . . . I don't suppose they've heard of the Internet in Scotland.'

Jack groaned. He had hoped that this huntin', shootin' and fishin' holiday of Milton's would keep him off their backs for a week or two.

'What's he got up his sleeve for us now?' he demanded.

'I don't know, but whatever it is, it was important enough for him to call at twelve noon our time which means very late in Argyll!'

Jack felt a stirring of interest at Maggie's news. Was it possible that Milton had a new project for him at last? Could he be planning something over there in Scotland?

Jack's family had emigrated to Western Australia early in the century, from somewhere in Scotland . . . his mother had always been rather hazy about where exactly. Mariette McDougal was a third-generation Australian of Czechoslovakian origin and had very little notion of geography outside her home state of South Australia. She had never ventured far from Adelaide until she met and married Jack's father and was whisked away to spend the remainder of her life on the McDougals' family property in Western Australia.

Jack had often thought he might like to make a pilgrimage to the land his grandfather still called 'home'. It would be great if Milton wanted him to join him over there.

He lifted the phone and dialled an internal number.

'Delia, it's me. I'm afraid I shall be late picking you up tonight. MTH wants me to ring him at eight. What d'you want to do, go ahead on your own or wait for me?'

There was a petulant little sigh from the other end. When she had come here to be close to Jack, Delia Aldred had expected her life to be all dinner dates and dancing with the rich and famous clients of the Kookaburra Resort. She had had visions of gentle cruises among the reefs on the luxury vessels she had seen in the travel brochures, bathing by moonlight and barbies on the beach under cloudless starry skies. The reality was seldom so romantic. The chances were that when any such opportunity presented itself, it would be the cue for Jack to be called out to settle a disturbance in one of the several bars in the resort or pacify some irate guest whose allocated room had been mysteriously double booked. The couple seldom had a minute alone together and Delia's carefully laid plans hardly ever worked out satisfactorily.

'Sam promised to take us to the outer reef this evening,' she said, disappointed. 'He'll sail on time, you can be sure of that.'

'Then you go ahead without me,' Jack suggested. 'There's no way I can ignore this instruction to phone Milton.'

'I don't know what you want with a fiancée,' she muttered miserably. 'You're already married to your boss!'

'Hiya, Jack! How's it going?'

'Settling down nicely, Milt. A few hiccoughs but nothing that can't be handled either by Maggie or myself.'

Under no circumstances did any employee of Milton T. Humbert admit to failure. In any case, nothing had occurred which needed to be related to him over the telephone. All the little problems would be ironed out long before he reappeared.

'I'm real glad to hear that, Jack.' Milton's voice was purring, a sure sign he had something new up his sleeve. 'Because I want you to drop everything and get over here just as fast as you can.'

'Where's here exactly?' Jack demanded, aware that Milton might well have moved a few hundred miles from his last location if the mood had taken him. 'Are you still on that Scottish estate you went to?'

Milton hesitated before answering.

'Yes,' he said at last. 'But since you mention it, it might

be best if we met somewhere a little more out of the way.'

Jack wondered if there was anywhere more out of the way than the coast of Argyll.

'Let's say Glasgow,' Milton decided. 'There's an exclusive little place in Kelvin Grove . . . Maggie will know. Book the two of us in there for the weekend. I'll be with you for dinner on Saturday evening.'

Whatever it was, thought Jack, it was not so vitally important that he must leave immediately. Wednesday would do . . . he'd get Maggie to book him through on a direct flight via Darwin. That should give him time to sort something out with Delia. She was sure to kick up.

'OK,' he replied, knowing that Milton would not divulge any more over the telephone line. 'See you Saturday.'

He allowed his boss to be the first to put down the phone and replaced his own handset with a sigh of relief. He glanced at his watch and found that if he got his skates on he could make it in time for their evening engagement after all. He shut down his computer and made for the exit.

The General Manager of the Kookaburra Resort Hotel had been allocated accommodation on the side of a steep hill, overlooking the harbour and the innermost parts of the reef. To reach it he used one of the tiny buggies, a development of the motorised golf trolleys used in the States, modified to negotiate the island's steep gradients. It had been Milton's inspiration to introduce them when confronted by local planners who were adamant that ordinary vehicles should not be allowed to clutter up the island's few roads. Each buggy was driven by a two-stroke engine and had a maximum speed of ten miles an hour. Without gear shift or indicators, these vehicles could carry four people and could be driven by anyone. The ten square kilometres of territory open to guests were easily accessible by this means. Rental on a daily or weekly basis was cheap.

Accommodation in a variety of styles sprawled across the hillsides in regular patterns and it was only in the oldest part of the settlement, the area which had existed before the intervention of Milton T. Humbert and his associates, that the lack of uniformity, coupled with a certain appropriateness to their surroundings, gave the buildings a charm absent in the more recent additions.

Jack had acquired one of these older properties a few weeks after his installation as manager and was now in the process of modernising it before moving in. Meanwhile his staff accommodation, although a trifle cramped, provided every luxury and Delia in particular was delighted with it. Several times a day she expressed a desire to remain there rather than move into the ramshackle old house he had chosen. It was in a most inconvenient site, remote from all the resort's amenities. Why, there wasn't even a pool in the yard!

Jack, however, had insisted that he needed to have some small part of his life which was not provided for, managed and completely controlled by the company. Delia could not understand his attitude and still hoped to change his mind about the move.

Except for this one matter concerning the house he was to live in, Milton T. Humbert owned Jack McDougal as he owned every one of his employees. He treated them well enough, but expected total obedience to his commands and absolute loyalty in all matters.

Jack pulled into his allotted parking space outside the neat little villa which was his temporary home. He slipped out from behind the wheel, dragging his briefcase with him. There were figures he would have to go through later, in preparation for the weekly staff meeting in the morning. Delia had insisted that they accept the invitation for this evening which meant that he must later stay up half the night to make up for the loss of time. This did not concern her, of course. While he sweated under the angle-poise in his study, she would be fast asleep.

He stumbled up the outside staircase and into the main living area. Clothes lay scattered over both furniture and floor. Spilt face powder had been ground into the carpet. The half-eaten remains of a meal still lay upon the glass-topped coffee table. Any normal house owner might have assumed that the place had been broken into by a particularly inconsiderate team of burglars, but Jack recognised the signs of Delia making a hurried departure.

He wandered about picking up the scattered garments and making a neat pile of them in one of the chairs. Only when he carried the dirty crockery into the tiny kitchen did he see her note, hurriedly scrawled on a piece of the resort's headed paper.

SAM HAS DECIDED TO MAKE A LONGER TRIP OF IT – PROBABLY AS FAR AS COOKTOWN, MAYBE FURTHER. I'M GOING WITH HIM. SEE YOU IN ABOUT A WEEK. DEE.

'Damn!' He rifled through the telephone directory, searching for Sam's mobile number. If the launch hadn't left the harbour he might still be in contact.

Jack found the number and pressed out the code but after a few moments of strange background noises he was told by an electronic voice, 'The number you have dialled is unavailable at the moment. Please try again later.'

Angrily he slammed down the phone.

She would return to find him gone and it was her own damned fault! He had no idea when he would be back. She should have waited for him, not gone rushing off on impulse like this. Perhaps she would never come back. Maybe he didn't care!

After a few moments his temper began to subside. It might be just as well that things had worked out this way. A break was just what they both needed . . . from this place and from each other. Maybe it was true what they said about absence making the heart grow fonder. He wondered if it also brought with it a measure of understanding for the other's point of view?

'Are you quite sure this isn't taking you out of your way?' Pierre asked again as the doctor pulled his ancient black limousine on to the gravel at the side of the road and climbed out.

'Och, not at all,' Ewan exclaimed. 'It is high time I called on Bill Douglas. It must be six months since he was last in my surgery.'

'Well . . . if you're sure it's no trouble.' Pierre followed the doctor down the slipway to where the ferry boat rocked gently on the waves.

'Good of you to wait, Angus.' The doctor handed his bag to the ferryman and allowed him to take an arm to steady him as he stepped down into the boat.

'The Postie saw your car pull up,' Angus Dewar told him, grinning across at the woman already seated in the bows.

'And how are you the day, Jeanie?' McWorter demanded, casting a shrewd glance at the rather too highly coloured face of Jeanie Clark, the village post-mistress. She had been to see him a week or two ago complaining of headaches and dizziness. An alarmingly high blood pressure reading had caused him to put her on to a course of Nifedipine.

'Och, a lot better, thank you, doctor,' she replied, rather too quickly. He held her gaze long enough to let her know he didn't think so, cleared his throat and said, 'Best call in at the surgery in a day or two . . . just to see if the tablets are doing their job.'

Pierre, who had followed Ewan McWorter on to the boat, fished in his pockets for some change.

'What's the fare?' he asked, holding out a fistful of coins.

'Pay on the way back,' said Angus. 'No chance you'll get away without paying, unless you decide to swim.' He let out a peal of laughter at his own, well-used joke and pulled at the starter cord. The Yamaha engine roared into life making further exchanges difficult.

The passengers remained silent while the boat was manoeuvred carefully out of the narrow harbour entrance and into the channel between Seileach and Eisdalsa

Islands. Once outside the harbour the doctor stood up beside the ferryman and asked, 'The Captain on the island today, Angus?'

'Well, I have nae seen him the day, so I suppose he must be.'

'Been out and about as usual, has he?' The question was casually put. The doctor knew that the islanders, while appearing to keep themselves to themselves, were entirely aware of what their neighbours were doing.

'Aye . . . he was out with his sextant only yesterday. I saw him mysel'.' The two men exchanged knowing glances. They were both aware that the old sea captain took his sextant to the northernmost part of the island every day when the sun was shining in order to find his position on the chart. If his calculations were not always as accurate as they might once have been, at least he would normally calculate the island of Eisdalsa to be within a metre or two of where she was meant to be! Islanders were used to being told Eisdalsa had shifted a couple of points to the west or five hundred metres to the south according to the number of drams Captain Billy had swallowed the previous evening.

Angus concentrated now on steering the boat towards the calmer waters of the island's one navigable inlet. In order to negotiate the tricky tidal flow in the channel, he was obliged to steer the ferry boat north-westwards to the point where Jamie McPhee's little red buoy danced on the waves. The *Lass of Lunga* was the only working fishing boat now operating in the sound. Morning and evening McPhee took her from her mooring in the lee of Eisdalsa Island and out past the offshore reefs, laying and collecting in his lobster pots. Apart from the prawns for which he trawled, lobsters and crabs were the most valuable harvest still remaining for local fishermen to gather.

Pierre was surprised by the strength of the current. The sea was quite choppy and he could quite imagine that there must be times when it would be too rough for a safe passage in this open boat. He read the sign REGIS-TERED TO CARRY NO MORE THAN TEN PASSEN-GERS and was surprised that the vessel could take so many. The turbulent waters settled down as the boat entered the jaws of a narrow inlet. The entrance to the harbour, from which fifty or more sailing boats had once plied their trade, was now silted up. After every storm the dredger must be brought in to make a passage wide enough to allow for movement of the passenger ferry and the few privately owned craft still anchored there. Waste slate, which had been cast into the sea during the hundreds of years when the quarries were operating, had been moved by the currents, around the island and across the harbour entrance.

The tide was on the ebb. Water was running out through the harbour entrance now with such speed that in half an hour or so the ferry would be obliged to beach itself and passengers would have to wade ashore.

Angus had swung the boat round to face the harbour entrance and closed with the quay by the time the island's patrol of dogs appeared, tails erect, ears pricked, eyes and noses scanning the passengers for friendly signs.

The recruits to this canine band came in all sizes. More mongrel than pure bred, the favoured variety for island living was the gentle, good-natured Labrador but the

Border Collie came a close second. Bringing up the rear, but no less prominent in all proceedings, was a Jack Russell of considerable age and fat as a barrel. Despite his lack of stature and the encumbrance of his wide girth, he was no less energetic than the rest when it came to singling out a particular passenger for his attention. He chose the doctor, an old friend, while the Collie attached himself to Pierre. The Labradors had more specific duties at this time of day: escorting the post. Two black and one chestnut, they fell into step beside the Postie, the senior dog, Red, leading the way, with Smoke and Judy to the rear. The Postie's route had been carefully calculated over the years to take in every house in the village with the least amount of backtracking and to ensure that the Museum would be reached at precisely eleven o'clock when Celia Robertson's kettle would be boiling for morning coffee and ginger biscuits. The entourage must then leave Celia in time to reach the Captain's house just as his lamb chops, or on high days and holidays fillet steak, came out of the frying pan.

Pierre stood watching while the post party departed for the first of the cottages and felt the Collie's damp nose nudging at his hand. He allowed his fingers to wander over the silky brow towards a particular spot behind the neatly pricked ear and looked down to find the dog gazing up at him with limpid brown eyes.

'What's your name, fella?' he enquired as though expecting an answer.

The doctor obliged. 'That's Ruff, and this little chap here is Dodger.' At the sound of his name the Jack Russell leaped up to lick the doctor's ear – a jump of at least three times his own length. He tumbled back, rolled over, regained his feet and was immediately out ahead of them once again.

'Whose dogs are they?' Pierre asked, intrigued.

'Oh, they belong to various residents on the island, I suppose, but they're regarded as an integral part of the community. You can't leave a dog cooped up all day in one of these cottages so most people let their pets out during the day. They seem to see it as their responsibility to escort visitors to the island. When the weather gets bad in the winter and there are few people about, they get pretty bored, I can tell you! They're also a bunch of scroungers . . . aren't you, eh?'

He stooped to tug affectionately at the Collie's ear and set off up the path from the ferry landing with Dodger leaping at his heels. The rough, unmetalled path led them past the ferry waiting room and along the track which skirted the harbour.

In this part of the village the long, low, white-painted cottages were arranged in three neat rows parallel with the southern wall of the harbour. Their uniformity was broken by a larger building, higher than the rest, with a uniquely shaped roof in the shape of a pyramid. Pierre came to a halt before the ramshackle wooden door which hung forlornly from its one remaining hinge, swinging occasionally in the brisk morning breeze and giving a piercing screech of protest at its neglect.

'Interesting roof,' the doctor remarked as he witnessed Pierre's critical observation of the building. The expanse of slate tiles was interrupted here and there by patches of unsightly roofing felt where attempts had been made, after successive storms, to keep the building watertight.

'Look inside . . . it always reminds me of an umbrella or perhaps a wigwam.' He forced open the door and the two men stood for a moment allowing their eyes to adjust to the gloomy interior. The roof was supported by a centrally placed pillar made from a single tree trunk. From this, supports radiated to the four corners and to strategic spots along the edge of the roof line. Angled reinforcing struts emphasised the likeness to an umbrella.

'This was built in the 1860s,' the doctor told Pierre. 'That central support was said to have been the mast of a ship which foundered in the Sound. The people had no money to buy materials so they used whatever came to hand. The building was intended for a drill hall for the Volunteers but I suspect it had considerably more varied uses than that. I reckon many a *ceilidh* was held under this roof in the old days.'

'Volunteers?' Pierre queried.

'A kind of militia . . . at the time there was a renewed threat of invasion from the French.' He grinned awkwardly, wondering how Pierre might react to this reference to his ancestors. The Canadian was unmoved. The doctor continued, 'The Government of the day raised an army of local volunteers and the Eisdalsa Quarrying Company, having the largest workforce of able-bodied men in the district, formed the first Artillery Company on this coast. They called themselves the Eisdalsa Volunteers. One battery was set up here on the island and a second on Caisteal an Spuilleadair.' He indicated the rugged escarpment across the water on Seileach. 'Annie and I have done a lot of research using the records of the

45

Volunteers as a guide. You'll see it all laid out in the museum.'

Pierre had noticed how, during the course of any conversation, these people assumed complete strangers knew the characters to whom they referred. McWorter had mentioned Annie on numerous occasions. Pierre supposed her to be the doctor's wife.

'Annie is a historian?' he asked now, hoping for a lead.

'Only an amateur like myself. When we came here to live in the 1960s we discovered that many of the village houses had been left virtually untouched for fifty years or more. There was a major exodus just after the first world war and many places had been left deserted just as they stood: with furniture, household goods too cumbersome to carry overseas, ornaments, family documents. Once we had permission to go in and clear them out, we found all kinds of interesting stuff in the roofs. The houses had been held for the most part on long-term leases so no one was empowered to go near them until the leases ran out in the 1960s. As various properties changed hands, the new occupants wanted to get rid of the junk which had been left behind. In the beginning, much of what they considered rubbish was burned. It was only when Annie found one fellow throwing Friendly Society records on to a bonfire that we realised what valuable material there was to be collected. A group of us set about trying to preserve some of it. That was how the museum started. Once it was proposed, and a suitable building acquired for the display, articles began to flood in from all around. It was simply amazing what a variety of items had been stored away in attics and coal cellars. You must go and see the collection for yourself. You'll not be disappointed.'

When Ewan McWorter had suggested the previous evening that Pierre might like to visit the island, the Canadian, reluctant to spare the time from his sporting activities but not wishing to offend his new friend, had pleaded lack of transport as an excuse. Not to be put off, the doctor had turned up at the castle after breakfast that morning, with the offer of a lift to Eisdalsa.

'I have patients to see over there myself. While I'm working you can spend a while in the museum and then I'll take you around the whole island. Ye canna come all this way and no' visit Eisdalsa. I'm telling ye, man, it's the most rewarding visit you'll make during your stay.'

Thus confronted, the Canadian was unable to offer any further excuse, and felt obliged to forego the pleasures of a morning's clay pigeon shooting in order to accompany the doctor on his rounds.

As he followed McWorter out on to an open green, with cottages on three sides and with the harbour forming the fourth boundary, he knew that the doctor had been right. He would not have missed seeing this for the world.

To outward appearances the cottages were small, and seemed to be composed of two rooms with a door placed centrally. According to McWorter one and a half or two of the old houses had been incorporated to form each of the present dwellings, the majority being clad in any material other than slate.

When questioned about this the doctor explained, 'By the 1950s, when there was an upsurge of interest in acquiring property on the island, the occupants were anxious to make the decaying roofs watertight. Local slate was no longer available so felt tiles and corrugated asbestos were substituted. It's a different story now. The village is "listed" and any renovations must be made in slate or an approved slate substitute. That's why there are now a few slated roofs. The hope is that in time they will all be repaired in the same manner.'

'But I thought you said there was no more slate available?' Pierre commented. Ewan was pleased to find his audience so attentive and interested.

'Not new slate, no, but there are plenty of old slated buildings coming down in the cities. The local builders buy up the used slates and reuse them on the cottages.'

'Expensive business.' It sounded like a statement born of knowledge of the construction industry. Ewan wondered if that was Pierre's business . . . he had so far hesitated to enquire. No doubt the Canadian would reveal his interests when it suited him. It was not in Ewan's nature to be inquisitive.

They followed the path along one side of the square until they came upon a sign pointing in the direction of the museum.

'I'll pick you up from there in about half an hour,' said the doctor. He turned to the Jack Russell. 'Coming to see the Captain then?' he asked. The little dog scampered ahead in the direction of another group of cottages at the head of the harbour while the Collie, torn between his new friend and the promise of lamb chops, succumbed to the latter temptation and sped across the green in Dodger's wake.

The doctor spotted Bill Douglas when he was still two

hundred yards away. The retired sailor strode along with head erect, his hands clasped behind his back as though still walking the bridge of his last command. Around his neck was slung a pair of binoculars which had seen forty years' service at sea before being retired like their owner. Now they were used as much for spotting sea birds as sailing vessels, but many a stranded yachtsman had had cause to be grateful for the Captain's keen eye and his instinct for recognising when a craft was in difficulties. Since his retirement, Captain Billy had become a voluntary coast guard, reporting on his own short-wave radio any incident worthy of note and also receiving and conveying messages to the local seagoing fraternity. It was the ferryman's duty to go to the assistance of any vessel in distress if the lifeboat was not immediately available and when the need arose, the Captain, octogenarian or not, was always at hand to render assistance.

Ewan was relieved to see his old friend looking so spry this morning. Flora had spoken of a certain breathlessness and a marked lack of energy sometimes in the morning. The doctor wondered if it was not perhaps time to check up on the old sea dog.

One lesson that Ewan McWorter had learned early on in his career was to know his patients well enough to recognise most of the problems they were going to present, before they occurred. Prevention was better than cure and often, by reducing the chances of delay in applying the correct treatment, he had managed to save lives. At his own request he saw as many fit patients as those who were acutely ill. Regular check-ups were compulsory if one wished to remain on good terms with Dr Mac.

'What brings you over here on such a bright morning?' asked the Captain.

'I brought a guest of the Marquis over to see the island. While he's looking around the museum I thought I'd take the opportunity to check on you. Haven't seen you in the surgery for quite some time.'

'Business must be bad if you have to go looking for patients!' laughed the old sea dog.

'Not really,' the doctor replied, 'but there was some suggestion of an excess of cholesterol in your last blood test and I think it's time to take another.'

'Bloody vampire, that's what you are.' Captain Billy grinned at his own joke. 'Oh, well, I suppose I'd better invite you in, seeing as you're here.'

They went inside the tiny cottage which Bill Douglas had made his home for the last twenty years. The doctor was obliged to duck as he entered the low doorway and walked straight into the overcrowded living room.

Even on this summer's morning a fire burned in the grate and a kettle sang on the hob. A pair of well-used armchairs were drawn up to the fire. In one, the ancient velvet cushions were heavily dented, showing clear evidence of recent occupation. The second was piled high with shipping and yachting magazines. The Sunday papers for weeks past were heaped below the single sliding sash window and every spare inch of wall carried makeshift bookcases.

From long experience, McWorter knew that his friend could produce a reference on almost any subject one chose to bring up. His life had always been filled with books and he had kept every one he had read. Above the bookshelves, the walls were covered with photographs and paintings of shipping of every kind, the most prominent spot above the fireplace having been reserved for his last command, a container ship which had worked the Australia, New Zealand route.

The heavy scent of shag tobacco permeated the atmosphere and McWorter, accustomed to a smokeless zone in his own house these days, took shallow breaths until he became inured to it. As he opened his case and began to fiddle with his equipment, the Captain reached for a half-empty bottle of malt whisky and a couple of glasses.

'You'll take a dram while you're here.' It sounded more like an order than an invitation.

McWorter nodded. 'But only after I've helped myself to some of your blood. Now strip off that jersey and roll up your sleeve.'

'I suppose Flora has been getting on to you, is that it?' Bill demanded while he did as he was asked. 'Fusses around me like an old biddy hen these days.'

'A daughter might be expected to be concerned for her father's welfare, don't you think?' asked McWorter as he shot the needle into his patient's arm with a deft flick of the wrist and began to draw back on the plunger.

'Och, I suppose so,' grumbled Bill. 'She's a good wee girl and she looks after me fine. Calls in once or twice a week. You know,' he added, 'to see everything's shipshape.'

McWorter, grinning at the unintended pun, nodded.

Flora Douglas had lived in the village on Seileach for most of her life, occupying the house which her parents had bought soon after they were married in the early-50s.

During the war Bill Douglas, at that time a Sub Lieutenant in the Royal Navy, had been directed to Tobermory for convoy duties. He had made the most of his time spent ashore in Argyll, exploring the countryside around and finding delight at every bend of the road and every view from a hilltop. After the war he had rejoined the Merchant Navy and when he married in the 1950s at the age of thirty-two he brought his French bride, Marie, to Argyll, fulfilling the promise he had made to himself that if he survived the war he would make his home here.

Bill celebrated his fortieth birthday at sea, the year Flora was born. When he at last came home to stay, she was already in her first year at University. In 1983 Flora graduated in Pharmacology and accepted a post in a hospital dispensary in the Borders. Called home to nurse her sick mother she found herself living continuously under the same roof as her father for the first time. Father and daughter were virtual strangers, having nothing in common but their love of the dying woman. When Marie was gone, they tried to get on with their lives, but it soon became clear that they could not continue to share the same house.

Soon after her return home, Flora had discovered that the doctor was looking for help with his practice. When Ewan McWorter let it be known that he needed a receptionist, he never anticipated that his only applicant would be qualified to dispense also. McWorter had welcomed Flora into the practice with open arms.

Her mother's death had removed any barrier to Flora's returning to her former life, but for some reason she had never been tempted to seek more lucrative employment elsewhere. She redecorated the family cottage, furnished it in her own taste and took a full and active part in community life.

Bill Douglas was a man used to his own company. Having no desire to remain living in the same house with Flora he acquired one of the unoccupied cottages on Eisdalsa Island, leaving his daughter to continue living in the family home in the village on Seileach.

Bill had never in his life been obliged to keep house for himself, however. At sea there were stewards to see to his every need. On leave, his wife had provided every comfort. Left now to his own devices he cooked his meals tolerably well, but he relied upon his daughter to sort out the domestic chores.

Many a time Flora wished he would move over to the village so that they could share her house, but he insisted upon his independence, ignoring any inconvenience to herself.

'I'll just take your blood pressure while I'm here,' McWorter decided, preventing Bill from rolling down his sleeve. He fussed with the sphygmomanometer, and the Captain began to lose patience.

'If you work yoursel' up like that, the reading will be too high and I'll be obliged to put ye on some tablets, you silly old man,' the doctor complained.

Instantly, Captain Billy settled back in his chair. In no way was this quack going to find anything wrong with him.

McWorter grunted as he watched the mercury rise and fall in the tube. He might have had something further to say on the matter of the patient's blood pressure had not a commotion at the door heralded the arrival of the Postie and her entourage. In the scuffle which ensued, the doctor silently replaced his equipment in his bag and with a quick reminder to Jeanie about keeping her appointment at the surgery, he was on his way. As he rounded the corner he could hear the Captain talking to the dogs,

'Now then, Red, you've had one chop . . . leave a bit for the others. What's that Judy? Nothing for you . . . well, how about this little bit of steak then?'

The doctor wore a worried frown. If there was a cholesterol problem he would have to get Flora to persuade the old man to eat more sensibly. His blood pressure was a trifle on the high side, but he had been a wee bit worked up. Ewan resolved to keep a closer eye on the old devil – he wouldn't want him to take a stroke if it could be avoided.

Chapter Three

Pierre ducked his head as he entered the low doorway and paused for a moment while his eyes adjusted to the light. Large sepia photographs formed the dominant exhibits in this neatly displayed collection of artifacts of a hundred years before.

A middle-aged woman, her hair tightly swept back from her forehead, spectacles perched on the tip of her nose, looked up from the keyboard on which she had been working, and smiled.

'Good morning. Just one adult, is it?'

She gave him a thorough appraisal. 'Concession rate?' she enquired.

'*Pardon?* Oh . . . I'm retired, if that's what you mean,' he replied.

'One twenty-five then, thank you.'

He searched in his pocket, withdrawing the money in small change.

'Oh, thank you,' Celia exclaimed with relief. 'Most visitors arrive first thing in the morning with nothing but a twenty-pound note . . . empties my float straight away.'

'Do you have a great many visitors?' he asked. He was fascinated by the lilting Highland tones of the woman's speech and consciously sought to prolong the discussion.

'Quite a few, particularly from overseas.' She smiled, teasing him. 'Lots of them are from the Colonies.'

He smiled back politely, not at all put out. 'I suppose quite a few people left here for the New World in the old days,' he commented.

'It's possible that some of your own ancestors came from here,' she told him. 'In the eighteenth and nineteenth centuries the Marquises of Stirling, who held all the land hereabouts, owned the province of Nova Scotia as well. When the estate workers sought new lives elsewhere, it was natural they should look first towards Canada.'

He felt strangely pleased that she should have distinguished correctly between the Canadian and American accents.

'It's unlikely in my case, I'm afraid,' he replied, jovially. 'I'm a French Canadian from Quebec.'

'Oh, one of the enemy.' She grinned. 'Be careful who you talk to around here. Some of us have long memories.'

'You'll be telling me soon that Eisdalsa men fought under Wolfe on the Plains of Abraham!'

'Almost certainly they did,' she answered.

'I was always led to believe that the Scots had a particular affinity with the French,' Pierre observed wryly.

'In the Western Isles, where the Catholics held sway. It was only the Jacobites who supported Bonnie Prince Charlie in 1745. The Campbells of Argyll hedged their bets . . . some even fought for King Billy under the Duke of Cumberland. We know for sure that a hundred years later we raised an army here against the French. That was in 1860. Some photographs and a lot of documentation are on display over there along the wall. It's as good a place to start your tour as any. If you want to learn something about the slate industry hereabouts you'll find that display in the far corner, and the island's social history is portrayed by the collection of household equipment and documentary evidence . . . church, Poor Law records and reports of the medical officers for the quarries.'

He thanked her and wandered off towards the section on the Volunteers. The woman returned to her keyboard.

There was a slight disturbance from outside and a family group appeared at the reception desk. A quick admonition from the parents prevented two small boys from tearing around the exhibition screens and their piping voices were quickly subdued by a sharp word from their father. What a pity, Pierre thought. It was a place to evoke comment and discussion. He was pleased to hear the cashier exchange a few words with the children and set them chatting about a display of school photographs and children's books.

He half-listened to the explanations given in answer to their questions about the island and smiled when the mother asked innocently enough, 'Does anyone live here permanently now?'

'Of course,' the cashier replied patiently. 'There is a population of fifty or more, from infants in arms to octogenarians. It's a very well-balanced community.'

'But how do you manage? Is there running water? Electricity?'

'Yes, indeed.' The woman politely pointed out the spot-lights illuminating the exhibits all around them and the husband nudged his wife, embarrassed that she should ask such a stupid question.

Pierre moved away, becoming absorbed in a collection of ancient documents relating to the formation of the original quarrying company. A Minute Book of 1745 indicated how long it had been since slate was first removed from the island for commercial purposes. Reports of accidents attended by the physician of the day gave an insight into the dangers experienced by the men, and relics of blasting tools and equipment reminded him that these were engineers who knew a thing or two about explosives. No wonder they had been formed into an Artillery Company!

Pierre was deeply engrossed in the collection of docu-ments relating to the churches of the district when he found the doctor at his elbow.

'Seen enough?' Ewan asked cheerfully.

'I don't think I could see everything if I stopped in here for a week,' sighed the Canadian.

'Most people feel like that,' Dr McWorter chuckled. 'You must sign your name in the visitors' book before we leave. Come on, it's over here.'

Before signing, Pierre turned back the pages, noting the countries from which previous visitors had come. There were other Canadians like himself, Americans, Australians and visitors from New Zealand as well as Scots and English. There seemed to be quite a few Europeans even from as far afield as Finland and

Czechoslovakia, Holland and Switzerland. Pierre looked closely at the last signature and recognised it as the Swiss gentleman staying at the castle. He wondered why the quiet little man had not told his fellow guests about his visit to the museum.

Pierre signed his name and was simply going to put 'Canadian' where it asked for an address. He caught the eye of the woman watching him from the other side of the counter. He wrote something swiftly in the book and handed her the pen.

'Thank you,' he said, as the doctor hovered by the open door. 'This is a great little museum . . . I wish I could have stayed longer.'

'Tell your friends about it,' was her reply. As the two men slipped outside she glanced at his entry in the book.

He had left his complete address and in the 'Comments' column he had written 'Worthy of better publicity'.

She was both mystified and gratified at the same time. She turned the page and found that he had slipped a ten-pound note between the leaves. It was, by any standards, a generous donation to the museum's upkeep. She entered it in her book and slipped the note into the till.

Pierre and Ewan McWorter took no more than twenty minutes to circumnavigate the entire island. Outside the village, where individual houses sported some very well-tended gardens, the land lay fallow. For the most part slate waste covered the surface, making a poor foundation upon which to grow anything. Where it had weathered to a fine soil, plants had taken hold. Heather, thyme and an abundance of summer-flowering meadow plants made it a constant delight for amateur botanists and laymen alike. Gorse grew where the soil was deepest and nettles indicated the presence of foundations of old buildings.

Rusty ironwork lent an additional dimension to the landscape, its association with past activity on the island giving it the status of historical monument rather than rubbish left to rot.

The old slate workings, huge pits which the doctor explained to Pierre were, in some cases, eighty metres in depth, were now filled with water. So clear and unpolluted were they that on this calm sunny day it was possible to see far down into their depths.

From the hill behind they had a clear view of the entire island. Pierre was surprised to see that at the southern end some of the cottages were perched right on the lip of two of the quarries. Their gardens sloped down to the water's edge.

'Isn't that a bit dangerous if people have children living down there?' he asked.

'There are walls marking the edges of the quarries,' the doctor replied, 'and in any case, the island children seem to be born with a natural respect for these deep pools. In all my years here, I've never had to deal with a drowning in any of them . . . the harbour, yes. But even then it has been drunks, not kids who have come to grief!'

They strolled across the meadow and clambered back down the path to where a group of ruined buildings stood, their rough stone walls softened by creeping vines.

'These are the old pump houses which served the

largest quarries . . . kept them free from water while the men were working. It's a shame they have been allowed to deteriorate so, they really should be preserved.'

'Who would do that?' asked Pierre.

'No one will take the responsibility. George Monteith owns the island, of course, but he needs every halfpenny he can lay his hands on just to keep that castle going. We've tried to interest the Heritage people in the island but they don't have any money either.'

'It seems to me that the whole place could do with some financial help,' Pierre observed. 'Maybe you should send round a begging bowl. You know the kind of thing – Friends of Eisdalsa!'

'You could be right,' said the doctor. 'Although who you would find around here to make that kind of effort, I can't imagine. It takes more co-operation and organisation than these folks are likely to give. Generally speaking the locals find it difficult to agree on anything. I can't see them getting together over a project like that.'

The Castle Burn, Eas a' Caisteal, drained crystal-clear waters from the surrounding hills across shallow gravel beds and into a deep dark lochan. Surrounded by reed beds and stunted willows and protected by the mountains on every side, this isolated stretch of water was visited only occasionally by man. It was the watering place of the wild mountain sheep and the red deer that roamed the high peaks.

'I suggest you each take a stretch of yon bank where the river runs out of the lochan, gentlemen.'

The gillie directed George's guests towards a spinney

of stunted oaks and alder through which the river tumbled in a series of shallow rapids and deep dark pools. The two men wandered away and in a few moments each had selected his spot and cast his line. The gillie watched them, nodding his approval at the manner in which the Canadian conducted himself. Here was a fit man familiar with woods and high mountain country.

By contrast, the old doctor had made rather heavy weather of the climb out of the glen. As they had forced a way through the airless undergrowth of the forest floor, he had begun to wonder if Dr Mac would make it to the top of the path. He was breathless and sweating profusely before they had covered half the distance, although he had certainly rallied quickly enough once they topped the rise and walked out on to the flat open heathland on the floor of the coll. The gillie allowed his gaze to wander across the crags in hopes of spotting deer. Tomorrow His Lordship's party would be out seeking that all important trophy to carry home in triumph: the head and antlers of some magnificent beastie to hang on their living-room wall at home.

He knelt down on the mossy bank and gazed into the deep dark peat-brown waters of the still lochan. What was going on down there in the depths? he wondered. Were there young salmon as he hoped, growing to a size and strength to carry them away on their momentous journey to the other side of the ocean. He saw a flash of silver as a large trout, startled by his shadow, darted from the bed of reeds at his feet. It was a well-grown fish . . . one of the many with which the Laird had stocked this reach of the river two seasons ago in hopes of providing something stimulating for his guests to fish. It was a pity the salmon could not be replenished in the same way.

Every year for centuries the salmon had come in their thousands to spawn in the shallows above the loch. Every year that is until just a decade ago. In just a few weeks, foreign fishing fleets using illegal nets had swept the waters clear of fish which were weak and weary after their long journey home to the spawning grounds from the far side of the Atlantic. The greed of the fishermen had almost destroyed the stock of wild fish.

When the wild salmon had been brought to near extinction, other entrepreneurs, encouraged and supported by local enterprise, had turned to farming salmon, setting up their cages along the shores of lochs and on the shallow reefs surrounding the islands in the sound. The farmed fish polluted the waters, killing much of the marine life in the vicinity, and as disease spread amongst a species weakened by inbreeding, escapees passed their infection to the few wild salmon remaining.

Those fish which had escaped the fisherman's net and avoided disease, now struggled to re-establish their numbers. The fish farms had begun to close within a few years of first making their appearance in the sound but it was almost too late, for the wild fish stocks had nearly disappeared from George Monteith's stretch of river. It was a rare occasion indeed when one of his guests hooked a salmon in the river that flowed swiftly beneath the castle walls.

Trout there were in plenty, since the upper reaches were stocked with young fish. A weir, constructed at a point down river where the burn emptied into the sound, prevented all but the most adventurous of young trout from escaping. At the same time those salmon which had managed to survive despite all vicissitudes could leap across into the burn and make their way upstream to the spawning ground.

A few hundred metres downstream from the lochan, Dr McWorter had taken up position on his favourite stretch of the river. He stood, legs astride, feet firmly planted in the bed of the stream. Near where he stood a huge boulder parted the waters into two separate courses. Beyond the rock, on its steepest side, they met again. To one side of the rock, the water was shallow and tumbled over a bed of loose pebbles, creating a flow of white water. Here a thin blanket of mist hung above the stream, blurring the vision of hunter and hunted alike. To the other side, the sandy bed of the stream was deeply gouged and the overhang of the bank cast a shadow over the still waters of a deep dark pool. From his commanding position on the bank above, he was just able to make out the sleek bodies of trout working their way steadily upstream against the strong current.

McWorter walked quietly downstream and crossed to where the white water of the further bank would disguise his presence. With a practised hand he cast his line. His fly rested on the surface of the water for an instant and was carried across the current towards the pool. He flicked it away almost at once but there was time enough for a sparkling rainbow-coloured fish to leap out of the water after it and swallow the bait. Ewan hauled in his line and released the fish into his keep-net. He turned triumphantly towards the figure slightly upstream of him and signalled his success.

Pierre d'Orsay acknowledged his partner's catch and quickly followed it with one of his own.

It was still early morning and he was determined to make the most of his last day on Seileach. He had risen before dawn, having agreed with Ewan McWorter to meet him by the old wooden bridge at five-thirty. This was the best time of day, when all was quiet and the fish were rising to insects newly released from their larval jackets by the first warming rays of the sun.

A kingfisher darted out from among the bushes and perched for a time upon a broken branch which bridged the stream just a few feet from where he stood. The bird dived and in one swift movement caught its fish, swallowed it and darted back across the smooth surface of the pool to disappear in the bushes overhanging the bank. The swift movement of jewel colours sent the Canadian's spirits soaring.

How he wished he did not have to leave tomorrow. One thing was certain: he would be coming back next season. Now he had found this wonderful spot he knew that it would continue to draw him.

Ewan felt the tug on his line and knew that this was a larger fish than anything he had caught all morning. His catch darted away down stream and the elderly doctor could do no more than allow the reel to run out. This was too large a fish to be a trout. With growing excitement he realised that he had hooked a salmon.

Suddenly the line slackened and in an instant the skilled fisherman, not wanting to alarm his prey, gave a gentle tug and took in just enough of the line to ensure

that the hook would be firmly embedded in the fish's car-
tilaginous lips.

His quarry was on the move again. Paying out line and
letting him swim until his strength was gone, the old man
followed the salmon downstream, all caution abandoned
in the excitement of the chase.

It was a big fish, eight pounds or more in his estimation.

He felt a jerk right through his arm and wound in more
line. The wild creature darted away once again, fully
aware that it was captive and determined to regain its
freedom. Ewan could feel the giant fish gaining in
strength while his own drained away at an alarming rate.
If he did not land the fish soon, he would have to cut the
line and lose his precious fly.

He shortened the line as far as he could, winding in on
the reel each time the salmon turned upstream, and at the
last minute he gave a mighty heave and swung line and
fish across the stream and on to the bank. The beautiful
creature lay in the long grass, its body writhing, its tail
flapping. If he did not reach it quickly and strike it with
the gaff it would almost certainly regain the river.

Plunging up to his armpits into the deepest part of the
water, he part waded, part swam to the opposite bank and
crawled towards his catch. He lifted a stout piece of
branch and smashed it down on the salmon's head, stunning it for long enough to haul it clear of the bank. The
effort had, however, proved too much for the elderly
doctor. He sank to the ground exhausted and Pierre,
having seen the commotion from afar, came up with him
in time to see both fish and captor gasping for breath and
laid out side by side.

'Say, are you OK?' he demanded, alarmed at the doctor's appearance. All colour had drained from his face and it seemed as though he might faint away at any moment.

'Just lost m'breath for a wee minute,' the doctor replied, shakily. 'My, but he was a tough fighter, was that one.'

'I'm not surprised,' Pierre observed, straightening out the fish and judging its weight and length at a glance. 'A nine-pounder if he's an ounce,' was the verdict. 'Here, let me help you up. No, I'll carry the salmon. This calls for a celebration!'

Dr McWorter scrambled to his feet. Pierre was relieved to see that the colour had returned to his companion's cheeks, but as he struggled to keep up, Ewan was dismayed to find that the dull pain which had been annoying him all morning was now increasing. It began somewhere close to his left elbow and travelled up his arm and across his chest, making his breathing difficult. These were symptoms often described to him by his patients but until now he had never experienced an attack of angina for himself. He was obliged to stop to catch his breath and Pierre, walking ahead, waited patiently for the older man to catch up.

'Are you sure you can make it on foot?' he enquired anxiously. 'If you'd like to wait here, I'll send McGreggor back to the castle and get George to bring out that little Mini Moke of his.'

'No need,' said the doctor, recovered after a moment's rest, 'I can manage if we take it slowly.'

Pierre carried the salmon and their two creels of fish,

their morning's catch, while the gillie gathered up all the paraphernalia of their expedition. Ewan held their two rods, using them as a prop. Slowly the little party made its way to the road where the doctor's ancient black Bentley was parked close up beside the hedge.

'You'd better let me drive you,' suggested the Canadian. The doctor frowned. 'D'you have a licence? I know Tam here disna drive.'

'Does it matter out here?'

'Probably not . . . but remember which side of the road you're driving on.'

'So far as I can see there's only one side . . . straight down the middle.' Pierre got behind the wheel and after a few moments familiarising himself with the controls, all of which were situated on the wrong side so far as he was concerned, decided he could manage. With only a few hiccoughs, they made their way along the narrow track, the doctor crossing his fingers in the hope that they would meet no other vehicles at such an early hour. In the back, the gillie, who preferred to walk and could not abide the smell of petrol, concentrated on the view from the rear window. There would certainly be talk if the Canadian were seen to be driving the distinctive vehicle through the village. While Pierre gripped the wheel tensely as he struggled to remember the reversed positions of brake and clutch pedals, Ewan told himself he'd better have a word with a colleague about this morning's incident . . . but in his own good time. He nodded wisely, agreeing with himself. He didn't want Flora to get wind of what had happened and start fussing.

*

'I wonder if I might ask a tremendous favour, ma'am?'

Cissy very much enjoyed the polite manner of speech of their Canadian guest. To her untutored ears Pierre's accent differed little from that of the American, but the two were streets apart when it came to civility.

'How can I help you?' she asked. He made so few demands upon her that it was a pleasure to be asked to do anything for him.

'Dr McWorter has been so very obliging, taking me to all his favourite fishing spots . . . I am sure he has gone out of his way on my behalf.'

Cissy laughed. 'I happen to know that he is always glad of any excuse to go fishing!' she assured him.

'Nevertheless I would like to repay him by inviting him to dinner this evening. Would that be in order?'

'Dr McWorter is an old friend. He often dines here during the winter . . . out of season, you understand.'

'But on this occasion I would like to invite him as my guest. And his wife too, of course.'

'Annie McWorter died two years ago,' Cissy told him.

'Oh, really?' The Canadian sounded puzzled. 'He speaks of her all the time, as though she were still around.'

'I know. They were very happily married for forty years. Ewan finds it difficult to come to terms with her death, I'm afraid. The rest of us have become used to his way of including her in all his conversations and hardly notice it.'

'Well, just the doctor then,' Pierre confirmed. 'Thank you ma'am.'

'The only thing is . . .' She would have to give away

the secret. 'I am not preparing the meal here for this evening. We've laid on a last-night treat for the whole party. It was going to be a surprise but if you are to invite the doctor you will need to know. We are driving all our guests down to the village and crossing to the island for a *ceilidh* in the Tacksman's Bar.'

'That sounds delightful,' Pierre responded, noting her anxious expression.

Cissy's idea had seemed a good one at the time. George had certainly thought so. Now she was not so sure.

'Do you think the others will want to go?' she asked him.

'I would have thought so. Mr Lucerne has already paid a visit to the island and would, I'm certain, be happy to go a second time. The German gentlemen will be happy enough, so long as their plates are full and the wine comes from your husband's own cellar. The same goes for the Dutch gentleman. I am not so sure about Mr Humbert . . . he seems a little harder to please.'

At first Milton had been pretty circumspect, maintaining an unusually low profile while he came to terms with his new surroundings. Overawed by the experience of rubbing shoulders with the Scottish aristocracy, he had initially showed some caution in his approach and was tentative with his questions, but during the course of the past few days he had resumed his normally assertive manner, expecting immediate compliance with his every requirement and making impossible demands upon the limited facilities offered by his hosts.

'If he wanted five-star accommodation he should have

stayed at the Glasgow Hilton,' Cissy had told her husband only that morning. It made her angry to think of her struggles with the antiquated ice tray with which she did battle on Milton's behalf several times a day.

'Iced water, iced whisky, iced beer . . . anyone would think he had a fire in his belly!' she had complained.

George had merely laughed. 'To look at him I would imagine that sort of fire was quenched long ago. You can't deny the poor old man what he asks for at the prices he's paying. Anyway, there's only a day or two left before he leaves.'

'You're right, of course, 'she had conceded gracefully. Now, she smiled broadly at the Canadian.

'If Milton makes a fuss about our arrangements for the evening, he can stay here. I'll leave a cold buffet for him so that he can help himself. Maybe he'll be happier with his own company.'

Much to the surprise of both Cissy and Pierre, when informed of the evening's arrangements, Milton T. Humbert appeared to be delighted at the prospect of a visit to Eisdalsa Island and declared with exaggerated enthusiasm how much he looked forward to sampling a little of the local culture.

Cissy, coming across her husband preparing for the last day's shooting, told him about her conversation with Pierre.

'He'll be bringing Dr Mac along this evening,' she explained. 'I do hope Ewan won't mind haggis with tatties and neaps. It's not the menu he's accustomed to when he eats here.'

'Ewan's a good sort,' George laughed. 'He'll understand the need for showing our guests a little local colour. We'll make up for it by inviting him to dinner here when the next party arrives.'

'I thought I'd invite Flora and Captain Billy to liven up the conversation at dinner and Kirsty will enlist the support of the islanders for the *ceilidh*, afterwards.'

'Good. I hope we won't be going on for too long, though,' George cautioned. 'Some of the guests want to get away very early in the morning . . . our friend Milton in particular. He's expecting a car to pick him up at nine.'

'Not going back by helicopter then?' Cissy could not get used to the ease with which these business tycoons could commandeer a helicopter or even an executive jet, if they were prepared to drive twenty miles north to Connel airport.

'No. It seems he has a yearning to see the Bonnie Banks of Loch Lomond. I suspect that the truth is he wants to find out what sort of a journey it is by road.'

'Why, he won't ever come again, will he?' She sounded quite anxious.

'I don't know. Despite his constant complaints about the lack of amenities, I have the impression that he's really interested . . . especially in Eisdalsa. He has been asking around.'

'What sort of questions?' Alarm bells were ringing. Cissy liked to know something of her guests' backgrounds and it had not taken her long to discover that Milton was a big name in American real estate. She did not know quite what kind of business he ran but she had ascertained that he was a self-made man and a millionaire several times over. She was happy enough to take his money as a guest but she had no desire to see him settling in the district. The Caribbean seemed a more suitable playground for the likes of Milton T. Humbert.

'You don't mean he's looking for somewhere to live?' she demanded anxiously.

'Oh, no. I shouldn't think so,' replied George, his mind already on the next thing. 'It's just his manner . . . he's the kind of person who likes to poke his nose into everything. It's the way these guys get to be what they are.'

'Which is what?' Cissy demanded.

'Rich, I suppose.'

'Who has he been questioning?' She was still concerned.

'I don't know exactly, but he has been spending an inordinate amount of time in the Badger Bar talking to Baldy McGillivray.'

'And keeping his glass well filled, I'll be bound. Well, he'll not learn a great deal to his advantage from that quarter. Baldy never told a tale to anyone without adding a large measure of his own invention. Milton would probably get a better insight into the community from the other side of the bar. Marty Crane knows just about everyone in the district.'

'But like all barmen, he rarely exchanges gossip,' George insisted. 'No, I think Milton's colourful notion of Eisdalsa is a picture painted by our friend Baldy alone.'

'He said the strangest thing to me the other day,' Cissy added, suddenly recalling an early-morning exchange. 'He asked if the ferryman was employed all year round, and when I said yes, he muttered something about the

73

Local Authority having money to burn. When I said the residents had to get on and off the island during the winter whether there were tourists about or not, he seemed very surprised, as if he thought everyone abandoned the island for the whole of the winter.'

'That sounds like another of Baldy's exaggerations to me,' George laughed. 'I'll be working down on the machair after lunch . . . that barley is ready and if I don't get it in, I could be too late.' He glanced across towards the outer islands where the clouds were gathering low on the horizon. 'That belt of rain will be on us by sundown.'

'I'll not have time to help you,' Cissy warned, disappointed that she could not join in a task which they both enjoyed. 'I've promised to pop over and give Kirsty a hand with the preparations for this evening. Oh, and by the way, Dr Mac is joining us . . . as Pierre's guest.'

'Good, that'll raise the tone of the conversation a bit. Those two German fellows are pretty heavy going, aren't they?'

'Rather stodgy, yes,' she agreed, 'but not nearly such hard work as our Milton. I can't tell you how glad I shall be to see the back of that one!'

'What I can't understand, George,' Milton was warming to his subject while the last morsel of Kirsty's delicious blackcurrant flan was chased around his plate, 'is why you haven't realised the full potential of this whole area. There's been habitation here for centuries. Surely someone found a way of making a living in the days before tourism.'

'This was at one time an important industrial commu-

nity,' Dr McWorter told him. 'It was the centre of the
Scottish slate quarrying industry, sold its output to most
of the major cities in Scotland and the north of England
and exported roofing slates all around the world . . . at
one time as many as seven million slates could be produced in a year.'

'So what went wrong?' demanded Milton. 'Did the
slate run out?'

'No, although it did become more costly to take out
once the quarries reached a depth of two hundred feet
below sea level. They found ways of pumping the pits
free of water and invented all manner of means of getting
the slate to the surface and on to the ships . . . no, it
wasn't that that killed the industry, it was fashion.'

'How do you mean?' asked Pierre who enjoyed
hearing the old doctor's accounts of the history of
Eisdalsa. McWorter had lived in the district for much of
his working life and probably knew as much as anyone
alive about the demise of the quarrying industry.

'Architects started to use clay tiles after the First
World War. They were cheaper, lighter to handle and
came in different colours. You'll see all over the country
a distinct difference in the appearance of houses built
before and after 1920. The change came about a little
more slowly here in Scotland where, other than thatch-
ing, they had used only slate roofing for more than six
hundred years.'

'Fashion trends can always be reversed,' said Milton.

'The cost of extracting the slate nowadays would be
phenomenal,' George chipped in. 'It would need a major
investment to extend the existing quarries out under the

ocean. There's very little bedded slate remaining on the island itself. I'm sure the technology exists to get it out, but think what such an enterprise would do to the appearance of the place.'

'Nevertheless,' Milton observed, 'with the right financial backing it might help to put Seileachan Castle back on its feet.' He had refrained from comment all the time he had stayed there but it irked him that nothing seemed to be done to improve the rotting fabric of the building. A major investment was required to set the castle to rights and here was George sitting on a potential gold mine in mineral resources.

'There's one point you seem to have overlooked,' said the doctor, not liking the implications of Milton's outburst. 'For some years, Eisdalsa has been designated a site of outstanding natural beauty. No additional buildings and no industries can be developed in the district unless they are sympathetic to the environment.'

'Who says?' demanded Milton.

'The local Council. Their planning officers vet every application to build anywhere in the County. There is no chance of anyone being allowed to reopen the slate quarries now.'

Milton laughed out loud.

'Do you really think a bunch of elected amateurs would hold back from a development like that if they thought there was money in it?' he demanded rudely. 'Increased prosperity for everyone, jobs for all . . . those guys would be queuing to get into the act, if only to increase their vote at the next election.'

'I hope you're wrong,' said McWorter, coldly. 'Not

every country in the world operates on a system of legalised corruption, you know!'

Milton reddened. 'What are you suggesting? That your local officials are any more honest than ours when it comes to making a few extra dollars?'

'What I'm saying,' insisted McWorter, 'is that we have laws and restrictions to prevent unwanted intrusion into our way of life and we have means of dealing with people who try to get round them.'

'You may consider your own way of life satisfactory,' said Milton, 'but I've met a few people around here who have been out of work for years, who are scratching a living by performing services for their neighbours and would welcome a steady form of employment.'

'Oh, really,' said George. 'Anyone we know?'

Whether or not Milton noticed the twinkle in his eye, Cissy certainly did and kicked her husband under the table.

'Mr McGillivray for one,' said Milton, convinced this was a name to impress.

'Baldy McGillivray would never work for anyone but himself,' declared Flora Douglas. 'What's more, given the opportunity of real employment he would run a mile. When he needs money for drink he builds a wall or mows a lawn. If he's really stretched he will dig out a septic tank or empty a cesspit. I've never known him be without money, a place to sleep and a glass in his hand, but he hasn't worked three days consecutively in twenty years. If he was given a pay packet on a regular basis he would be out on a binge for the first three days of every working week. It's fatal to pay Baldy McGillivray until the job's done . . . everyone knows that!'

'I'm sure there are plenty of others who do want a job,' Milton insisted.

'Maybe,' said McWorter, 'but not down a slate mine. The conditions in which those old quarrymen worked were appalling. No one today would be expected to do what they were obliged to do to make a living.'

'There's modern machinery that would do most of the heavy work.' Milton was not to be shouted down in this. His aim had been to get them thinking about change but they were a reactionary bunch, that was for sure. Still, once George Monteith understood what kind of dividends his piece of Scotland could be bringing in . . .

'Once the economy improves, everyone benefits,' Milton continued. 'Wealth brings more people to a district and people require services so the house builders, the painters and decorators, the road builders and motor vehicle repairers, the shop keepers and hoteliers, will all have more demands on their services. Everyone gets a taste of the action.'

Despite his resolve not to be baited by this man, McWorter was annoyed. With his flushed face turning purple around the mouth, he stood up and leaned across the table towards the American.

'Why, mon,' he declared, his Scottish accent accentuated by rage, 'what kind of a place would Eisdalsa be with twice as many people in it, wider roads and more cars . . . houses everywhere? Why do you think those of us who live here came in the first place? To make money? We came here because it's quiet and peaceful, because folk can go out at night without fear of mugging. The kids don't take drugs and the local drunks are treated as poor sick individuals, not as a menace to society. The old people are cared for and the young are nurtured and tutored by the whole community. We came to a village where we don't lock our doors because, no matter how much we might argue with them, we trust our neighbours.'

He sat down again suddenly and began to tug at his collar. Flora, realising something was wrong with her employer, ran to his side and as his head went back, she finished removing his tie. The doctor clutched at his left arm and gasped, 'Floor . . . lay me down!' By the time they had him stretched out on the quarry tiles of the restaurant floor he had already lost consciousness. In an instant, Pierre was at his side, kneeling and preparing to give him mouth to mouth resuscitation. As he took a deep breath and pulled down on the doctor's lower jaw, Flora turned to Kirsty Brown.

'Call 999,' she said. 'They'll send an ambulance. And tell them it's Dr McWorter himself otherwise they may expect us to have called for him.'

Kirsty was back in a few moments.

'They're sending the helicopter. Fortunately it had just delivered an expectant mum from one of the islands, and was still on the hospital landing pad with the engine running.'

McWorter's eyes flickered and he came round, looking dazed. He struggled to rise, but Pierre held him down gently.

'Stay there, Ewan,' he insisted. 'Help is on its way.'

'Nitro . . .' McWorter managed to gasp and moved his hand towards his breast pocket.

Pierre looked puzzled and turned to Flora who pushed her hand into the jacket pocket and withdrew a small pink phial with a spray attachment. She forced the doctor's mouth open and lifted the tongue. Spraying the underside with a short burst, she then held his jaw closed until the drug had taken effect. The doctor's recovery was almost instantaneous. He struggled to rise but Pierre persuaded him to remain where he was until the helicopter appeared.

Flora glanced down at the phial in her hand. Now what was he doing with that thing in the pocket of his best suit? she wondered. Was he expecting just such an attack as this? Well, she had told him he was overdoing things . . . a man of his age, on call for twenty-four hours a day, seven days a week. When Mrs McWorter was alive she would never have countenanced such a thing. It just proved Flora right, didn't it? Although it gave her no pleasure to say so. Fortunately she had already persuaded the doctor to make provision for just such an eventuality as this. Help was due to arrive within a day or two. Good job too . . . otherwise what would the islands have done for a doctor? Once Ewan McWorter was in the hospital he wouldn't be getting out for ten days at the very least.

They all stood on the harbour wall to watch the helicopter take off with the stricken doctor on board. Then, feeling the autumnal chill in the night air, they returned to the Fish Kettle for the evening's entertainment.

The company, much subdued by the events of the last

half-hour, was beginning to wonder whether they should call the evening off but the: arrival of the helicopter and the news of the doctor's collapse had filled the bar with concerned islanders. With a few drinks taken the conversation became noisier and by the time the musicians were ready to play, the mood had changed to one of cheerful optimism. Old Dr Mac was a survivor. In no time at all he'd be back on his feet!

The fiddler struck up the first tune, quickly joined by his comrades on concertina and penny whistle, chairs were pushed back and feet began to tap.

The party from the castle had returned to the dining room to finish their meal, although no one had much appetite left after all the excitement.

Milton, who had remained very quiet during the first moments of panic and the well-disciplined procedures which had followed the doctor's heart attack, could restrain himself no longer.

'That was pretty impressive by any standards,' he said. 'Those guys in the helicopter . . . don't they want to know who's going to pay the bill?'

'Of course not,' said Cissy. 'It's part of the National Health Service.'

He could not believe what he was hearing.

'In the States they would be making enquiries about the man's bank balance while he was still lying on the ground. I can't conceive of a chopper being called out where an ambulance would do just as well.'

'The resource was available, so why shouldn't it be used?' George was amazed to hear the American's question. 'After all, the sooner Dr Mac gets into hospital, the

Mary Withall

sooner they'll put him right and send him home. Why prolong the journey when he can be in hospital and receiving treatment almost immediately?'

'More important from our point of view,' said Cissy, 'is what shall we do for a doctor, with Dr Mac indisposed?'

'Fortunately, that problem should be solved in a day or two,' Flora told them. 'Dr McWorter was expecting the arrival of an Associate Practitioner. He was supposed to work between this and the practice at Kilglashan, but I daresay they will forgo his services until Dr Mac is back on his feet.'

'I'll contact the local Health Board and explain the situation,' said George. 'I expect they'll manage some emergency cover for the next day or two.'

'Is Dr McWorter all the health cover you have around here?' Milton looked askance.

'The population of the entire parish doesn't amount to more than three thousand,' George replied. 'Some GPs with urban practices have lists of twenty thousand patients. Our situation doesn't justify more than one doctor with an occasional relief. We rely on a young woman who has given up general practice to have a family. She steps in when Dr Mac has the odd day off or his annual leave, but she couldn't be available on a twenty-four-hour basis, as he is.'

'That's a point,' said Flora, suddenly. 'We'd better let the Chairman of the Community Council know. He'll be able to put it about that people should nurse their own wee problems until the new doctor arrives. I expect the hospital will send someone out if there's a real emergency.'

'What's this Community Council?' asked Milton, intrigued.

'It's a body of volunteers, elected by the local inhabitants to represent their interests to the County Council,' George explained. 'When there are problems with any services . . . roads, bus timetables, ferry hours, unsatisfactory planning applications, that sort of thing . . . the Community Council sends someone to talk to the County Councillors. It's known as representation of the people by the people, if you know what I mean.'

Pierre had difficulty disguising his obvious amusement. All week they had been obliged to listen while Milton praised the openness of the United States government to the detriment of the British system. It was good to hear George getting his own back for once.

Chapter Four

The passengers from the 747 had been waiting so long beside the carousel that Jack McDougal began to feel he knew each one of them personally. Some he recognised from his long wait at check-in at Sydney airport; others he had noticed joining the aircraft in Singapore and Bahrain. Aboard the plane he had spent the long, lonely hours speculating about his fellow passengers and their reasons for travelling. By now some faces were so familiar that he regarded them as old friends and nodded in farewell as the carousel began to move at last and, one after another, they gathered their possessions and moved away.

Jack turned his concentration to the extraordinary assortment of luggage which passed before him on the carousel, none of it remotely resembling the expensive, carefully matched set he was looking for. As one exceptionally battered suitcase made its third circuit, it was seized by an individual who had appeared from nowhere. He walked casually forward and lifted it easily off the moving belt. Jack wondered how it was that he had not spotted such an arresting figure before this for the newcomer was a tall, broad-shouldered fellow with a tan to equal Jack's own and hair so red it reminded the Australian of his two young cousins, back home. His hair was sufficiently long for him to have been described as a hippie twenty years earlier. He wore a white singlet and a pair of rumpled khaki shorts, while beneath the strap of his oversized back pack hung the khaki bush jacket which completed his tropical ensemble. Even in high summer this clothing appeared to be quite inadequate for the British climate.

The fellow deposited his back pack on the floor at Jack's feet while he selected a second well-travelled piece from the carousel. Then, having lifted the heavy pack on to his shoulders, he bent to pick up a bulging case in either hand, striking Jack on the shins as he turned away.

'Oh, I say . . . sorry, old chap. Did I hurt you?'

It was a surprisingly cultured voice considering his appearance.

Jack rubbed ruefully at his shin but replied automatically, 'OK, mate, no harm done.'

With a cheerful nod and a polite, 'Enjoy your stay in England, digger,' the stranger strode off in the direction of the immigration desk.

That's one who'll be getting a thorough going over by the Customs boys, Jack decided rather smugly, and turned back to the carousel in time to see the first of his own pieces of luggage disappearing through the screen, returning to the loading bay.

'Oh, blast it!' he muttered and withdrew the second of his two immaculate pieces from the carousel. He placed the case carefully on the trolley with his lap-top and waited for the other to reappear. When at last he was able to retrieve it he joined the queue at the immigration desk.

Once he had cleared Customs, Alan Beaton made straight for the bar on the airport concourse and ordered his first malt whisky in two and a half years. It was good to be able to relax properly at last. Quickly downing his Bruichladdich, he called for another. He normally stuck to beer when actually flying because he considered that spirits exaggerated the symptoms of jet-lag.

He settled back in a comfortable upholstered chair and stretched his legs with relief. The Boeing 747 was never designed to accommodate passengers over five foot ten in height and he had been sitting in a centre seat for hours.

He picked up his copy of the *Lancet* and turned immediately to the article headed 'Health in Rural Communities: a pattern for the future?'.

Alan had spent the last three years in the oil fields and would have been there yet had Saddam Hussein not set his sights on Kuwait. Early in 1990 troops and heavy equipment were brought up to the border and there was every reason to suppose that there might be an invasion. The oil companies immediately warned their European and American staff to prepare for evacuation. While waiting for instructions to leave, Alan had had the foresight to get off a letter in response to an advertisement in the *British Medical Journal* and had actually made contact with a pair of General Practitioners who were seeking an Associate Partner. He would be required to divide his time, covering for two doctors whose country practices were, neither of them, large enough to sustain more than one full time practitioner. In a sparsely populated area it would mean a great deal of travelling but at least he would be introduced gradually to the NHS routines. Things had changed radically since he completed his training in General Practice.

He was looking forward to the challenge. Although his work in Kuwait had centred on the health and welfare of the oil workers themselves, many had brought their families out to the Gulf, with them. Alan had found himself dealing also with women's problems and a full complement of children's diseases, experience which had given him a taste for general practice.

When the word came to move out, he was faced with a long drive through the desert to Abu Dhabi in the United Arab Emirates and a further wait of a week, before a transfer could be arranged to Bahrain for the flight home.

Alan rather hoped he would be able to snatch a couple of weeks' holiday with his parents in Aberdeen before setting out for his new appointment but he had to get to work soon because he needed the money. The oil company had paid well, but most of what he had earned had gone to clearing the debts he had accumulated during his medical training. Apart from a few hundred pounds to tide him over, he was near enough skint.

He had served five years as a resident in a Newcastle hospital, taken his Fellowship in Surgery, and spent the last two years as Medical Officer to one of the largest oil-producing companies in the Gulf. He had had no experience of general practice under the NHS, apart from the six weeks' compulsory work experience which he had undertaken during his medical training. He had worked at that time for a practice in the suburbs of Newcastle. His employer was an elderly GP who, during thirty years of practice, had witnessed, successively, the closure of three local pits and the disbandment of a great steel industry. Years of unemployment had created a society in which two major diseases took precedence: despair and despondency. Valium had been top of the drugs chart. Alan was very pleased to be going now to a rural practice where there were unlikely to be similar problems. Anticipating a leisurely month or two in which to find his feet, he saw this new job as a stepping stone towards the next stage in his career, hopefully in surgery.

His coming sojourn in the Highlands was going to be a complete change from the experience of the past few years and Alan was looking forward to gaining a little breathing space and a chance to look around for more permanent employment.

He swallowed the remainder of his drink and got to his feet. Still holding his copy of the *Lancet*, he trundled his trolley towards the nearest telephone.

In a matter of minutes he was through to the number on the letter he had received just a few days ago. Was it his imagination or did he detect a note of relief in the answering voice?

'Thank you for contacting us so soon, Dr Beaton. Things have changed somewhat since my employer wrote to you . . . we have something of an emergency on our hands—!'

Alan listened intently while the woman related the

problems which had arisen within the practice he was to join.

'I'm speaking from Heathrow,' he told her, 'about to board the shuttle for Glasgow. I shall need a day in the city to settle my business affairs and then I shall have to go home to Aberdeen to retrieve my gear and see my parents . . . I've been away for more than two years, you know.'

He registered the sympathetic note in her reply.

'I really am sorry to have to press you,' she said, 'but we have three thousand registered patients and goodness knows how many tourists without medical cover, and we must have a doctor as soon as possible.'

Alan made a rapid calculation. An overnight stay in Glasgow was essential. He hadn't slept properly for nearly thirty-six hours. He could get to Aberdeen on Tuesday, spend the remainder of the day sorting out his things and making up for lost time with his parents, and be on the road the following day.

'Look,' he said, 'I'll be there some time on Wednesday. Which hospital did you say the doctor had been taken to?' As she replied he scribbled the name on the back of his copy of the *Lancet* and replaced the handset. Thrusting the magazine into the pocket of his rucksack, he trundled his trolley towards the Internal Flights boarding lounge, arriving just as his flight for Scotland was called.

Jack McDougal, who had been seated awaiting the same call for the last twenty minutes, wanting a coffee but daring only to spend a few minutes in the gent's lest he miss the flight, boarded at the head of the queue and settled himself in the Business Class section. He did not see that the 'hippie' he had encountered earlier had followed him on to the plane.

Among the first of the shuttle passengers to emerge from Glasgow airport's arrivals lounge, Alan Beaton hailed a taxi and directed the driver to take him to Hillhead. There was a little barber's shop there he remembered from his student days. First a haircut, then something decent to wear . . . he had only tropical gear in his luggage and all his other stuff was at his parents' home in Aberdeen. There was no time to get there and back before tomorrow morning, so he would have to squander most of his spare cash on a decent outfit. A medical practitioner doing the rounds of the various departments of the local Health Board needed to appear in something more prepossessing than a pair of crumpled Daks and a T-shirt. Once he was suitably kitted out, he would book into the Park Hotel near the hospital where he, and his father before him, had always stayed if their work involved a visit to Glasgow.

Jack McDougal's taxi turned into a quiet tree-lined crescent of houses whose fine proportions, granite-faced exteriors and slated roofs denoted a more affluent time, when middle-class city dwellers could afford to accommodate their families on several floors together with the servants to wait upon them.

Today these buildings served a multitude of purposes. Many were the offices of professional men: architects, accountants, solicitors, medical specialists. Others housed Local Authority offices: the Strathclyde River Board, Regional Department of Land Reform, and so on. There was little to distinguish the Park Hotel from its neighbours in the terrace, the façade of the three houses which constituted it having been left unchanged, despite extensive alterations to the interiors. The Georgian windows and sturdy oak doors looked identical to those of other buildings in the row. Only the discreet sign above the main door gave any hint that this was indeed a hotel.

The Australian was reminded of some of the more prestigious buildings in Adelaide. Places where, as a first-year student, he had stood on the far side of the street imagining what life behind those heavy brass-studded doors could possibly be like.

'Score one point for Maggie,' he told himself.

The last thing he wanted on this trip was one of those modern bedroom factories of the kind that Milton T. Humbert and his competitors felt compelled to build all around the world.

The main door swung open and a porter in a discreetly elegant uniform, which included, of all things, white cotton gloves, bounded down the stairs to collect his luggage. He paid off the taxi and, being unfamiliar with the currency, offered a more than generous tip. The driver politely explained how much Jack had given him and suggested he might wish to reconsider. Too embarrassed to retract, the Australian waved a hand nonchalantly and said, 'That's OK, mate. Thanks all the same. Keep the change.'

The driver, honour satisfied, pocketed the Scottish bank-note. It wasn't every day he made twice the fare in tips.

The entrance hall was impressive to say the least. Thick pile carpet in subtle shades of red, purple and blue covered the floor from wall to wall. Two great chandeliers hung from the ceiling twenty feet above, unlit on this bright afternoon but sparkling in the sun's rays which penetrated a row of oriel windows set above a broad gallery on the first floor. Heavily embossed pale wallpaper covered all the walls, giving the place a feeling of light and space which could not be expelled even by the preponderance of heavily carved, warm-coloured and richly grained wood. Jack whose experience of timber was limited to the hardwoods of Australia, supposed this to be mahogany of some kind.

A wide sweep of staircase, carpeted like the floor, led up to the gallery and the first-floor guest rooms. The place carried an aroma of beeswax and metal polish which was overlaid by a faint mustiness born of age and perhaps a vestige of dry rot within those magnificent old timbers. Jack was again transported to Adelaide and his grandmother's house of which he still held the most vivid memories.

'Mr McDougal?'

The sombrely dressed receptionist repeated his name as he searched the bookings register.

'Ah, yes, here we are. Your booking was made by a Miss Turner, speaking from,' he hesitated over the name, 'the Kookaburra Resort, Queensland. A Mr Humbert is expected also?'

'Yes, he will be arriving tomorrow morning, I believe.' Jack wished Maggie had not been so explicit as to their address. She probably thought she would get Milton a better deal if the proprietors realised they were in the hospitality business, too.

'Ah, yes, the details are here. Do you know how long you will be staying, Mr McDougal?'

'No. It will depend upon my discussion with Mr Humbert, but two nights certainly, maybe a third.'

'Your room will be number six, on the first floor. Mr Humbert is in number five.'

'You don't mind if I have a look at the rooms first, do you?'

If the receptionist was taken aback by this request, he did not show it, despite the fact that guests rarely questioned the acceptability of the rooms in the Park Hotel. Noting the source of the bookings, he suspected that this Australian visitor, being something to do with the hotel trade, was probably trying to make a point. Confident that the room would be acceptable, he called the porter.

'Please take Mr McDougal to number six. If he finds the room to his liking you may carry up his bags later.' He handed the boy the keys to both rooms. 'Perhaps you would also like to confirm that Mr Humbert's room is suitable, sir.'

It was all so smooth, so polite yet so disparaging. Jack winced, but made no sign that he was in any way disturbed by the man's attitude. He had stayed in some of the best and also perhaps the worst accommodation in the world, and chandeliers or no chandeliers in the entrance hall, he had no intention of taking a room he hadn't seen first.

He followed the porter up the broad staircase and around the gallery until they came to a door with a shining brass number five. The man opened up to reveal a spacious room with a real four-poster bed standing on a low dais. The draperies to bed and windows were in subtle shades of greyish-green and orange which were set off elegantly by a deep-pile carpet in warm beige. With a practised hand, Jack lifted back the top cover on the bed and checked that the sheets were spotless. He nodded with satisfaction as he wiped a finger across the top of the bedside table and found it clean. He checked the bathroom and turned to the porter.

'Right, shall we take the room next door?'

Number six differed from the room assigned to Milton in only two respects. The double bed was a modern divan and the furnishings were in shades of blue rather than green. Jack carried out his inspection as he would have done in any room at the Kookaburra Resort.

'OK,' he said. 'These should do very well. Bring up the bags, will you?'

The man opened the door on to the gallery and left it propped open ready for his return. From the entrance hall below Jack heard the sound of voices raised in merriment. Someone was receiving a very different welcome from that afforded to himself. The receptionist's accent appeared much more Scottish and was readily distinguishable from the second voice which also seemed oddly familiar. Curious to see who the newcomer might be, Jack stepped out on to the gallery and looked over the rail.

At the counter stood a tall figure dressed in an immaculate business suit. His shoes were so highly polished that they reflected the light from the chandeliers which had now been switched on, giving the hall the appearance of a Regency ballroom. His hair, which had been neatly styled to control its tendency to form curls across the forehead, was fiery red but even this did not give Jack a clue as to where he had met the owner of that voice before. It was only when the tall figure stooped to hoist a scruffy, overloaded back pack on to his shoulder, that Jack realised who it was. The last person in the world he would have expected to encounter at the Park Hotel that evening was the hippie he had met at the airport.

The receptionist was shaking Alan Beaton warmly by the hand.

'Aye, but it's good to see ye home safe and well, Doctor,' he exclaimed, handing Alan his key. 'You'll be wanting your old room, as usual?'

'If it's available, William.' The doctor laughed good-naturedly, as the porter attempted to lift his case and failed.

'That's all right, Harry. I'll do it myself. Is the lift working today?'

'Aye, but she might object to both you and your luggage, sir,' laughed the receptionist. 'She's been a wee bitty cranky of late.'

'Tell you what, I'll put the bags in the lift and run up the stairs myself . . . how will that be?'

All three found this suggestion so amusing that further gales of laughter rolled around the vaulted ceiling.

Not wishing to appear to be eavesdropping, Jack returned to his room and was taking in the view from his window when the porter re-appeared.

'What's the big red building on top of the hill?' he

enquired, when he had watched the man place his two suitcases side by side on the rack.

Harry came to stand beside him.

'On the very top, that's Glasgow University,' he replied. 'Below it is the Western Infirmary, and the other large building at the foot of the slope, that's the Art Gallery.'

'Some of those places look pretty old,' said the Australian, to whom anything over more than a hundred years was ancient history.

'The University was founded in 1451 but that particular building was built in 1870. Of course it's been very much altered over the years. Much of what you see from this side is Victorian, but the newest parts of the Infirmary were built after the last war.'

'So the original building is over five hundred years old?' The question was asked almost reverently.

'Oh, no, the original building was down here, on High Street. That was pulled down to make way for shops and offices, more's the pity. Glasgow Cathedral and Paisley Abbey now, they date from the time of the original University, nearly five hundred and fifty years ago,' the porter explained proudly.

'I've spoken to one or two Scotsmen since I arrived. Most of them don't speak like you at all,' observed Jack. 'In fact, you sound a lot like an elderly relative of my father. He came from Argyll.'

'I am from the west coast myself,' said the man. 'From a wee island called Eisdalsa. D'ye see yon blue slates on the roof of the University building? They came from quarries dug out by my great-grandfather and his pals.

You'll not find better slate than that anywhere. It was sold all around world. You could probably find some of it on roofs in Australia.'

Jack was impressed by Harry's loyalty to his home. It reminded him of the way his grandfather once spoke of Scotland. The man was talking about slate quarries similar to those which had figured so largely in the old stories he had heard at his grandfather's knee on those quiet evenings when the men had gathered around the campfire after a long day at the shearing. He recalled how often an old grey head would nod wisely in recognition of the often-told stories of 'back home', and, under the bright panoply of the Southern Constellations, a surreptitious tear of regret would be shed for times long past.

As he listened to the note of pride in the porter's voice, Jack wondered if he himself might ever get to see this island which could inspire such loyalty in a man even when it had failed to provide him with a living.

Milton seemed remarkably fit after his holiday in the Highlands. Jack, who was still feeling jaded from the after-effects of jet-lag, was quite overwhelmed by his employer's enthusiasm for Maggie's choice of hotel, his four-poster bed, the view of the University from his window . . . everything! These high spirits could mean only one thing. He had a new project in mind and nothing was going to deter him from carrying it out.

'Oh, gee, McDougal . . . how could your folks ever have left such a wonderful country? Scotland's the greatest place on earth.'

'I believe it was a question of emigrate or starve,' he replied, laconically.

'Wait until you see those mountains, boy, and that coast! It beats the Gold Coast any day. It's so rugged. The colours are amazing. The greens are so green and the blues so blue. There is absolutely nothing to beat the western sky at sunset. It's a sin more people don't get a chance to appreciate it. Would you believe, that castle gets no more than five thousand visitors to its gardens in a year, and the islands provide accommodation for a mere couple of hundred tourists at a time?'

'It's got to be something mighty special for you to have dragged me all the way over here to see it,' said Jack. 'I presume that you've found some spot that is presently untouched by the hand of other entrepreneurs and intend to rectify that situation?'

'In a nutshell, boy!'

'What do the locals have to say about expanding the tourist trade?'

'Oh, mum's the word for the moment, Jack. Don't want any minority lobbyists getting wind of what we're doing until we've made a few more enquiries and got things straight with the powers that be. You know how it is. No one thinks of a thing until some outsider comes in and shows them the way, then they all want to get in on the act.'

Jack, who had fought a number of similar battles on Milton's behalf, knew only too well what it was to go against opposition from the public.

'Did you try sounding out local opinion?'

'Only in the most discreet way, but there's no doubt

about it – the economy of the place is at rock bottom, there are plenty of people without permanent employment and what they have doesn't pay too well so our labour costs should be low. I can't see anyone arguing against a development which is going to bring money into the place.'

'So, what's the plan?'

'They recognised me as a potential developer straight away, of course,' his boss declared.

Jack, only too aware of his inability to hide his light under a bushel, could imagine the impact that Milton would have had upon a group of naïve country folk.

'No doubt you bought their confidence with free drinks all round?' he suggested, having employed similar strategies himself, in the past. It was a project just like all the others so why, he wondered, did he feel so uneasy about this one?

'I bought a few rounds for my particular friends, yes,' Milton agreed, cheerily. 'What's wrong with that?'

'And did you make any suggestions about how they could improve this economy of theirs?' the younger man demanded. If Milton had put forward some suggestions, no matter how casually, his own task would be made all the more difficult. They might already be considering acting on those suggestions off their own bat or, worse still, have begun to formulate arguments against Milton's proposals.

Jack could see all kinds of problems arising from this venture. Except in the very early days, when Humbert Developments was a minor real-estate organisation, Milton had had no hand in the preliminary negotiations

for any new project, choosing always to remain anonymous until the last possible moment. He kept a team of
men in the field seeking out suitable locations for
exploitation and wisely restricted his own input to those
discussions which took place behind closed doors.

Quite oblivious to any doubts there might be in Jack's
mind, Milton proceeded on the assumption that the
matter was already decided.

'I want you to turn up at Seileachan as if by chance,'
he said. 'You have Scottish ancestors. What could be
more natural than that you should be over here seeking
your roots? I'm told there's a museum on the island,
where one can go and look up family records. That might
be your best way to start.'

'You haven't explained what you have in mind for this
little piece of paradise you've discovered. Am I to
assume we're talking about another Kookaburra?'

'What else? Because the place is so isolated we shall
have to provide everything . . . transport from Glasgow,
our own ferry to the island . . . the present arrangement
is too restrictive. Did I mention that the plan will be
centred on this cute little island? – Eisdalsa they call it.
That's where we'll build the hotel accommodation. There
might be a few problems with multi-storey but we'll go
for that to begin with, see what they say. I'll leave you to
work out with the locals the kind of sporting activities
which will be most appropriate. Boating of different
kinds is obvious. and diving . . . the water's not too cold
and I'm told there are reefs in plenty to be explored . . .
even a few wrecks. We'll have to provide a couple of
pools – at present the islanders swim in one of the old

slate quarries but only in hot weather. One pool under cover for the winter season would be essential. George Monteith's shoot doesn't provide for more than a limited number of guns every season. Maybe we shall have to negotiate our own grouse moor. There shouldn't be any problem laying down a golf course, and then of course we can fix rights of way for nature walks, abseiling, all that stuff. We'll need evening entertainment. There are some talented local musicians and dancers – people will be expecting to see a bit of tartan. There are a few crafts-men we might set up in a craft village where tourists can buy locally made objects. In short, everything the average tourist's heart could desire!'

'It seems you'll have to rely heavily upon local labour. Are you sure there will be enough people around to run the thing?'

'If not, we can bring ours in.'

'That will mean even more accommodation. I thought you said boarding facilities in the village were practically non-existent?'

'We'll have to build additional accommodation for staff.'

'You don't seem to have considered the weather.'

'How do you mean? It was fine all the time I was there.'

'Did you take the trouble to find out how many days in the year it rains? Scotland is notorious for its wet weather. It's the rain that makes everything those glorious colours you were eulogising about a few minutes ago.'

Milton's enthusiasm was not to be dampened by mere practicalities. 'OK, so we build a dome over the whole damn' lot and give them a perfectly controlled environment.'

'Who's going to put all this to the planners?'

In a warm and confident gesture Milton threw his arms about his young protégé and said, 'Why, you are, my boy. Why do you think I sent for you from among all my smart executives? You're one of *them*, after all! Oh, I know you don't have the accent, but you only have to spread the word about your ancestry . . . you might even be able to come up with some genuine connection with the island itself. Who knows?'

'Argyll was a big county even before it became a part of Strathclyde Region,' Jack observed. 'All I know is that my grandfather's folks came from Argyll. They were farmers, for God's sake. That means they could have lived anywhere!'

'Are you telling me you don't want this opportunity I'm handing to you on a plate, boy? Because if that's the case I can as easily get Paulo Sanchez over from Miami. He won't be so picky.'

Jack could see Milton was determined to go ahead with his plan. And maybe it wasn't such an outlandish idea after all. Not everyone wanted to lie on a hot beach and bask in the sun for weeks at a time. Presumably there was already a nucleus of tourists attracted to the place.

From what Milton had told him about Seileach and Eisdalsa he tried to envisage a holiday environment like that the company had created on the coast of Queensland. With the exception of the weather, the other aspects were little different from the Kookaburra. Sea, boats and fishing, hiking, cycling and horse riding through wild, open countryside, together with a flavour of quaint rural activities . . . all these could well be a terrific pull with the tourists. Jack began to feel a little of Milton's enthusiasm rubbing off on him.

'OK,' he agreed. 'I'll give it a whirl.'

'That's my boy. Now then, I'll arrange for a new four-wheel drive to be delivered here tomorrow morning. You'll need a car that will go anywhere and the roads are like sidewalks. I don't suppose you have suitable clothes for the Highlands? No, well, use your company credit card. Any expense within reason.'

In a moment he would be suggesting a visit to Sauchiehall Street to purchase a complete outfit of Highland dress.

'Now hold on,' Jack interrupted him before he could get too carried away. 'If I'm supposed to be a travelling Australian looking up my ancestors, I don't think I should be turning up in a new off-road vehicle and an expensive wardrobe, do you? If I'm to work my way in with the locals, I think I should look the part of a digger taking a holiday. You know the kind of thing. A cheap ramble around Europe. You'd better leave the vehicle and the clothes to me.'

'If you say so. There's a neat little hotel just outside the village on the mainland side. It's called Tigh na Broch – the House of the Badgers or the Badger's Sett or something.'

'That'll do for a start,' Jack agreed, 'but I think I might do better to find less expensive accommodation . . . a room in a private house perhaps? Hotels don't come cheap for impecunious travellers.'

'Up to you.'

'What about the Kookaburra?' Jack asked. 'I left in such a hurry, Maggie only had instructions for about ten days and Delia was away when I left. She's going to be real mad if I'm not there when she gets back.'

'Maggie can hold the fort and if you get delayed for too long I'll send one of the West Indies team out to take over for a while. As for Delia . . . well, I'm sure she won't grumble when she hears about your promotion.'

'Promotion?'

'Get this thing sorted out for me and you'll be Vice President, UK Enterprises, before the year's end!'

They finished their drinks and moved into the dining room. Just as they entered, Alan Beaton brushed past the two businessmen. The newcomer hesitated when he saw Jack, trying to remember where he had seen that face before. He took a cursory glance at the second man and dismissed both of them as casual guests.

Chapter Five

The Argyll Hospital for Respiratory Diseases stood high on a hill above the port. Built in the late-nineteenth century, mainly for the treatment of tuberculosis, it had in its day been as popular with Scottish physicians as any of the more expensive establishments in the Swiss Alps. The Argyll had specialised in the treatment of lung diseases during and after two world wars and for a long period of economic depression between the two. As a result of overcrowding and a meagre diet, there had been a huge increase in the incidence of the disease locally until well into the 1950s. The introduction of modern drugs had since led to the demise of TB, but the affluence which had followed had resulted in an upsurge of a different group of diseases: those more closely associated with over-indulgence in the good things of life.

The hospital had, under the Regional Health Board, been designated a centre for the treatment of vascular conditions of all kinds. With the exception of the introduction of a helicopter pad for the receipt of patients from the outer islands, the drab collection of single-storey brick buildings, which were still euphemistically called pavilions, had changed little since 1901 when the last major extension had been provided. A few huts had been erected as a temporary measure during the 1950s but forty years on, these were still in use as laboratories, treatment and consulting rooms. A new building had been suggested for many years, but cutbacks by successive governments and an extensive County boundary change had provided grounds for prevarication. A project which twenty years before would have carried a six-figure price tag was now expected to cost the taxpayer several millions and in the present climate seemed to be out of the question.

Alan Beaton's red, vintage model E-type Jaguar, took the steep road with a roar and a puff of blue smoke from the twin stainless steel exhaust pipes. This one luxury was all he had allowed himself from the grinding hours he had invested in his profession in the past few years. As well as clearing his debts, he had been able to raise just enough money to carry out the restoration of the magnificent machine. During the rebuilding of the Jaguar he himself had handled every nut and bolt. Under the bonnet there were three litres of cylinder space, and when she fired the engine purred like a cat. The dashboard was polished walnut and the instrument panel was reminiscent of the flight deck of a Boeing 707. The solid leather upholstery exuded that peculiar scent, evocative of the high life, which is found only in the most prestigious of vehicles. Alan took little interest in accumulating material rewards for his labours. He did not expect wealth, although he hoped for satisfaction, even success, from his chosen profession. He envied no one. This car was his only indulgence and when he was behind the wheel, he was king of the road.

The car slowed on its approach to a hairpin bend. He changed down to second gear, pumped the accelerator and roared away along the final straight and level stretch which led to the gates of the hospital.

He was not the first to consider this an unfortunate choice of site for a heart hospital. Access must be very difficult for those without their own transport and the strenuous climb must sometimes contribute additional problems.

Sister herself conducted him to the ward where Ewan McWorter had been installed, following his transfer from intensive care. An oxygen trolley was drawn up beside the bed alongside another carrying an array of electronic equipment. A heart monitor bleeped insistently and Alan's gaze fell upon a dark screen where the trace told its own story of an elderly heart weakened to the point of surrender. His diagnosis was confirmed by the fact that the patient was obliged to seek the aid of the oxygen mask rather too frequently.

'Dr McWorter?' Sister touched the old man lightly on the shoulder to attract his attention.

His was a very different appearance from that of the carefree fisherman of a week ago, so keen to show off his favourite stretches of trout stream to his Canadian friend. Ewan's face wore the hollowed cheeks and prominent bone structure of the seriously ill, while deep purple shadows emphasised the feverish brightness of his eyes and the grey pallor of his skin. He seemed to be in a daze, but whether from drugs or sheer exhaustion it was difficult to tell.

'What's that, Annie?' Ewan McWorter, roused from his torpor, seemed not to recognise the sister immediately. He squinted at her and murmured feebly, 'Sorry, I must have been dreaming.'

'This is Dr Beaton, your new colleague, Dr McWorter,' she told him. 'He's called in to see you.'

'Beaton?' McWorter stared at the newcomer for a long time, trying to focus more clearly on the eager young face. There was something about that shock of curly red hair and those piercing grey eyes that reminded him of someone . . .

'Beaton . . . I wondered, when I read your application . . . that was a name well-known in these parts half a century ago.' He paused, gathering strength to continue. 'Hugh Beaton was the consultant in surgery here during the war . . . He set my arm when I broke it falling down a cliff. I must have been twelve or thirteen at the time . . . must have been well past retiring age – he'd served in the first war too, you know.'

'I believe that could have been my great-grandfather,' said Alan, moving forward and leaning over the bed to take hold of one pale, heavily veined hand. The skin was dry and paper thin, the handshake feeble. 'My father mentioned visiting him when he was very young, but he couldn't recall where exactly – only that the house was somewhere near Oban. My people have always lived in England – until Dad retired a year or two ago.'

The elderly doctor seemed confused. He tried to make a calculation of his visitor's age and failed.

'Funny to have a Beaton in these parts again,' he muttered. 'Thought they'd all died out . . .'

'No need for you to worry about your practice now, sir,' Alan told him. 'Once I find my way around, I'm sure I'll be able to manage. I had a pretty varied experience out in the Middle East.'

Although he tried to appear cheerful, he was filled with dismay. They had told him back in Glasgow that it was a mild heart condition and that McWorter would be back on his feet in a few weeks. It had been suggested to him that he might be needed to take the full weight of the practice for about six weeks, despite only being appointed on an Associateship basis. Now, however, he saw little prospect of this frail old man ever taking up the reins again. Alan's heart sank. For it would probably be a matter of days only before a decision was made as to Ewan McWorter's future. Once it was formally agreed that the old doctor would not be returning to work, wheels would be set in motion and the practice reallocated, almost certainly leaving him without employment in a matter of weeks, rather than months.

'You know Eisdalsa?' McWorter asked, rallying his thoughts.

'No, I've never been there. My father's work kept us in London until after I left home in 1980, to start my medical training. My only connection with Scotland is that I took my degree at Glasgow University and trained at the Western Infirmary.'

There had never been any doubt as to choice of career for the adolescent Alan Beaton. The male members of the family had trained in medicine and surgery at Glasgow University for generations.

'Eisdalsa's a grand wee place,' said the old man. 'Good

people . . . A bunch of cantankerous old curmudgeons . . . some of them, but once they take you to their hearts . . . there's nothing they won't do for you.' There was a tear in his eye as he remembered how supportive his patients had been after Annie's death.

These past days he had thought of her so much. Finding himself *in extremis*, he had finally accepted the fact of her dying. Until his heart attack, he had continued to hope that her death was just a bad dream. He had continued to listen for her step in the hallway, for the sound of her singing as she went about the house. He had convinced himself that one day he would walk into the kitchen and there would be a basket of newly gathered vegetables from the garden which she had always tended so lovingly.

Certain, now, that she would be there, waiting for him when his time came, Ewan felt he could at last face up to her absence. They would not be apart for much longer . . .

Alan could see that his visit was tiring the patient.

'I must go now,' he said. 'Is there anything particular you want me to know about?'

'It's all in the notes,' McWorter replied. He inhaled deeply through the mask and, while he did so, a sudden thought struck him. He raised himself off the pillow and reached out as though to hold Alan back for a moment longer. 'Mrs Clark . . . the Post Office . . . need to see about her blood pressure . . .'

Alan grasped the restless hand, and replaced it gently on the white candlewick cover.

'Don't worry yourself,' he said. 'I'll take care of it.'

As he passed Sister's office he paused to thank her.

'I may be seeing you again?' he suggested.

'No doubt,' replied the woman crisply. 'Most of the local GPs pop in and out of here like yoyos. I suppose they think we don't know what we're doing with their precious patients.'

'I was thinking more of calling back from time to time, to report to Dr McWorter. He seems very disturbed about the condition of some of his patients. I thought I might perhaps be able to relieve his anxieties.'

Her expression softened.

'The poor wee man,' she sighed. 'He'll be glad to hear how his people are getting on. I'll look forward to seeing you then, doctor.'

With a rustle of starched cotton she hurried off, leaving behind her a whiff of Chanel No. 5 subtly blended with the more familiar aroma of iodoform. Some patients were obviously generous with their presents to the staff.

Flora Douglas watched the little red sports car draw in to the parking lot and made hurried adjustments to her appearance, before hastening to greet her temporary employer. She smoothed her spotless white overall over neatly rounded hips and straightened the lace collar of her new blouse from McKay's. A quick glance in the mirror reflected a pale, delicately featured face, perfectly framed by dark, silky locks, cut fashionably short. It was important to make a good first impression. Satisfied that there was not a single hair out of place, she opened the door. The new doctor seemed to be younger than she had been led to believe. This was not the sort of practice favoured by most ambitious young men.

'Dr Beaton?' she asked, admitting him to the tiny entrance hall.

'I'm a little later than I anticipated,' he said apologetically, placing his medical case on the step while he shook her hand.

'Miss Douglas, isn't it?'

'Flora,' she smiled in return.

'I stopped off at the hospital to introduce myself to Dr McWorter. I hope I haven't kept you waiting about?'

He had been told that the receptionist worked a half day on Wednesdays to compensate for being on duty for the occasional Saturday surgery.

'Not at all, doctor,' she replied. 'I couldna' allow you to arrive with no one to greet you. It will do no harm for me to spend an hour or so showing you the ropes.' She blushed, wondering if he would think that presumptuous.

'That's very good of you,' he replied. 'I suppose there is already quite a backlog of work? Has anyone been covering for Dr McWorter since he was taken ill?'

'Only Dr Pullson. She normally works one day a week and takes emergency calls alternate weekends. She has a couple of small children so can only spare a few hours, keeping her hand in as it were until the children are older. Anyway, she has been dealing with emergencies but the regular surgery and home visits have been postponed, so there are a few urgent matters to be dealt with. If you like, we can go through the list when I've shown you the surgery.'

'Do you have an appointments system?'

'No, it's not really necessary. The waiting room is rarely full. If there's going to be a long wait for any reason, I telephone the regulars to put them off coming in.'

Alan recalled the huge numbers of patients seen every day by his colleagues in Newcastle. As he had hoped, this did not appear to be a busy practice.

Flora showed him the consulting room and dispensary, explaining her own part in its operation, and they spent some time going through the method of keeping the records.

'No computer?' he asked, somewhat dismayed to find that records were confined to an outdated system of card indexing.

'Oh, yes, we have one.' Flora indicated a mound of equipment hiding beneath a grey plastic sheet. 'Dr McWorter never quite got the hang of it.'

Alan could well imagine McWorter's response to the Regional Health Board's insistence that he install modern technology.

'I use it myself,' she hastened to add, 'for stock control of drugs, letters, invoicing and so on, but we never quite got around to computerising patients' records.'

'Have you had any lunch?' Alan asked suddenly. He glanced at the clock. 'There must be a pub or something where we can get a bite to eat?'

'The only place to eat out is the Badger Bar . . . along the road towards Eisdalsa. On a Wednesday I go home to eat,' she explained. 'Other days I just bring in a sandwich.'

'And I've held you up,' he said. 'I'm so sorry. You must

let me make it up to you by buying you a meal. Will they still be serving food at this time?' It was nearly two o'clock.

'Usually not after two . . . but I could ring ahead and ask them to make up something.' She went into the office and Alan heard her one-sided conversation with the landlord of the local inn.

When she returned she was smiling.

'He will make us some fish and chips,' she said. 'It will be ready in twenty minutes. Are you very hungry? You must have been travelling for hours.'

'I left Aberdeen at seven this morning,' he told her. 'It took longer than I anticipated. The roads were crowded with holiday traffic – lots of caravans on the move. Going home for the winter, I suppose.'

'Yes, it's always bad at this time of the year.' She handed him a set of keys.

'You'll need these,' she said. 'This is to the outer door, and this is the surgery key. The corridor door to the dispensary has a special lock, by order of the powers that be. It's such a palaver opening it that we don't use that door at all. We gain access either through the surgery or the office. The lock is of course a precaution against casual theft but I can't imagine anyone attempting to break in here.'

She searched in her handbag for several seconds before triumphantly extracting a set of car keys. 'If you'll follow me in your car, I can show you the way to the hotel.'

'I can see I'm going to have to rely heavily upon you for the next few days,' said Alan. 'Until I get the hang of things.'

'Of course.' She felt her flesh tingling and her knees weakening in the warmth of his charming smile.

'Do you have anywhere to stay? I did explain to the chap in Glasgow that the doctor's private accommodation would not be suitable.'

'I've been told to look for accommodation as close to the surgery as possible, but in the meantime they will pay me a hotel allowance. Depending on how long this appointment is likely to last, I had thought of trying to rent somewhere. There must be a few holiday cottages which are not let for the winter months?'

'I'm sure you'll find something,' she assured him. 'I'll ask around. You might talk to Jean Clark at the Post Office, she always has her ear to the ground in these matters.'

Her mention of the Post Office jogged Alan's memory.

'Dr McWorter was anxious about a Mrs Clark . . . she has to have a check on her blood pressure?'

'He did mention it, the day before he was taken off to hospital,' Flora answered. 'I'll look out her notes for you in the morning and ask her to come along to the surgery if you like.'

'Fine. Well, hadn't we best be going? The pub won't keep that food for us forever.'

She reddened. 'I'm so sorry, you must be starving. I was getting a little too carried away . . . there seems to be so much to talk about.'

'I'll follow you then, shall I?'

As he waited for Flora to start up and move away, Alan glanced up at the house. It looked as though it might have been an ordinary crofter's cottage at some time. It was single-storey with a high-pitched slated roof whose attic rooms had clearly been added at a later date. He wondered vaguely if this had always been the doctor's house. If so, was it possible that this was the place where his ancestors had lived? He hardly thought so. His father had intimated that the Beatons had been a typical Victorian middle-class family. He couldn't see them living in a crofter's cottage.

There was little charm in the outward appearance of the building because a mid-twentieth-century extension had been added to provide a surgery and waiting room. This was flat-roofed and constructed of block rather than local stone, the bonding clearly visible where the blocks grinned through the well-weathered paintwork. The large modern casements of the extension contrasted adversely with the sliding sashes and small panes of the original cottage. Like the walls, the timber window frames and doors had once been painted a uniform white but now were mainly bare wood. There was a general air of dilapidation about the place and it was clear that poor McWorter had been letting things slide. Alan prayed that the practice itself had been conducted more efficiently.

Despite the late hour, there was still a sizeable gathering in the Badger Bar of the Tigh na Broch Hotel. As they entered, Flora was greeted on all sides and it was clear from the jocularity of the exchanges that some of the clientele had been taking an unusually long lunch break.

'This is Doctor Mac's new assistant,' Flora announced, making a general introduction. 'Dr Beaton will be taking care of things for the next few weeks.'

There were general polite acknowledgements from all around and Alan found himself being introduced to Jock and Tam, Jamie, Theo and Baldy. He knew he would not remember their names the next time he saw them but they would all know him. He felt at home instantly and was soon participating in the general banter appropriate to the last half hour before closing.

'I thought pubs stayed open all day in Scotland,' he ventured to remark, when the bar slowly began to empty until only the two of them and the permanent fixture in the corner of the bar, who answered to the name of Baldy, remained.

'They can,' Flora explained, 'but by this time of the year there isn't sufficient tourist trade to warrant staying open all afternoon, so Marty closes for a few hours before the evening session.'

Each having consumed a piled plateful of the most delicious fish and chips that Alan had tasted in more than two years, they lingered over their drinks until the landlord reappeared.

'Do you have a spare room for a few nights?' Alan enquired, 'Just until I can find somewhere more permanent to stay.'

'Of course,' Martin Crane replied, pleased to be able to let a room so late in the season. 'If you've finished your meal, I'll show you what I have by way of accommodation.'

'Well, I must be going.' Flora got to her feet. 'Will I be seeing you in the morning? Thursday is normally Dr Mac's day off and Dr Pullson will take surgery.'

'I think I'll take the opportunity to sit in with her, if

she's agreeable. Anyway, I'll be in early,' he told her. 'When do you usually arrive?'

'I start at eight o'clock.' She went to the door.

'Thank you, Flora,' he called after her, using her name for the first time.

She blushed.

'I'll probably go back to the surgery this afternoon and go through some of the records, if that's all right by you,' he added. 'Oh, yes . . . and I'll take any emergency calls. Did you leave a telephone number for Dr Pullson, by any chance? I'd best get in touch with her as soon as possible.'

'In the address book by the phone.' Flora felt an inexplicable twinge of jealousy. She did not feel like sharing this delightful new colleague with anyone, especially Janice Pullson who, married though she might be, was not only exceedingly attractive but also on Alan's own level professionally.

'Right, doctor.' Martin came from behind the bar, wiping his hands on a tea towel. 'If you'll just follow me?'

He led the way out into the main hallway of the hotel. A stained glass window in the front door cast a rainbow pattern of colour on the black and white marble-tiled floor. A dado of dark oak panelling gave a gloomy atmosphere which was accentuated by the sepia photographs, images from a hundred years before, which covered every inch of wall space.

Seeing Alan's expression, Martin hastened to say, 'I know . . . terrible, isn't it? I only took the place over eighteen months ago and so far we've concentrated on the guest rooms which I hope you'll find more cheerful. If I take down those old photos I shall have to decorate the walls, so they'll need to stay as they are for a while longer. This was how the house was when my predecessor first bought it and turned it into an hotel,' he continued. 'Before that it was a family home complete with farm . . . the old farm house is where my wife and I live ourselves. It's a bit of a mess at present but I intend to have the whole place restored once we get the hotel on its feet.'

He led the way up a wide staircase to the floor above and halted before the first of a number of doors opening from a broad landing, lit by a single window at the far end. Through this Alan could make out the slopes of a mountain, rising up behind the hotel. 'Caisteal an Spuilleadair,' Martin told him. 'The path you see going up the hillside is the route of the annual hill run . . . one of the events in the Highland Games.'

'Do they still hold the games in these parts?' Alan asked, intrigued.

'Every summer each of the villages produces a team and invites participants from all the others. From the last week in June there's "games" almost every week until the end of August. Ours is held on the meadow alongside the hotel. Makes quite a difference to our trade for a few days, I can tell you.'

He opened a door.

'This is one of our larger rooms.'

It was comfortably furnished with a modern bed and chairs but the tallboy and wardrobe were clearly from another era and probably valuable antiques. A Victorian cheval mirror stood to one side of the bay window which offered a sweeping view across the hotel's grounds to the sea shore and the ocean beyond.

In the bay itself stood a heavily carved oak desk of the same period as the tallboy.

The soft furnishings had been tastefully selected from modern Laura Ashley prints which lent an added charm and softened the otherwise austerely plain white walls. In this room the landlord had been more selective with his pictures. A pair of watercolours depicting sea and boats, and some colourful flower prints, completed the decoration.

'This is splendid,' declared Alan, pressing the mattress and finding it more than satisfactory.

'How many nights do you expect to stay?' asked Martin.

'Let's say a week in the first instance . . . if that suits you?' replied the doctor. 'By then I may have had time to sort out some more permanent arrangement.'

'I could offer a special tariff if you decided to stay on longer during the slack period,' Martin suggested, hopefully.

Alan, who was accustomed to fending for himself, shook his head, doubtfully. 'I was hoping to be able to rent somewhere,' he said, 'but we'll see how it goes, shall we? I'll just go and fetch my gear from the car.'

'I'll give you a hand.' The landlord followed behind the younger man.

The house had had a peculiar effect upon Alan. He had never been anywhere near this part of the country, he was quite sure, not even in his childhood, and yet every turn in the stair, every rail on the balustrade, seemed familiar. At the foot of the stairs he instinctively turned into a narrow passage and came to a stop.

'Where does this go?'

'Quiet lounge – library, if you like,' said Martin. 'There's a TV in the main lounge which not everyone wants to watch, so we provide an alternative room. Used to be the doctor's surgery, I understand. This was the home of the local GP right up until the end of the war. After that, it was sold to my predecessor and the next doctor bought the present house along the main road.'

When they reached his car, it was clear that Martin was hugely impressed by the Jaguar and the two men quickly discovered a mutual interest in vintage cars of all kinds.

'She's beautiful,' said the landlord, running his fingers lovingly over the shining paintwork. 'Looks ready to enter for a *Concours d'Elégance* this afternoon!'

'Nice of you to say so,' said Alan, 'but I think she'd need a bit of a polish up first.'

'Any time you want some help with that, just say the word.' Martin attempted to lift the first of Alan's cases out of the boot.

'What on earth have you got in here?' he gasped, straining under the weight.

'Oh, don't bother with that one . . . I'll take it down to the surgery. It's mostly books. Unfortunately it's necessary to carry a library around with you in this job. I had to send that lot on ahead when I left Bahrain. They were waiting for me when I got home. Not knowing what sort of a reference library Dr McWorter has, I thought it best to bring them along.'

'There's a fair number of old medical books in the library here,' Martin told him. 'You might have a look through them some time, if you would. They'll be out of date, of course, but you may find them interesting. I was thinking of handing some of them over to the museum.'

'I doubt if I'll have much of a chance this week,' Alan replied, 'but I'll be glad to take a look later on.'

He removed his back pack from the boot and hoisted it on to his shoulders while Martin carried in the remaining suitcase.

Pausing in the hallway, Alan found himself staring at the enlarged photograph of a young man, seventeen or eighteen years of age, wearing the stiff collar and silk cravat which were everyday dress in the late 1900s. It was a sepia print like the rest, but had been lightly coloured in by hand. The hair was swept back with macassar oil and cut severely short, but it had been given a reddish tinge and the eyes, which were quite striking in their intensity, had been tinted a light grey. Alan felt a stab of recognition. Where had he seen that face before? he wondered. It was only when he had reached the privacy of his room and set down his luggage that he chanced to glance into the long mirror. The reflection he saw there was a slightly older version of the portrait in the hall below.

It was in a two-year-old, dark green Ford Escort, hired from Clyde Cars, that Jack McDougal drove over the brow of the hill on that bright September afternoon when he saw Eisdalsa Island for the first time.

He pulled in to the side of the road and parked the car.

Reaching behind him for the binoculars which lay on the rear seat, he stepped out, stretched his cramped legs and began to climb. A series of steep steps led to a look-out point from which he was able to view the entire coastline.

He spread out the Ordnance Survey map which he had purchased in town at the tourist information centre and studied it as best he could, all the time fighting the breeze which threatened to tear it from his hands.

The nearest island, Eisdalsa, lay a short distance offshore in the midst of a sparkling ocean upon whose surface only a modicum of white horses could be seen. At the southernmost point of the island, creaming surf broke upon the dark rocks, while against the skyline a small hill rose up behind a village of white cottages. A narrow inlet widened into a substantial harbour where a number of sail boats and small dinghies rode at anchor. There were more boats drawn up on a narrow beach and others lay upturned on the grass beyond the harbour wall. Amongst these smaller craft the massive red and black hulk of an old puffer seemed to be quite out of keeping. These coastal steamers which had been the most common bulk carriers to service the Hebridean islands in former days, had almost entirely disappeared.

Jack, who had in his youth absorbed much of his awareness of British culture from television programmes exported to Australia, had at his father's insistence watched every episode of the *Para Handy* series. While he had found the language difficult to comprehend at times, he had come to love the true hero of the piece . . . an old puffer called *The Vital Spark*.

With an exclamation of delight, he took out his notebook and wrote down one word: PUFFER. He added a question mark.

There were more islands which he struggled to identify. The Islands of the Sea, all of them triangular in shape, rose out of the waves due west of where he stood. Positioned midway between the larger islands of Mull and Scarba, they formed part of a circle of islands surrounding the southern shores of Mull. Closer to hand, he was able to identify the northern tip of the long island of Lunga which was approached across a narrow strait from the isle of Seileach. To the south-west, on another small island which barely rose above sea level in any part, were the skeletal remains of an abandoned settlement whose roofless cottages, their gable ends protruding above the narrow strip of green machair, were all that was left of a once thriving industry. Jack studied the map. Clearly this too had been a slate-quarrying site, for the entire centre of the island had been gouged out and the area bearing the title OLD QUARRY, was now filled with water. He made another note: ISLE OF ORCHY? MARINA?

He saw from the map that the main village of Seileach, which had been mentioned particularly by his employer, must lie behind that promontory of rock which at present obstructed his view. The rock, part of a hill named Caisteal an Spuilleadair, represented the coastal end of a range of mountains which stretched eastwards across the island of Seileach. At its foot was a large white house under a slated roof. Built at the seaward end of a wide fertile glen and sheltered from the sea breezes by trees and dense shrubbery, this must have been an important private residence in its day. On the map it was marked as an hotel.

To his right, way up the glen, shaggy, red-coated Highland cattle grazed the lush meadows, while the hillside beyond was dotted with sheep. Behind the hotel, Jack noticed a group of farm buildings. It wouldn't take a lot to extend a complex like that, and planning consent for converting existing buildings was much easier to obtain than building on a green field site. As an added advantage, according to the map, this was the only hotel in the area.

He made another note: HOTEL, and drew a rough sketch of what he could see from this point. He completed this brief preliminary survey by taking a few photographs and then climbed back behind the wheel. He drove cautiously down the steep winding road to the shore. In half a mile he turned in at the gates of the Tigh na Broch Hotel.

At six o'clock in the evening, the Badger Bar was almost empty. A few late holidaymakers sat over their beer and salt and vinegar crisps while, in his usual corner, surrounded by a pall of pungent blue tobacco smoke, Baldy McGillivray engaged the patient landlord in conversation.

'Aye, it is good that we have a new young doctor for once,' he was saying. 'Perhaps he will find one of these famous wonder drugs to cure my poor old lungs.'

To make his point he coughed productively, caught the landlord's eye just in time and withdrew from his pocket a well-used handkerchief of indistinct colour with which he wiped away the spittle.

'The new doctor'll tell you just what Dr Mac's been telling you for years,' Martin Crane assured him. 'Stop the smoking and you'll cure the cough for yourself!'

'Och, away.' Baldy dismissed the obvious truth. 'If I canna get a bottle of medicine, he's no doctor. My throat's gey sore,' he whined now. 'A wee dram would be just the thing to put me right.'

In Martin's opinion, it was far too early in the evening for Baldy to be starting on the whisky. By eleven o'clock closing time, he would be unable to stand and Martin would be obliged to prevail upon someone to drive the silly old codger home. Ignoring the request for a dram and leaving Baldy to the remains of his beer, Martin retired to the far end of the bar to serve the stranger who had just walked in.

'Good evening, sir. What can I do for you?'

The landlord's English accent took Jack by surprise. In the past few days he had become accustomed to the variety of Scottish intonations and the harsher, English pronunciation quite jarred with him.

'A cold beer, please.' He had discovered it was necessary to stipulate.

'From New Zealand, are you?' Martin enquired, taking a bottle of Heineken from the refrigerated counter and pouring the light-coloured liquid into a tall glass.

'Australia.' Jack swallowed a long draft.

'On holiday?'

'Taking a look around. My folks came from Argyll, way back. I thought I might try looking for any records of them . . .'

'If it's the old quarry workers you want to know about,

Baldy there is the only representative of the trade still living. He was just a lad when the last slate was taken out of the Eisdalsa quarries.'

'Oh, my people weren't quarrymen, so far as I know. Farmers, more like.'

'From these parts, were they?'

'That I don't know,' Jack replied. 'Name of McDougal. They left Argyll in company with a family called McGillivray. Now *they* might have been quarriers, because the son went gold mining out near Kalgoorlie. The two families were related by marriage, that I do know, and I have very early recollections of an elderly aunt who was Mary McCulloch before she married Dougal McGillivray . . .'

Jack had been rehearsing the history of his family so far as he knew it, in order to sound sufficiently convincing about his search for his roots.

'Ma mither used to take me to visit an old clerical gentleman of the name of McCulloch,' said Baldy, joining the discussion at Martin's bidding. 'He survived the Great War and lived to be over ninety. Now, as I recall, he had a daughter who emigrated to Australia.'

'You could do worse than go through the parish records,' suggested Martin. 'The Minister is the one to ask, and the other place to go for information is the museum on Eisdalsa. They have all manner of records there. You might come across the combination of names you're looking for.'

'The County archives are down south at Kilmory.' A tall, thin figure in Harris tweed jacket and wool check shirt, the standard uniform of the country gentleman, had

129

left his companions in order to join in the conversation at the bar. As he waited to have his glasses replenished, he continued, 'You'll find a series of census returns for Argyll which might give you a lead, but without knowing the village your people came from, you are going to have a problem. What did you say your name was?'

'McDougal, Jack McDougal.'

'George Monteith.' The other held out his hand. 'Welcome to Seileach,' he said pleasantly. 'Will you be staying here long?'

'That depends a bit on whether the landlord can let me have a room for a few days,' said Jack cautiously. He wanted to create the impression that he had come upon the place by chance and had no definite plans.

'Delighted to have you,' said Martin. 'As soon as I've dealt with His Lordship's order, I'll call my wife and get her to show you the rooms.'

Jack made no sign that he had registered the reference to the Marquis's status. So this was the man who owned most of the property that Milton was interested in acquiring. When Ruth Crane appeared a few moments later, Jack thanked his new friends for their helpful suggestions, ordered a fresh glass of beer for Baldy and followed the landlady's comfortably rounded figure into the main body of the hotel.

'We don't normally provide full board at this time of the year,' Ruth explained as she preceded him up the stairs. 'Breakfast and an evening meal are served in the dining room. We do snacks in the bar at lunchtimes.'

'Oh, that will be fine,' said Jack affably. 'I expect to be out and about during the day. It seems I shall have to do a fair bit of travelling.' He explained how he had been given advice to visit Kilmory.

'Is it far?' he asked.

'About forty miles,' she replied, 'but it's a winding road and the traffic is pretty slow. It usually takes us about an hour and a half to get down there but it's a very pleasant drive.'

Used as he was to the long straight roads in Western Australia and the featureless highways of the USA, Jack still could not get over the length of time it took to get anywhere by road in these parts.

'Well,' he said resignedly, 'I'm on holiday so I've all the time in the world.'

'You might find it useful to make an appointment to see the Archivist,' Ruth suggested. 'It will save you making the journey for nothing. Mr Munro is not always in his office. He spends a fair amount of time at museums and so on around the county. I'll fetch you the telephone number while you're settling in.'

She opened a door on the main landing and showed him into his room. He curbed a strong desire to examine the sheets and glanced into the bathroom just long enough to note that there was no tell-tale ring around the bath. There was a scent of beeswax and turpentine which suggested old furniture well cared for. He could hardly expect Kookaburra standards in a place like this. The room would do very well for his purposes.

He shuddered inwardly at the predictable Laura Ashley prints, but managed a smile as he turned to her and said, 'What a delightful room, Mrs Crane. This will do splendidly.'

*

Alan Beaton had spent the afternoon familiarising himself with the surgery and its contents. Despite his age, Dr McWorter had clearly made an effort to keep abreast of medical advances. If his housekeeping had been neglected since the death of his wife, his practice certainly had not. His library of reference books was up to date and he had an excellent system for filing relevant information abstracted from magazines and advertising publications. His pharmacopoeia was the current year's edition.

The system of recording patients' treatment was easy to follow, and if it lacked the efficiency of a computer data base, it was adequate. As a matter of interest he turned to the one patient whose name had already been made known to him.

Jeanie Clark had a history of high blood pressure going back to the first of her three pregnancies. Alan studied the readings of her previous visits and noted the drugs which McWorter had prescribed. She ought to have been brought under control with that lot, he thought. McWorter must know his patient well and if he had noticed no change when he had last met her, then there must surely be something wrong. Alan noted the telephone number for the Post Office and dialled.

'Mrs Clark?'

'Yes,' she answered a trifle suspiciously. The shop was closed but that did not stop villagers from ringing up at all times of the day and night for something they had forgotten to buy at the supermarket in town. Willie Clark stocked a few items of groceries, just the basics to help the old folk who depended on a weekly shopping trip by the one bus which ran each day between the town and the village of Seileach. It was a convenience which some of his less considerate customers tended to abuse.

'This is Dr Beaton. I'm standing in for Dr McWorter.'

'Yes, doctor?'

'Dr McWorter expressed some concern about your health, Mrs Clark. He asked me to make a point of seeing you within the next few days.'

'Och, the poor wee man,' she cried in dismay. 'Fancy him thinking of me and him lying there in the hospital.' She was clearly moved.

'Something seems to be on his mind, Mrs Clark. I would like to reassure him that I have seen you by the time I next visit him . . . as much for his sake as your own, if you understand me. Could you manage to call in to the surgery as soon as possible?'

'If it will put the old man's mind at rest, I'll come, doctor, but really there's no need.'

'Perhaps you will allow me to be the judge of that?' Alan replied. 'I'll look forward to seeing you then.'

'Aye . . . I'll be there.' She replaced the handset.

'Who was that, Jeanie?' demanded her husband.

'Och, just the new doctor checking up on his patients. I'm to call in for some tablets is all.'

Willie Clark nodded. These doctors were all the same. Forever fussing around people. Anyone would think they hadn't enough to do without going out looking for work.

Chapter Six

Alan Beaton was first in the surgery the following morning. By the time Flora Douglas arrived on the scene he had been through the list of patients from A to D and was beginning to understand how Dr McWorter conducted his practice. Additional notes intended for the eyes of those in the practice only included such items as: *rough farm road, take boots; vicious Jack Russell, avoid front entrance; ferry stops 2100hrs, call ferryman 709*. Against Mrs Dingle's official medical card was attached a sheet carrying the information: *mother died of breast cancer. Regular screening essential*, while Hamish Watt was considered at risk from gall stones: *father suffered from chronic cholecystitis*. In the course of twenty years or more, the old doctor had meticulously mapped not only the medical histories of all his patients but their habits and social histories also. The letters *HS* and *MS* puzzled Allan for a while until he came to a patient with chronic emphysema whose card carried this annotation. Heavy smoker, of course. Then an *A* or an *MA* might mean an alcoholic or a moderate drinker. He would have to check with the old man.

Alan could see how by matching telephoned symptoms to recorded history he should be able to make sensible assumptions as to the cause of sudden collapse requiring urgent attention. It meant that when turning out on a stormy night to cross to one of the islands, the doctor had at least an idea of what he was likely to encounter.

Flora Douglas was, as always, in place to receive the first telephone calls of the morning on the stroke of nine and so busy was the line that she had taken three calls before she realised that her temporary boss was standing behind her in the tiny office with a sheaf of patient record cards in his hand.

'Good morning, Flora. I've just been going through these cards and I see that a Mrs McLeod on the island of Lunga is due to have her baby next week. Fill me in on the procedure with respect to pregnancies, will you? Surely the mothers don't wait until the last minute before getting into the hospital?'

She started at the sound of his voice and was overcome by an unexpected rush of adrenaline. 'Oh, good morning, doctor,' she blurted, her cheeks suddenly warm.

'It's usual for the ladies to go into hospital well in advance of labour. They see the midwife every week during the final month and she advises when they should go in.'

'It's a bit different from Newcastle,' he observed. 'Twenty-four hours was the maximum stay allowed for any but the most complicated cases.'

'A helicopter or lifeboat journey is rather more costly than a hospital bed for a day or two,' Flora told him, rapidly regaining her composure. 'The maternity ward is seldom so full that they can't accommodate a mother before she goes into labour.'

'It's a relief to know I won't be called out too often in the early hours,' he commented. 'I had visions of being rowed across angry seas in the pitch dark!'

'Not rowed, at any rate,' she laughed. 'The ferries all have quite high-powered engines, but there will be night calls involving trips to the islands, I can assure you. Dr McWorter keeps wellingtons and a set of oilskins in the boot of his car . . . mind you, it means he is also always prepared for an hour or two's fishing should the opportunity arise. Perhaps you'd like to borrow them?'

'Thanks, I will, until I can get some of my own. That reminds me, what about the car? I hardly think my E-type is suitable for this job.'

'The doctor has an elderly Bentley. It's quite useful for taking emergency cases to hospital and will probably be safer than your sports car on these roads, in really bad weather.' She lifted down a set of keys from the hook. 'Dr Pullson always uses the Bentley for house calls so I'm sure Dr McWorter would expect you to do the same.' She handed him a large mortice lock key. 'For the garage,' she explained. 'His Lordship drove the doctor's car back after his heart attack and insisted we locked it up. I must say, it's the first time the old bus has been under cover for about ten years, but he was adamant that it should not be tampered with in the doctor's absence.'

Alan took the key and examined it curiously. 'Must be an old lock,' he suggested.

'As old as the house, I should think,' she replied. 'What is now euphemistically described as a garage was once a cattle byre. It's well aerated to say the least so it doesn't smell too badly of dung!'

Alan found the Bentley just where Flora had said and with nothing better to do until his colleague arrived, lifted the bonnet, fearing the vehicle might be in the same sorry state as the house.

He need not have worried. Dr McWorter had neglected nothing which might affect the welfare of his patients. The car was obviously serviced regularly, and if the bodywork was a trifle scratched and dented, beneath the bonnet the engine was clean, the wiring connections immaculate, the oil and water reservoirs full and the battery fully charged. He checked the tyres and found nothing wanting there and although the chassis showed a few patches of rust, understandable in the salty atmosphere of the coast, there was nothing to prevent her from passing an MOT tomorrow.

Alan struggled out from beneath the offside wing to find himself faced with a pair of substantial brogues and two shapely legs clad in serviceable tights. His gaze travelled up the folds of thick tweed skirt and comfortable suede jerkin, coming to rest on a pert round face beneath a soft felt hat.

'Good morning,' she said, 'you'll be Dr Beaton?' Then turning her attention to the Bentley, she asked, 'What's wrong with the old bus? Nothing too drastic, I hope. I've a trip down to Craignish scheduled for this morning after surgery. The road's a bit dicey . . . I wouldn't like to chance my old faithful down there.'

She indicated a Citroen 2CV which had certainly seen better days, drawn up on the hard standing beside Alan's E-type.

'The Bentley looks fine to me,' he said, uncoiling his tall frame from beneath the chassis of the car and struggling to his feet. 'I'm a bit of a connoisseur,' he explained. 'Just having a look, that's all.'

'Ewan has her serviced every month . . . she should be in good lick. I'm Janice Pullson, by the way.' She thrust out her hand and Alan glanced at his oily fingers and wiped his hand on the seat of his trousers before taking hers.

'Alan Beaton . . . pleased to meet you.'

'Yes,' she said, eyeing him thoughtfully, 'I'm afraid we hadn't anticipated these circumstances when the decision was made to go for an Associate Partner. They'll have told you I can only do a limited number of hours at the moment? The children do really need me. They're only wee.'

'I have to get in touch with the other practice at Kilglashan,' he told her. 'They have already been informed of the problem here and don't expect me to join them until Dr McWorter is back on his feet. Nevertheless, I feel I owe them a visit.'

'Of course,' she agreed, 'but I can't help feeling relieved. I have been relying on my neighbour to baby-sit when there's an emergency but it is a bit much to ask a seventy-year-old widow to turn out late at night. My regular days on duty are arranged to coincide with my husband's free time. He works with the Hydro Board and is sometimes called out at night himself.'

They had wandered back into the surgery by this time and Flora was disappointed not to be required to make the introductions.

'The waiting room's filling up,' she told them, handing Dr Pullson a collection of record cards. 'Jeanie Clark is first. She's particularly anxious to get back to the village in time for the post van.'

'We'd best get down to it then,' said Janice Pullson. 'I presume you want me to take surgery as usual this morning?'

'Oh, yes, of course,' Alan replied hurriedly. 'I wondered if I might sit in . . . just to get the feel of things?'

'Sure. It might be an idea for you to come out on this morning's house calls as well. I'm visiting a few rather out of the way houses. It will be a chance to show you around the district.'

'That would be great. Thank you.' He beamed at his new colleague.

Flora knew she should be pleased to see the two of them getting on so well. Why was it then that she felt such a strong wave of jealousy as he stepped aside to allow Janice to enter the consulting room before him and then closed the door behind them?

Jeanie Clark's blood pressure was certainly higher than it should be. While Janice went through the procedure with the sphygmomanometer Alan studied the notes. McWorter had scribbled a few words on the back of the buff envelope. The writing was weak and spidery, not nearly so precise as on other documents. Could it be that he had made this note while he himself was already feeling unwell? *Village shop failing Is it stress?*

Janice had already introduced her colleague and since Jeanie Clark had already spoken to the new doctor on the telephone, it was no surprise to her that he should be present at this morning's consultation.

'Pressure's still a wee bit over the top, Jeanie.' Dr Pullson tried not to show that she was worried. Any sign of concern on her part would serve to exaggerate the symptoms. 'I'll just listen to your chest, if I may?'

Alan busied himself with the notes while the elderly postmistress disrobed. He could see that his presence embarrassed her and would have made some excuse to leave had he not noted for himself her alarmingly high reading. There was a problem here right enough and the sooner it was diagnosed the better. Both doctors listened in to the abnormal sounds of blood trying to force its way through clogged arteries.

'I think it's time you had an ECG, Jeanie,' Janice wrote hurriedly on the record card. 'If you'll wait just a moment, I'll ring the hospital now and make you an appointment.' She glanced briefly at Alan, seeking his confirmation, and at his almost imperceptible nod, dialled the hospital.

A cryptic conversation ensued of which the others heard only half the exchange. At last Janice covered the mouthpiece with her hand and glanced at Jeanie. 'Can you manage tomorrow morning . . . twelve o'clock?' she demanded briskly.

Jeanie, alarmed at the apparent urgency of the situation, could only nod miserably. 'I suppose Willie can hold the fort for an hour or two.'

'I'm afraid he'll have to,' said Janice, her insistence confirming Jeanie's worst fears.

'What sort of a season have you had?' Janice enquired, attempting to lighten the atmosphere. She could not have chosen a more unfortunate subject.

'It's been worse than ever this year,' Jeanie replied, and Alan noticed how mention of the family business had set her to picking nervously at the sleeve of her cardigan. 'That wet spell in June . . . we had the lowest turnover in the store I can ever remember. There have been lots of campers and all the holiday lets have been fully booked, but people don't come here to spend their money. They bring most of what they eat with them. One woman actually admitted she had shopped for the entire fortnight in her local Sainsbury's before she came away, because the prices are so much lower down south. How are we expected to compete with that? The Tourist Board are forever telling us that the region is becoming more prosperous by the year with such a large influx of tourists but we don't see any benefit from it. The gift shops do all right with their customers coming in on the tour buses, but ordinary traders can't make a living here.' As she spoke her colour rose to an alarming degree and Alan sought to calm her.

'Do you have a means of getting in to the hospital in the morning?' he asked.

'I'll need to catch the nine-thirty bus,' she replied.

'That means a long wait in town,' Janice commented. The woman made no reply.

'Only the one bus?' asked Alan. He was not unduly surprised by this. Where he had just come from there had been one bus a week from the oil field into the nearest town.

'Yes. There's a return service which leaves Oban at two o'clock, but it's all right,' Jeanie added hastily, 'I'll find plenty of things to do while I'm in town.'

'I shall be going in to see Dr McWorter after surgery,' Alan told her. 'How would it be if I called for you and took you in the car? You might like to have a word with the doctor yourself. I'm sure he'd be relieved to see you there.'

This was blackmail and she knew it. Left to herself, she might have found an excuse for not keeping the appointment. If Dr Beaton was going to give her a lift, she would be obliged to go through with the test. She resigned herself to the inevitable.

'All right,' she agreed. 'Thank you.'

'I'll pick you up soon after eleven then,' he told her, 'always assuming the morning surgery doesn't run too long over time.'

Jeanie rather hoped that it would.

Jack McDougal had made two appointments for the day of his visit to Kilmory. At Ruth Crane's suggestion he had arranged an interview with the County Archivist, but since Stephen Munro would be out all morning, the meeting was not due to take place until three o'clock in the afternoon. Jack made a second telephone call to arrange a morning meeting with the Chief Planning Officer.

'I wish to discuss a planning proposal with your Chief Officer,' he told the girl who answered his call.

'I'm afraid that Mr Campbell does not normally see planning applicants in person. May I put you through to one of our Assistant Planning Officers?'

'I think that your Mr Campbell will wish to speak to me himself,' replied Jack. 'What I have to discuss is very much in his interests.'

'I'm sorry, sir, I have my instructions. Mr Campbell sees no one except by appointments initiated by himself. If there are matters requiring his personal attention, these are brought to him by his assistants when and if necessary.'

The words came out pat, as though she used them several times a day.

'This is an application of some importance which will involve a major investment in the district. I believe your Principal will wish to talk to me personally.' Jack's tone was insistent and authoritative. The girl's determination wavered. If the matter was as important as the caller suggested she would be in trouble for intercepting it. She'd better risk it.

'One moment, sir. I'll see if Mr Campbell is available. Please hold the line.'

The popular classic orchestration was turned up to such a volume that Jack was obliged to hold the receiver away from his ear. He narrowly missed the moment when the music cut out and an impatient voice shouted, 'Campbell here. What's all this about . . . hello? Are you there?'

'Mr Campbell, I represent the Humbert Development Corporation of America. My company is interested in investing in a major new tourism development in your area. You will appreciate that at this early stage we would not want our plans to be broadcast and I would therefore respectfully request a personal interview with you, at your earliest convenience. I wondered if tomorrow morning would be too soon?'

Mr Campbell, unused to being addressed in such a direct manner, was temporarily lost for words. He was clearly intrigued by what Jack had to say. A major development? That could have quite an impact on the powers that be in Strathclyde and might have far reaching effects on his own position.

There was a move afoot to abandon the large Scottish regions created in the 1970s, in favour of a return to the old County system. The word in the corridors of Glasgow's Regional Council chambers was that jobs were going to be slashed. Colin Campbell had no intention of being one of those who went to the wall.

'Very well,' he said at last. 'Shall we say ten o'clock, Mr . . . ?'

'McDougal . . . Jack McDougal.'

'Well, I shall be very pleased to see you tomorrow, Mr McDougal.'

'Thank you, sir. Ten o'clock it is.'

Alan could truthfully say that he had enjoyed his first day at work in his new job.

Dr Pullson might at first glance seem a trifle drab and ineffectual, but looks were deceptive. Not only had she proved to be an excellent driver, handling the heavy Bentley on the narrow rutted roads with consummate skill, but she had taught him in just a few hours a great deal about handling the independent, strong-willed people who made up the population of the parish of Kilbrendon.

He had particularly admired her manner in handling a farmer who had insisted that he had come to the surgery for a bottle of linctus for his cough and nothing else. It was Janice who had spotted the possibility of a work-related disease.

'What has been the trouble?' she had asked the elderly gentleman in his old-fashioned plus fours and tweed shooting jacket. He had made some attempt at scraping the muck off his leather gaiters before coming into the surgery but there was still a strong whiff of the country-side about him.

'I thought it was just an ordinary bout of 'flu at first,' the farmer began. 'It started with sneezing and a cough . . .' The effort of speaking had brought on heavy, laboured breathing and he paused to catch his breath. 'You see,' he choked on the words, 'this happens all the time. It was as much as I could do to get the cattle out on to the machair this morning. If it had nae been for my old Jess, I don't know what I should have done.'

Alan looked bewildered. Janice murmured, 'The dog.' He nodded and remained silent.

'Do you smoke, Mr McLeod?' she asked him.

'Not for years,' he replied. 'Not since the last time I had a bout like this, in fact.'

She listened in with her stethoscope and then stood aside, allowing Alan to do the same. He heard the dull sounds of a lung which was severely congested, but sur-prisingly there was no wheezing such as he would have expected to hear in a normal case of bronchitis.

'How was the harvest last year?' Janice asked, to the surprise of both men. The question appeared to have little relevance to what was going on, but the farmer answered nonetheless. 'Och, it was a better summer last year as you ken well, Mrs Pullson. We managed to make plenty of hay in the meadows down by the shore . . . I know the experts tell us that silage is better for the cattle but the beasts love a bit o' sweet hay in the depths of winter.'

She nodded thoughtfully.

'Have you made much hay this season?'

'In all this rain?' He spoke as though he thought her quite daft. 'No, I have not!'

'And all last season's hay has now gone?'

'Just used the last few bales this week,' he replied, wondering what all this was about.

'Good, because I'm going to ask you, or preferably someone else, to burn what's left and I think you should stick to silage from now on.'

He had come for medical advice. If he'd wanted a lecture on farming he'd have gone to MAFF. Come to think of it, with all her sharp questions, she reminded him a great deal of those Ministry men.

She asked him to cough up sufficient phlegm to examine a little under the microscope. After adding a drop of staining fluid she studied the slide in silence for a few moments then, apparently satisfied with what she had found, stood aside for Alan to have a look. What he saw was a collection of spores such as he recalled drawing assiduously when he was still at school and taking his A level in Botany.

He looked up, mystified.

'*Micropolyspora faeni*,' Janice announced, with some satisfaction. 'It's a mould found on hay . . . causes what is commonly known as Farmer's Lung.'

He nodded, only half remembering what he had learned about certain diseases more commonly found in the countryside.

'I can give you a course of steroids,' she told McLeod, 'but the only way to avoid the disease is to stay away from the cause. No more hay making. Is that understood?'

He nodded half-heartedly. It was difficult to resist the temptation of carrying out the old-fashioned task, beloved by true farmers everywhere.

'This is very serious, Mr McLeod,' she insisted. 'Another bout like this one could kill you.'

She wrote rapidly on the prescription pad. 'These tablets must be taken precisely as directed and you must take them all. You do understand, don't you?'

'Och, aye.' The farmer appeared to be sufficiently impressed by her warning.

'Now, Duncan,' she was emphatic, 'this is no idle threat. You cannot afford to have another attack of this disease. The cortisone I have prescribed acts against the symptoms only; it cannot cure the disease and your lungs will not withstand another bout like this one.'

He returned her long hard stare, nodded briefly and struggled to his feet. When he reached the door, he turned. ' 'Tis a pity all the same, the beasts do so love a handful o' sweet hay,' he repeated, his protest almost drowned in the fit of coughing which it brought on.

'Will he take notice of what you said?' asked Alan when the patient was out of hearing.

'I doubt it,' she replied. 'How can you change the ways of an old man born and bred to a particular way of life?'

'He stopped smoking,' Alan observed.

'Yes, so he said.'

'You don't believe him?'

'From the discoloration on his fingers, no. If he really gave up three years ago,' she had been studying the farmer's notes as they spoke, 'the nicotine stains would have gone by now.'

Alan realised he had not even noticed the man's hands . . . he really must smarten up his powers of observation. He had become lazy and complacent dealing with strong, generally healthy men and their young wives and families, all of whom were accustomed to doing what they were told. These people had minds of their own and were not subject to any company rules.

That afternoon the Bentley covered mile upon mile of narrow, pot-holed roads through the wild hill country of Argyll. The doctors visited the elderly and the bedridden and also a young housewife, newly discharged from hospital following the birth of her third child. She was the wife of a shepherd whose cottage lay three miles off the road along a rutted track which must be a quagmire in wet weather. Unable to afford a car, the family had no means of getting to the surgery and relied upon the doctor and health visitor calling when the children were sick. A weekly bus ride to Lochgilphead was their only means of supplying their needs, although from the evidence of neat rows of vegetables in the kitchen garden, the nanny goat tethered in the lane and the hens rooting around in the yard, Alan suspected that much of their food was home-produced.

'Did you ever see such a healthy, happy bunch of kids?' Janice demanded as the eldest of the children, a boy of ten years or so, handed her a glass of milk still warm from the goat.

'Thank you, Bobbie.' She accepted the milk gratefully and drank it with relish. 'You must have known how thirsty I was!'

'Will you have some too, doctor?' the child asked Alan. 'I just did the milking myself,' he explained, proudly.

Alan, who had had more than enough goat's milk and cheese in the last few years, declined with a polite smile.

'I'm sure it's very good,' he said, sorry to disappoint the boy, 'but I'm really not terribly thirsty.'

Having pronounced both mother and baby to be very well, they returned to the car, accompanied by a noisy collection of dogs and infants, and as she settled herself behind the wheel, Janice reached into the glove box and pulled out a handful of Werther's Originals. 'Good old Ewan,' she murmured, 'I knew he wouldn't let me down.' She opened the window and handed round the sweeties.

'Goodbye,' she called to the children. 'You take great care of that lovely new sister now, and see you help your mummy with all the hard work!'

To a chorus of squealing children and barking dogs they drove through the farm gate out of sight.

A short distance from home, Janice turned into a

narrow side road which climbed steadily for a couple of miles between tall hedges and overhanging trees until it ended abruptly, barred by a farm gate. She drew the car in to the verge and shut off the engine.

'This is as good a place as any, to see the full extent of the practice,' she told Alan and, stepping out of the car, she preceded him through the gate and along a dusty track. In due course their path petered out and they found themselves on a broad plateau of close-cropped turf. The entire panorama of the islands lay before them.

With a wide sweep of her arm Janice indicated the boundaries of the practice.

The large Isle of Seileach lay across a narrow waterway connected to the mainland by an ancient hump-backed bridge.

'At one time it was the only bridge in the British Isles which could truly be said to span the ocean,' she told him. 'Now of course there are others . . . Skye for example, but in its day this one was quite unique and visitors still travel great distances to see it.

'Eisdalsa Island lies to the north of Seileach,' she reminded him, 'and to the south-west lies Lunga, not a great deal further offshore than Eisdalsa actually, but it's a larger island with a number of villages so there is a car ferry.'

'Why is it that all the maps and signboards talk about Eisdalsa when they really mean Seileach?' Alan asked. It was something that had confused him since his arrival. Even the surgery which was in the centre of the Isle of Seileach, was described in the literature as the Eisdalsa surgery.

'Eisdalsa Island was the first island to be exploited for slate and was for a long time the headquarters of the industry here. When the first Ordnance Survey maps were drawn the entire district was labelled Eisdalsa. It's always been the postal address for the Islands.'

She turned her attention to the smaller islands surrounding Lunga naming them one by one. 'Most have no more than a couple of houses on them and they are only inhabited in the summer months but of course we can receive requests to visit when there is a problem, nevertheless.'

'How do we get there?' Alan was no great sailor and was certainly unable to handle any kind of a boat on his own.

'Oh, it's easy. The ferries are used for emergencies and of course, there's always the lifeboat.'

Satisfied with this explanation, he allowed her to continue her lecture.

'The large island in the distance is Scarba, largely uninhabited but again, we get the occasional call from campers and there is sometimes a school party on an adventure course. Those are always good for a fracture or two and a few sprained ankles. Between Scarba and Mull you have the Islands of the Sea. There's a lodge on the largest island which can be rented and frequently houses an author or artist looking for seclusion for a few months.'

She turned to face due south. 'The remainder of the practice includes this peninsula and the next, with the village down there on the loch and the marina which again brings in a fair amount of work for us during the summer.'

'I can imagine the local Health Board wincing a bit at the statistics. It looks as though you only have patients to deal with for six months of the year.'

'Don't you believe it,' she laughed. 'In the winter we have all the usual problems, colds and 'flu; accidents caused by the weather conditions and of course, the chronic conditions which people have had no time to complain of all summer!'

She glanced at her watch. 'Best be getting along,' she said. 'I'd like to pop in and check on my kids before the evening surgery.'

As they drove homewards in the late afternoon, around every bend some new delight appeared to lighten the spirit and gladden the eye. Craggy grey rocks were touched with pink from the setting sun. Green meadows gave way to ancient oak woods and twentieth-century forests of tall dark pines. High mountains, scoured by tumbling streams and waterfalls, were separated by lush valleys through which brown peaty rivers meandered towards the green machair at the sea's edge. On these low-lying, flower-strewn meadows, red Highland cattle ruminated contentedly, while high on the hillsides sheep, startlingly white in their new winter wool, grazed among the swathes of purple heather. At every turn of the road, Alan glimpsed the blue ocean, sparkling in the early-autumn sunshine, its waves breaking white along the black shoreline of exposed slate rocks.

'You must have some sleep to catch up on, after all your travelling,' Janice suggested as she parked the Bentley beside Alan's sports car. 'Besides which, you ought to take some time to get to know a few people, socially. How are you finding the hotel?'

He did not recall mentioning to her where he was staying. Already he was aware of a system of jungle drums at work. Around here, people knew things about a person almost before he knew them himself!

'It's very comfortable,' he replied to her question. 'The Cranes are delightful people and Ruth is an excellent cook . . .'

'Do I detect a *but* in that?'

'It's just that I'm used to fending for myself and value my privacy. When I've completed a long day's work, I like to avoid bar room consultancy as much as possible.'

She laughed. 'Old habits die hard,' she told him. 'In the days when people had to pay for a consultation they would waylay the doctor on the street and engage him in casual conversation in hopes of avoiding a fee. Now they do it to save a trip to the surgery.'

'I'm really looking for a place to rent for the next few months. It's been suggested that Jeanie Clark might help.'

Alan ducked his head as he entered the tiny cottage on Back Street and stepped into the single living room.

'I'm afraid it's awful wee, doctor,' Jeanie Clark apologised, following him in. 'Yon lintel has been the cause of more than one cracked head over the years.'

When Alan stood up straight, his head was within inches of an antique oil lamp which swung from a central beam.

'It's electric now, of course,' Jeanie explained hastily. 'In my grandfather's day it was the only light in this room.' She went to the wall and switched it on. The dingy little room was instantly bathed in a warm comfortable glow which disguised the somewhat worn upholstery on the two small armchairs set either side of a Victorian grate in which stood a simulated coal fire apparently fuelled by Calor gas. She bent to light it.

Immediately, china ornaments, brass knick-knacks, and heavily framed sepia prints sprang into view and Alan once again experienced that same feeling of *déjà vu* which had been haunting him ever since he had arrived in Seileach.

'The bathroom is through the wee kitchen.' Jeanie showed him how the galley-like kitchen had been built into what had originally been a central closet and a space containing a box bed separating the two rooms of the cottage. The bathroom, containing a shower but without a tub, had been installed in what had clearly once been an outhouse, probably a coal shed. The rough stonework was lined with plaster board and covered with a plasticised wallpaper which clung half-heartedly to the almost square walls. It appeared to be a pattern of underwater worlds where garishly patterned fish wove in and out of the fronds of amazingly bright green and red seaweeds.

'Willie thought the paper might cheer it up a bit, and it's appropriate for the position of the cottage.' She indicated the view through the window which was across a disused water-filled quarry, to the sea beyond.

Alan grudgingly agreed that fish were quite appropriate and silently wondered if they'd mind him doing a bit of redecoration, himself.

'The bedroom's through here.' She had returned to the

main room and the small square entrance hall. The brass latch caught when she lifted it and she struggled to release it.

'Here, let me.' Alan reached across and opened the door for her. The bedroom was approximately the same size as the living room, a small double bed occupying the greater part of the space. A wardrobe and dressing table completed the furnishings. Not much by way of storage space, he thought, but then, what did he have to store anyway?

'There's access to the loft through there.' Jeanie indicated the square hatch set into the ceiling of the nearly square hallway. 'There's an extending ladder fixed on the floor of the loft . . . let me show you.'

She took a rod which hung beside the front door and hooked into a ring on the ceiling. With one deft movement she pulled down a hinged trap door and an aluminium ladder slid down and into position.

'There's a light up there beside the hatch,' she explained. 'It's a well-floored, useful roof space and there's a beautiful view through the Velux windows. You might consider using it – for visitors, perhaps?' Did he have a family or a girl friend? she wondered. So far she had done all the talking. The doctor had remained silent.

'I won't bother to go up now,' he said. Jeanie was breathless from all her exertions and he was concerned for her. 'Shall we sit down and talk about it?'

When they had settled themselves in the surprisingly comfortable armchairs, she said, 'The one good thing about this cottage is that we don't take advance bookings for it. It's not furnished to a sufficiently high standard for the holiday lettings agency so we just offer it to casual visitors looking for a few nights' stay in the village.'

'So it's free immediately?' he asked. This interested him because he really was anxious to get away from the hotel and all that it implied in terms of socialising in his time off.

'You can move in when you want,' she told him. 'Lizzie McIntyre cleans for me after visitors have been in. I expect she will be happy to make a regular arrangement with you, if you would like. She'll also do your shopping for groceries and so on, if you want her to. I don't suppose you'll have much time for that sort of thing.'

Alan hesitated to commit himself. 'The trouble is, until we know whether Dr McWorter is going to be able to continue working, I don't know how long I shall be staying in the village. I should be hearing what is happening by the end of this week. If I am to be staying on, I'd like to have a proper short-term tenancy agreement . . . maybe for three months. Do you think you and your husband would agree to that?'

Jeanie was pleased. The prospect of having the house off their hands for a definite period was comforting, especially when she was feeling so very down these days and so inordinately tired.

'I'll talk to Willie about that,' she answered, 'but for the time being it would be just on a weekly let, at the usual rates.'

'That seems very satisfactory,' Alan told her. 'Shall we agree that I move in on Saturday then?'

*

Alan stayed a long time in the bath that evening, adding more hot water as it became chilled and almost sleeping over the book which he had taken into the bathroom with him. The clock striking eight reminded him that he would soon be too late for dinner. He dried hurriedly and dressed in a clean shirt, rummaging in his as yet unpacked suitcase for a suitable necktie.

A glance in the long cheval mirror told him he would pass muster here if not at the Savoy. He smoothed down a tuft of hair left standing after his protracted sojourn in the bath and took the stairs two at a time. There was a hushed atmosphere in the dining room. An elderly couple sat over coffee and brandies while in the window seat, gazing thoughtfully out upon the wide sweep of the bay, sat a single gentleman. As Alan entered this individual turned his head and smiled in surprise.

'By a remarkable coincidence we arrived at Heathrow on the same plane,' he said in an Australian accent. 'You dropped a bag on my foot, remember?'

'Good Lord, of course. I say, did I do any damage?' Alan glanced down at the other man's highly polished brogues.

'No, not at all.'

'Did you catch the next shuttle up here, then?'

'Yes.'

'So we were both on the same plane, again?'

'And in the same hotel. The Park.'

Alan suddenly remembered seeing the young man enter the restaurant with a smartly dressed thickset man.

'Yes, of course,' he said, and indicated the Australian's beer.

'Can I buy you another?'

'Thanks, but no thanks,' replied the Australian affably, then added, 'This really is a remarkable coincidence, isn't it. What are you doing here anyway?'

'I'm a sawbones,' Alan explained. 'I'm taking over a local practice for a colleague who's ill. It'll probably only be for a couple of months, maybe weeks. What brings you to Scotland?'

'As a matter of fact my folks came originally from somewhere round here. I thought I might have a look round . . . see if I can find any reference to them.'

'There must be a lot of Australians with Scottish connections,' Alan observed. 'I'm told there are a few members of my own family Down Under.'

'Ever been to Australia yourself?'

'No, but I've often thought I might give it a go. I suppose they allow Brits to practise out there? There are enough Aussies over here, running our Health Service!'

'Thank God for that!' Jack kidded him. 'I was dead worried I might get sick over here and no decent doctors to look after me!'

They both laughed.

'The name's Jack McDougal by the way.'

'Alan . . . Alan Beaton.'

He offered his hand and they shook heartily. 'So have you traced your ancestors to hereabouts?' he asked.

'I'm not sure,' Jack answered. 'I came because of something the porter at the Park Hotel said about his own people coming from Eisdalsa. Their history seemed to coincide with mine in a number of ways so I thought I would look into it. I'm off to Kilmory in the morning to meet the County Archivist and have a look at the census returns for the last century.'

Alan settled down and ordered his meal. 'I'm beginning to wonder if I am going to come across traces of my own family,' he said. 'My father tells me that my great-grandfather was the medical officer for one of the quarrying companies in this area.'

'While I'm looking up my people, I'll let you know if I come across any Beatons, shall I?'

'That would be grand,' said Alan, 'thanks very much. The way things are looking at the moment, I shan't have too much time to go looking for antecedents myself!'

'I heard the local doctor had a heart attack,' observed Jack. 'Bad, is it?'

'Could be . . . only time will tell.' Alan was immediately on his guard. He could not answer questions about patients, no matter how kindly meant. Their discussion only served to emphasise his need to get his own home as soon as possible.

'Are you staying in the district for long?' he asked, steering the conversation away from Dr McWorter.

'It depends a bit on what I find out tomorrow,' Jack replied, and then added rather too hurriedly, 'about my ancestors, I mean.'

They ate in silence for a while, both men lost in their own thoughts. Jack attempted further conversation but Alan found himself unable to answer in more than monosyllables.

'I'm afraid that the jet-lag is catching up on me,' he said at last, refusing the recommended dessert. He said, 'I'll have a pot of coffee and a double whisky brought up to my room in about ten minutes, if you don't mind.' He made his excuses to Jack McDougal then, folding his napkin, he bade the Australian good night.

Jack watched him go, wondering how he might win over this young doctor. A newcomer to the district, without preconceived notions of loyalty and tradition, surely he would be on the side of progress and increased prosperity for all.

Chapter Seven

'Now then, Mr McDougal, what is of such importance that it is fit only for my ears?'

Jack had taken an instant dislike to the pompous little man who had introduced himself as the Chief Planning Officer for the Argyll District of the Strathclyde Regional Council. Nearly bald, with long wisps of greying hair stretched across his polished pate from ear to ear, it was as though this simple attempt at deception was the key to the man's character. He had the air of one who thought a great deal of himself and seemed to assume that everyone else did the same.

'It was good of you to see me at such short notice, Mr Campbell.' Jack swallowed his natural aversion and smiled.

'You mentioned a proposal of some considerable value. Could you be more specific?'

'My organisation has global interests in tourism,' Jack began. He noticed an immediate furrowing of the other's brow. Campbell had hoped for a project involving silicon chips or clean energy. During his term of office, many tourism schemes that had promised so much on paper

163

had failed ignominiously . . . it only took one poor summer season to decimate the visitor numbers for years ahead. By the time another good spell of weather came around, the new project had, as like as not, gone into bankruptcy through lack of support.

'We would like to set up a major holiday complex in your area,' Jack carried on swiftly, not allowing Campbell to interrupt him. 'The plan would be to take over an entire village and an adjoining island and make it into one large self-contained holiday unit.'

He opened his briefcase and withdrew a number of glossy brochures depicting Humbert resorts in several parts of the world.

'You will see that our plans include building a variety of holiday accommodation to suit every pocket, leisure facilities associated with activities on land and sea – maybe even paragliding and airborne trips by light aircraft or helicopter. We would naturally, be prepared to contribute towards the cost of local infrastructure to support these.'

Campbell's eyes widened. The furrows on his brow receded and he relaxed into his leather-upholstered executive chair. This was no proposal for a roadside restaurant, offering bagpipes to go with a menu of haggis and smoked salmon, nor was it some peep show of Hebridean culture. This man was talking roads, sewage systems and housing, all items which made huge holes in the local authority's budget.

'Tell me more?' he breathed, hardly daring to hope that Jack was not exaggerating.

'What we are proposing is a complex to be centred on

Eisdalsa Island and parts of the larger island of Seileach
. . . taking in the village, the surrounding hills, including Caisteal an Spuilleadair, and the glen which runs up
beyond the Tigh na Broch Hotel.'

Jack spread his Ordnance Survey map out on the
desk and outlined the area intended for development
with a red marker pen. 'Where necessary we are prepared to purchase land and buildings but we would hope
that the existing property owners would come into the
scheme of their own accord and continue to carry on
their various enterprises under the umbrella of the
company. In order to encourage this, we are prepared to
offer them financial aid for the purpose of upgrading
those properties which do not already conform to our
standards. We want the area to be a showplace, using
the existing nineteenth-century buildings to enhance its
unique character.'

Campbell had blanched a trifle when Jack named the
villages under consideration. In the mid-70s the larger
part of the area he'd described had been designated a conservation site, the old slate workings having particular
significance within Scotland's industrial history. Now he
breathed more easily. No one could object to the refur-
bishment of deteriorating property if it was renovated in
the traditional style.

'I'm glad to see you have noted that there is a conservation order on the area,' he commented now, and Jack,
to whom this was news, betrayed no sign of surprise. The
fact that he and Milton had agreed the designs of future
buildings should fit in with 'those cute little workers'
cottages' was purely fortuitous.

'There would be no question of your obtaining permission for any multistorey buildings, you understand.' Colin Campbell had noted Jack's brochure for the Kookaburra Resort and shuddered at the photograph of a twenty-storey hotel which dominated the skyline there. He waited for an acknowledgement from Jack before continuing. 'So what sum of money is your company thinking of investing?'

'About eight million.' Jack tossed the figure into the discussion as an angler might cast his fly.

Campbell caught his breath. 'US dollars?'

'Pounds sterling.'

Campbell cleared his throat, trying unsuccessfully not to sound too excited.

'Do you have any firm plans to show me?' he asked, attempting a matter-of-fact air which was quite unconvincing. Jack knew he had already caught his fish.

'Not as yet.' The Australian smiled confidently. 'I wanted to hear your opinion about a development of these proportions, before setting out on a lengthy and expensive preliminary investigation. If you consider such a scheme to be viable and likely to be accepted by your Planning Committee, we shall proceed immediately to draw up a formal application.'

'It will of course be necessary to consider the plan in some detail,' Campbell reassumed his authoritarian attitude. This outsider needn't think he would be having everything his own way. 'A number of bodies have to be consulted. The Clyde River Board for water and sewerage considerations, for example,' he explained. 'Then there is Scottish Natural Heritage, Historic Scotland,

Commissioners for the Crown who own the foreshore below high tide mark, and a number of other bodies who will declare an interest. I'll have my secretary send you a list of the authorities involved who will require to approve the plans.'

Jack, no stranger to bureaucracy, wondered what it took in the UK to get such bodies to come into line. Elsewhere in the world, a few thousand dollars scattered amongst the bureaucrats was enough to get the wheels turning but he had been given to understand that such methods were frowned upon here.

'I shouldn't worry too much about these other bodies,' Campbell was saying, smoothly. 'They usually take their cue from this office. Provided your plan satisfies our own requirements, they won't object. If you will provide me with sufficient copies of the plans to send out to every-one with an interest, I will cover your application for outline approval with my own recommendation. There shouldn't be a problem.'

'And what about the elected members of the Council?' Jack had not wasted his time on the long flight from Sydney. He had studied the Scottish system of local gov-ernment in the greatest detail and probably knew more about planning procedures here than most of the elected members themselves.

'No problem there,' Campbell told him, rather arro-gantly. 'They do as they are advised by their officers. They pay us to do just that . . . advise them!'

'Thank you for your time.' Jack rose to go. 'You will be hearing from me within a few weeks.'

'I shall be interested to see what you come up with.'

Colin Campbell accompanied him to the door. 'That's an Australian accent, is it not?' he enquired. 'I was rather anticipating an American.'

'Humbert Developments is a world-wide organisation,' Jack explained. 'You might equally well have met a Barbadian or even a Japanese.' He let this notion sink in before continuing. 'As a matter of fact, my ancestors came from Argyll . . . emigrated just before the First World War. I'm about to visit your Archivist to see what he can tell me about them.'

'Your local connections might have some sway with the Council,' Campbell advised as he shook Jack's hand. 'The locals tend to be wary of incomers.'

Jack climbed into his car, well satisfied with his encounter with the Planning Officer. Convinced that his ability to trace his ancestry to somewhere near Eisdalsa would be of tremendous help to Milton's plans, he drove along the side of the loch with one eye on the traffic and the other on the road names. Houses and side streets became more frequent as he entered the long stretch leading into the centre of the little town which nestled comfortably between the hills at the head of Loch Gilp. He drew up before a stone-built school house whose windows had been set too high in the walls for the children to see out and whose stark tarmac playgrounds were carefully divided between boys, girls and infants. A battered and nearly illegible sign indicated the old school was now the County Records Office and a series of arrows pointed him in the direction of the County Archivist.

'McDougal?' Stephen Munro took down an index of local names. 'There were plenty of those throughout Argyll,' he said. 'Can you not narrow it down to a particular district? A few family Christian names would help.'

'John occurs most commonly.'

The archivist glanced sourly at Jack. McDougals were as common as Smiths in this part of Scotland and John Smiths were universal!

'They were farmers, I do know that,' Jack added hastily. 'My great-grandfather started a sheep farm in Western Australia about 1912 or 1913, and family tradition had it that he brought his first sheep dog with him from Argyll. Another branch of the family were miners or quarriers of some kind. They headed for the gold fields at about the same time, but their name was McGillivray . . .'

'Would that be ordinary stone quarriers or slate miners? If it was slate, that narrows the search to the slate islands of Lorn or to Ballachulish, which is out of my district.' He continued to rummage through a pile of ancient ledgers. 'The McDougals were not too popular further north so the Eisdalsa quarries are the most likely.'

'Surely there wasn't that much clan rivalry by the turn of the century?' Jack was intrigued. As a child he had heard many tales of the troubles between the Highland clans, but he had been led to believe that all the hatred and bitterness had died out long ago.

'You'd be surprised. In some of the more isolated places the people are still suspicious of incomers, particularly fellow Scots belonging to the wrong clan.'

Jack suspected Munro of exaggerating the problem for

the benefit of his visitor. He obviously enjoyed taking a rise out of any simple colonial who came his way. The Americans, in particular, were suckers for any far-fetched tale which had anything to do with their historical connections.

'If we concentrate for the time being on the quarriers and assume we are talking about the slate islands, we may find the two family names connected somehow.'

The archivist took down a well-thumbed tome, studied the index for some moments and turned to the Census returns for 1861.

'It's further back than you might be hoping for, but most of these families remained for several generations after the slate quarries went into commercial production in 1745. McGillivray, did you say?' He reached down a second volume. 'Here, you might like to browse through this while I search.'

It was an account book recording the slates made and the amounts earned by the gangs working in the Eisdalsa quarries in the years 1875 to 1879. Several times Jack came across the name McGillivray. It seemed that James McGillivray was the senior man in his team which was, in the earlier years, way ahead of the others in terms of slates made. In 1878, however, the name McGillivray slipped out of the list and Jack searched ahead to find it was still missing from the records of slates made in 1879. Then he came across a scrawled signature at the end of the year's entries. 'Jas. McGillivray'. Was it possible that James McGillivray had been promoted to tallyman?

'Ah, here we are, McDougal spelt with one L. Now

that's significant because the usual way of spelling the name was with two Ls.'

Jack leaned forward. He took up the book for himself. Under 'Eisdalsa Island' he found the entry for:

an gabhail-fearainn	McDougal, John	farmer
	McDougal, Katrina	wife
	McDougal, John	farmer (son)
	McDougal, Ellen	scholar (daughter)

'What does the Gaelic house name mean?'

'It simply means the farm or croft. Eisdalsa is a pretty small island, I doubt if there was more than one farm.'

'So it would be like . . . Eisdalsa Farm?'

'Yes, that's about it.'

'How could I verify that these are my ancestors?'

'What else do you know about them? Are there any wedding dates, births, or deaths we could check on?'

'I know that my great-grandfather married twice. His second wife was a McGillivray . . . it was she who accompanied him to Australia. That's the connection I mentioned with the quarrymen. Her name was Anne . . . Anne McGillivray.' Jack could not contain his excitement. What a coup if he were to prove that his family had actually originated from Eisdalsa itself!

'Any idea of the marriage date?' Munro enquired.

'No, but it must have been about the time of their departure for Australia. I know the two of them were both widowed for many years. Let's say 1911 or 1912.'

Munro pulled out a couple of large dusty volumes and laid them on the already crowded bench.

'They expect me to get all this information into the

computer,' he said, indicating a PC carefully shrouded in its grey PVC cover. 'The trouble is, I've never had time to learn how to use it!'

He was a man in his fifties with the wide intellectual brow and earnest appearance of one used to browsing amongst books and papers. Jack could understand the archivist's natural aversion to the new technology and sympathised with his reluctance to give up his enormous collection of leatherbound papers, smelling strongly of mould and old, distinctly organic, glue. There was no romance attached to feeding a floppy disk into a computer. Nothing to compare with the excitement of turning the pages of some ancient record, written in the immaculate copperplate hand of earlier times.

Parish of Kilbrendon
Registrar of Births Marriages and Deaths,
John McCulloch, DD.
1895–1914

This must be the one. Eagerly, Jack turned the pages, hoping to see the record he was after. Yes here it was.

'*26 December 1911, John Douglas McDougal, farmer, widower of this parish, to Anne Mary McGillivray, widow of this parish.*' He strained his eyes, trying to make out the signature of the witnesses. No, he was not mistaken. The name was Beaton . . . David Beaton, MB; ChB; BSc.

Hastily he noted down these details along with those of his own ancestors. Alan Beaton would be pleased at what he had found, he felt sure.

He flipped back the pages, casually glancing at the names recorded there. A second entry caught his attention.

'*June 1893, Dougal James McGillivray, engineer of this parish, to Mary Ellen McCulloch, schoolmistress of this parish.*'

Mary McGillivray, or Great-aunt Mary as Jack had known her, was for many years the teacher in the township of Kerrera where he was born. She had lived to a very great age.

Hurriedly he searched the columns of births recorded in the years following 1893 and found two further entries which interested him.

Dougal McGillivray and Mary had had a son, Hamish, in 1894 and a daughter, Flora, in 1896. Jack remembered them well. He had been a schoolboy of twelve when he'd attended Hamish McGillivray's funeral in 1974, and Cousin Flora, who had spent all her working life as a nurse and was for many years matron of the Kerrera Cottage Hospital, had been eighty-six when she had died and he attended her funeral in 1982. Suddenly the years between seemed to fall away and he felt a close connection with this remote community which he was about to transform, providing a whole new era of prosperity for all. Warm feelings of benevolence and self-satisfaction flowed through his veins.

With a satisfied grin, Jack closed the books and thanked Munro for his time.

Alan was pleased he had not taken the trouble to unpack

his things. All he would have to do on Saturday morning was load up the car and drive down into the village. This time tomorrow night, he thought, I shall be unpacking in my own wee house.

It was a relief to know that he was going to be an independent spirit so soon after his arrival. He would take time while in town to stock up with a few necessities. Enough to keep him going for a while at least.

Shedding the formal lounge suit and tie which he had thought appropriate for work, Alan changed into comfortable jeans and T-shirt before making his way downstairs in time to take a drink before dinner.

Jack McDougal had preceded him.

'Good evening, doctor.' The landlord reached for a whisky glass when he saw Alan approaching. 'A dram, is it, sir?'

'Yes, thank you.' Alan waited while Marty drew a double measure from the optic. He exchanged greetings with Jack and felt obliged to apologise for not remaining to talk. 'I think I'll take this into the lounge,' he explained, 'I'd like a quiet read before dinner.'

'I went down to see the archivist as was suggested,' Jack called after him as he turned to go. 'The name Beaton was mentioned in some of the documents relating to this area. One of your ancestors witnessed my great-grandmother's wedding certificate . . . would you believe that!'

Reluctantly, Alan returned to his place at the bar.

'Is that so?' he asked. 'Actually I did rather wonder . . .' He addressed Marty Crane who was silently polishing glasses behind the bar. 'Do you happen to know the name of the previous owners here?'

'George Monteith owns the property even now,' Marty told him. 'The house was converted to a hotel and leased by a family called Wilson. We took over from them. I haven't seen any earlier deeds.'

'So those photographs, the sepia ones in the entrance hall, belonged to these Wilsons?'

'I shouldn't think so. The photographs would probably have been inherited with the lease.' Marty considered for a moment. 'Come to think of it,' he continued, 'they probably go back to the time when this was the residence of the local doctor.'

'You don't happen to know what they were called . . . the doctor's family, do you?' Alan demanded, quite excited now.

'No, but George Monteith would know. He should be in later.'

'One gets the impression that he's the big noise around here,' Jack intervened, and immediately cursed himself for blurting out something which might make him appear overly interested and inquisitive. No one appeared to notice, however, for at that moment the permanent fixture in the corner of the bar, Baldy McGillivray cleared his throat and declared, 'Beaton . . . that was their name, the doctors hereabouts. There was the old quarry doctor, Hugh Beaton. He had three children, two boys and a girl . . . all doctors too, even the girl. She was a surgeon, a rare thing for a woman in those days. I remember my old mother talking about how Morag Beaton had worked up in Lochaber with the Commandoes during the war . . .' He gazed sorrowfully at the emptiness of his glass and Alan signalled to the bartender to refill it.

'Beatons, you say?' he demanded, his voice raised in his excitement. 'Do you happen to know if they were still here after the war?' Alan's father had spoken of a visit to relatives – a family wedding in the late '40s. All he could remember was arriving by train at Oban station.

Baldy seemed uncertain about this and disguised his ignorance by taking a long uninterrupted draught of Heineken.

A quietly spoken, cultured and broadly Scottish voice now joined in the discussion. It was Captain Billy Douglas who took up the story.

'I believe that the Hugh Beaton who was still here during the last war, had several children, just as Baldy says. They all went elsewhere to work. Earlier, there had been two generations of medical officers from the same family. From the 1880s right to the end of the first decade of the twentieth century, David Alexander Beaton was the official medical officer of health to the Eisdalsa Quarrying Company, as was his father before him. You'll find their official records in the museum. That David died in the 1920s. His grandsons were David and Ian. I suppose there could have been a daughter, but there is nothing about her in any of our more recent records. The first Hugh Beaton's tombstone is in the churchyard near St Brennan's church over yonder, the other side of the brae. It was sometime in the 1870s when he died.'

Alan's grandfather had been Ian Beaton. Was that perhaps the connection he was seeking? He thought again of the portrait in the entrance hall, that of a young man so like himself as to be almost indistinguishable.

Jack could see the bottled-up excitement in the doctor and knew a little of what he was feeling from his own experience earlier in the day.

'Bit of a coincidence, your being a Beaton too, isn't it?'

'Well, yes and no,' he said, trying to modulate his reply so not to sound too excited.

'Beaton is a name which goes way back in the history of Scottish medicine,' Captain Billy interrupted. 'There were physicians called Beaton or McBeath on the island of Mull and others on Skye, in the time of the early medieval kings of Scotland. A Beaton was physician to the first Lord of the Isles.'

'So, you're in good company then,' Jack's tone was bantering although he was truly envious of his companion. He, himself could only lay claim to kinship with an insignificant sheep farmer. Nevertheless he intended to make full use of his local antecedents.

'I managed to establish that my great-grandfather held the croft on Eisdalsa Island in 1881 before he emigrated to Australia . . . how about that!'

'Congratulations to him,' muttered Baldy. On getting away from this place, I mean. Some of us never got the chance.'

'Some of us never took the trouble to get off our fat backsides,' observed Jamie McPhee, who having anchored his fishing smack in the sound was enjoying a rare evening with his friends in the bar.

'Ye havenae gone that far frae hame yersel',' said Baldy. 'I remember you when y'wus in short pants and climbing the sea wall searching for whelks.'

'What d'ye mean, I never left hame?' Jamie objected. 'Didn't I serve my twenty-one years in the Royal Navy?' As he spoke he pulled himself up to his full height and flexed well-developed muscles. Baldy, backed into a corner, defended his observation with, 'Och, aye, so ye did, but ye still came running back here afterwards. What sort of initiative does that show?'

'Maybe I like it here,' Jamie replied. 'Did that thought never penetrate that thick heid o' yours? There's some of us hereabouts like the place the way it is.'

'City folks complain it's so quiet here at night they can't sleep,' Marty Crane explained, then took it upon himself to introduce those customers whom Alan had not yet met.

'I don't think you know Captain Billy.' He indicated the erect, smartly dressed octogenarian who had related the history of the Beaton family. 'Mr Douglas is a fount of knowledge about the clan system, the Lords of the Isles and all things Scottish. Billy, this is our new doctor, Alan Beaton.'

'No wonder you were so interested in our Beaton doctors,' said Captain Billy, shaking Alan's hand with a remarkably firm grip. 'With that name, anyone hereabouts will be glad to welcome you.'

'You live on Eisdalsa Island?' Alan asked politely, remembering seeing the old man's records during his preliminary search the day before. McWorter had highlighted the need to watch out for diabetes. The Captain was a reluctant patient and required regular checks.

'You may be just the man I'm looking for,' Jack

chipped in, rather rudely. 'I need someone to show me over the island. I'd like to know where my great-grand-father had his croft.'

Alan realised that here was an opportunity to call on the old sea dog himself, while not appearing to be making a professional visit. 'I'd quite like a conducted tour too,' he declared, 'if it wouldn't be too much trouble.'

'Come over whenever you like, both of you,' said the obliging old gentleman. 'I never stray too far from home these days. As to the site of the croft house, that will be difficult to locate. So much slate spoil has been tipped in more recent times that the majority of the old ruined buildings have been quite inundated. There are a few stretches of cultivable ground left which might have been part of a croft, I suppose, but most of those are now gardens belonging to the island's residents.'

'I'm not free until Sunday,' said Alan to Jack, 'but if you want to go earlier. . . it's up to you.' He would have preferred to spend time alone with the Captain and hoped McDougal would avail himself of the opportunity to go ahead without him. Surprisingly the Australian did not seem keen to go alone to the island.

'I can wait until Sunday,' he declared. 'Now that I have located my ancestors, I'm reluctant to leave them . . . not until I've found out a great deal more about them anyway. These hotel bills are beginning to mount up, though,' he explained. 'I shall have to spend some time tomorrow, finding somewhere else to stay.'

'You'll need to make a visit to the museum on the island,' suggested Marty Crane. 'Celia Robertson is the woman to talk to over there. She has all manner of documents relating to the slate industry, although I don't remember seeing anything about a croft on the island.'

Ruth, the landlord's wife, put in an appearance at this moment to announce that dinner was ready and the two resident guests made their way into the dining room where she had laid their places at a table for two.

'I hope that's all right,' she said. 'There's no one else dining this evening and it seemed stupid to have you seated in splendid isolation.'

It would have been impolite for either man to protest at the arrangement, although Alan could have done with some time alone with his thoughts. There was so much to plan in the next day or two. He wanted to get straight in his mind the questions he would ask Dr McWorter when he saw him the following day. He also wanted to think about what he would need to buy in order to make his new home comfortable enough to live in during the long winter evenings. A TV set was a must, and he thought a small microwave cooker would save a lot of time . . . he would stock up with ready-made meals when he was in town. Was there a deep freeze? He couldn't remember. If not he would need to hire something of suitable size. A couple of bottles of malt whisky and a few cans of beer were also added to his mental list.

'. . . you thought about moving into something more permanent?'

Alan came to with a start. Jack had addressed him directly while he had been just on the point of dozing off over his steak.

'Sorry?' he said apologetically. 'This sea air has really

got to me today. I can hardly stay awake.'

'Delayed jet-lag, perhaps?' suggested Jack. 'I asked if you had any thoughts about a more permanent home?'

'Already settled as a matter of fact.' Alan was quite pleased to be one step ahead of the well-organised Mr McDougal for once. 'I move out in the morning.'

'Somewhere in the village?'

'Next door to the Post Office, a very convenient little place.'

'I'm told that the Captain's daughter sometimes lets out a room for short periods,' said Jack. 'I thought I might try there.'

'I wasn't aware the Captain had a daughter,' said Alan, wondering why he had not seen her name alongside that of her father in the doctor's file.

'You know her all the same . . . Flora Douglas, your own receptionist.' Jack was laughing at his ignorance.

Of course. Why had he not seen the connection? Alan wondered why Flora herself had not pointed out that her father was one of his patients.

'She lets rooms?' Alan asked.

'Bed and breakfast,' Jack replied. 'Usually only in the summer months, I'm told, but I hope to persuade her to extend her season.'

'You won't mind being on the island? I understand the ferry is rather limited . . . doesn't run late at this time of the year.'

'Oh, Flora lives in the village, in a place of her own,' said Ruth Crane helpfully. 'You wouldn't find that particular father and daughter sharing a household . . . too much friction by far.'

She set a plate of fruit and ice cream in front of each of them.

'Oh, I see.' Alan did not know why he found Ruth's disclosure so disquieting. It should be no concern of his if Flora agreed to take McDougal in as a lodger. Even so . . .

'Coffee, gentlemen?' Ruth asked.

'Not for me,' said Alan, 'though I'd like some in my room in about half an hour, if that wouldn't be too much trouble?'

He pushed his plate aside and stood up, excusing his abrupt departure on the grounds that he had packing to do and must settle up with the landlord.

Jack nodded dismissively, drained the dregs from the bottle of Australian red they had shared and repaired to the bar.

'I'll see you before Sunday, to arrange a time to visit the Captain,' he said as Alan passed him on his way upstairs.

The village of Seileach boasted two streets of quarrymen's cottages, Front Street and Back Street. An open square beside the harbour allowed room for the buses to turn and gave access to a scattering of houses opposite the jetty, where passengers for Eisdalsa Island boarded the ferry.

The room which Flora Douglas was able to offer Jack McDougal, occupied the entire loft space of her small terraced cottage in Back Street. It was accessed by a narrow stair and the only windows were two small lights set into the steeply sloping roof. Each of these tipped open to reveal a view across adjacent roof tops towards the lowering crags and the sheep grazed hanging valleys of Caisteal an Spuilleadair. If he craned his head sideways to the left, he could just catch a glimpse of the shoreline; enough, at least, to judge the state of sea and tide. It was hardly the room with a view which he might have hoped for, but isolated in the roof space as he was, he would at least have the privacy he sought. On the plus side, there was space here in which to lay out his maps and plans . . . there was even a folding trestle table stored under the eaves which would be ideal for his purpose.

'This will do very well,' he called down to Flora who waited below to hear his verdict. She had been reluctant to agree to his renting the room and half hoped he would turn it down. During the winter months she enjoyed having the house to herself but he had made her a very good offer, one she really could not afford to refuse.

'I'll only want breakfast,' he assured her, once they had settled on a price which was well over the odds. 'I shall be out and about much of the time and can grab a midday meal in town or at the pub. I believe there's a bar on the island as well as the Tigh na Broch?'

'There aren't too many restaurants which stay open for evening meals once the season ends,' she told him doubtfully. 'Many people close down for three or four months during the winter. I don't mind making the occasional dinner for you but I can't guarantee to have anything ready on a regular basis . . . sometimes evening surgery lasts longer than expected or the doctor is called out for an emergency and I have to man the telephone.'

'Oh, really, there's no problem,' Jack protested. 'I can

easily fend for myself, provided you have no objection to my using your kitchen occasionally? I can always make myself a sandwich or something if the need arises.'

He was determined to persuade her and she felt unable to refuse. He had, after all, assured her that it would only be for a week or two.

Jack looked at his watch.

'Good heavens,' he gasped, 'is that the time? When do they stop serving dinner at the hotel?'

'Not until eight o'clock,' she replied, tempted to invite him to eat with her.

'I could rustle up something, if you like,' she suggested. 'I have to cook for myself anyway.' She knew she could be making a rod for her back, breaking her rule right away like this, but it was his first night.

'I have a better idea,' he said. 'How would it be if I took you out to dinner? We could go into town and do the job properly . . . there must be some decent restaurants. You choose.'

'It's a bit late to go so far,' she said regretfully. It was not often she was invited out. 'If I give Marty Crane a ring, I'm sure he will be able to fit us in at the Tigh na Broch.'

She moved into the living room and he heard her lift the telephone. That was something else he had to arrange. He needed a mobile phone. If he were to use the one she paid for, there might be questions about the number of overseas calls he would have to make.

Again he wondered if he was wise, renting Flora's room. Perhaps he should have looked for a cottage to rent, like Alan Beaton.

*

Flora was the belle of the bar that evening. She had put on a new, very flattering dress which she had had no opportunity to wear during the uncertain weather of the past summer. Her clear, rain-washed skin, having little need for artificial enhancement, glowed with a pink flush which was due only in part to the two glasses of Chablis which Jack had persuaded her to drink. She revelled in the unusual experience of being the object of the attention of the most personable and interesting man in the room. Jack McDougal oozed charm, sophistication and confidence, all of which were sadly lacking in the other men of her acquaintance. She was very aware of the envious looks of the rest of the women.

It was Friday night, the bar was crowded and Jack assumed that the additional clients were those who had regular work to go to during the week. 'What do people do for a living around here?' he asked.

'As little as possible.' Baldy McGillivray was well into his third or fourth pint of lager and getting to the point in the evening where he aired his resentment against all incomers, particularly those from across the border. 'Most of them are spending their pensions,' he continued, 'or their Social Security, which amounts to the same thing.'

Jamie McPhee thumped his empty glass on the bar and turned to Jack. 'How can anyone be expected to make a living when foreign boats are destroying the fish stocks? They come inshore where there are no restrictions, trawl the sea bed for prawns and destroy everything there, including the young white fish and the shellfish larvae

. . . everything which represents a food chain for the larger fish. The sea bed out in the bay is like a ploughed field. There was a time when there were wild salmon to be caught all around these shores. You could go out for a few hours and bring home king prawns the size of young herring. When I was a lad I used to be sent out to catch a cod or a saithe for our tea by casting a line off the end of the pier. There was never any doubt that I would come home with the supper! These days you'll be lucky to pick up half a dozen lobsters and a few crabs as the total night's haul.'

The fisherman carried his newly filled glass to the corner table which was occupied by his cronies and Flora reminded Jack that he shouldn't take too seriously anything that was said this close to closing time on a Friday night. 'Whatever he tells you, Jamie gets a good price for his fish,' she assured him. 'His prawns and lobsters are flown out of Glasgow daily and find a good market in London and on the Continent. Like farmers, fishermen enjoy a good moan.'

'You wouldnae talk like that if you'd been up at the market last Tuesday,' said Duncan McLeod. He coughed, stubbed out a cigarette and took a long pull at his glass of Seventy Shilling. 'Full-grown lambs selling for as little as twenty-five pounds apiece and beef prices not worth the cost of taking the beasts to market.'

Jack listened intently while those around him engaged in their usual Friday night gloomy overview of the world and was gratified to have his suspicions confirmed. It was quite clear that the area needed, and would surely welcome, an increase in employment.

'So what have you been doing with yoursel' since you arrived?' asked Baldy. 'Apart from getting yourself fixed up with Flora Douglas, that is.'

Flora blushed when everyone within hearing roared with laughter, but Jack quickly replied, 'I've been offered a comfortable room at a price I can afford. It suits me very well.'

'Did you get down to Kilmory as George suggested?' enquired Marty Crane.

'Indeed I did,' replied Jack, pleased not to have to introduce the topic himself. 'I discovered that my great-grandfather had a croft on Eisdalsa island. I'm going across on Sunday to see if I can locate the site.'

'There never was a croft house on Eisdalsa.' Baldy was adamant. 'There's nae soil for to grow anything.'

'The census of 1861 makes it very clear that there was a farmer called McDougal who lived on Eisdalsa,' Jack insisted. 'Maybe the ground was covered in spoil at a later date?'

'I recall my old grandfather telling us how he used to help round up the sheep on Eilean Uan in the old days,' said Duncan McLeod. 'They took the animals off by rowing boat and sold them in the market at Oban. No one lives over there but there must have been a farmer nearby who ran his flock on it. Can't say I ever heard of a farm on Eisdalsa, though.'

'Captain Douglas seems to think he can locate the site,' suggested Jack, not to be deterred. It didn't matter whether they believed this bit of his story or not. He had sown the seed by declaring his ancestry. Just when and where his people were present in the district mattered

187

little. The important thing was to have established a connection.

'Funny thing is,' he turned to Baldy, 'farmer McDougal married a widow by the name of McGillivray. We might be related.'

'Oh, aye.' Baldy was not impressed. 'There's plenty of that name in these parts.'

'Why anyone wants to live on Eisdalsa, I can't imagine.' The speaker, although casually dressed in jeans and a sweater, spoke with a cultivated accent and with considerable authority.

'Oh, how can you say that?' demanded Flora. 'It's a beautiful place, so quiet and peaceful without cars and street lights, and there are some lovely wild flowers . . . If it wasn't so inconvenient for work, I'd live there myself any day.'

'The place is one monumental tip,' declared the speaker. 'Tell me, what is there to look at apart from a few old cottages built with whatever materials came to hand and repaired on the same principle, and a number of enormous holes in the ground filled with stagnant water? The quarries are green with algae because, no doubt, sewage seeps into them and they serve as a repository for all the old junk thrown out of the houses. Add to that the heaps of rusty old iron lying about in the long grass and a few derelict industrial buildings and you have the historic island of Eisdalsa.'

'That's a bit harsh,' Marty Crane intervened. 'It's mostly rough grass and slate spoil, I'll give you that, but if there is stuff lying about, it's because people live there and it's not easy to get rid of what you don't want when there's no motorised transport to take it away. You try moving a broken down washing machine on a wheelbarrow. Anyway, they do have a clear up every now and again. They get a special boat in and a Council lorry to remove the heavy rubbish to the tip. The islanders pay their taxes the same as you and me,' he added. 'They're entitled to more help than they get at the moment. How would you like to be confined to the island after six o'clock in the evening for five months of the year?'

'I wouldn't,' came the snappy reply. 'But then I'm not so foolish as to want to live on an island anyway.'

'You already do,' observed Baldy McGillivray, laconically.

'In name only,' was the reply. 'At least Seileach is connected to the mainland by a bridge.'

'How about that?' asked Jack. 'Has anyone ever thought about building a bridge across the channel?'

'Often,' said Jamie McPhee, 'but it's a navigable channel for one thing, and anyway it would cost too much for anything more than a footbridge.'

'Can't see any flimsy structure lasting more than a couple of winters in this situation,' muttered McLeod.

'The islanders wouldn't want it anyway,' declared Flora, who had frequently been obliged to listen to her father on the subject.

It was past eleven when Marty Crane placed the towels over the beer pumps and called time.

Jack helped Flora into her coat and escorted her outside into the night. A heavy mist had settled over the sea and there was a definite feeling of autumn in the air.

At this time of the year, the nights grew darker and longer and while there were a few lamps scattered about the village where residents had fixed outside lights above their doorways, these only served to emphasise the dense blackness of the shadows.

'You should have let me bring the car,' Jack protested.

'Och, it's only a wee way,' she replied, 'your eyes will soon get accustomed to the dark.' She stopped, felt about in her handbag and brought out a torch. 'This will help a bit.'

By the faint light of a pencil-thin torch, whose battery was past its best, they picked their way across a cattle grid and turned on to the shore road headed towards the village, passing the school and the old manse along the way. Across the sound, the island of Eisdalsa lay in complete darkness except for the occasional square of yellow from a lighted window. The blackness was almost tangible.

Jack was reminded suddenly of his childhood back home, where their nearest neighbours had been twenty miles down the track and at night you could see the approaching headlights of a truck from ten miles away, through the bush.

'You don't want to take too much notice of Giles Scott,' said Flora.

'Which one was he?' asked Jack.

'The fellow who had so much to say about the condition of the island,' she told him. 'It's his proud boast that he went over there once, on a wet day and has never been again. He must have been living here for the best part of ten years. Things have changed considerably since he saw it but he swears nothing will induce him to return to Eisdalsa Island!'

'He talks with such assurance.'

'Yes, well, he's a retired university professor and is used to people accepting what he says as gospel truth. You should make up your own mind about the island. It has a certain mystery and is a real draw for some people. My father insists that the people who arrive intending to live over there are usually full of plans to change things, but they invariably end up either changing their opinions or leaving. Some folks are simply unable to come to terms with island life. Small improvements do get made from time to time and if they are gradual enough, people accept them, but I would defy anyone to attempt any major innovation . . . like your bridge, for example.'

'Surely people would be happier to park their cars near their houses and be able to unload their groceries at the door?'

'As I said, see the island for yourself and then tell me whether you think a bridge would be a good idea.'

Flora fumbled in her bag for the key.

'I have a spare somewhere,' she told him. 'I'll look it out for you, for the morning.'

She watched him mount the stairs to his loft room, slipped quietly into her bedroom and closed the door.

As he lay on the narrow bed close under the eaves, Jack stared out through the skylight. The mist had lifted during their walk home and now the whole panoply of the heavens was within his view. He sighed contentedly and then laughed to himself. A few days ago he would have walked out of the Park Hotel if he had found a spot of dust on any of the furniture. Tonight he lay in a sparsely furnished room with a carpet which had seen better days, under a roof so low he could barely stand upright except at the very centre, and yet he felt quite content. His forebears must have slept much like this, except that their mattresses would have been stuffed with heather and it was doubtful if the roof lights would have been made of glass.

He drifted into sleep thinking of his great-grandfather and the children he had sired . . . what had their lives been like? he wondered. What dire circumstances had prompted their emigration to Australia? It had taken a great deal of courage to take such a step into the unknown. They must have been tough . . . and very determined.

Chapter Eight

'There . . . see that . . . those flat spots? That's after only fifteen seconds. Fatigue set in almost immediately. We've got a pretty sick lady on our hands here.' The cardiologist switched off the machine and returned to his desk.

'What's the prognosis?' asked Alan.

'An angiogram will tell us more, of course, but I would suggest that she needs a by-pass, and soon.'

'Would you do that here?'

'No, it's a job for the boys in Glasgow. We don't have the resources or the trained staff for that kind of work. Unfortunately it means your lady will have to wait in the queue. The best we can do is offer her the rest and observation she requires to keep her alive while she's waiting.'

'As bad as that?' Alan was wondering how the Clarks were going to take the news. Even though he scarcely knew them, it was enough to realise that the couple worked as a team. If Jeanie was withdrawn from the scene the entire village would feel the effect.

'I think she should come in right away. Meanwhile I'll set the wheels in motion to put her on the first available list. Do you want to be there when I tell her?'

'Yes. I'll need to reassure her about things at home.' Alan followed his colleague into the cubicle where Jeanie Clark was resting after the tests they had given her. Her colour was alarmingly high this afternoon and although the hospital heating system had kicked in efficiently enough at the first hint of cold weather, the temperature was not so high as to be entirely responsible for her distress. She was sweating profusely and even at rest struggling for breath. The consultant lifted an oxygen mask off a hook and adjusted the flow.

'Just draw on that, Mrs Clark, whenever you feel the need,' he suggested, fixing it over her face. Almost at once Jeanie's colour returned to normal and she began to breathe more easily.

'I shall need to take further tests.' The cardiologist drew up a chair and sat down beside her, taking her wrist in his fingers as he spoke. 'For that we'll need to keep you in for a day or two.'

Frightened, the woman glanced quickly from one to the other of the two men, seeking reassurance.

'It looks as if you will have to have an operation,' continued the consultant, 'but all in good time. At present complete bed rest is called for. Dr Beaton here tells me he will be going back straight away to tell your husband so there's no need for you to worry yourself about anything. Nurse will come along in a few minutes to take you to the ward.'

He stood up. 'I'll see you again later,' he told her, and to Alan he said, 'I'll let you have the results of the tests, Beaton. Perhaps you'd call into my office on your way out. We need to talk about Dr McWorter.'

Alan nodded and turned to Jeanie whose anxiety was plain. She removed the oxygen mask to speak.

'What did he mean? What sort of an operation?' she demanded anxiously.

'It's a fairly commonplace procedure,' he told her. 'A production line job these days. The only trouble is you have to wait your turn and there's a big demand. That's why Mr Fergusson wants you to stay in here. You need absolute rest to get your strength up for the operation.'

'But I have to get back home . . . what's Willie going to do without me?'

'What's he going to do if you're never there to help him again?' asked Alan. He knew his words sounded brutal but she had to appreciate the seriousness of her condition. 'I said the operation was commonplace but you must understand that a successful outcome depends largely upon the co-operation of the patient.'

Too exhausted to argue further, she sank back upon the pillows and Alan replaced the oxygen mask.

'I'll be going back to Seileach quite soon,' he told her. 'I'll let your husband know what's happened. No doubt he'll want to bring in what you need himself so if you want to speak to him later on, just ask the nurse for a telephone. I'm going to pop in to see Dr McWorter and then I'll be off.'

'Dr Beaton,' she called him back, 'you'll manage all right . . . in the cottage?' she gasped, struggling for breath to continue. 'I expected to be there when you went in . . . there are several little things . . .'

'Don't you worry about that,' he told her. 'I'm sure I'll

manage. And if not, I can always slip next door and ask Willie.'

As he left, he glanced back. Jeanie had already closed her eyes. That was good, she needed to relax.

Ewan McWorter was fully dressed and sitting in an armchair reading a newspaper when Alan appeared on the ward.

'Ah, Dr Beaton, good of you to come,' he called across the room.

'How are you feeling now?' asked Alan as he shook the doctor's hand. It was far firmer and steadier than it had been on the previous occasion and the old man was a much better colour. It was surprising what a change could take place in just a couple of days.

'I'm fighting fit, as you can see, and badgering them to release me.'

'I'm glad to see you up and about at any rate,' said Alan. 'Have they had you walking yet?'

'I was allowed to take a few steps outside this morning,' replied Ewan proudly. 'Had to stay in full view of Sister's window, you know, but nevertheless it was good to be on my feet. There was a time back there when I wondered if I'd ever get off the bed again.'

'Well, don't try to do too much too soon,' said Alan, and then grinned as he remembered he was talking to someone with a lifetime's experience of such cases. Ewan knew just as well as Alan how he ought to behave.

'How are things on Seileach?' Ewan demanded, anxious to hear of Alan's experiences in the practice.

'Everything's under control. Dr Pullson and I spent

yesterday together. She certainly has her hand on the pulse of things, if you'll forgive the pun.'

'Yes, Janice is a good girl,' McWorter nodded. 'The women like her and that's always a good sign. Nurses can be right bitches, you know, if they think one of their own isn't up to snuff. Now, tell me, Jeanie Clark . . . have you managed to catch up with her yet?'

'I brought her in for an ECG myself, this morning,' Alan told him, rather reluctantly. McWorter was a sick man and had no business to be worrying about his patients.

'And?'

'Not good, I'm afraid. It seems she may be in need of a by-pass. Fergusson is keeping her in for a rest. I gather there's quite a queue for heart surgery.'

'Yes, gluttony and smoking are the downfall of too many Scots these days,' agreed McWorter. 'Still, that's unfair so far as Jeanie is concerned, she's the last person I'd describe as self-indulgent in any sense of the word. Just a hard-working wee woman who's brought up a handful of kids and served the community with a smile, all her working days.'

'I'm renting her cottage, next door to the Post Office,' Alan told him.

'That sounds like a good idea . . . convenient for the practice and close to the bulk of the patients. I hope you don't get too many out-of-hours calls, just because you happen to be so centrally situated.'

'I thought it was a twenty-four-hour-a-day job anyway,' Alan laughed. 'It's what I've been used to.'

'I wish some of those Savile Row-tailored dummies in

the city could hear you say so,' said McWorter fiercely.
'You wouldn't believe the tales I hear about so-called
doctors refusing to attend patients out of surgery hours.
Never heard of such a thing in my young day!'

He was getting too worked up and Alan knew it was
about time for him to be leaving. 'I have to have a word
with Mr Fergusson before he begins his afternoon
rounds,' he said, 'but there are one or two things I did
want to ask you . . .'

During the next fifteen minutes their talk was of the
day-to-day operation of the practice. It was well into the
afternoon when Alan was at last able to speak with the
cardiologist again.

'How did you find McWorter?' Fergusson asked him.

'If I hadn't seen him two days ago in a much weaker
state, I would have thought he was shamming,' declared
Alan. 'He seems full of fight.'

'Yes' Fergusson sounded a note of caution. 'They
always tend to be like that after the first few days. It's a
different matter, however, once they start getting out and
about. That's why I thought I should have a word with
you while I had the chance. I understand that you are
appointed as an Associate GP, is that correct?'

'Yes, sharing time with the Kilgashan practice.' Alan
noted the consultant's look of consternation.

'Ah, I wondered about that. The fact is, McWorter's not
going to be one hundred per cent for some months . . .
if ever. He needs a permanent partner rather than a shared
associate.'

'The Health Authority have already agreed to my
delaying my start with the Kilgashan people,' Alan told

him. 'I suppose I shall have to get in touch with them again and let them know the latest position. After two days, I can't really say to what extent I shall want to commit myself to the Eisdalsa practice, but suffice it to say I would not let Dr McWorter's patients down. Maybe the Health Board themselves can come up with some alternative arrangement.'

'I'll put in a word on McWorter's behalf,' said Fergusson. 'Meanwhile I'd be obliged if you'd continue to pop in from time to time. The old fellow does worry so about his patients.'

'Well, I hope I have settled some of his concerns today,' said Alan, 'but I shall certainly make a point of coming in every day or two until we know what's happening.'

'Thank you.' Fergusson rose to shake Alan's hand and conducted him to the front entrance.

'Poor Jeanie.' Flora was genuinely upset at Alan's news. 'And poor Willie Clark, too, he'll need help in the Post Office . . . he's a dear wee man and willing to turn a hand to anything, but he's no so good when it comes to keeping the books. Jeanie is the brains behind that business.'

'Surely there's someone in the village can take the job on for a while . . . there must be people who are being laid off for the winter,' Alan suggested.

'Well, yes, but it's not that simple,' said Flora. 'The Post Office expect to vet all counter staff and you know how long that sort of thing takes. They'll probably put in a locum and that might be anyone. I don't think Willie will take too kindly to a complete stranger taking over.'

'He said he would contact head office directly,' Alan told her.

'Perhaps I'd better pop in and see if I can do anything to help,' she suggested. 'They probably won't find anyone for a day or two.'

'Well, everything seems pretty quiet here this evening.' Alan glanced through the glass panel into the empty waiting room. 'Why don't you get off early and see what you can do to help? No doubt Mr Clark is anxious to go in and see his wife.'

'Oh, are you sure you don't mind?' She was clearly relieved at his suggestion. 'What about locking up?'

'I can attend to all that,' Alan assured her. 'What happens tomorrow morning? I gather there's no official surgery.'

'Normally patients come by appointment only on a Saturday. There are a number of private patients in the practice, mainly the landed gentry and some of the farmers. There's a retired English stockbroker and a couple from Holland who own the big estate on the Ballahuan road. Visitors to the castle can be a bit troublesome at times. They're often Americans and you know how demanding they can be, but George Monteith handles them pretty well. On the whole they're not too demanding, but they do tend to call in at the weekend and we can't afford to turn down any extra income in this practice! Some private patients expect a house call, of course, but they know they have to take their turn just like the ordinary mortals. On the whole they're not too much bother.'

'Are there any appointments for tomorrow?'

'Fortunately, no. People have been putting off making an appointment if the matter can wait. Everyone has been hoping that Dr Mac would be back.'

'No chance of that for a while yet.' Alan repeated what the consultant had told him. 'I'm afraid folks will be stuck with me until the Health Board decide what they're going to do about the situation. That reminds me, before I go I'd better send them a fax. All right to use the computer?'

Flora was a little taken aback. Dr McWorter had studiously avoided contact with the new technology, leaving her to handle the computer without his intervention. If he wanted to write a private letter, he used an ancient Imperial typewriter on which he picked out the keys with two fingers and much cussing.

'There are some new floppy disks in the drawer,' she told Alan. 'We tend to keep the important records on the hard disc and individual correspondence on floppies . . . saves the space for the data base.'

'That sounds like a good idea,' he agreed. 'I'll keep a few floppies for my own personal use, if that's OK?'

As Flora gathered up her coat and handbag, Alan settled down in front of the PC. She watched him start up, find his way through the initial menu and get up the word processing package. Satisfied that he knew what he was doing, she left him tapping out his report to the Board. 'I've switched the telephone through to the answering service,' she called as she opened the front door and shivered in the blustery autumnal breeze. 'If you should get a call for the morning and find you need me, just let me know. I'm only a couple of doors down from you, in Back Street . . . number fifteen.'

Alan had taken advantage of a quiet Saturday to sort out his living accommodation. When he found no calls had been fed through to either his home telephone or the surgery, he took the opportunity to drive into town and pick up a few items which would make his life more comfortable.

It was gone four o'clock when he returned to the little cottage beside the Post Office. Willie had long since shut up shop and gone off to visit his Jeanie in the hospital so Alan was forced to wait to discuss a couple of problems which he had found with the electrical system. There were a number of socket outlets that did not appear to have any function and to which there was no power, and although there was an impressive aerial attached to the roof of the cottage, television reception was appalling.

It was a fine afternoon, the first really bright day since he had arrived, so once he had unpacked his personal possessions and rearranged the furniture to his liking, he decided to take a stroll around the village.

Apart from the Post Office, which doubled as a general store, there were two other shops, one of which sold books and casual clothing suitable for the rugged climate of the west coast. On impulse he went in and bought a waxed jacket which cost much more than he could afford. He could imagine the wet nights in winter when he would be glad of it though, and did not begrudge the money.

The second was a rambling emporium occupying a

series of single-storey buildings set higgledy-piggledy alongside the harbour. Here visitors, pouring forth from a collection of tour buses parked in the private space beside the shop, purchased trumpery souvenirs decorated with thistles, tartan and highland cattle, tammies with bright red wigs attached and the kind of postcards which depict happy campers and overweight hikers in shorts and boots enjoying typically wet Highland weather. Through the open doors Scottish music, played continuously throughout the day, carried on the breeze across the water to where a small group of visitors waited patiently for the ferry.

Opposite the Post Office was a small restaurant advertising morning coffee and cream teas. This establishment was open for the first time since Alan's arrival in the village. He concluded that the Quarry Tea Rooms opened its doors only when coach loads of tourists were anticipated.

He wandered between the houses, finding behind the two neat rows of cottages a sprawl of unrelated buildings, some derelict, others with obvious commercial purpose. In a stone shed which might once have been a cattle byre, a car mechanic worked on an old rust bucket which looked as though it was a candidate for the breaker's yard. In a corrugated iron shed J. McTavish, BUILDER, stored his materials in such a fashion that disused doors and window frames, sanitary ware, timber, wallboard and building blocks tumbled haphazardly into the surrounding space which was shared with an ancient and very rusty band saw and a broken-down dumper truck.

Turning sharply to the left, Alan found himself

approaching Front Street and turning out of the village he came to the community hall. This was a substantial stone building under a slated roof bearing the date of its construction, 1869. The date had been carved into a stone placed above a loosely fastened door from which the brown paint of several summers before had peeled in long strips, leaving the silvery wood exposed beneath. Alongside the hall, a timber shed some ten foot by six, bore the sign 'Strathclyde Fire Brigade'. Alan wondered what size of pump could be housed in such a small building and was reminded that he should contact the Fire Brigade headquarters to inform them he had joined the practice and to find out how he fitted into their emergency procedures.

Beyond the school house Alan discovered a footpath leading up on to the hill which towered above the village. There was time before dark for him to climb up and get a better view of his surroundings. He turned on to the muddy path, his feet slipping on the moss-covered stones, and began to climb.

For a while, the path followed a burn which tumbled past him down the steep hillside towards the sea. As he climbed, glorious autumnal tints in a wide variety of trees and shrubbery came into view. Many of the plants were clearly not indigenous to the district. Created more in hope than expectation by an enthusiastic amateur towards the end of the last century, Fear Bogha gardens were hidden from the road by a solid stone wall some twelve foot in height. When Alan had first spotted this grim structure, so reminiscent of a prison, he had wondered at its purpose. Now all was made clear. It was to this ugly edifice that the glorious garden owed its survival.

He had been climbing steadily for some time and was well above the tree line when a sharp turn in the path led him out on to a wide grassy plain. Falling away on the seaward side in a vertical cliff, to the north-east the meadow stretched back between great jaws of overhanging igneous rock. As he approached the head of this hanging valley, Alan came upon a sheltered lochan of crystal clear water.

Fed from the heights above, its waters were free from plants save at the very margins where iris and watercress, the fleshy leaves of marsh marigold plants, spiky brown bulrushes and the fluffy white tufts of bog cotton, marked the boundaries of the pool. Close to the bank, dark shadows hovered motionless above the gravelly bed of the loch. Only when Alan drew near enough to be seen did the fish, with a sudden flash of silver, dart in amongst the rushes.

He settled himself upon a rock and gazed out to sea. In the clear September light, the islands in the sound stood out sharply, darkly silhouetted against the light blue of the sky. White mist, gathering at the base of the rocks, made each distant island appear to be magically suspended above the waves. Up here, sheltered by the surrounding cliffs, the air was still, the silence broken only by the occasional cry of a ewe to her lamb, or seabirds, wheeling above the craggy heights, noisily defending their territory against all comers.

From higher up, perched on a bluff which enabled him to see the entire panorama of the coast, the village and the island of Eisdalsa, Jack McDougal watched the doctor, fervently hoping he had come to the end of his explorations. On his lap, Jack supported a large sketching block on which he had drawn everything he could see. Superimposed upon his plan were a number of structures which did not yet exist.

From this vantage point, he could see the village on Eisdalsa, quite clearly. He had noted that the houses were largely situated on the southern side of the harbour and had consequently sketched in the boundary of his new hotel within yards of its northern wall. Since the ferry landing was on the southern side, he had shown a second landing stage sufficient to allow a sizeable vessel to unload close to the hotel. A covered way would conduct visitors into the central reception area which, incorporating in addition, restaurant, lounges and bars, occupied one side of an oblong green. Around this the accommodation blocks were laid out in two rows, echoing the arrangement of the quarry workers' cottages on the other side of the harbour. A dotted line indicated the position of the glass roof which would cover the entire green and its centrally sited swimming pool, thereby providing an area for rest and relaxation in inclement weather.

On Seileach itself, in the valley running up behind the Tigh na Broch Hotel, he had located a golf course, while the existing car park had been extended to take in a wide area of rough pasture running behind the gardens of the houses in front street. The shoreline along that part of the bay which had not already been built on showed a large compound and a jetty for storing and launching dinghies, canoes and pedalo boats, while the deep-flooded quarry between Back Street and the sound had been converted into a marina for larger vessels. A second marina, destined for use by visitors to the hotel and other facilities on Eisdalsa Island, had been sited in the most northerly of the flooded quarries. He had sketched in the position of the seaward entrance, to be achieved by blasting through the quarry wall. The mounds of waste from this operation were going to prove a problem but his sketch suggested a way to handle this by bulldozing much of the spoil into the remaining shallow quarries on the eastern section of the island. By importing topsoil it should be possible to grass over the flattened area which could be made into bowling and putting greens, gardens and perhaps an additional outdoor swimming pool. He confidently sketched in round umbrellas and a band stand where, in fine weather, there could be concerts held under the stars.

Access to the island was his worst problem. A bridge would be the best solution and a road bridge would allow cars to be brought over – not to drive around the island, of course, but to be kept under the eye of their owners. He could envisage certain types of visitor feeling uncomfortable about leaving their BMWs and Porsches to the mercy of the teenage population of Seileach.

Lightly he drew in a line to indicate the path to be taken by a Sky Rail, starting from a point on the cliff at the edge of the hanging valley which lay below him, and ending on the island, close to the harbour wall. A lift would carry passengers from the car park in the village to the top of the cliff.

He reached into his haversack and withdrew the Ordnance Survey map, which was already becoming tattered from constant handling. Laying aside his sketch book, he spread the sheet out on the rocks and studied the terrain inland of where he was sitting. The hill behind him rose another fifty feet or more before dropping away gently towards an estate which, according to a brochure he had picked up in the Post Office that morning, bore the rather ignominious title of Johnstone's. From the brochure which he now studied more intently, the main house was a large, somewhat drab and unimaginative stone building of late-Victorian date, but the attraction of the estate was its garden, world famous for its rhododendrons in particular and for the hundred-year-old plantings of tree species from around the world. Jack wondered whether it would be worth the cost of extending the Sky Rail to end at Johnstone's. He made a note to pay a visit there and to enquire about the ownership. He felt pretty certain this was not part of George Monteith's domain or Milton would surely have mentioned it.

Alan, attracted by the flash of white which caught his eye when Jack handled the map, attempted to identify the figure on the hillside, way above him. All he could make out was an orange cagoule and a shock of dark hair.

A shout, coming from somewhere to his right and further down the slope, caught the doctor's attention.

'Help! I say . . . up there . . . could you help me, please?'

A head had appeared over the edge of the hanging valley. This was quickly followed by the shoulders and soon the entire form of a portly man in baseball cap, short-sleeved shirt and shorts. He lumbered towards Alan as the doctor got to his feet and started down the slope towards him.

'Thank heavens,' cried the man as soon as they were near enough to speak normally. 'I despaired of finding anyone up here at this time of the year.'

He sank down in the heather, out of breath and clearly out of condition. He could have done with losing a couple of stone, Alan concluded while the stranger struggled to regain his breath.

'My wife . . . she's down there . . . on the cliff. She slipped and fell . . . turned her ankle . . . it could be broken. She's obviously in great pain and can't put any weight on her leg. I wonder if you could help me to carry her down to the road?'

'Point me in the right direction and I'll go on down to her straight away,' said Alan. 'I'll see what I can do to help her.' Then, by way of explanation, 'I'm the local GP, Alan Beaton.'

'Well . . . there's a bit of luck,' exclaimed the other. 'Fancy finding a doctor out here in the wilds, just when you want one!'

'If we do need to carry her down,' said Alan, 'it will take more than the two of us. Why don't you go on up and have a word with that chap up there?' He indicated the figure perched on the rock way above them. 'Take your time, though. I don't want a heart case as well as a twisted ankle to deal with.'

Alan set off in the direction the distraught husband had indicated, while the man himself carried on up the slope, more composed now he was satisfied that something would be done.

Led to the spot by the intermittent cries of the injured

woman, Alan found her balanced precariously on a narrow shelf about ten foot down from a rough sheep track. One leg was stretched out to the very edge of the shelf, while the other was drawn up to her chest.

When she heard his footsteps on the path above, the injured woman glanced up, her drawn features suddenly illuminated by a smile of relief. When she attempted to move, however, pain got the better of her and she gave a sharp cry.

Alan scrambled down beside her.

'Hello,' he said, 'I met your husband on the path up there. He tells me you are in a spot of trouble. Perhaps I can help? I'm a doctor.'

She was clearly shocked and was trembling with cold. Both she and her husband had come ill-equipped to be climbing about on the cliffs. The ground was slippery underfoot and the temperature had fallen considerably during the last half-hour.

Alan removed his newly acquired waxed jacket and wrapped it around the woman's shoulders.

'It's my ankle,' she moaned. 'I seem to have twisted it.'

Her injured foot, from which the shoe had been removed, was already badly swollen and her torn tights did little to disguise some ugly bruising. Alan supported the injured foot in his left hand whilst he felt gently above the ankle and then down towards the toes. When he reached the instep, she yelled out in pain.

'I don't think you've broken it,' he told her, completing his examination. 'But it is a bad sprain. How did you come to fall?'

'I was having difficulty in keeping from slipping,' she

told him. 'The grass was damp and my shoes don't have much grip.'

The shoe which she had removed was of the court variety with a two-inch heel. The sole was of smooth leather without any tread at all. How she had been able to keep such footwear on, even on level ground, was a mystery.

'I suppose you think me very foolish to be up here wearing those,' she said. She smiled bravely then winced with pain once again as he replaced her foot on the grass and helped her to shift into a more comfortable position.

'I don't think I can walk,' she told him nervously, and then, glancing around her as though to emphasise the absurdity of her situation, she asked, 'How will I get down?'

'I've sent your husband to get some help. When he comes back we'll see if you can put any weight on that foot. If not we'll have to try and carry you down between us.'

'But it's so steep . . . I don't think I like the idea of being carried.'

'There's really no alternative,' Alan told her. 'Don't worry, you'll be all right.' He felt in his pockets, finding nothing suitable, then looked about him, hoping for inspiration. The woman wore a sleeveless dress with a straight skirt and that was all.

'I need to support that ankle with something,' he said. 'I don't suppose you have a scarf or anything like that?'

She shook her head, thought for a moment and then said, 'I am wearing a cotton slip under this dress, if I can get it off, you could tear that up.' She pulled her skirt above her knees to reveal a glimpse of lace and fine white cotton.

'That would do fine,' said Alan. 'You don't mind tearing it up?'

'Oh, that's all right,' she replied, dismissively. 'It's only an old thing. The trouble is, you'll have to help me to take it off.'

Alone, on a bare hillside in full view of the village below and with the woman's husband about to reappear at any moment, Alan hesitated. He could be placed in a very compromising position here . . . Quickly he dismissed his reservations; it was an emergency and there really was no alternative.

He unzipped her dress at the back and helped her to wriggle forward, so that she was not sitting on the skirt. He pulled the dress up over her head, nearly falling off the ledge in his embarrassment. When it came to removing the slip, they were hampered by the woman's inability to control her giggles. He put her hysterical behaviour down to shock and embarrassment.

Struggling to remain professionally composed, he caught hold of the flimsy slip, and as she wriggled free, peeled it off over her head. For a split second he was treated to an expanse of white thigh, a flash of champagne-coloured bikini knickers and a bra which scarcely contained her ripe bosoms. Deftly she snatched up the dress and in seconds, was drawing the skirt back over her head.

Alan busied himself tearing the dainty, lace-trimmed undergarment into strips. Dipping his makeshift bandage in a nearby burn, he rolled the strips into the semblance of a bandage.

'As the material dries it will tighten up,' he explained. 'That should give the ankle enough support.'

It was at that moment that her husband reappeared, with a rather disgruntled Jack McDougal following behind.

'How is she, doctor?' enquired the anxious husband.

'I suspect it's nothing more than a bad sprain,' Alan replied, 'I'll just support the damaged ankle with this and then we'll see what we can do about getting her down to the road.'

The husband watched while Alan made a professional job of the bandage, splitting the last ten inches of the material and tying it off neatly, above the instep. With Alan on one side and her husband on the other, the doctor persuaded his patient to try placing weight on the injured foot. Her scream of pain must have alerted the residents over on Eisdalsa Island.

'OK, OK,' he decided. 'We'll have to carry her.'

'But how?' The husband was showing signs of distress himself now.

'We'll make a chair.' Alan turned to Jack, acknowledging his presence for the first time.

'Good of you to come so quickly, McDougal,' he said. 'I saw you up on the hill but didn't recognise you.'

'Just doing a bit of sketching,' he said, in order to explain his earlier behaviour.

Alan held out his clasped hands and Jack grasped them with his own, thereby completing the knot.

'If you will assist your wife to sit on our hands, sir . . .'

Between them they lifted the woman into a sitting position and the two younger men staggered upwards the few feet to the sheep track. Here they set their burden down on a boulder and paused, waiting for the husband to catch up.

'It might be easier if we had a name to call you by,' suggested Jack, addressing the stranger. 'We can't keep on saying: Hey, you!'

'Oh, I'm sorry, my name is Thornton-Mowbray, Alexander Thornton-Mowbray, and this is Alicia, my wife. We're staying on Eisdalsa Island. It's a holiday cottage belonging to a Mrs Marie McCallum. Do you know her?'

'I'm afraid not,' said Alan. 'We're both only recent arrivals to the district ourselves.'

'Did you walk up here from the harbour?' Jack asked, thinking of the distance to be covered carrying the woman right through the village.

'I'm afraid so,' said Thornton-Mowbray, 'my car is parked on the quay.'

'We'll take Mrs Thornton-Mowbray to the hotel,' Alan decided. 'There's a path leading off this one . . . a short-cut. I discovered it the other evening soon after I arrived.'

'Would you be kind enough to carry my stuff?' Jack asked Thornton-Mowbray, indicating the sketch pad and haversack he had been carrying.

'Of course,' said the other, collecting Jack's belongings.

After a hundred yards, the men let down their burden and rested their arms while they swapped sides. The woman weighed no more than nine stone. Nevertheless, the action of manipulating a heavy weight on a steep slope while walking sideways was very tiring.

'Let me take a turn,' suggested the husband.

Jack would readily have given up his position as one half of a human stretcher, but Alan clearly felt the strain would be more than the older man could bear.

Marty Crane was just opening up the bar when they eventually arrived at the hotel. He poured drinks all round while Alan hurried off to find a telephone.

'My name is Beaton, Dr Alan Beaton, speaking from Dr McWorter's practice. Can you put me through to Accident and Emergency please?' He was through to the switchboard of the Chest Hospital . . . the only one he knew of.

'I'm sorry, doctor, there's no Accident and Emergency department here. You will have to call the West Highland. Perhaps you would like to take down the number?'

The voice was cool and condescending. Well, he supposed he should have found out already what other hospitals there were in the district. He took down the number, thanked the attendant and redialled.

'Hello, this is Dr Alan Beaton speaking from Dr McWorter's practice . . . yes, I'm his locum. I have an ankle injury requiring X-ray and treatment. The patient is a woman, about forty to fifty years. She slipped and fell out on the mountain. She is shocked and in considerable pain. What happens . . . do we bring her in or will you send out an ambulance? Sorry?' He listened to a long explanation about how the ambulance was out of action for the weekend, undergoing repairs. 'No, that won't be necessary. I'll give the husband directions and send her in her own car . . . Well, we have to reach the vehicle first . . . say about an hour? OK, thanks very much.' Rather than ask for directions to the hospital, he returned to the bar and spoke quietly to Marty Crane.

'Some system,' he complained. 'There's no ambulance available until Monday. Goodness knows what happens if there's a real emergency.'

'That's easy . . . they either send out the lifeboat from Oban or order up a helicopter from the RAF base.'

'I would have thought it would be cheaper to have a stand-by ambulance.' Alan turned to Thornton-Mowbray. 'You'll have to take your wife in to the hospital yourself, I'm afraid, unless you'd like me to?'

'Oh, no, I can't impose on you any further,' he insisted. 'You have both done more than enough. I don't know how to thank you as it is.'

'Mr Crane will tell you how to get there . . . it's the West Highland Hospital. They know you are on your way. Just mention my name . . . Beaton, Dr Alan Beaton.'

'It will take me a while to get back to the village and collect the car,' said Thornton-Mowbray. 'May I leave my wife in your care?' he asked Marty Crane.

'Of course,' said Marty. To the patient he said, 'I'll just go and fetch my wife, Mrs Thornton-Mowbray.'

'Actually a cup of strong sweet tea is what she needs most at this moment,' Alan suggested. 'Do you think you could organise that?'

Marty Crane went off to find Ruth, while Jack and Alex Thornton-Mowbray prepared to walk down to the village together.

When Alicia had been settled more comfortably in the lounge with Ruth Crane for company, the doctor excused himself, saying that although he intended to wait to assist Alicia to her car, he would take this opportunity to fulfil his promise to Marty to take a look at the medical books in the quiet lounge.

He crossed the hall, glancing once again as he did so, at his Victorian counterpart on the wall beside the coat rack. He entered a short, gloomy corridor which ended in a half-glazed door whose tiny square panes of coloured glass provided the only illumination in that place.

It was a decidedly masculine room. The furniture was of heavily carved mahogany with the two armchairs upholstered in leather, now cracked and worn. A huge desk occupied the bay window with, behind it, a swivel chair of the Edwardian era. Apart from wall-to-ceiling glass-fronted bookcases, the only other item of furniture in the room was a leather-upholstered examination couch dating from halfway through the previous century.

As Marty had suggested, this must certainly have been the doctor's consulting room. Alan glanced into an adjoining room which opened directly to the outside: the patients' waiting room he felt sure. A further door opened into what had clearly been the dispensary. Used now to store cleaning materials and equipment for use in the hotel, the original glass-fronted cabinets for instruments and drugs had remained unchanged in a hundred years.

Alan returned to the consulting room and examined the rows of books occupying the bookcases. He leafed through an 1860 edition of Andrew Combe's *Physiology of Digestion* and then his hand came to rest upon a first edition of *A Manual of Surgical Operations* by Joseph Bell. Alan recognised the name at once. Bell, who had been a friend of Sir Arthur Conan Doyle, was the surgeon who was thought to have inspired the character of Sherlock Holmes. This book alone represented treasure trove.

He glanced along the rows of heavy, leather-bound tomes picking out *An Index of Treatment* published in 1913 which appeared to cover any and every eventuality which might present to a medical practitioner and a *Manual of Operative Surgery* which was dated 1912.

Alan smiled at the descriptions of heroic, kitchen-table surgery of a kind which the most adventurous of modern-day practitioners might well hesitate to perform even within the luxury of a sterile operating theatre. The book was stained and quite badly damaged. Alan imagined his ancestor carrying this surgeon's bible to France with him, during the First World War. He looked for a signature on the fly leaf. Yes, here it was. *Major Hugh Beaton, MB., ChB., Tigh na Broch, Eisdalsa, Argyll.*

At the end of the bottom row he found a large, slender volume with the name Beaton prominently displayed in gold lettering on the Morocco leather spine. It was too heavy to hold open in his hands so he laid it on the desk and carefully turned to the title page. *Beaton's Medieval Herbal, translated from the Gaelic by Stuart Cameron Beaton. Published in 1918 by Anne Beaton. Illustrations by Katherine McLean.*

Reverently, Alan turned the pages. Glorious illustrations of common wild flowers graced each of the pages which were written half in Gaelic and half in English. It was a work of monumental devotion. One could not but admire the effort which had gone into finding the correct translation for every description given by those ancient physicians, the Beaton doctors of Mull and Jura. How could such a precious volume have come to be left behind when the family moved out? He returned to the fly leaf and found there an inscription: *To Hugh and Millicent from Stuart, Annie and wee Stephen. Christmas 1918.* Intrigued to know more about these shadowy figures from the past, he replaced the volume. If Marty did not want it himself, it might be that he would be prepared to sell it . . .

'Mrs Thornton-Mowbray is ready to leave, doctor.' Marty was standing at the door watching Alan replace the book.

'Did you find anything of interest?'

'There are some medical books which might be of value to collectors,' Alan replied. 'One in particular could raise a fair price at auction . . . it's a first edition. The one I've just put back was written by someone I believe to be my own ancestor. I'd like to negotiate a price, if you will agree to sell it.'

'The library is part of the lessee's inventory,' Marty explained. 'The books aren't mine to sell. You'd have to discuss it with George Monteith.'

'Let's get Mrs Thornton-Mowbray on her way to hospital,' suggested Alan, 'then we can have another whisky and you can advise me how to go about acquiring it.'

Giles Scott trained his binoculars on the cliff at the spot where he had seen something fluttering in the breeze.

Yes, there they were. He adjusted the focus and saw what had attracted his attention. The woman had quite clearly removed her clothes. 'Well I never!' he breathed, 'a funny place to choose to be sure.' Momentarily he had a full view of the man. He gasped in recognition. He had seen that face, recently . . . in the bar at the Tigh na Broch.

'What is it, dear? Something interesting?' His wife asked, placing a laden tea tray on the table beside him and busying herself with pouring the tea. She handed him a cup and held out her hand for the binoculars. 'Can I see?' she demanded.

Enjoying the titillation, he was reluctant to hand them over. 'There's nothing much to see,' he replied, getting a firm control on his excitement, 'a bit of courting display . . . nothing more.'

'Too late in the year for that, surely?' She dismissed his suggestion out of hand, grabbed the binoculars and swept the mountainside, hoping to get a view of the birds herself.

'I can't see anything,' she said after a few moments. 'Maybe that party of walkers disturbed them.'

'Probably,' said her husband, taking back the instrument and hoping for further entertainment. Unfortunately, his quarry had already moved out of sight, hidden by the boulders which at that point, marked the cliff edge on the seaward side of the sheep track.

It was later that same evening when Giles pushed open the door to the Badger Bar and stripped off his jacket. As he placed it on one of a row of hooks by the door, he was passed by Marty Crane and another man whom he had already seen once before that afternoon. He sidled up to the bar and waited while Marty, without removing his jacket, drew two glasses of whisky from the optic. One he pushed across the bar towards the stranger. The other he downed himself in one swallow.

'Sorry to keep you, Giles,' he apologised. 'The doctor and I   have just been standing about out there in the cold. It's a raw evening and no mistake. Now what can I get you?'

Of course, now Giles knew why the figure on the hill seemed so familiar. He had seen the fellow here in the bar only the other evening. He gave his order and as he waited to be served, turned to the tall red-haired young man at his side.

'Scott,' he announced, 'Giles Scott. I take it you're the stand-in for Dr Mac?'

He eyed Alan with a look, tinged with . . . what? Envy . . . amusement . . . distaste? It was difficult to say.

Alan, ignoring Giles' rather impertinent stare, acknowledged his greeting, picked up his glass and excused himself, calling to Marty as he left, 'I've found something rather interesting amongst the books you asked me to look at. I think I'll go back and read some more.'

'Bit of a lad that one,' commented Giles when the doctor was safely out of the way. 'Not been here five minutes and already he's romping in the heather with some woman.'

Marty looked up sharply, ready to intervene. He didn't like this kind of talk in his bar.

'How d'ye mean?' demanded Archie McGillivray, his

eyes widening at the hint of gossip.

'Well, put it this way,' Giles lowered his voice to a stage whisper, 'he's not a doctor I'd want to have attending my wife, unchaperoned.'

More of the regulars gathered around as Giles relived the scene he had witnessed through his binoculars that afternoon.

The story spread around the village like a forest fire, first from one group to another in the Badger Bar and from table to table in Ruth's restaurant. The word was carried across the counter of the village store, soon to be distributed with countless mugs of morning coffee. By Wednesday afternoon, the story was even being whispered through tight lips over the bone china teacups at the monthly meeting of the Church Women's Guild.

Bill Douglas, who had had a slight cough and had stayed away from the Tacksman's Bar for a night or two, learned of the, by now highly embellished, incident with his first dram on the following Friday evening.

He knew better than to take village gossip at face value but nevertheless considered that his daughter should be informed. A fatherly word of warning could do no harm.

Chapter Nine

Almost before he became aware of the birds themselves, Alan noticed two silent shadows darting across the unruffled surface of the waves as a pair of cormorants flew beside the shore, in a direct line from south to north.

'Do you know, since I first retired in '75,' Captain Billy told them, 'I've strolled around the island most evenings. In all those years, I could have set my watch by these fellows. They fly past half an hour before sundown, as regularly as a couple of commuters boarding the 8.20 for Waterloo.'

'What are they doing?' asked Alan, edging forward, eager to get a better view of the birds.

The cormorants' flight path took them past the old flooded quarries, over the jutting rocks at the island's most westerly point and on across the sound, skirting Eilean nam Uan and disappearing somewhere to the north of Caisteal an Spuilleadair.

'Going home to roost.'

The Captain turned his back to the slight breeze, which had got up since they had reached the top of the hill and fumbled with his pipe. Alan caught a whiff of St Bruno tobacco and, although a convert of some five years standing to the non-smoking fraternity, he inhaled the familiar, rich aroma with pleasure.

The old man puffed steadily until he was satisfied that the tobacco was properly alight, then removed the pipe from his mouth.

'You wait. In another two or three minutes the rest of the commuters will fly past.'

Even as he spoke, they heard the high-pitched chatter of a flock of oyster catchers flying low along the shoreline. They rose in formation, seeming to miss by inches the jagged rocks on the far side of the quarry, and continued on across the sound in the wake of the cormorants.

Jack, lost in his own thoughts, was startled by the noise and heard only the end of Captain Billy's remark.

'I suspect that it's only since the quarries closed down that the birds have felt safe enough to come close to these islands. Can you imagine them becoming accustomed to the continuous noise of pump engines draining the quarries, the frequent explosions of blasting powder and the clamour of locomotives puffing backwards and forwards across the island with their loads of slate? It must have been a dirty, noisy old place in the old days.'

It pleased Jack to be able to agree with him. If industrial noise was the norm around here in the past, there could be little argument against the minimal disturbance which his own proposals would introduce. After all, if the Marquis were to restart the quarrying operation, something he was perfectly at liberty to do, the island's residents would have to put up with it.

While the three men continued to survey the scene

from their vantage point on the summit of the island's single hill, a large ocean-going yacht hove into view, its sails furled as it chugged slowly to its mooring in the sound. The area was no stranger to the noise of marine engines and Jack consoled himself with the thought that although speed boats made a bit more noise than this yacht, no one was likely to be bothered so long as the economy of the district improved and everyone got rich.

On Sunday, the ferry stopped running at ten minutes to six. Alan glanced at his watch, anxious to ensure that they were not going to be stranded on the island for the night. Jack seemed far more casual about the time, quite ready to spend the evening in the island's little bar.

'We're sure to find someone with a boat who's willing to take us across,' he told Alan, looking to Captain Billy for confirmation.

The old man nodded his agreement but the doctor was disinclined to be led astray.

'It's all right for you,' he said, 'you're on holiday. I'm obliged to stay within call in case there's an emergency.' He turned back to Captain Billy. 'Thanks so much for showing us all the old workings, Mr Douglas. Next time I come across I'll call in to the museum and find out a bit more about the quarriers and their families. They must have been a sturdy bunch of people to have lived here at all, given the lack of facilities in those days. One wonders how they ever got warm . . . or dry! It's a pity about those buildings down there.' He indicated the ruins of a smithy and engine houses which stood at the foot of the escarpment, between the hill and the sea-filled quarries. 'It's a wonder Historic Scotland or

Scottish Heritage haven't taken those in hand and preserved them.'

'Celia Robertson, in the museum, has tried, often, to
get both organisations over here to look at the place, but
she meets a blank wall every time. I'm afraid that in
general my fellow countrymen only recognise the value
of their heritage after it's been taken away from them.'

Jack took no part in this conversation. The Chief
Planning Officer had mentioned certain organisations
which would have to be appeased before he could obtain
planning consent. Perhaps he himself should take a look
in this museum. There might be something there he could
use to his advantage.

'Well, I'm off,' Alan decided. 'Are you coming or not,
Jack?'

'No, I think I'll take a chance on getting a boat later,'
said the Australian. 'I'd like to soak up some of the
island's culture while I have the chance.'

Captain Billy gave a little snort, but made no
comment. The most any stranger was likely to get out of
an evening in the Tacksman's Bar was a lot of idle gossip
and island politics but who was he to deprive Kirsty
Brown of some much-needed custom? He had observed
the Australian over in the Tigh na Broch, spreading his
largesse amongst the locals. Kirsty should make a nice
little packet this evening.

Bill Douglas and Jack McDougal watched the doctor
make his way down the steep path to the ruined buildings
and take the shortest route to the harbour. The ferry was
already loading up for the final run of the day as he
turned into the square and sprinted across the grass

towards the ferryman's hut.

'Ah, they've seen him,' observed Bill when the ferry, having already cast off, did a three-hundred-and-sixty-degree turn and secured to the harbour wall again.

As he and Jack descended to the lower ground, Captain Billy suggested his visitor might join him in a spot of supper before going to the pub. 'Things rarely get going in there before nine o'clock,' he explained.

'That's very good of you, sir.'

Jack was pleased to accept. During their visit, Bill's visitors had learned a great deal about the history of the island but what the Australian really wanted was information about the present-day population.

Bill's cottage stood in the middle of a row which was hidden from the harbour by the largest building on the island, the coalrea.

They glanced inside in passing. It looked as though the contents had been left undisturbed for many years. Bill pointed out a section of steel railway track left embedded in the floor.

'When I was here in the 1940s there was narrow-gauge track like this running all over the island,' he told Jack. 'George Monteith's uncle – he was the owner then, was offered a sum of money for the scrap metal so they came and tore it up . . . some time in the '50s that would have been. Pity, really. I could do with a train ride from the jetty these days. Never thought twice about the walk from the ferry then, of course.'

What if the railway could be re-established? Jack wondered. He pictured the scene. A small locomotive drawing a set of wooden waggons, constructed to look like slate trucks but fitted with seats and crowded with holiday makers . . .

'It wouldn't take that much money to reinstate the tramways,' he suggested, tentatively. 'The viaducts and bridges are still there. Has anyone ever thought about restoring them?'

'What for?' asked his companion. 'It only takes twenty minutes to get around the island on foot . . . half an hour at the outside. Who'd want to pay for a train ride?'

'I would have thought it would have made quite an attraction,' Jack insisted.

'There are a good many folk around here who would object,' said Bill. 'Most of those who have been here for a few years resist any form of change. Take the ferry, for instance. When the Marquis persuaded the Local Authority to take it over and run it as an extension of the bus service, there was an outcry, despite the fact that Argyll County Council wanted to provide a powerful motor boat to replace the old wooden dory. She had a Seagull engine so ineffectual it had to be assisted by oars in a strong tide! Many's the time I've seen old Tam, the late ferryman, pulling across the sound in a force-six gale with a couple of island matrons at the second oar. Islanders insisted they preferred the little boat and thought a more powerful vessel would only encourage unsavoury visitors to the island. The owner of the pub won the day . . . he wanted to improve his trade and suggested the existing boat was inadequate for night trips in bad weather.'

This was exactly what Jack wanted to hear. If there was dissension and division amongst the islanders, it was always possible to win over at least a faction to his own viewpoint. While they were squabbling amongst themselves he would be able to proceed with his plan unimpeded.

Bill Douglas lived in comfortable bachelor squalor, the despair of his daughter who came in weekly to remove clothes for washing and to clean the kitchen area in order to minimise the risk of food poisoning. Otherwise she left the clearing up to him, and a poor job he made of it! He shuffled a pile of old newspapers and magazines together, murmuring his stock phrase on introducing visitors to his living room: 'Time I put some of this on the bonfire.' Having cleared a space so that his visitor could sit down, he relit his pipe, throwing the spent match to the back of the simulated log fire, black and dusty from long neglect. Jack noticed a collection of similar burnt matches and grinned.

Catching his eye, the old man laughed. 'Flora goes mad when she sees me do that,' he said. 'It's a habit born of the time when I could cope with an open fire. These days I find carrying coal and clearing the grate too much trouble, but I can't ever remember that the electric fire won't burn the matches!'

He made his excuses, went into the kitchen and busied himself opening packets and lighting the Calor gas stove. In such cramped quarters, Jack could not avoid seeing that Bill had set a pan to boil and was busy placing a variety of polythene bags side by side in the water.

'I hope *Boeuf Bourguignonne* will serve?' he enquired cheerily. 'It'll take twenty minutes.'

Jack was very fussy about what he ate. The gourmet

cooking put before him in the course of his work usually met with his severest criticism. He shuddered at the thought of boil in the bag! 'What I do for the sake of the Humbert Development Corporation,' he muttered to himself, and made a mental note to claim danger money the next time he contacted Milton.

He could hear the old man humming to himself in the kitchen. It was a very pleasant voice . . . something from opera, Jack surmised. He thought he recognised the aria.

In one corner of the cluttered space stood a table covered in a chenille cloth, visible only where it hung below the edge. The surface was completely obscured by the plethora of articles piled there. Taking centre stage was an impressive array of hi-fi equipment which seemed totally out of place in such a confined space. Alongside this stood more electronic apparatus which at the moment was giving out a humming sound. From time to time, this changed to an irritating crackling. Suddenly the relative calm was shattered by a blast of Morse code.

The humming stopped and Bill called out, 'That'll be the Royal Yacht taking the Queen up to Balmoral. They come by here every year about this time. That message is from the yacht to its escorting submarine.'

He came in, wiping his hands on a tea towel, seated himself at the table and began to tap out a message of his own. There was an answering signal and then everything returned to normal.

'What was all that about?' Jack demanded.

'I just sent a message to the Royal Yacht,' said his companion.

Jack thought at first that the old man was pulling his

leg. 'What did you say?' he asked, sceptically.

'What I usually do. The people of Eisdalsa Island send loyal greetings to Her Majesty . . . that's all.'

'Is that allowed?' asked Jack, realising at last that Bill was serious.

'Why not? When Lizzie came up to review the Sea Cadets at Fort William, she told me how pleased she was to have received my signals over the years.'

'You mean, you always do that?'

'Of course. Supper will be ready in two ticks.' He disappeared once more, leaving Jack to contemplate Captain Billy's words. There was a lot more to this casual old fellow than met the eye, that was for sure.

The 'instant' meal was more palatable than Jack could have hoped and since it was washed down with Bill's ten-year-old malt he had surprisingly few qualms about after-effects.

'We didn't look for the site of the croft,' he reminded his host. 'Is there still light enough to go and see?'

'Well now, as I've already explained, there's nothing on the old maps to indicate the presence of any kind of farm on the island, but bearing in mind that a croft house would have been situated well away from the main village, that is not surprising. Since all the records we have relate to the quarrying company, they might possibly exclude a building outwith their control. There is one set of stone walls which always puzzled us . . . we could have wrongly identified them.'

He emptied his glass, piled their empty plates on the kitchen draining board, picked up his binoculars and opened the door.

'It's a fine evening and there's still enough light to see by. Follow me.'

They took a path which Jack had not noticed on their earlier circuit of the island. This led upwards towards the sheltered base of the escarpment. The path was overgrown and it was unlikely that many casual visitors to the island ever came this way. After a hundred yards or so, the old man stopped and bent down, examining the thicket carefully.

'Yes, I thought so,' he declared at last. 'Look, do you see . . . was there ever anything as perfect as that?'

He parted the brambles, exposing a tiny bird's nest woven of the finest grasses and incorporating here and there strands of cotton and string together with bright fibres of orange and blue nylon rope. The inside was lined with moss, dried up now after the long summer drought. This in turn was covered with soft down, plucked from the breasts of the parent birds.

'Jenny wren,' Bill breathed reverently. 'You don't often see them nowadays. They're easily scared off.'

He continued along the path for a few more yards and stopped again. 'Here, look at this.' He parted some long grasses whose flowering heads scattered their pollen liberally, making Jack want to sneeze. 'Here's something which will only grow where the feet of man never tread.'

Indicating a patch of fleshy plants whose broad leaves were strangely spotted, he stood back for Jack to take a closer look.

What the Australian saw was a substantial stem bearing a long raceme of flowers, each one a miniature replica of the gaudy blossoms he'd last seen on sale in the florist's shop back home at the Kookaburra Resort. He had never considered himself a naturalist; flora and fauna generally left him cold, but even Jack could not but admire the delicate blooms.

'They look like orchids,' he said, genuinely impressed.

'Correct!' Bill grinned with satisfaction. 'But none of your vulgar tropical blooms . . . those can only be grown under glass in this country. These are our own Scottish variety *Dactylorhiza maculata* . . . the Heath Spotted Orchid. One of the few orchids to grow on peaty soil. Common in name only these days, of course. The only reason they've lasted here is that few people know of their existence.'

He allowed the protective grasses to fall back into place. Jack was aware that, had he been on his own, there was no way in which he would have noticed the existence of the flowers.

The old man had moved on along the path and came to a halt at a spot where the track opened on to a flat area of ground, covered in a dense growth of long grasses, yellow and white umbelliferous plants and bramble bushes which were bent over under the weight of ripening fruit. Clumps of bracken were beginning to infiltrate the grassy areas and it was obvious that the invasive plant would soon be taking over the long-neglected meadow.

Using his walking stick to push aside the brambles, the Captain led the way into the middle of the largest clump of bushes and paused before a series of hummocks in the ground. Brightly coloured lichens and mosses covered a scattering of boulders. At this spot there was too little soil for the growth of anything other than short grasses and creeping alpine plants. Pale yellow potentilla, purple thyme and creamy bedstraw formed a soft carpet under their feet while an occasional waving stem of Scottish harebell broke the flat surface of the turf.

Stooping down before one of the boulders, Bill pointed out the smooth flat surface of the stone.

'See here . . . only a chisel could make marks like that. This rock was cut by a very skilful mason. This is whinstone, one of the hardest rocks you'll ever come across. The quarrymen in these parts were able to fashion stone like this into any shape you wanted – in this case the quoin of a building. I'm surprised this one hasn't been removed. The squared-off pieces are much sought after by the people here for constructing walls and out-houses. I don't doubt that's what happened to the rest of the stones. This one here was probably too heavy to lift into a wheelbarrow.'

He searched in the bushes on the far side of the clearing, his stick revealing a further series of hand-worked stones forming one wall of what had been a rectangular building.

'This is the part which I have always described as a steading, maybe even a stable to shelter the horses used for hauling trucks of slate. I suppose it might just as well have been a croft house.'

Jack stood in the middle of the clearing and looked about him, wondering if indeed this was his ancestor's house. He recalled the stories his grandfather had handed down from *his* father . . . another Jack McDougal who had forsaken the family croft to accompany his parents to Western Australia in 1913. It was a strange feeling to be standing on ground once inhabited by his forebears. Whether it was the evening breeze blowing up from the south or some spirit of the past which caused Jack to shiver at that moment, he would never know. He shrugged off a strange icy sensation in his spine and smoothed the hairs which seemed to have risen at the nape of his neck.

'Celia in the museum has more information about the families living here before 1914. She may be able to confirm that your people were here.'

Jack agreed that he would take the Captain's advice but he was already convinced that this was the place.

There was no further conversation while they wandered back towards the village. Jack was deep in thought and Bill seemed sensitive to his companion's need for silence. Only when they were again in sight of the main square did the Captain speak.

'Do you fancy a wee dram before we go across to the Tacksman's Bar?'

Startled out of his reverie, Jack hesitated before protesting, 'Oh, no, thanks all the same. I've leaned too much on your hospitality already today. Allow me to buy you a dram over in the pub.'

Throwing off the strange mood which had descended while they were at the old McDougal homestead, Jack now put his mind to more pressing matters. He needed to be well established at the bar in order to engage the bar staff in conversation before the bulk of the customers arrived. In his experience, the publican was always a fount of information about the locals.

*

Within a fortnight, Jack McDougal had managed to talk to most of the prominent members of the community. This he achieved in a variety of ways. Casual conversation with his landlady established precisely who were the spokesmen for the area – those most likely to put themselves forward for election to the Community Council, the various parish organisations and residents' associations and those most likely to form an opposition to change.

In the Badger Bar he spoke of his father's experiences during the war in the Pacific and was introduced to the local branch of the British Legion after he had declared himself active in the work of the Veteran's Association of Australia from childhood. One Saturday in September, he even found himself in charge of the white elephant stall at the annual fund-raising event in the old Volunteers' Drill Hall. In quieter moments he was able to view for himself the shabby condition of what was one of the older monuments to the slate-quarrying community.

He had been staying in Flora Douglas's house now for more than two weeks and, jealous of her privacy, she was beginning to regret having agreed to his continued occupation of the attic room.

It was not that he was a difficult lodger . . . far from it. He could not be more helpful in carrying out those small chores which were often a burden to her after a long day in the surgery. But because of his very presence she felt compelled to do some things she would otherwise have left undone. Her life was no longer her own. Despite her insistence that she would not cook anything other than breakfast for him, she had found herself providing supper for them both each evening, and thinking about what she would offer him when she should have been working during the day.

The other problem was his incessant questioning. Anyone would think he was writing a book, the amount of information he had absorbed about the place during his stay. She liked to relax in front of the television during the evenings but now found herself continuously engaged in conversations concerning the history of the islands and the people in the village. He was a glutton for family details, wanting to know all about everyone's associations with the islands and each other. In her capacity of receptionist at the surgery, who better to know just who had been in the district the longest, who had been born there and who were recent arrivals?

In the privacy of his attic bedroom, Jack had amassed a wealth of detail, had made sketches and photographs of every aspect of the Marquis's estates and copious notes following his encounters with the locals. He felt that now was the time for him to consider his findings from a distance. A much clearer picture would emerge when he spread all this stuff out in the air-conditioned sanctum of his office on the top floor of the Kookaburra Reef Hotel.

One last duty remained. There was no point in engaging architects and civil engineers to draw up the initial application for planning consent until he had established that the land he needed to acquire was actually available. According to Milton, everything apart from a few of the houses belonged to George Monteith. Jack would have to carry the Marquis with him if he hoped to sway the opinions of the rest of the community. He pondered for some time over how the approach might be made and had already decided that a formal meeting was what was required when, out of the blue, one evening in the Badger Bar, His Lordship gave Jack just the opportunity he was looking for.

'So, what do you think of the place now you've had a chance to look around?' George asked, blowing the froth off the top of a fresh pint of 'heavy'.

'It's so marvellous, I can't imagine how my folks ever brought themselves to leave,' was Jack's reply. He never missed an opportunity to press home the fact that he was one of them.

'Needs must,' George suggested. 'There was little work, few ways of making any sort of a living, for a good many years after the First World War, you know. The most the village lads could hope for was a chance to enlist in the armed services but it wasn't long before cutbacks brought many of them home again. A few became merchant seamen or went into the fishing industry and there were always farmers, but they too had a pretty thin time in the thirties. Had it not been for the Second World War and the coming of the Forestry Commission to the area, I doubt if there would ever have been a revival. Of course, the motor car has made a tremendous difference. Now folks can commute into Oban for work, the area has become a desirable residential backwater. People consider themselves fortunate to be able to have their cake and eat it, as it were!'

'But there are still a lot of locals who are unemployed,' Jack protested.

'It depends what you mean by unemployed,' the Marquis replied. 'It would be hard to find a single individual who has absolutely no means of support. In a community like this work arises simply from people living in close proximity. It's more convenient to get Charlie to fix your TV aerial than to have a firm come out from Oban. Val Struthers does the hairdressing for the entire village. Willie Clark will fix your car for half the price they'll charge at McTaggart's Garage in town. Critics may frown on the fact that this amounts to a black economy, but these people are paying their own way . . . few of them are claiming benefits and it could be argued that they pay over the odds in the form of direct taxation because of the high price of food brought in and the heavy duty on petrol.'

'But surely people would be happier to know that they had a steady job and a regular income?'

'I'm not at all sure about that,' George laughed. 'I sometimes think that uncertainty adds something to the lives of us all . . . it makes for a more ingenious and resourceful community.'

He ordered another round of drinks and, thinking the conversation had become far too heavy, changed the subject.

'So, how have you got on with your family researches?'

'I think I can safely say that my people came from Eisdalsa Island, and with the help of Mr Douglas I have even located the croft they occupied over there.'

'That's interesting,' said the Marquis. 'I've studied the quarrying records myself and never found any reference to a croft on the island, but of course there must have been a source of dairy products even if it was only a few cows. We have evidence of sheep being farmed from Eisdalsa, course . . . hence the name of the other island between Eisdalsa and Mull, Eilean nam Uan. No doubt the shepherd lived on Eisdalsa – Eilean nam Uan is uninhabitable. To provide food for over four hundred people, there must have been a few cows. Where there's cattle there has to be a supply of fodder, I suppose . . .' He continued to think about the matter, trying to envisage a situation in which a croft might have been situated in such a small area, amongst all that rock and rubble. 'Of course, the spoil spread over the island now may well have been dumped at a later date. There was an attempt to revive the quarrying after the first war, you know.' There was a pause and an awkward silence fell. Both men concentrated upon their drinks until at last George asked if the Australian had seen much of the rest of the district.

'The only place I haven't been to is the castle,' he ventured, and immediately got the response for which he had been angling.

'Why, m'dear fellow, you must come along and visit us . . . be delighted to show you round.'

'I'm afraid I shall have to be moving on at the end of the week,' he sighed. 'I have a flight home from London booked for Monday.'

'We've just seen off the last of our sporting visitors. There's nothing more booked for this year until the Hogmanay party. How are you fixed for tomorrow? Shall we say about eleven? You could stay for lunch.'

Although, like so many of his fellow Australians, Jack

claimed to have a robustly anarchic attitude towards the British monarchy and its aristocracy, he was quite overwhelmed by Monteith's offer of hospitality.

'Really?' he stammered. 'That would be marvellous . . . if you're sure it wouldn't inconvenience you?'

'Not at all,' said the Marquis, quite unaware of having suggested anything out of the ordinary. He rapidly went over in his mind the list of pressing tasks planned for the following day and reshuffled his timetable.

'That's very kind of you, sir . . . if you're sure Her Ladyship won't mind?'

'Of course she won't. Will you, m'dear?' He placed a protective arm comfortably around his wife's shoulders as she came to stand beside him at the bar.

'What's that?' she asked, smiling uncertainly at the Australian.

'Mr McDougal here is coming to have a look at the castle tomorrow and I've suggested he stay for lunch.'

Startled, Cissy hesitated imperceptibly before producing her usual friendly smile and holding out her hand.

'We'll be delighted to have you, Mr McDougal.'

'Oh, please, your ladyship, call me Jack.'

'Welcome to Seileach, Jack,' she gave him a sharp appraisal. 'I'm Cissy. We don't pay much attention to titles around here.'

He was very personable and appeared harmless enough, yet Cissy had the most curious sensation that this man was not all he seemed. There was a slight shiftiness about the eyes, his glance constantly darted in all directions. Even while they spoke, he gave the impression of someone who was trying to listen in to half a dozen other conversations at the same time. Still, George seemed happy enough to talk to him.

'. . . so what I'm looking for is an option to lease, or buy, a certain amount of land in and around the village on Seileach and the whole of Eisdalsa Island. My company will be happy to make a generous down payment in advance for such an option. The rent will be a matter for negotiation between our legal guys.'

Jack began to fold up the unmarked Ordnance Survey map he had spread on the Marquis's ancient refectory table half an hour before. George, cramped from bending double in order to follow Jack's finger as he pointed out the areas under discussion, now stretched painfully and walked across to the tall window. He gazed out upon a view of the sound and watched a small fishing boat coming up to its mooring in Bonach Bay. When he had invited Jack to visit the castle he had not expected anything like this. The detailed proposition had come as something of a shock. Jack's ideas were revolutionary, but he had certainly done his homework and his proposals appeared sympathetic to the situation. Eisdalsa was something of a holiday resort already . . . from what the Australian had told him, it would merely be a question of tidying the place up a bit and making the area more accessible for visitors. He wasn't too sure how Marty Crane would react to the idea of an additional hotel but he supposed that any move to get more visitors into the area would improve trade for everyone . . .

'So you are looking for an option only at the moment?'

He turned to face Jack. With the light behind him, his face was in shadow and Jack could gain no indication of his reaction from his voice. He waited in trepidation to hear George Monteith's response to his proposal.

'I have to take back with me some indication of your own response to the idea,' Jack explained. 'You will appreciate that drawing up a suitable planning application is going to be a costly business? There is no point in our going into too much detail without some degree of assurance that the land will be available.'

'And you will appreciate that there are several hurdles to be overcome . . . matters over which I have no influence,' said George, who in the past had had a number of brushes with the planning authority over developments on different parts of his estate.

'Yes, of course,' Jack replied. 'Any purchase agreement would be subject to our obtaining planning consent. That goes without saying.'

For a long time George had been seeking some source of finance to put right those defects in the castle requiring urgent attention. Merely to secure an option to buy, Jack McDougal had suggested an amount of cash which would enable him to start planning substantial repairs to the roof. He recalled that frightful American's assessment of the family portraits and his suggestion that by selling the painting of Lady Jane Monteith, George would raise sufficient money to put the castle to rights. The Marquis had recoiled from the idea at the time and now grabbed at this Australian's proposal, seeing it as a much more attractive alternative.

'I take it that the up-front money would be paid even

should your company decide, for whatever reason, not to develop after all?'

'Yes, indeed. That is a loss we would have to bear.'

This company, whoever they were, would have to convince the Regional Council that what they were suggesting was good for the area. Once the planning application went forward, the ball would be in their court and no one would be able to accuse George of taking sides in the issue. He had no doubt there would be opposition from the locals but some would benefit, either by the sale of their property or by obtaining regular employment. It was clearly his duty to encourage any development that brought added prosperity to the area. His conscience thus salved, George nodded.

'I see no reason to refuse such an offer,' he told Jack. 'There's a long way to go before any decisions can be taken, though, and I assume any wrinkles will be ironed out in the process.' Dismissing the subject before there was a chance of Cissy overhearing them, he rubbed his hands together and said, 'Now then, it's time to consider weightier matters . . . luncheon must be nearly ready.'

As Jack returned the folded map to his pocket, George went to the door and looked over the balcony into the hall below. The dining-room door was open and he could hear Cissy discussing table arrangements with the maid. There was time for a snifter before she called them down. He returned to the library and went to the drinks cabinet.

'You'll take a dram before we eat?'

As he poured whisky into two fine crystal tumblers, he said, 'Perhaps we might refrain from discussing your plans during the meal. I would prefer to talk the matter over with my wife in private.'

Jack accepted the well-filled glass with an appreciative nod. 'Of course, sir. Anything you say. Good health!'

'*Slainte mhath*,' George replied, taking a substantial draught of the unique single malt. He had a feeling Cissy was not going to take kindly to Jack's proposition. He would have to find some way of introducing it at a time when he could most readily convince her of the dire necessity of accepting it.

Chapter Ten

It was a bright morning in early October. Strong winds, high in the startlingly blue heavens, had whipped the clouds into fine wisps of white cirrus. The sprinkling of small islands, way out on the horizon, was today shrouded in mist and any local fisherman could have predicted dirty weather ahead.

In Jack McDougal's eyes, however, the morning was sheer perfection. He gunned the rented Ford and slipped it into third gear as he took the final steep slope and rounded the corner, leaving all that glorious panorama behind him . . . lost from view maybe, but printed upon his memory for all time.

Jack, his preliminary survey completed and having established the Marquis's willingness to participate in Milton's scheme, set off on his journey to Glasgow airport that morning with a light heart.

He took in the glory of the landscape; the hills standing clear and sharp against the light blue of the sky; the lochs absolutely still, their reflecting surfaces repeating mountains and forests, heather-covered slopes and neatly harvested fields . . . actuality and image standing toe to toe at the shoreline. He sighed with deep satisfaction. Rowan trees bowed under the weight of their scarlet berries; sycamores, high on the hill, highlighted the dark greens of the pine forest with the yellow, orange and red tints of autumn. On every pole there perched a buzzard or a hooded crow, patiently awaiting an opportunity to scoop up carrion left by passing vehicles, while overhead a sparrowhawk spotted some furry creature venturing out on to a sheep-grazed grassy slope and swooped down, scooping up the squealing creature between fearsome claws and carrying it to its eyrie high on some rocky crag.

The past weeks had provided the Australian with the rest and refreshment he had so needed. Far away from the pressures of his normal existence, even the frequent faxes from Milton had been ignored. When he saw his boss he would plead a failure in the system because of the mountains, the poor telephone connection. Milton, having experienced life in Argyll, would accept his explanation without question

During the long hours he had worked alone in his quiet little garret, above Flora Douglas's living room, Jack had been able to review his position and to see his life in a more rational perspective. If he had learned nothing more from this experience, he knew now that the time was fast approaching for him to make a radical change to the way in which he lived. He would see Milton's project out to the end, but after that he would be on his way.

Unknown to Jack, his departure for Bermuda and a meeting with Milton coincided with the expected onset of winter weather amongst the islands and highlands of

Argyll. As the afternoon shuttle took off from Glasgow for London, heavy black rain clouds were gathering over Scarba and the coastline of Mull disappeared in the mist. It was almost as though the elements had deliberately held back from venting their full wrath until the Australian was well out of the way.

The day after his departure, heavy seas and gale-force winds created havoc for those few boat owners who had had the temerity to risk squeezing the last vestige of use from their pleasure craft before putting them up for the winter. There was damage to the harbour walls in Seileach village and several householders, living close to the sea, complained of losing a few more feet from their shore-fronted gardens. For three days the ferry was restricted to essential voyages only and the island children could not be carried across to school.

On Friday the winds abated, the clouds cleared and things returned to normal. With the high winds now past, the islanders got on with their preparations for the coming winter months. The first of these activities being the Coal Weekend. This was an annual event in which the islanders collectively ordered their coal supplies for the entire winter and together hauled the fuel across on the barge, completing the delivery, door to door, by wheelbarrow.

After a gruelling day and a long hot bath the younger folk were ready to party. The Coal Weekend *ceilidh* was one of the highlights of the year and an event which enticed even the villagers of Seileach to risk a night crossing on the specially arranged late ferry.

*

'Is that you, Flora?' The woman's voice sounded almost conspiratorial. Who else would be answering the doctor's telephone?

'Doctor's surgery,' she responded, using what Alan jokingly called her pharmaceutical voice.

'Flora, will it be that new doctor who's consulting today?'

'Yes, Miss McColl, it is.' Flora had recognised at once the clipped, courtroom speech of the retired advocate.

'Oh, dear, and I've quite run out of my tablets. When will Dr Pullson be on duty?'

'Dr Pullson has now reverted to her weekly consultations, on a Thursday.'

'I see.' There was a long pause.

'I am sure Dr Beaton will be happy to see you, Miss McColl.'

'Oh! Oh, no! That wouldn't do at all!'

Whatever was the matter with the woman? Flora wondered.

'If it's only a repeat prescription, I am sure that Dr Beaton can do that for you without your seeing him,' she told the caller.

'Oh, could he? Yes, that would be more satisfactory. Would you ask him to do that?'

'When will you call in for the prescription?'

'Will it be all right if I come later this morning?'

'Yes, leave it until after surgery, say eleven o'clock.'

'Thank you . . . see you later!'

The caller replaced her handset and Flora sat gazing at her own instrument for some seconds before replacing it thoughtfully in its cradle. That was the fourth or fifth call of its kind which she had received in the past couple of days. She understood a certain reluctance on the part of long-standing patients to swap their allegiance overnight to another doctor. It always took a while for people to become accustomed to a new face . . . but never so long as this.

Since Flora had worked for Ewan McWorter, there had been a succession of assistant GPs coming along to share his workload. They had each experienced difficulty in gaining acceptance, but in the end there there had always been a nucleus of patients willing to take a chance on a new doctor. The reluctance of patients, particularly women, to consult Dr McWorter's stand-in had never been so marked as it was now, in the case of Alan Beaton.

Before the telephone could ring again, she gathered up the morning's post and sorted out the junk mail from the real thing. Someone at least had recorded Alan's presence here. A splendidly embossed envelope of best quality paper was addressed to the new doctor in person. She planted it, with a second also addressed to Alan, on the top of the pile and carried the bundle of mail into the consulting room.

'Looks as though your presence is beginning to be noticed around here.' Flora grinned as she placed the pile on his desk. 'These two are addressed to you personally,' she pointed out.

'Thanks!' He watched her turn back to the door, her smart pleated skirt swinging as she walked. Hers was a trim little figure, in sharp contrast to the majority of overweight matrons who made up the larger part of the female population in the area. McWorter put it down to

251

meat pies and scones; Alan considered that excessive smoking, lack of exercise and too many coffee mornings were to blame. Fortunately Flora had no time for the latter and did not indulge in the former.

He tore open the first envelope. It was a letter from the Health Board, informing him that his services would be retained for three months at the end of which time a decision would be made concerning the future tenure of the practice. This would be based upon the state of Dr McWorter's health at that time. Alan was pleased. It meant that he had a job until after Christmas . . . ample time in which to look for a more permanent post.

He set the letter aside and inspected the second envelope.

The flap was embossed with the address of one of the most prestigious Advocate's Chambers in Edinburgh. Alan recognised the name of the senior partner as being an old acquaintance of his father and wondered how it was that they should be writing to him when scarcely anyone, other than his parents, knew where he was working.

Apprehensively, he tore open the envelope.

> *Dear Dr Beaton,*
>
> *I am pleased to inform you that because of your prompt action and kindly assistance when my wife fell and injured her ankle on Caisteal an Spuilleadair a week or two ago, she has now fully recovered. Fortunately X-rays showed that she had not sustained a fracture and a protracted period of rest was all*

*that was required. She has asked me to convey
to you our sincere thanks for your part in the
episode.*

*I would also be grateful if you would pass on
my thanks to your assistant, whom I understand was a Mr McDougal from Australia. My
wife and I have been coming to Eisdalsa for
many years, using it as a retreat from the exi-
gencies of life in the city. I shall look forward
to meeting you again when we return in the
spring.*

Alan put aside the letter with a grin, remembering the
struggle they had had to carry Mrs Thornton-Mowbray
off the hill. That fellow McDougal had proved to be less
than fit when put to the test . . . so much for brawny
Australians who perform prodigious feats of weight
lifting. McDougal had been so flaked out he hadn't even
appeared in the bar that evening and come to think of it,
Alan hadn't clapped eyes on him since.

'What's happened to your lodger?' he asked Flora
casually, as soon as she reappeared. 'I haven't seen him
about for quite a while.'

'Oh, he's gone,' she answered with apparent indifference. 'It's nice to have the house to myself again.'

Alan gave her an amused glance.

'I thought that was a very cosy arrangement,' he
teased, grinning when he saw her colouring up. 'If you'd
played your cards right, you might have found yourself
on your way to Queensland by now!'

Flora was annoyed that he should think any such thing.

If he noticed her discomfort, he showed no sign of it.

'It's just that I have a letter here with a message in it for him. I don't suppose you have a forwarding address?'

She appeared reluctant to admit it.

'Well, yes, he did leave an address as a matter of fact . . .' he thought she spoke with exaggerated indifference, '. . . in case he had left anything behind.'

The explanation was a pretty feeble one and Alan suspected there was more to the relationship than she was willing to admit. It jarred with him a little, though he didn't quite understand why. He had been too busy to pay any attention to Flora's private life during the past few weeks. Perhaps he ought to make some attempt to be sociable.

'Anything happening by way of entertainment in the near future?' he asked, casually.

'There's a *ceilidh* in the Tacksman's Bar on the Island on Saturday, as a matter of fact.'

'Will you be going?'

'Oh I expect so. Kirsty usually asks me to lend a hand, serving behind the bar.'

Alan seemed disappointed.

'That's a pity,' he said. 'I was thinking of inviting you to partner me.'

'Oh, it's not a formal affair of that nature,' she laughed, pleased nonetheless. 'People just go along and if they feel like dancing, they join in with whoever comes to hand. If you turn up, I'm sure I shall be able to spare a few minutes for you!'

'I'll wait to see what the rest of the week brings,' he decided. 'I need to talk to Dr Mac,' he said, thinking of the contents of the letter from the Health Board. 'I could go in on Saturday morning, if there's no one down for a visit?'

Flora looked carefully through the appointments book.

'No, all clear for the moment. I'll let you know if there are any late calls.'

'How was Dr Mac?' asked Flora as she finished pulling Alan's pint and set the brimming glass down on an already soaking bar mat.

The noise was deafening and he was obliged to lean across the bar to make himself heard.

'Fighting fit,' he declared, 'and worrying the consultant to let him come home.'

'He won't be sent back to the house on his own, surely?' she asked. 'He usually does everything for himself, you know . . . apart from Sarah Nevis, who goes in three mornings a week to do the cleaning.'

'No. Apparently, the Monteiths have offered to have him as a house guest for a week or two, until he can fend for himself. I gather they're old friends?'

'Oh, yes, Cissy and Ewan's wife, Annie, were very close. He'll be well looked after there.'

'The hospital is discharging him on Thursday. I said I'd go and fetch him myself since it's my day off, and deliver him to the castle . . . perhaps you'd like to come too?'

'I'd like that,' Flora agreed. 'Provided Dr Pullson can manage without me for a while.'

'We'll see what she says. Now then, you promised me we would have a dance.'

The pipes and fiddles were tuning up in the restaurant,

cleared of extraneous furniture for the party, and the first bars of an eightsome reel heralded the start of the real business of the evening.

Flora put down her glass cloth, signalled to Kirsty who was chatting in a corner with some of the older islanders and preceded the doctor along the narrow corridor towards the restaurant. In a space no more than twenty-five foot in either direction, the dancers had managed to form up into three sets, Alan and Flora completing the third. As the music began, Alan got into his swing, the steps learned in his youth at college in Glasgow, movements he thought he had long forgotten, coming back to him. He found himself flying around the small room with Flora light as a feather in his arms.

'I'd forgotten how much fun this is,' he gasped as the music came to a stop and the dancers draped themselves in attitudes of exhaustion about the room. It was time for a rest and as though on cue, Celia Robertson, retired schoolmistress and curator of the island's little folk museum, got up to sing. There was a moment of hurried activity while her *clarsach* was brought out of the cloak-room and set up in the middle of the floor. As she settled herself, the chatting and laughter died and the expectant audience became still.

The words, mainly by Robert Burns, were set to old familiar airs. Her voice was a warm contralto, the singer's West Highland brogue entirely suited to the lyrics of the bard. When she had finished, there was not a dry eye in the room. Alan, carried back in time to his grandmother's living room in Peebles, where his grandfather had set up his practice in the 1930s, murmured, 'I had quite forgotten.' Flora, wondering at the degree of his involvement, squeezed his hand and led him out again for a group of waltzes which were rather easier to cope with in the confined space.

Then the tempo changed. The young people unearthed drums and a saxophone while someone discovered the socket in which to insert the lead for the electronic keyboard. Soon the building was rocking to the sounds of the nineties.

The last ferry was due to leave at midnight and those wishing to cross over to Seileach gathered in the bar, downing one final dram of *uisge-beatha* while they awaited the appearance of Angus, the ferryman.

Contrary to his usual custom, he had stayed away from the *ceilidh* that evening. Having brought over the revellers at seven o'clock he had disappeared into his cottage, complaining of a chill. His wife, Mairead, had left him to nurse his ailments before the fire while she went across the green to join in the fun.

When he had not appeared by twelve-fifteen, someone went to knock on his door and a few moments later returned to the bar and whispered in Alan's ear.

'The old feller's nae sae guid, doctor. I think maybe you should come and take a look at him.'

Anxious glances were exchanged between those wanting to get home to their beds. Alan hurried out and felt his way in the darkness to the door of the ferryman's house. He knocked gently and went in.

Although Angus Dewar had been born in the Gorbals district of Glasgow, he had spent his holidays on the island since childhood and well remembered his father's tales of the old days when it was being worked for its slate and the quarries rang to the sound of hammers from dawn until dusk. When the shipyards began closing down in the 1950s, he had grabbed the opportunity of a job on the Eisdalsa ferry and had served the islanders well for over thirty years.

Now in his sixties, Angus was nearing an age when he should be thinking of retiring, but despite Dr McWorter's warnings following two winters in which he had been laid low by bronchitis, had refused to give up his job and also resisted the doctor's advice to give up smoking.

Alan found him crouched in a low armchair beside the open grate, wheezing noisily and almost comatose.

'I hear you're feeling poorly, Mr Dewar,' he said quietly, not wishing to alarm the man.

Angus opened his eyes, a glint of recognition giving Alan the permission he sought to proceed with his examination.

Gently he undid the buttons of the fleecy check shirt and laid bare a chest caved in by years of persistent coughing and covered in a thick mat of grey hair. Lacking a stethoscope, Alan could examine the chest by percussion only. Skill and experience told him almost immediately what was wrong. There was a dullness to one side, indicating that the right lung was choked with phlegm. He did not need a thermometer to tell him the man was running a high temperature.

'How long has he been feeling unwell, Mrs Dewar?' Alan turned to the ferryman's wife who, alerted by her neighbours, had followed him across the green from the pub.

'He complained of a tightness in the chest when he woke up yesterday but it seemed to go off when he was working on the boat. He always says the fresh air is the best thing for what ails him,' she replied. 'Of course, he wakes up every morning to a fit of coughing . . . but that's the fags, as I'm always telling him. The amount of time he spends in front of that thing,' she indicated the impressive twenty-nine-inch TV screen in the corner, 'you'd think by now he would have got the message, but he always uses the old excuse. "Ma faither smoked all his life and lived to be ninety!" ' She made a pretty good attempt at an impression of her husband's Glaswegian accents.

'Well, he has a nasty touch of pleurisy now,' said Alan, 'I really think we should get him away to hospital just to be on the safe side. May I use your phone, please?'

While he was busy arranging for his patient's removal to hospital, there was a tap at the door and a whispered conversation between Mairead Dewar and the caller. She returned as he replaced the handset.

'They're sending the ambulance down to the pier,' said Alan, 'but I wasn't able to tell them who would be running the ferry. Is there a standard procedure for getting someone off the island in an emergency?'

'Joe McCluskey is the standby ferryman,' said Mairead. 'He wasn't at the *ceilidh* so someone has gone to fetch him out of bed. He'll take the people off the island and wait for the ambulance.'

'Can we get a message to him before he goes?' asked Alan. 'He may not appreciate the seriousness of the situation. Perhaps you could arrange for him to meet me back here when he has taken the people over from the dance?'

'Och, dinna worry, doctor. The men are well versed in how to manage a carry-off by ambulance. Joe'll bring the ambulance men straight here just as soon as they arrive.'

'But they'll need to bring across a portable oxygen supply . . .'

'Och, aye . . . they'll do that anyway.'

She dismissed his concerns but nevertheless went out into the night to find her husband's replacement while Alan returned to his patient.

Angus's breathing had become more laboured during the past few moments and he was struggling for breath. Alan had no idea how long they were going to have to wait for the ambulance. He cursed himself for having come out without his medical case . . . at least he would have had something to relieve the man's distress. He made a mental note never to be without an emergency pack of equipment again.

Mairead had set a kettle to heat on the top of the range. Now it began to boil and as the steam began to pour from the spout, half-remembered images of his childhood came to him. When, as a small boy, he had developed a bad cold, his granny had made him sit over a steaming bowl, with a cloth over his head. He remembered now how much his chest had hurt and how breathing in the fumes had relieved the pain. Half hoping that he might find something useful, he took a look in the bathroom cabinet. There, right at the back, in a small bottle whose label was smeared with oil and blackened with age he discovered Friar's Balsam. In the kitchen he found a suitable bowl and poured boiling water into it before adding the balsam. He grabbed a towel from the bathroom and came back into the living room. Forcing his patient to sit up, he drew up a side table and arranged the bowl so that Angus could lean right over it. Then he draped the towel over the man's head.

'Try to breathe . . . deeply as you can. Get those fumes right down into your lungs. Come on, man, try.'

Angus drew in one painful breath after another, each accompanied by an extraordinary chorus of grunts and wheezes. After a few minutes, however, his breathing became easier. Alan added more boiling water to the bowl and a few more drops of the pungent liquid and replaced the towel. The two men were concentrating so hard on this operation that neither heard Mairead return and it was not until she presented Alan with a steaming cup of coffee that he realised she was there.

'Aye, that's just what ma mither would have recommended,' she remarked, a twinkle in her eye. 'I would have thought that at this end of the twentieth century there might be other remedies for difficult breathing . . .'

'Indeed there are, Mrs Dewar,' Alan laughed, 'but in an emergency, let us never forget the ways of our forefathers! Even today they can still teach us a thing or two. Oh, by the way, I hope you don't mind . . . I found some Friar's Balsam in your bathroom cabinet and helped myself.'

'I didn't even know it was there,' she told him. 'It's years since I cleared that cupboard out properly.'

'It's just as well you haven't, because you would have been sure to have thrown this out.' He showed her the dirty little bottle and grinned, remembering the entreaties from the Health Board to see that patients did not hoard out-of-date prescriptions.

The removal of Angus Dewar from the island on a pitch dark night in a howling north-westerly gale was a model of efficiency born of practice and experience on the part of both the islanders and ambulance men. Angus, wrapped up warm in blankets and covered by a waterproof sheet, was transported to the boat in a stretcher chair. He was a heavy man and it took six islanders taking it in turns, to carry him across the rough turf and down to the ferry landing. Alan climbed into the boat after the ambulance men and Joe McCluskey handled the little craft with consummate skill. In ten minutes they were tying up on the other side of the sound and Alan, full of admiration for the way in which this tiny community worked together when the chips were down, thanked the ferryman and climbed out of the boat to assist in getting the stretcher chair to the ambulance. Joe, having tied up securely to the quay, came and gave a hand also. Together the four of them transported their bulky load up the steps and into the ambulance.

'I'll follow on in my own car,' Alan said to the men. It was late at night and he had no idea what kind of cover would be available in the hospital at this hour. He might be needed.

As the ambulance drew away Alan turned to bid Joe goodnight. Already the ferry boat was half way across the sound, its engine puttering quietly so as not to disturb those living close to the harbour.

Only then did he remember that he had not seen Flora for hours and had not even been able to say goodbye.

Flora had remained in the Tacksman after Alan was called away, serving behind the bar. As the number of customers was reduced by the departure of the last ferry, Bill Douglas sidled across to have a word with his daughter.

'Lost your partner, I see,' were his first words.

'Hallo, Dad, enjoying yourself?' she asked cheerily. It was a while since she had seen him. He looked well enough.

'Oh, aye, just having a wee crack with the old fellas,' he indicated a collection of retired residents of the island, most of them years younger than himself.

'If they're so old, what does that make you?' she laughed.

'You've missed the last boat,' he observed. 'Do you need a bed for the night?'

She appreciated his offer but shuddered at the thought of sleeping in his spare room. It was unheated and there was the suspicion of a leak in the roof. She did not fancy spending such a freezing cold night in a damp bed.

'Thanks very much, Dad,' she answered, not wishing to offend him by refusing, 'but I shall be up for a while yet, helping Kirsty to clear up. You get along home now. She'll let me sleep on her sofa, I feel sure.'

'The doctor gone off then, has he?'

'I believe he intends to go to the hospital with Angus, in case there's a problem,' Desmond Bartlet, who had been one of the party carrying the patient to the ferry, chipped in.

'Good.' Billy sounded so relieved that Flora looked at him, a puzzled expression on her face. She replenished Desmond's glass and waited until he had returned to his companions before confronting her father.

'What is it?' she demanded. 'Something I ought to know?'

He told her the rumour which had been circulating for the past week.

'I don't believe a word of it,' she said. 'He doesn't strike me as that sort at all!'

'I've no doubt the story has become exaggerated in the telling,' he agreed, 'but I thought you should be warned. I wouldn't like to see you hurt, m'dear.'

'What's it got to do with me?' she asked, defensively. 'We simply work together, that's all.' But she was more disturbed than she cared to admit. What was being said about Alan just could not be true. Whatever Giles Scott had witnessed, she was certain he must have misinterpreted what he had seen.

George was lingering over his third cup of coffee and stretching for the remaining piece of toast, putting off until the last possible moment any move towards the outdoors and his waiting tractor which McGreggor had parked ready for him outside the kitchen door.

Cissy came in bearing an armful of post and tried to hurry him up. 'If you don't get a move on, you'll lose the best of the weather. There's rain forecast for this afternoon.'

She began tossing junk mail into a conveniently positioned waste paper basket. 'There should be some means of off-loading this stuff straight into the waste paper col-lection in Tesco's car park,' she muttered. 'It would save the poor old postie having to deliver it to all the doors in the district for immediate consignment to the bin. I don't know why the Post Office accepts it all.'

'Economics,' replied her husband, rescuing a per-sonal letter from the heap she had just discarded. 'Hey, watch it . . . you never know, there might be a cheque inside.'

He slit the envelope open with the butter knife. It was not a cheque, but it was a letter from a satisfied customer which was almost as good.

'Do you remember the French Canadian fellow who was here for the August shoot?'

'Pierre d'Orsay?' Cissy answered quickly. How could she forget the quietly spoken gentleman who had stood out like a sore thumb from the crowd of self-opinionated egoists who had formed the bulk of their clientele that summer.

'He seems to have been very pleased with his stay here. Says he will recommend us to his friends and wants to come again next year . . . how about that?'

'Let me see.' She snatched the letter from him and began to read.

'Anything else?' George enquired, and noticing a larger than usual brown manilla package, reached across for it.

'This seems a little more important than the latest insurance scam from the banks,' he said, noticing the impressive embossing on the flap and the exotic postage stamp. 'What's more, it's from overseas . . .' he screwed up his eyes to read the country of origin '. . . Bermuda. Do we know anyone in Bermuda?'

'Oh, don't be such a pain,' she cried. 'Just open the thing and be done with it.'

Ignoring her plea, he investigated the address on the flap. 'HDC?' he queried. 'Who might they be when they're at home?'

'Well, there's only one way to find out.' Cissy handed him a sharper knife. Even then he only managed to cut through the linen-reinforced covering with some difficulty.

She waited impatiently while he scanned the letter which accompanied a whole heap of documents. Glimpsing the heading, which addressed George by his full title, she realised this was no ordinary communication. He read the contents through a second time before handing the letter over to her. While she read, uncomprehending, he spread out a large map which turned out to be of their own area, covering the greater part of his estate. Several areas were highlighted in red pen. He started to read from the wad of documents attached to it.

'I don't understand.' Cissy looked up, bewildered. 'You have never mentioned selling off any of the land. What makes these people think you might be interested?'

'Do you remember the Australian guy who came here ostensibly to look up his family? McDougal . . . Jack McDougal?'

'Yes, though I only met him a couple of times.'

'Before he left, he paid me a visit. It seems his employers had expressed some interest in developing this area for tourism. He wondered if I would be interested in their taking up an option to buy Eisdalsa Island and some of the land in Seileach village. He wasn't very specific about what they intended to do with it, but it seemed to be little more than building a second hotel, on the island this time, and tidying up the approaches to the village . . . more car parking space, a little more accommodation for holiday letting, that sort of thing. I could hardly say I wasn't interested, could I? After all, we're desperate for money to restore this place and the land in Seileach is really no use to us . . . it's just so many patches of waste ground. As we've learned to our cost, apart from slate, which is unworkable now, Eisdalsa has no commercial value. Maybe a small hotel on the island is just what's needed to improve tourist interest.'

'If the island really has so little to offer, why are they after it?' Could they be looking for mineral rights? she wondered. It seemed ludicrous, but these days you never knew. Everywhere there were entrepreneurs waiting to pounce on any prospect which might bring them in a few dollars.

'Who knows?' George shrugged his shoulders. 'The way I see it, if these people want to purchase an option on the land it's no skin off our noses. They'll have to go for outline planning consent first. If they jump that hurdle, then they'll have to put in a detailed plan which the Council may or may not approve. Whatever they aim to do will be vetted by the Chief Planning Officer. If they don't get consent, they won't buy, but they'll still forfeit their option money. In the meantime, I can't see anyone else wanting to buy that land, so we have nothing to lose and everything to gain.'

'How much are they offering up front?' Cissy asked. Something was bothering her but she was unable to articulate her fears.

'Six thousand . . . just about enough to cover the cost of a temporary repair to the glass dome over the hall.'

'What do they want to do with the land, do they say?'

'This is a copy of their submission to the Planning Department for outline planning consent. If they get it, then they have to provide details of their exact intentions.'

'And can we put a stop to it at any point . . . if we don't agree with what they want to do?'

'Anyone is entitled to lodge an objection at the appropriate time.'

Cissy was still not entirely comfortable with the idea.

'We only have to sell if they receive the go-ahead from the planners?'

'Precisely.'

'Do you think they'll get it?'

'Probably, so long as their ideas are not too outrageous.'

'It does mean that the village people and particularly the islanders are going to have their lives disrupted. Don't you think you should talk to a few people before you agree to the option?'

'Frankly, no. It's my land and I'm entitled to do whatever I want with it.'

Cissy wondered why he was being so defensive. Had he given more assurances than he was willing to admit to?

George was anxious to end the debate.

'Look, I can't hang around here all day. You go through all that bumf if you want to . . . we'll talk about it this evening.' He couldn't say fairer than that, could he? It might be a good idea if Cissy did have a look through the proposal . . . she was amazingly good at figuring out the small print.

He swept the papers together into a tidy pile and left them for her to put away. As he went out of the door he called over his shoulder, 'Remember, we can't expect things to stay still for ever. That's something our tenants will have to understand. It could well be their homes or ours, and when it comes to the crunch, the castle comes first!'

It wasn't the tenants so much as those members of the community who owned their own houses who worried Cissy. They were a force to be reckoned with, many of them retired professional people who were unlikely to welcome any intrusion into the comfortable existence they had built for themselves. She hated conflict of any kind and numbered many of her neighbours among her best friends.

Alan found the work of the practice fairly routine; Dr McWorter had made his life easy with his careful notes concerning each of their patients and he rarely met any real crises during his first few weeks.

The incident with Angus Dewar had shown him how smoothly things could be handled by these island dwellers. He had been very much impressed by the effi-ciency with which the evacuation of the ferryman to hospital had been accomplished. Angus had recovered quickly from his bout of pleurisy and was now at home recuperating.

The only patient causing any real anxiety was Jeanie Clark and she was in the hands of the experts. The cardiologist had placed her in a priority position on the waiting list and she was expecting to travel to Glasgow within days for her heart by-pass operation. From time to time Willie expressed to Alan his concerns about her forthcoming operation and the young doctor found himself applying all his psychological skills in counselling the poor fellow.

He had eventually convinced Willie that Jeanie would not be fit to return to work for a long time and that it would not be disloyal to her or tempting the fates in any way for him to approach the Post Office for an official temporary replacement.

As luck would have it, there was on their waiting list, someone who was conveniently situated on Eisdalsa Island.

During the late '80s, Desmond Bartlet had been a casualty of a major cut-back in one of the most affluent of the silicon chip valleys in the South of England. Rather than hang around the offices of the Executive Register, scrambling for crumbs falling from the tables of those American and Japanese-owned high-tech companies, still investing in Britain, he had brought his family to the one place where he knew they could live free from the stresses and uncertainties of the past few months. His late grandfather's holiday cottage on Eisdalsa was a place he had enjoyed visiting as a child and had often dreamed of occupying permanently. Unemployment and the negative equity on his suburban semi had forced him into taking a decision which he would never have had the courage to make in normal circumstances. It was a move neither he, nor his wife, Molly, had for one moment regretted.

He had equipped his attic office with state-of-the-art hardware and set himself up as a designer of web sites for the Internet. In this new world of advertising, he was a pioneer in his field and quickly gained a full order book which included some of the most prestigious organisations in the country. The work required long hours of concentration, alone in front of his PC. In a short while he had found himself becoming isolated from the very life he had come here to experience and cut off from the people around him. Seeking some employment of a part-time nature, which would not impinge too heavily upon his private business but which would bring him in contact with other people, he had registered with the Post Office as a locum counter clerk and been accepted on to their roster only a few weeks earlier. Being so close to the Seileach Post Office, he was the first person to be called upon in the emergency and within days of Willie's plea for help, Desmond was installed behind the grill in the village store, as the Seileach Postie.

Willie, a trifle intimidated by his new colleague's obvious capabilities and having little knowledge himself of the operation of Jeanie's part of the business, left Desmond to find his feet alone. Apart from two days' instruction at the hands of one of the clerks from the Oban office, the younger man was left very much to himself to discover the intricacies of working behind the counter of a village Post Office. When, towards the middle of November, a thick brown A4 envelope arrived addressed to the Post Master, from the Western Division of the Regional Council, he cast an inexperienced eye over the document, read the words 'Notice of Planning Application' and put the package on the 'difficult' pile for later consideration. The envelope had sat under the counter for a week before Bill Douglas, scanning the Public Notices in an old copy of the *Oban Times* while tearing it up to light his bonfire, read of a proposal to develop Eisdalsa into a holiday complex and decided he needed to see the plans which the Local Authority claimed to have lodged in the Post Office at Seileachan.

It was about eleven o'clock when Bill Douglas thrust open the shop door, accompanied by teeming rain and a gust of wind so strong that he had to struggle to close it behind him. Water streamed off his oilskins and he was obliged to wait until he recovered his breath before speaking.

'I hope your journey was really necessary?' Desmond laughed as the older man shook himself and watched the puddle he had created, spread across the slate flags.

'Sorry about that,' he apologised to Willie, who reached for a mop.

'Nae bother,' was the reply. 'I've been doing this all morning. My Jeanie would be that pleased to see the floor sae clean!'

'What can I do for you?' asked Desmond when Bill approached the Post Office counter.

'I'm looking for the development plans they talked

about in last week's *Oban Times*,' Bill told him. He scanned the notice board where Jeanie usually displayed such items but could find nothing.

'I'm not sure what you're talking about,' said Desmond, with an uneasy feeling he had been in some way remiss.

'It'll be quite a large packet, I expect,' said Bill. 'There'll be a plan and some notes . . .'

Desmond, with vague memories of having handled a large brown envelope at some time during the past few days, searched desperately through a pile of correspondence addressed either to Jeanie personally or to the Post Office itself. At last, with a tremendous feeling of relief, he came up with the communication from Strathclyde Council.

Bill spread the contents of the envelope out on the counter and, Willie having joined them, all three men pored over the plans for some moments before Desmond let out a long, low whistle. Willie, a slower reader, frowned when he came upon mention of the village shop and Captain Billy's face turned purple with annoyance.

'This needs to be gone over very carefully,' Desmond decided. 'I'm going to make a few copies and hand them around to the folks who know about these things. There's a few people around here are going to want to make a stand against this . . .'

Two doors down, a Seileach resident had rented one of the smaller cottages and converted it into an office from which to conduct his architectural business. Since he worked abroad much of the time, this merely served as a base through which to filter correspondence and provided a space in which to work when he was at home. The building contained an array of office machinery to gladden the heart of anyone used to the facilities of a big organisation. In the absence of his friend, Desmond retained a key to the office and permission to use the equipment whenever he wanted.

'Hold the fort here for a few moments, will you?' he asked the Captain. 'I'll make a few copies of this . . . you'll want one yourself, Bill, and then we'll need one for the Community Council and one for the Residents' Association . . .' He was still chuntering away to himself as he retrieved a ream of copier paper from a back shelf and opened the door to the street.

Willie, who had turned away to serve a customer with groceries, looked up and seemed surprised to see Bill standing behind the counter in Desmond's place.

'Is everything all right?' he asked. 'Where's Desmond gone?'

'Just down to Wilson's place to make a couple of photocopies. He'll be back in a minute.'

'It sounds bad, doesn't it?' observed Willie.

'What's up?' asked his customer, as she packed her purchases into her shopping bag. Generally speaking, planning applications referred to replacement windows or extensions to one or other of the old houses. The restrictions on building alterations were so stringent that there was seldom anything for anyone to argue about.

'It looks as if George Monteith has sold out to some development company,' Willie grumbled. 'They're after planning consent to change the village and the island into some kind of a holiday resort.'

'Sounds like a sensible idea to me,' said the woman, whose modern bungalow stood outwith the village, overlooking the bay. Her house was a comfortable mile down the road and would not be affected by developments around the harbour. 'Anything which brings a few more people to the area will be a good thing,' she decided. She ran a complex of holiday cottages, just over the brae. A succession of poor summers in the past three years had reduced her income considerably.

Bill Douglas did not disagree with the idea that a few more people would be an improvement to the area. These plans, however, indicated a positive influx of additional bodies, enough to alter the nature of the place entirely.

In ten minutes Desmond had completed his copying and returned. In the process of handling the papers he had read more of their detail and was by now so incensed he seemed like a mine primed to explode.

'If it wasn't so damned well thought out, it would be laughable,' he declared. 'Whoever is responsible for this knows the area intimately . . . they use all the Gaelic place names for a start and even the terminology is Scottish vernacular. It has to be some local firm.'

'What do they call themselves?' demanded Bill, searching the front page for a name. 'Ah . . . here it is. It's a company calling itself HDC International with a head office in Bermuda.'

'That'll be for tax purposes,' commented Desmond, whose blood pressure had by now begun to return to normal. 'These guys don't miss a trick.'

'But why would an international development organisation want to move in on a tiny backwater like this?' Bill wondered.

'Why indeed?' muttered Desmond. 'If they're attracted to the natural qualities of the area they must see that any development of this kind is going to destroy the very thing they're seeking to sell!'

'But I don't understand,' said Willie, bemused. 'Surely George Monteith wouldn't agree to turning this village into a pleasure park?'

It was Bill who put two and two together at last.

'That's got to be it,' he said. 'George has been moaning for months about the state of the castle and the cost of restoration. I know he's been trying, unsuccessfully, to get some kind of a grant for essential building works. He's even offered the place to the National Trust but they're not interested.'

'But surely he realises how we would all feel about such a development?' Willie seemed bewildered.

'He must know something more than we do, that's for sure,' muttered Desmond.

'There's nothing for it but to fight,' Bill decided. 'It's a pity we have already lost so much time . . . this is an old copy of the *Oban Times*. It was quite by chance that I read the notice as I was lighting a bonfire.'

Desmond shuffled uncomfortably, avoiding his glance. He knew he was partly to blame for not having read the documents from the Council more carefully when they had first arrived and making their presence known to the customers.

'How much time do we have?' he demanded.

Bill re-examined the notice in the newspaper. 'Any

observations to be in the hands of the Chief Planning Officer by 28th of November. That's not very long in which to make sure everyone knows about the proposal and puts in a protest. Perhaps one of us should produce a summary of what's in this plan and see that everyone gets a copy.'

'We'll suggest everyone comes here to view the plans,' Desmond added. 'Then we'll call a public meeting.'

'I don't know what my Jeanie will say to all this.' Willie literally wrung his hands. 'Her people have lived in the village for four generations. It will break her heart.'

'Don't you worry,' said Desmond. 'Communities do have some rights in these matters. We must just be certain that we lodge our objections to the plan at the right time and in the right way.'

By twelve-thirty Desmond had completed the books for the day. He shut up the Post Office counter and took the ferry back to the island. Before making his way to his own cottage and the lunch which awaited him there, he called on a number of people including Margaret McColl, a retired lawyer, now the proprietor of a small B&B. Her home was larger than many of the houses on the island, consisting as it did of two cottages joined into one, and her living room was furnished to seat up to a dozen people in comfort.

'Do you think we might use this room for a meeting?' asked Desmond. 'I think we ought to get together a few people with experience of planning objections, don't you?'

'I certainly think it is important to co-ordinate any effort we *do* make to contest this application,' Margaret confirmed, echoing his own thoughts. 'In my opinion, what's needed is a small committee of those people most willing to put their energies into it. You know how it is if a committee is elected in the normal way. We tend to get the wrong names put forward for all the wrong reasons. In a case like this, you want only those who can offer something concrete to the campaign by way of expertise or experience.'

'We shall need your help for a start.'

'Oh, I've been too long out of the business to act in any professional capacity,' she protested, 'but I know a few useful people, and am happy to offer my advice. You need someone with experience of planning law . . . I wonder if Mr Wilson might join us?'

'His work is mostly abroad,' Desmond explained. 'I doubt if he has had much to do with Scottish planning applications. In any case, he's away just now. I don't know when he's due back.'

'Nevertheless . . .' She thought for a moment. 'We shall need someone with a good knowledge of the past history of the place . . . someone who knows which are the buildings which must be protected and so on. Celia Robertson is the person with that kind of knowledge. Then there's the wildlife, any noisy development could affect the birds, and too many additional domestic pets will play havoc with the otter and badger population.'

Accepting one of the copies which Desmond had made, Margaret agreed to give the plans her undivided attention and he proceeded to the home of the museum's curator, Celia Robertson.

Nor surprisingly, she did not immediately fly into a passion. Her museum depended for its continued existence upon the number of bodies coming through the door during the tourist season. A spell of bad weather or some economic downturn which interrupted the flow of tourists from over the border, or even overseas, could spell disaster. She saw little but good coming from an increase in holiday makers to the area. Not wishing to antagonise Desmond, however, she kept these opinions to herself and agreed to read the document carefully.

Chapter Eleven

Margaret's living room was spacious enough to seat the small representative gathering of Eisdalsa residents in comfort.

'Someone had better take the chair,' Desmond said importantly, as soon as everyone was settled and the coffee and biscuits had been circulated. He fully expected at least one voice to pipe up, 'You've made all the running so far, Des, it had better be you.'

'I propose that Margaret be our chairman.' Bill Douglas removed his pipe from his pocket and concentrated hard on stuffing it with tobacco, so as not to catch Desmond's eye. He had thought long and hard about the person to lead their band of protesters and was convinced that Desmond was the wrong man. A loose cannon was what they would have called him in the Service.

All eyes turned upon Margaret McColl.

She hesitated before replying. She had intended to put this sort of thing behind her on the day she folded her Advocate's gown and wig and stuffed them into their drawstring bag for the last time. But looking at the anxious faces around her, she realised that this was one situation from which she could not distance herself.

'All right,' she replied.

There was an audible sigh of relief.

'But I'm going to need a good Secretary because I don't even have a typewriter, let alone a computer, and I have no intention of learning to use one at my time of life!'

Desmond was about to volunteer when the ferryman's wife, Mairead Dewar, piped up, 'I propose Celia, if she's willing to take it on.'

Celia had equipped her museum with computer, fax machine, photocopier and office storage, all the facilities in fact which would be needed for this campaign, and what was more she carried in her head and in her filing cabinets a detailed history of the island for a hundred years and more. Everyone agreed that she was the right person.

'I don't mind taking it on now, at this end of the season,' she told them, 'but if this affair goes on into next year, I might have to think again.'

'Oh, it will all be over by Christmas,' Bill assured her.

'That's what they said about two world wars,' muttered an unidentified voice from the darkest corner of the room.

'We shall need a treasurer, too,' said Margaret.

Everyone else looked a trifle surprised.

'Why, is there likely to be any expense?' asked Angus, anxiously.

'There'll be postage for a start,' Margaret replied, 'and we can't ask Celia to carry the cost of paper and photo-copying just because she happens to have the facilities.'

They relaxed again. A fiver each would cover those costs.

'If this protest should go to appeal,' Margaret added, 'we could be looking at advocate's fees of anything up to three thousand pounds.'

Now they were really worried. Words were exchanged all around the room. They had not reckoned with any such level of expenditure.

'It probably won't come to that,' she hastened to reassure them. 'Initially we have only to put our objections to the Planning Officer. If he agrees with us, that should be the end of it. The problems will arise if the applicants appeal against the ruling.'

'I'll look after the books, if you like,' offered Bill, before Desmond could open his mouth. There were no other nominations and Bill was formally elected Treasurer.

'Well now,' said Margaret, slipping easily into her Chairman's role, 'the first thing we have to do is to rally the support of the rest of the islanders.'

'Sunday's a good day for meetings,' suggested Kirsty. 'You may use the restaurant,' she offered.

Sunday trade was slack at this time of the year. She was always ready to support any event which might end with a full bar and a late-night session.

There was a general murmur of approval.

'How about preparing a letter to the Council in advance of the meeting? We could get everyone to sign it on the spot. The Local Authority will find it easier to read one letter rather than fifty,' Desmond suggested.

Those who were unlikely to write anything more than

a few Christmas cards once a year were quick to support this suggestion.

Bill puffed on his pipe and cleared his throat in that way which meant he had something important to say. Margaret invited him to speak.

'A year or two back,' he looked fixedly at Desmond, 'when there were fewer of us living on the island, we had a tussle with the Authority about the ferry. They were threatening to change the hours of running. On that occasion we acted together, sending one letter signed by forty people. Six or eight others wrote individually, in support of the changes. At the Council meeting, where the matter was discussed, the Roads Department officer was asked for the numbers of letters received protesting against the proposal and those in favour. The answer given was that one letter had been received against and eight in favour. The fact that the first letter contained forty signatures was ignored.'

Bill's speech was slow and deliberate and his voice rather monotonous. Most of those present were well aware that once into his stride with his reminiscences, he would be hard to shut up . . . experience had told them that it was best to let him ramble on until he ran out of breath.

Desmond, unfamiliar with accepted practice, jumped in immediately.

'Surely someone got up and said that the letter represented the opinions of the majority?'

Bill replied patiently, 'At a meeting of the Council, members of the public are not invited to speak, just to listen. The Clerk was asked a question – How many letters? – and he gave a straight answer.'

'What Bill is saying,' Margaret intervened, 'is that if we want to make an impact, we have to get everyone to write their own letter. The people at the Council Offices will surely sit up and take notice of a sackful of correspondence all on the same topic. One single letter might easily be overlooked or ignored, even if it carries a hundred signatures!'

'What we could do,' said Celia, thoughtfully, 'is draft a model letter giving all the points we want emphasised and ask people either to copy it or change it as they see fit. It doesn't much matter if we all say approximately the same thing . . . in fact, it would lend the arguments more weight.'

'Are we all agreed then?' Margaret demanded

'Who's going to write this letter?' asked Desmond, petulantly.

'I think you can leave that to Celia and myself,' suggested Margaret. 'We'll find an opportunity to discuss the draft with the rest of this committee before we take it to the meeting on Sunday.'

She glanced across at the newly elected Secretary and Celia nodded.

'Shouldn't we decide now what our main objections are?' demanded Desmond, determined to have his say despite having been snubbed so consistently. He was beginning to get the message that, as a newcomer, he was not going to be allowed to play a leading role in this affair. He was determined, however, to demonstrate the importance of his technical skills and ready access to the most sophisticated of communications systems. For the moment he would have to bide his time. When a web site was needed, they would soon come running.

'I think we have to be careful,' Margaret was saying, taking his point that they should discuss the contents of the model letter. 'It is obvious that there are some advantages for the community in this scheme. The development ought to provide employment for local people. It looks as if this HDC lot are prepared to improve the infrastructure, essential works that the Council have been putting off for years. What is being proposed includes attractions for tourists which could bring three times the number of visitors to the area and that will be welcomed by the shopkeepers, the B&Bs and the hotel.'

'So what do we have against it?' asked Celia, only too aware that most people resented change of any kind, simply for its own sake.

'I am opposed to anything which encourages crowds of visitors who have no regard for the ambience of the place, who know nothing of its history and ignore all those aspects which make Eisdalsa so attractive just as it is,' Bill declared. 'They probably won't appreciate the lack of street lighting, for example. There's no mention of that on the plan but there is a clear implication in the words – "the company plans to put forward proposals for upgrading the infrastructure to modern-day standards". A large influx of people is likely to impose upon the loneliness of these wild spots outwith the villages, the peace and quiet . . . all those intangible things which combine to make this the place we love could be lost. Once gone, they will never be regained. What these developers seem to have overlooked is that it is the very uniqueness of this area which attracts tourists to it. Remove that and you will make Eisdalsa like any other seaside resort or worse . . . a grotesque caricature of itself.'

'I don't think it will be quite as bad as that,' suggested Margaret, attempting to cool the tone of the argument. People were obviously becoming very apprehensive. 'Until we can see the detailed proposals, there's no point in raising blood pressure all round. I get the impression that this company is looking for a more up-market clientele than Bill envisages . . . visitors from abroad who can afford to pay fancy prices. Nevertheless, some of the activities suggested would impinge severely on the local fishing grounds and it's well known that fast motor boats, used frequently, can disturb the wildlife.'

'I'm worried about this idea of opening up the northern quarry as a marina,' said Jamie McPhee. He spoke slowly in a West Highland brogue. His softly voiced intervention caused the rest of the company to be silent in order that they might hear what he had to say.

'I don't think their surveyor can have realised the impact that winter storms might have, and if the causeway between the two quarries was to collapse, the whole of that side of the island would be cut off. In any case, I don't see how they can hope to open a channel of sufficient width and depth to allow the passage of yachts . . . it would take a very wide and pretty deep opening to allow some of these amateur yachtsmen to sail through in safety. At low tide the rocks across the gap they're talking of widening are actually exposed. It would mean blasting away the rock to a depth of as much as four metres to accommodate the deepest keels. What's more, you don't need me to tell you that the larger that gap becomes, the greater will be the danger of the walls of the quarry collapsing. I might add that, because of the nature of the tides and the strength of the prevailing wind, there are likely to be very few days in the year when it would be safe to sail a boat through there, no matter how wide and deep the opening.'

'I'm no marine engineer . . .' intervened an unfamiliar voice. Heads turned to examine the stranger in their midst '. . . but I would suggest that the cost of opening a passage of the dimensions just suggested would run into hundreds of thousands of pounds.'

'I don't know how many of you know Gerry Wilson,' Desmond said hurriedly. 'He arrived home from Hong Kong unexpectedly, only yesterday, so I took the liberty of asking him along. He lives in Seileach of course, but I thought, since he is an architect, he might have something useful to contribute.'

If the islanders were uncomfortable at what many of them might regard as an intervention from 'the other side', as they were wont to describe the village across the water, most of them were too polite to show it.

Bill Douglas, however, incensed that Desmond, a comparative newcomer to the island, should have taken such a liberty, could not avoid a note of sarcasm.

'Oh, no, the more the merrier,' he said. 'No doubt there will be plenty of others wanting to put their oar in from over there.' He had already had an argument with Flora, who could see only the benefits of the proposals and had accused him of being a reactionary old fool who should wake up his ideas and realise that at this end of the twentieth century, people had different values and different requirements. They were not so ready to accept the primitive conditions with which he had been content forty years ago.

Margaret, while recognising the tension created by Desmond's initiative, welcomed the newcomer politely. 'I think we would all value the opinion of someone versed in the business of obtaining planning consents,' she said, smiling at Wilson. 'Would it be possible for you to obtain a realistic estimate of the likely cost of opening the quarry, to put to the general meeting on Sunday?' Her smile melted the frost in the air and elicited a cheerful nod from him.

'I'll have a word with a friend of mine who is concerned with this kind of work . . . see what he can come up with.'

Hurriedly, she began to draw the meeting to a close.

'To sum up, is it the will of this committee, that we call all the interested parties to a meeting in the restaurant on Sunday next?' There was general assent. 'Then Celia and I will draw up a letter containing the points raised here tonight and Mr . . .'

'Wilson,' Desmond intervened.

'. . . Mr Wilson will look into the feasibility of the proposed quarry modifications.'

Heads nodded.

'If you will permit me?' Wilson, having been snubbed once, was cautious in his second intervention.

'Mr Wilson?'

'While I can see that this proposal has serious implications for Eisdalsa Island, it will have a significant effect upon those living in Seileach as well. The community over there is not quite so well co-ordinated as here.' His flattering words did not go unappreciated. 'They are unlikely to get anything organised in time for a collective protest. Since you people are so clearly on the ball, it would seem sensible to hold your meeting where others affected by the scheme can also make a contribution to the debate. May I suggest you consider holding your meeting in the village hall over there?'

There were a few hostile murmurings and Bill, who had made the former remark, looked rather uncomfortable. He quickly saw the wisdom of the fellow's suggestion but did not know how to wriggle out of the uncomfortable situation into which his earlier disagreement with his daughter had led him.

Celia it was who spoke up for those present.

'I think Mr Wilson is right,' she said. 'Whatever we may feel about the way things are done "over there", this is one occasion when we should all be pulling together. I propose we accept his suggestion that the meeting be held in Seileach.'

'You could find yourselves out-voted,' suggested Angus. 'There's plenty over there would welcome street lighting and better roads and the suggestion of a lot more tourists will produce a deal of support for the developers.'

'That's up to the community as a whole,' said Margaret. 'If the vote should go against us, we can still revert to the islanders taking unilateral action. That is, of course, always supposing the vote from over here is substantially against the development. We don't know yet that that is the case.' She appeared to be addressing Bill in particular when she added, 'Maybe we are wrong to assume that everyone on Eisdalsa is likely to be on our side?'

'Let's have an official minute,' Celia suggested. 'If the Seileach lot turn down the idea of a protest, I propose that we proceed with action on our own behalf.'

'I think we should take one step at a time,' suggested Margaret. 'We don't know yet what the outcome of the public meeting is going to be.' She noticed Celia's crest-fallen expression and added hastily, 'However, I see nothing wrong with having a contingency plan ready. Now, if there is no other business?' She paused, and receiving the silence she had hoped for. 'Then I declare this meeting closed.'

While the remainder of the company rose to their feet and began a frantic search in the tiny entrance hall for overcoats and a matching pair of wellington boots, Bill Douglas, wishing to make amends for his rudeness, turned to Wilson. 'The late ferry won't be leaving for another forty minutes,' he said. 'How about a wee dram in the Tacksman before you go?'

'Splendid idea,' said the other, and turned to Desmond. 'How about you, Des? Are you going to join us?'

Chagrined by the off-hand treatment he had been given by the company in general, he shook his head.

'Sorry. I've got a job on at the moment . . . burning the midnight oil, I'm afraid.' He strode off into the darkness, leaving the others to pick their way across the grass in the direction of the pub.

*

'There's a public meeting called for Friday evening . . . in the village hall.' Cissy placed George's bacon and eggs before him, forcing him to discard yesterday's *Scotsman* which landed in an untidy heap on the floor.

'Do you know, I remember when my father's *Times* awaited him on the breakfast table every morning,' he mused. 'And even then, Mattheson had had time to iron it before he came down!'

'That would have been in the days when the house-maid had been up since five, lighting the range to boil water so she could carry the pitchers up the back stairs to all the bedrooms,' Cissy said sharply.

'The night mail would have brought it up from Glasgow so it arrived on the doorstep with the first post,' he continued, ignoring her interruption. 'The first post, mind . . . there were two a day then.'

'Times change,' she insisted, spreading low-fat mar-garine on her toast.

'Yes, despite the villagers of Seileach and Eisdalsa,' George reiterated.

'Oh, so you did hear what I said?' His wife looked up sharply. 'What do you intend to do about it?'

'How do you mean?'

'Will you go to put your case?' she demanded. The atmosphere had been pretty chilly during recent days. Cissy was still smarting from the fact that she had not been consulted about HDC's offer to buy land although she had been forced to agree that such a sale might be necessary if they were to restore the castle before it crumbled away entirely.

'No, I will not,' was George's reply. 'It's no business of

anyone but myself to whom I sell my land.'

'But it is their business if the sale is likely to make a significant alteration to their lives!' Cissy insisted.

'You go and hold our end up, then,' he replied. 'If you're willing to spend the evening listening to a bunch of old fogies debating a subject on which they have little or no information.'

'How do you mean? They have access to the same plans as you received.'

'Outline plans only. You don't suppose they contain the entire story, do you?'

'You mean . . . the Council might grant outline planning consent and still hold out on the detail?'

'Precisely.'

'Meanwhile, having received their outline consent, HDC will go ahead with the purchase of the land, which will certainly suit your agenda.'

George grinned in a self-satisfied way and spread himself a slice of toast.

'It seems a bit off-hand, not to go along and explain, though.'

'Tell me what has been proposed so far that anyone could legitimately protest against?' he demanded. 'HDC want to improve the roads, maybe even add street lighting. They're talking about a golf course. How often have we heard it suggested that if we are to get any credibility as a tourist centre, we have to have an eighteen-hole course? And why not a marina? Most people around here have their own boats and just look at the support given to the Tobermory race every year. Another hotel should improve Marty's trade, not diminish it . . . a little competition never did anyone any harm. How could any of these things seriously disturb the everyday lives of the islanders, other than by giving some of them regular employment for a change?'

'Maybe you should go along and tell them that . . . allay their fears?'

Cissy's tone softened as she tried to persuade him. In her heart, she wanted to support him. Who better than his wife to understand George's desperate need to restore his family home? Her instincts told her, however, that if he did not align himself with the community at this point, George might well become a pariah amongst those whom they had always regarded as their friends. She did not want a new roof at the expense of life-long associations.

'Let them speculate as they will.' He had made up his mind and nothing was going to change it now. 'I see no reason at all to go to a public meeting to explain my own private business.'

'Well, I shall go anyway,' Cissy told him. He gave her a warning glance. 'Oh, I won't say anything one way or the other,' she assured him, 'but you ought to know what is being said. We can't alienate ourselves entirely from the people . . . this isn't the eighteenth century, you know.'

The shaft found its mark.

At their very first meeting, George had confessed a passion for the eighteenth century, seeing it as an idyllic period in history . . . one in which he would have preferred to live. Cissy never missed an opportunity to tease him on the subject. Like the time when the septic tank ceased to function and they were obliged to revert to chamber pots and commodes until the plumbing could be sorted out.

'Imagine coping with a situation in which every bucket of water had to be brought up from the burn to be fed into the storage tank,' she had pointed out.

His instant response had been to protest, 'But I wouldn't have had to do it – there were plenty of servants around for that kind of work!' For that insensitive remark he had received a mighty thwack across the buttocks and they had fallen on the bed, laughing.

They were not laughing now.

The lightness had gone out of the argument. Cissy wondered if they were about to have their worst row ever, and shuddered at the thought. Nevertheless she was not about to give ground.

'I still think you should go to the meeting,' she insisted, 'and if you won't, I will!'

'Please yourself,' he murmured, and returned to yesterday's news.

On Friday night, George dropped Cissy off at the hall on his way to the harbour.

'I've been wanting to have a few words with Kirsty about the lease on the Tacksman's Bar,' he told her. 'This might be a good opportunity, while everyone is at the meeting. I'll return on the late ferry and pick you up on my way home.'

For the last few days, the atmosphere between them had remained chilly. Cissy hoped that after the meeting tonight, she might be able to clear the air. No matter what George said, it really was important for them to know how the villagers felt about the proposed changes. Maybe they would approve the scheme and there would be nothing to worry about. After all, not everyone was opposed to change, She could not believe that her husband could remain so arrogant as he had appeared over this matter, and wondered if it was not merely embarrassment and apprehension which kept him away.

The old drill hall had changed little in the course of a century and more. One end sported a stage whose ugly brown-painted proscenium arch dominated the space and whose curtains had seen better days. The overhead lighting was painfully inadequate so that Cissy, who had noticed a marked deterioration in her sight in recent weeks, had to strain her eyes to read the agenda. The room was cold and cheerless and, for the moment, sadly lacking in people.

She settled herself near the back of the hall, shuffling uncomfortably on the canvas seat which was stretched over a too narrow and very hard steel frame. The chairs were fixed together so that when one moved, they all moved. Every few moments a newcomer would move between the rows, dislodging them and causing those already seated to rearrange themselves.

'Good evening, Cissy. George not coming?' Marty Crane joined her, waiting while she moved along one seat to allow him to stretch his long legs into the aisle.

'No . . . afraid not,' she answered, unwilling to be led into confessing her husband was unwilling to face the music.

'I would have thought he would have wanted to come along and hear praises heaped upon him for services to the community.'

She regarded Marty coolly. Was he making fun of her or did he mean it?

He seemed perfectly sincere.

'You're not against the development?' she asked, surprised.

'Why should I be ? Anything that raises the profile of the place is bound to do my hotel business a bit of good. I would have thought that would have gone for all the others too . . . No, I'm not here to protest. Far from it.'

Margaret McColl, realising the resentment which might be generated if, as Chair of the Eisdalsa Residents' Action Committee, she were to call a meeting in Seileach Village, had taken the wise precaution of persuading the Community Councillors to call the people together. Since she had gone to considerable trouble to analyse the contents of the planning document, however, it was she who was called upon to open the meeting.

'I have no wish to pre-empt the discussion by putting forward the opinions of representatives of the Eisdalsa community with whom I have already spoken,' she began, guardedly. 'I will simply outline the plan as I see it, and leave it to you to voice your own opinions.' She glanced at Giles Scott, who was in the Chair, and received his approval.

'On the face of it, the plan is a simple one: to build a new hotel on the island of Eisdalsa. Also it appears that a golf course is envisaged, probably taking in a portion of the farmland at Tigh na Broch.'

Old Duncan McLeod half rose in his seat to make a protest at this suggestion but his wife, Elizabeth, pulled him back. She would be quite pleased to see her husband working a smaller area of land. Whatever the new doctor had said to him about his cough had made little change to his working and smoking habits. Perhaps this would force him to take things more easily.

'Apart from the hotel on Eisdalsa, there is a proposal to open up the most northerly of the quarries as a marina and to provide facilities for yachtsmen . . . a ship's chandlery, a general store, an ablutions unit and launderette.' As Margaret spoke she realised how innocuous it all sounded. It was not for her to mention her own gnawing suspicion that the detailed plans would have a far greater impact upon their lives than this document suggested.

'It is clear,' she continued, 'that these additional facilities will require an improved infrastructure in terms of water, waste and sewage disposal and access to Eisdalsa Island. It seems certain that street lighting will be called for and metalled roads and footpaths will be essential even on Eisdalsa. The extent of these alterations will no doubt depend upon the requirements of the Local Authority.'

There were murmurs of agreement amongst those who had, for a long time, requested an improvement in the roads, including lighting, and in the water and electricity supplies to the villages. The islanders kept mum at this point but they were certainly opposed to any suggestion of paved footpaths over there and were united in their opposition to the introduction of motorised vehicles.

'Here on Seileach, an area of the foreshore outwith the village is designated as a small boat park with a floating jetty for launching.' Margaret paused to allow for a few mild guffaws and the unidentified voice which spoke for them all. 'I'll give that five minutes. First autumnal equinox will see it blown away by the gales.' The general laughter went some way to relieving a mounting tension and she paused to allow Giles Scott to regain the audience's attention.

'That just about sums up the plans which have been released so far,' she concluded, when all was quiet. 'What is not stated is the means by which HDC intend to get cars across to their hotel car park which is clearly marked on the plan. They have not stated what provision will be made to improve access by a ferry or other means.' Here she put in her one personal comment. 'It is clear that an open ferry boat carrying a maximum of ten people will not suit this company's plans and we must anticipate the introduction of a vehicular ferry or,' she paused for effect, 'maybe a bridge.'

There was derisive laughter from the villagers of Seileach while the Eisdalsa residents were quick to protest. The suggestion of a bridge had been the subject of a long-standing dispute between residents on Eisdalsa and those on the larger island, with the Seileachans arguing that the cost to the rate payers of running a high-powered ferry boat was too much, while the islanders were determined to maintain their isolation at all costs.

Margaret regained her seat and Giles acknowledged the work she had put in, in investigating and summarising the proposals. There was spontaneous applause from the meeting.

'Does anyone have any comment to make?' asked the Chairman.

'It seems to me,' Marty Crane imagined that he spoke

for them all, 'that nothing but good can come from such a proposal. Let's face it, the whole community needs a face lift and this sort of cash injection should put us all on our feet.'

Again applause drowned out the one or two feeble protests from members of the local Historical Society and the more conservation-minded members of the community.

Cissy noticed a cloud of blue smoke rising from three rows in front and gagged as the pungent odour of St Bruno tobacco caught her in the throat. So Bill Douglas was here after all. She had wondered whether he would be making an appearance. From what Flora had told her, he was totally opposed to the scheme. Clearly he was about to tell them why.

'I have lived here since the war,' he began to a chorus of sighs. They had heard it so many times before. 'I have seen a depression in the years when the cottages hereabouts were falling into ruin, the young people were moving out just as soon as they finished school and the only folk one met in the village store were twenty years older than oneself. I have seen the better times arriving, too. By ones and twos they came, the incomers with their idyllic view of life on the west coast, bringing with them not only their much-needed retirement pensions but also their fancy suburban ideas of the importance of window boxes and flush toilets. Readily, we accepted their financial input into our economy and, in due course, experience changed their views about the window boxes.' There was general laughter. 'The idea of the flush toilet we took on board, together with the electric cookers, the night storage heaters and washing machines. But it has all happened slowly. So slowly that one hardly noticed the changes until one day one looked around the villages and remarked on the new paint, the double-glazed windows and the lack of oil lamps in the houses, with some surprise.'

Giles Scott cleared his throat rather obviously. Even the garrulous Captain Douglas understood the significance of the gesture.

'I can see that I am overstepping my time,' he apologised, but continued just the same. 'What I am saying is this. Change is all very well when it happens slowly and doesn't interrupt the flow of life around us. I fear for all our futures if this development is allowed to take place. It will transform the whole area into something different overnight and we will live to regret it.'

He sat down to some facetious quips, a few mild cheers and just a smattering of clapping in agreement. Bill had had his say, now they could all get down to the business in hand.

George chased his third whisky down with a pint of heavy and realised that he was drunk. The strain of recent days was telling on him. Why couldn't Cissy see that what he had arranged with Jack McDougal was the answer to all their problems? Jack's estimate of George's slice of the cake amounted to millions of dollars. How could she expect him to turn down such an offer?

'I'll never understand women . . .' he slurred his words so that Kirsty could hardly understand them '. . .

never happy. When you work all the hours God sends, they want to know why you don't pay attention to them like you used to. Give 'em the chance of an easy life in the lap of luxury, and they quote duty and responsibility at you until it's coming out of your ears . . .'

'I've heard of the Royal *we*,' said Kirsty, in an attempt to lighten the tone of the conversation, 'the Royal *they* has hitherto escaped me.'

'Wha?'

'Look, George, I don't mind you drowning your sorrows at my bar but I think you owe it to Cissy to keep your private quarrels to yourself. Besides . . .'

He looked up, suddenly surprisingly alert.

'Yes?'

'I'm inclined to agree with her. If I have interpreted your ramblings correctly, she is not happy about your selling off land to these developers. Well, I think she's right. Just because you happen to have inherited these few acres from which we all derive our livelihood, doesn't mean you have the right to disrupt our existence without even asking our opinion. You're worried about a new roof on the castle. Some of *us* have sunk our life savings in little enterprises around here which could be squeezed out entirely by the big boys.'

'Oh, no. McDougal promised there would be no damage to the existing economy. Quite the opposite, I would say.'

'Do you really believe that a fifty-bedroomed hotel with a covered swimming pool and glassed-in recreational areas will have absolutely no effect on Marty Crane's business?'

'There will still be the traditional holiday makers who like to walk, take a small boat out fishing, watch the wild life . . .'

'Will there? Do you honestly believe that members of the RSPB and the National Trust will still come flocking to a seaside resort with candy stalls, fish and chip bars and amusement arcades?'

'Oh, I don't think that's what's intended,' he blustered.

'All right then, the up-market version of such amusements . . . a casino; motorised buggies for getting around; a steam train carrying tourists around the island; a bridge to Eisdalsa or, even worse – a Sky Rail!'

'A Sky Rail?'

'You know, like a cablecar. One of those aerial torpedo things slung across the sound, in order to dispense with the ferry.'

George's brow clouded in a puzzled frown. 'Where did you get that idea?'

'They have them in Australia – Queensland, where your friend McDougal comes from. Angus Dewar was out there last winter visiting his sister – he told me all about the one he went on.'

'I don't see any reason for anything more being needed than a slightly larger ferry boat. The men are always complaining about being exposed to the elements. They're constantly angling for a covered deck, as well you know.'

'These plans show an area for parking the cars of hotel guests *on* the island.'

'They won't be able to drive around. Why should they want to transport their vehicles to the island? It's no more than a couple of miles around the shores even at low tide!'

'I don't know. Maybe they'll feel their BMWs and their Saabs will be at risk on the other side. Let's face it, with the proposed influx of people into the area all of a sudden, there'll be a greater chance of unsavoury characters arriving too. The one thing folks around here still pride themselves upon is the fact that they never lock their doors.'

'That's a pretty feeble reason for refusing a multi-million pound investment into the villages.' Remarkably, their discussion had overcome the effects of George's excessive drinking. He suddenly felt stone cold sober.

'It depends what price you put upon our present environment,' she argued. 'Such things as a shoreline uncluttered by anything other than a few wee fishing boats; villages where you can actually see the houses without the inevitable row of cars hiding them from view; a place where there are very few sounds loud enough to drown out the crashing of waves on the shore, the cry of sea birds and the howling of the wind around the chimney pots; a place where the only two-legged predators are crows and an occasional heron. More important than all these things is the peace of mind of the people.

'Here folks manage on what they can make by the skill in their hands or the services they are able to provide. People around here are not continuously striving to be richer than the chap next door. OK, some of them may be more comfortably off than others, but generally speaking you would never know it. There's a common denominator among both the people who live here permanently and those who visit on a regular basis. They seem to have a deeper understanding of what really matters in life:

good neighbourliness, friendship, compassion for strangers and those weaker or less able than themselves . . . some of those old-fashioned principles which seem to have been lost in the scramble to find a place in the capitalist society of which our politicians are so proud, the one which supports companies like HDC.

'There are people on these islands who have given up promising careers in order to live a simpler life, without the pressures of the commercial rat race. They have come here to rear their children within a lifestyle which is more in sympathy with our natural surroundings. By an accident of birth you are in a position to destroy everything these people hold dear. Do you really see yourself in the role of a despot, enslaving everyone to your will?'

'Oh, come on, that's a bit strong, isn't it?' Things had gone badly wrong during this encounter. George had anticipated an ally in Kirsty and now found her firmly of his wife's opinion.

'Can't you see any advantage to yourself?' he demanded. 'With greater numbers of people on the island after ferry hours, you're bound to do more business.'

'Yes . . . but at what price? I can see these fancy hotel guests coming in once or twice, to gape at our quaint island folk, but once they've sampled the atmosphere of the Tacksman, I have no doubt they'll begin to compare beer prices and you'll be one of the first to complain if mine are higher than the hotel's. I can't hope to ask for the kind of concessions from the brewery a multinational organisation like HDC can demand.'

'I'm sure it will have some mechanism for incorporating all the retail outlets in the district and gaining joint concessions from wholesalers. After all, I too have something to lose if they undercut *my* business in any way.'

'The only mechanism I can see is one in which HDC takes over all the businesses and runs them under one banner. How do you know that's not their ultimate aim?'

George paled. He had not considered anything like a wholesale takeover.

'Wouldn't it be funny if you found yourself kowtowing to some giant American mogul?' Kirsty grinned, but George looked decidedly sick. For some inexplicable reason there flashed across his mind a picture of Milton T. Humbert, striding across the heather with McGreggor in his wake, shouldering that elegant case of Purdeys.

'One for the road,' George said, glancing at the clock, aware that the last ferry crossing would be in just a few moments.

'You driving?' she asked, concerned. A public meeting in the hall was just the occasion when Sergeant McNab would be out and about, on the lookout for late-night drink drivers.

'No, I left the car at the hall. Cissy will be waiting to drive me home.'

'Funked the meeting, did you?'

He suddenly remembered the excuse he had given his wife for coming across to see Kirsty this evening. He was going to tell her that they had reached the end of their initial agreement and that if she wanted to renew her lease, he would have to increase the rent by seven and a half per cent to keep abreast of inflation. He couldn't face another argument now. With the lease due for immediate renewal, he had to make his approach to her tonight or hold his peace for a further twelve months. He decided to do just that . . . after all, in twelve months her paltry fifty quid a week would be like a pimple on an elephant's hide.

He pulled his flat tweed cap down firmly so as not to lose it in the evening breeze, and unexpectedly leaned across the bar, grasped both her hands in his and gave her a light peck on the cheek.

'What was that for?' she demanded, feeling the blood surging towards her face.

'Oh . . . just for being you,' he murmured. Then, embarrassed that he should have revealed feelings he had no business to disclose, he deliberately slurred his speech as he bade her, 'Goodnight'.

Kirsty was used to the inebriated exaggerations of her customers' compliments and would, he felt sure, immediately forget his momentary indiscretion.

The door slammed behind him. She stood staring at her reflection in the glass panel for some minutes, her fingers caressing the spot where his kiss had landed. She knew that George was out of her reach and wished she could put him out of her mind, also. There was little point in carrying a torch for the Marquis – people like George could philander with impunity. It was almost expected of them. She on the other hand, could not afford a whiff of that sort of scandal in this close-knit community. With a deep sigh, she picked up a cloth and began to polish glasses.

Chapter Twelve

'So . . . how did it go?'

George laid his head back against the rest, finding it difficult to keep his eyes open.

Cissy stared straight ahead into the darkness. Even the dimly lit dashboard of the Range Rover was enough to cause distracting reflections in the windscreen.

'Quite well, from your point of view,' she answered grudgingly, changing gear in order to creep around the buttress of rock which created a tight hairpin bend before the long straight stretch to the foot of Smiddy Brae.

'A bit of lighting wouldn't go amiss here,' he muttered sleepily.

'But think what it would do to the atmosphere of the place if there was lighting all along the shore. We wouldn't see those marvellous night skies as clearly as we do now.'

'So, people were largely for the scheme, were they?' he pressed.

'I wouldn't say that exactly. There were many doubts expressed. Old Bill Douglas made an impassioned speech about the breakdown of our society and the destruction of the environment, but I don't think too many people were listening. They tend to switch off as soon as he gets to his feet.'

'But we're not being accused of selling their birthright for a mess of pottage, or anything like that?'

'What a curious question. Whatever prompted you to ask that?'

'Oh, just something Kirsty said.' He fell silent and she thought he must have dropped off to sleep. She would have to tell him in the morning about the plans to write individual letters of protest. He wouldn't like it, but Cissy was determined to add her comments to the flow of opinion expressed in the hall that evening. She had anticipated out and out dismissal of the scheme, but what she had heard was reasoned argument in favour of waiting for further details before condemning the proposals out of hand. In order to publicise the depth of feeling over the plans, everyone who could manage it had agreed to attend the Council meeting at which the application for outline planning consent was to be discussed. Whatever George said, she was determined to be present.

Desmond Bartlet did not attend the debate in the village hall. He had heard enough at the meeting of Eisdalsa residents to summarise their general feelings on the HDC proposals. Far better to devote his energies to enlisting support for their fight from elsewhere.

He sat down before his state-of-the-art PC and began to design his web site. Naturally, he would show it to Margaret McColl when it was done . . . before he sent it out.

The children were both in bed and Molly would not be back until the late ferry. He worked away steadily, and by eleven o'clock was well satisfied with what he had produced. He tampered slightly with the depth of colour, realigned one of the margins to give better balance and sat back, proud of his achievement. How could anyone find fault with his message? He had put down only what they had said. OK, he hadn't received any input from the Seileach lot, but Wilson had given him a pretty good idea how they would all be feeling. Anyway, if anyone was going to suffer from this invasion, it would be the Eisdalsa people first and foremost. He 'saved' his final result and sat back. Molly would be in at any minute and he would have time to go round to the pub for a pint before bed. He drew on his wellingtons and his waxed jacket.

The page was still on the screen.

He read it once more, smiled in a self-satisfied way and then, on impulse, brought up the transmission file and clicked on OK.

It was done. For better or worse, the plight of Eisdalsa Island had been broadcast around the world at the press of a button.

'What d'you think of this plan to turn the villages into a holiday resort, doctor?' Barbara Fullerton enquired, rolling down her sleeve and reaching for her cardigan.

'Oh, I'm afraid I have no opinions either way,' Alan replied. He was beginning to make some headway with McWorter's patients, but not so much that he dared risk antagonising any of them by a careless word for one side or the other. 'Well, your blood pressure readings seem to be consistent at last, but I think you had better continue with the tablets for the time being. Maybe we'll cut them down to one a day after your next visit.'

He wrote out the required prescription and handed it to her. It was her cue to leave.

'My Robbie is concerned that they'll stop him using Eisdalsa harbour once they start tarting it up,' she continued as though she had not heard him.

'What does your husband do?' Alan asked, thinking he must be one of the small band of fishermen still left on the west coast.

'He's the master of the puffer . . . the *Eilean nam Uan*. Haven't you noticed her in the harbour? She sailed in yesterday.'

'I haven't been across to Eisdalsa for a day or two,' he answered. 'To be honest, I didn't realise there were still any puffers in working order.'

'This is the last one actually carrying cargo. Most of her sister vessels, those that are still afloat, have been turned into cruise boats. Although, as Robbie says, who'd want to spend two weeks tossing about in an uncomfortable old barge like that and call it a holiday?'

In an attempt to encourage her to leave, Alan half-rose from his chair but she was determined to monopolise his attention for just a few moments longer.

'Have you heard how Dr McWorter is getting on?' she enquired, wishing to prolong the conversation for as long as possible. Barbara Fullerton led a lonely life, with her man away at sea for weeks at a time and her children boarding in the school hostel in Oban. She was enjoying the undivided attentions of this personable young man and was in no hurry to go.

'He's doing very well,' Alan replied, replacing the sphygmomanometer in its box and closing Barbara's file, very deliberately, before throwing it on the pile in front of him. 'In fact, he should be coming back home soon after Christmas.'

'Och, the poor wee man.' She expressed the feelings of all his patients. 'He'll never look after himself properly on his own.'

'We're trying to arrange some kind of help for him,' Alan explained. 'I believe there are a few women in the neighbourhood who might be approached?'

'Oh, aye, you'll likely find someone willing to do a few hours a week. Well, I mustn't take any more of your time, doctor, I'll be getting along now.'

She gathered her belongings and made for the door. As she reached for the knob, Flora entered, a worried frown on her face.

Barbara hesitated and would have waited to hear what was amiss but Alan dismissed her with a polite, 'Good morning, Mrs Fullerton,' and before she knew what was happening, she found herself out in the corridor with Flora closing the door quietly behind her.

With a sniff, she tucked the prescription into her purse. Having been so summarily dismissed, she would hand the paper in at the chemist's rather than wait for Flora to dispense it. Dr Mac had once told her that every pre-scription filled at the surgery was additional money for the practice. Well, they would just have to do without hers.

*

'There's a message from Dr Pullson's husband,' Flora explained. 'Janice won't be able to take surgery tomorrow. It seems she has been in a high fever since yesterday afternoon. She's insisting it's just the beginnings of 'flu, but Gordon thinks it's something more serious. He didn't ask for a house call, but he sounded very concerned.'

'Ring back and tell him I'll be there as soon as surgery is finished,' Alan told her.

Flora turned to go.

'By the way, you'll have to fill me in about the planning meeting last Friday,' he called after her. 'People keep asking me to give an opinion, and while it would be politic to sit on the fence about the whole thing, I feel I should take an interest in what is going on . . . if only to be able to tell Dr Mac when next I see him.'

'That reminds me,' she answered, avoiding his question. 'I have found a woman in the village willing to come in three days a week, to look after the doctor as soon as he is ready to come home. That may be sooner than you think, by the way. Once he gets to hear about George Monteith's part in this affair, I suspect that the fur will begin to fly.'

'Why on earth should it affect the old Doc in any way?'

'He's a champion of conservation,' Flora explained. 'When his wife was alive he and Annie spent all their spare time nurturing local wildlife and doing what they could to preserve the heritage sites, of which there are a great many in these parts. He will never agree to any development which threatens either.'

'And what about you? Do you think this plan is a good idea?'

'As a matter of fact, I do.' She surprised him with her defence of the changes. He had thought her decision to remain in this backwater was associated with the same lethargy which appeared to affect many of the local people. She was, after all, well qualified and very able at what she had been trained to do. She could go anywhere in the country and get herself a decent job, but she preferred to stay on.

'I love this place,' she explained, 'but I can see that if it is to survive as a viable community there must be progress. People need work, something to sustain them through the winter months as well as during the height of the tourist season. This project seems to be the answer to all our dreams.'

So far, Alan had paid little attention to the talk he had heard about the development. Clearly, Flora had given it a lot of thought. If she said it was a good thing for the district, who was he to dispute it? he had no wish to be at odds with her; far from it.

'OK, you'd better send in the next patient. Oh, and don't forget to give Gordon Pullson a call.' He looked at his watch and gave a low whistle. Ten-thirty already and he still had three more patients to see.

Janice lay back on her rumpled pillows, a pale shadow of her normal self. Alan was quite shocked by the sudden change which had taken place in the four or five days since he had seen her last. Her eyes were closed, the lids red and sore, the sockets deeply sunk and violet-coloured. The flesh had fallen away from her cheek bones so that the outline of her skull was clearly visible beneath the thin, parchment-coloured skin. He advanced toward the bed, trying to disguise his concern at her emaciated appearance.

'She's been bringing up anything I've managed to persuade her to take,' said Gordon, 'even boiled water.'

'How long since the sickness began?' asked Alan, searching for a pulse and finding it feeble and irregular. In cases like this the greatest danger was dehydration.

'It started after lunch the day before yesterday,' Pullson answered. 'She wouldn't let me call you . . . insisted it was something she'd eaten and that it would all be over by morning. At suppertime her temperature had risen quite alarmingly but it seemed to die down as the evening wore on and she slept reasonably well until the early hours of yesterday morning, when she woke up complaining of a headache. At her suggestion, I gave her a couple of Aspirins but they didn't seem to help much.

'The fever returned twice yesterday, morning and evening, but each time, after I had helped her into a tepid bath, she seemed better and slept for a few hours. When the fever returned last night I was all for calling you in straight away, but she insisted upon leaving it until this morning. I was up half the night, changing sheets and sponging her down. Then in the early hours her temperature dropped dramatically and she seemed to be on the mend. She said she felt hungry and I really thought it was all over. She had a cup of tea and a little scrambled egg and immediately brought it all up again. Then the fever returned and at that point, despite her objections, I insisted we call you.'

'We doctors make pretty bad patients, I'm afraid,' Alan told him, trying to sound casual. 'Look, why don't you go and make us both a cup of tea while I have a proper look at Janice. Have the kids been near her, by the way?'

'Why? You don't think it could be contagious, do you?'

'I can't be sure of anything until we've taken a blood test, but in the meantime . . . just to be on the safe side, I should keep them out of the way. Is there anyone who could keep an eye on them?'

'I can get my mother-in-law to come over if you really think it's necessary.' Gordon had quite clearly been putting off the inevitable. Alan could only assume that he and Janice's mother didn't get on.

'I think it would be advisable. Presumably you ought to be working and it doesn't look as if your wife is going to be able to cope with the family herself, not for a while, anyway.'

All this time, Janice had lain with her eyes closed.

'I *am* here you know,' she protested feebly. 'It just hurts to open my eyes. I'm not really asleep. I'm so sorry, Alan, I told Gordon not to bother you. It's just a mild dose of food poisoning, I'm sure.'

'It's not *mild* anything,' he observed, 'and you know it. Now come on, stop your talking and let's see what sort of a temperature you're presenting at the moment.'

Gordon had disappeared by now. While he waited for the thermometer to tell him the worst, Alan took Janice's wrist once more. The activity of speaking had increased the pulse rate and the beat seemed a little stronger, but it was still erratic. He pulled back the sheets and examined her glands. There was definite swelling of the lymph nodes all over her body. That didn't indicate food poisoning but rather some kind of bacterial or viral infection.

'If you think this is food-related, what do you suggest you might have eaten to cause it?' he asked. 'Has anyone else in the family shown similar symptoms? If not, what have you eaten which the others didn't have?'

'I've been lying here asking myself those very questions,' she admitted. 'I can't for the life of me identify any one thing. We had mussels on Sunday night, but I would have thought that if one of those was a bit dodgy, it would have come to light much sooner.'

'Yes, I agree. Look, I'm going to give you a shot of antibiotic for now, just in case it's an infection. How about the pain? Do you want something for that?'

Almost on cue her headache returned with such excruciating ferocity she could only nod in response.

He got her to swallow a couple of tablets of a sulphonamide product and gave her an injection of morphine. 'You'll not be getting too much of that, my lady,' he said jokingly, trying to make light of the situation. 'Don't want to go making a junkie of you, do we? I'll need some blood,' he told her, taking out a larger syringe and swabbing a spot in the crook of her elbow. He tightened the rubber cuff he had placed around her arm and slowly withdrew the dark, venous blood. 'I'll get this straight along to the lab, and see what they make of it.'

She nodded feebly.

By the time Alan had finished, Janice was already

dozing. He replaced the covers and slipped quietly out of the darkened room.

'Not much we can do until I've identified the bugs,' he said, taking a chair opposite Gordon at the kitchen table. He stirred his tea thoughtfully, remaining silent for a few moments. There was something niggling at the back of his mind. He had seen all these symptoms before, of course, but where had he encountered them in this combination? There was something about the timing of the fevers . . .

'Keep trying to get her to take liquids,' he blurted out at last. 'If she really can't keep anything down, we'll have to get her into hospital and put her on a drip . . . and try to keep her temperature down,' he added. 'The tepid baths were a good idea, but if she becomes too weak to manage that, just sponge her all over with warm water with a little vinegar added.'

'What does the vinegar do?'

'Don't ask me, it's something my granny always used to recommend! I'd like you to make a note of exactly when her temperature goes up . . . can you keep a chart for me?'

'I think I can manage that,' Gordon replied, irritated that Alan should assume he was not capable of nursing his wife properly. 'You don't have to be a medic to read a thermometer, you know.'

Alan looked at him properly for the first time. The man was exhausted. He had lost two nights' sleep and clearly needed to rest.

'As soon as your mother-in-law arrives, I suggest you get some sleep,' he advised. 'This business could go on for a while yet and I certainly don't want *two* patients on my hands.'

He stood up and looked at his watch. It was well past lunchtime and he had other calls to make.

'I'll be back this evening. If she's no better then, we'll get her into the hospital. Should that temperature rise above thirty-nine degrees, you'd better give me a call.'

Jack McDougal, jet-lagged after travelling almost continuously for the past month, sank gratefully into the cushions of the couch in his comfortable apartment and poured himself an ice-cold beer, straight from the fridge. There had been no word from Dee since he'd been away. He presumed she was still aboard Sam's boat and half hoped a cyclone would clobber the two of them. 'Good riddance!' He swallowed the last of the beer and sauntered over to the mini-bar to get himself another. He had been unable to raise a flicker of interest in any other women since his encounter with Flora Douglas. She had shown no sign that his presence had meant anything more to her than extra income coming in for a couple of weeks, and yet he had felt a strange compulsion to remain at her side. For some reason he couldn't get her image out of his mind.

He glanced at his reflection in the long mirror behind the bar and wondered what she had seen when she looked at him. Most women appeared impressed by his bronzed complexion and finely chiselled features. He was particular about his dress and frowned instinctively when he saw the crumpled appearance of his lightweight mohair suit. His silk shirt, made for him in Hong Kong, was soiled and his tie awry. He loosened the knot and undid the buttons of his shirt to the waist, revealing a thick mat of dark hair. He waited for the cool air from the fan above his head to dry him off. He used to think he liked the tropical heat of Queensland, but since his return from Scotland he had found it difficult to readjust. 'I must be a Highlander at heart,' he mused.

'But, Jack McDougal, you have a lot going for you,' he told himself. 'Good prospects, a healthy income and an attractive lifestyle.'

Any girl would be glad to become his partner . . . any girl that is except the one he most wanted.

Taken with a sudden desire to gain any information relating to Flora and her environment, he flipped open his lap top, brought up the Internet and sent his server searching for the word 'Eisdalsa'. There were the familiar pages he had seen before: an historical account of the Scottish slate industry, another on the beginnings of Christianity in Argyll, something about the Eisdalsa Museum. Hello, what was this? A new page he hadn't seen before . . . what was all this about a threat to their natural environment? Foreign developers wanting to take over . . . destruction of the fishing industry . . . the island under siege. Furious, Jack printed off the entry. While the gist of the message that someone was planning to turn the idyllic villages into a holiday resort was true enough and based upon the facts displayed in the Public Announcements column of the *Argyll Observer*, the response of the public was unbelievably biased against Humbert Developments.

'Oh, well, forewarned is forearmed,' he told himself as,

with a highlighting pen, he went over the points raised one by one. If they wanted a fight, they were going to get one! He would just have to take a little more care with his presentation to the Councillors.

On the far side of the globe someone else was surfing the net for want of something better to do. In his lakeside bungalow, twenty miles from Quebec, Pierre d'Orsay savoured the last of the splendid malt whisky he had brought back with him from his holiday, and scanned the web pages, looking for something to interest him. Under Scotland he ran the cursor down the list of titles and quickly arrived at Eisdalsa. He had read most of the entries before but here was a new message, a plea for support against a planning application. He read on, becoming more and more incensed at the inflammatory information given. Angrily he began to compose a reply.

Having worked for some time, he cooled down and as he went over what he had written, correcting a word here and there, realised that his reply was a bit over the top. Abandoning a response by e-mail, therefore, he decided to write an ordinary letter to the one person who would give him a balanced opinion on the matter. He drew a sheet of elaborately embossed note-paper from a little-used packet and began to write:

> *To Lady Christina Monteith*
> *Seileach Castle, Argyll.*
>
> *My Dear Cissy . . .*

Chapter Thirteen

Ewan McWorter was sick of his own company. It had been all right in the hospital. There was always someone to talk to in there, gossip to exchange with old acquaintances. There were after all very few folk he did not know in this close-knit community, and there was always one or other of the young nurses to tease. When all else failed, he was able to exercise his mind by mulling over the symptoms of his fellow patients. Even if the consultants excluded him from their deliberations, he enjoyed making his own diagnoses and comparing them with the conclusions of the experts.

There were very few conditions Ewan hadn't encountered in a long life of general practice, following six years' service in the army as a medical orderly. At the age of nineteen, he had served in the Western Desert and was in the first wave of attack at the Sicily landings in 1942. He had even had a spell in India and Malaya at the last knockings. There wasn't much that escaped his old eyes even today.

In the course of his work he was accustomed to studying people for their reactions to situations, as an indica-

tion of their state of health. Living in close proximity to
George and Cissy Monteith for a couple of weeks after
leaving hospital, had convinced him that all was not well
between them. In the absence of other guests at the
castle, Ewan took his breakfast in his room, but joined
the Monteiths at other meals. Most evenings he spent in
the television lounge or the library, where occasionally
one or other of the pair would join him for a short while
. . . but never both.

George rarely appeared at lunchtime, though this was
to be expected if he was working in some distant part of
the estate. Just where he took his midday repast was
never mentioned, but Ewan noticed that frequently the
Marquis seemed a little the worse for drink, long before
sundown, and assumed that his activities on those days
must have taken him near the Tigh na Broch or even the
Tacksman's Bar.

It was a week or so after he had moved into his very
pleasant room overlooking the Sound of Seileach, that
Ewan found himself, unwillingly, at the centre of the
argument which divided his two good friends.

Dinner had been served in the breakfast room, the
main dining room having been placed in mothballs until
the beginning of the new season. The three of them sat
together at a round table in the bay window, overlooking
the gardens. Despite their obvious efforts to be pleasant
whenever Ewan raised some new topic of conversation,
the bright log fire burning in the grate added little
warmth to the frosty exchanges between George and
Cissy.

'Sheep all down from the hills now?' Ewan enquired of

George. 'It must be a relief to have them under your eye, during the worst of the weather.'

'Yes, they're all tucked up in the glen, alongside McLeod's wee flock. I like to have them protected from the worst of the gales and he's grateful for the bit extra I pay him for the grazing.'

'And where do you propose to graze them next year?' Cissy asked, the apparently innocuous nature of her question belied by the sharpness of her tone.

Recognising undisguised frostiness, McWorter looked inquiringly from one to the other.

'Oh, I'll find somewhere suitable,' George retorted. 'I don't suppose the golf course will take up more than a few acres.'

'What's this about a golf course?' asked the old doctor. 'I've always thought one would be a great asset to the area . . . going to be by the Tigh na Broch, is it? Marty will be pleased with that idea. It's just what he needs to boost the flow of clients into his hotel.'

'Oh, a golf course is just a small part in the great scheme of things,' declared Cissy, 'to turn Eisdalsa into the Disney World of the west coast!' She deliberately ignored George's warning glance. 'It'll fit in nicely,' she concluded, 'alongside the dry ski slope, the roller coaster and Sky Rail – and I don't suppose the noise of power boats in the bay will disturb the golfers too much!'

George was furious. They had agreed they would not air their differences before their guest and here she was deliberately bringing up the subject of the planning application.

'I've agreed to lease a small parcel of land to an

outside company to put in a golf course,' he explained.

'Only thing is, the wealthy punters will be staying at a swish new hotel on Eisdalsa . . . not at the Tigh na Broch or even here,' Cissy interrupted scathingly. 'Once people get the message that the new place has an indoor swimming pool and a glassed-in garden for the wet weather, the chances are poor Marty will lose even the few customers he gets now. Oh, and perhaps George hasn't mentioned that, owing to its size, the new place will be in a position to cut prices and put both Marty and ourselves right out of business.'

'What?' Ewan was laughing at her suggestion. 'You can't be serious?'

'Oh, yes, I can,' she replied, anger getting the better of good manners. 'And that's not the half of it,' she continued. 'There are to be marinas, holiday chalets, car parks all over the place – and a bridge across the sound to Eisdalsa.'

'We don't know that,' George protested. 'They haven't given out the full details yet. Everyone is getting upset about something which may never happen.'

'You wish!'

Cissy would have stormed out then, had it not been for the presence of Doctor Mac. Instead she muttered something about water skiing destroying the fishing and concentrated on her pudding.

Ewan finished his meal abruptly and rose to go.

'Will you excuse me, Cissy? There's a programme on BBC2 I particularly want to see. Might I take my coffee in the lounge?'

'Of course,' she replied, happy to oblige him but not

apologising for her outburst. 'I'll tell Mary.'

He had scarcely settled down to watch his programme when Ewan overheard a muffled conversation outside in the hall and Cissy burst in, followed closely by Alan Beaton.

I'm really sorry to call so late,' the doctor was apologising. 'I had a home visit to make after evening surgery.'

'I thought Thursday was your day off,' said Cissy, remembering Doctor Mac's own routine. She had only met Alan Beaton twice before, once when, in company with Flora Douglas, he had brought Ewan home from the hospital, and the second time a day or two after her guest had been installed at the castle. Used as she was to Dr McWorter, whom she had known for the greater part of her life, she had considered the locum doctor to be extraordinarily young. On those other occasions, Alan Beaton had seemed immature and rather brash and it had taken some convincing from Ewan for her to accept that he was not newly out of medical school. This evening, however, he looked tired and perhaps showed his true age more plainly.

'Is this a professional call, Dr Beaton,' she asked, 'or may I offer you a dram?'

'No . . . and yes, thank you, my lady. I'm really here looking for advice.' This last was directed at Ewan. Cissy poured the whisky and excused herself. 'I can see you two have medical matters to discuss so I'll leave you to see yourself out, Dr Beaton,' she suggested. To Ewan she added, 'I'm rather tired, Dr Mac, I think I'll have an early night. I'll leave you in charge of the whisky decanter!'

'Of course,' he replied while Alan opened the door for her.

'Thanks for the drink,' he said. 'Good night, ma'am.'

Unusually, she did not invite him to use her Christian name.

Alan didn't know Cissy Monteith well, but the strain in her bearing was obvious. The woman looked positively ill . . .

'What's your problem?' Ewan demanded the moment she was out of the way. 'And why *are* you working today? As Cissy said, this should be your day off.'

'It's Janice Pullson. She's not at all well, and to be honest . . . I haven't a clue what's wrong with her.'

He went on to describe events leading up to his most recent visit to their colleague an hour ago.

'What do the blood tests suggest?'

'Nothing as yet. It's going to take a day or two to get a positive identification and meanwhile I'm struggling to keep her hydrated.'

'Hospital?'

'I've been in touch with the local boys but they're reluctant to take her in without a positive identification, in case of cross-infection. The only alternative is an isolation wing in Glasgow, but the thought of being sent so far away seems to distress her more than the condition itself. I've set up a saline and glucose drip and I've got the nurse going in every four hours to keep an eye on it. She's stabilised satisfactorily for the moment, so at present I'm treating the infection with a cocktail of antibiotics and keeping down the fever by all means possible.'

'In the absence of a positive identification, you're doing everything you can,' Ewan assured him. 'Mind you

. . .' he appeared to be thinking out loud '. . . one might hazard a guess. The timing of the fevers is significant. On the dot each time, you say?'

'Regular as clockwork.'

'If this were the Middle East, I wouldn't hesitate,' the old man deliberated. 'You've been out there more recently than I . . . they still live on goat's milk products in Kuwait, I suppose?'

Suddenly it all clicked into place.

'Undulant fever, of course!' Alan exclaimed. 'Out of context like this it never occurred to me, although I have to admit to a nagging suspicion I had seen the symptoms somewhere before.'

'Don't get too carried away,' cautioned the older man. '*Brucellosis melitensis* is specific to goat's milk. Unless Janice has visited the Mediterranean in recent weeks, I don't see where she could have picked it up.'

His words were sufficient to jog Alan's memory. A picture formed in his mind of Janice Pullson at the remote farm on the southern borders of the practice. It was his first day, and he clearly recalled the admirable manner in which his female colleague had handled the many differing facets of the widespread practice. She had an easy rapport with their patients and he recalled how she had accepted, without hesitation, the frothing glass of goat's milk proffered by the patient's eldest child.

'I was with her when she drank some fresh goat's milk,' he confessed, now. 'The little lad who offered it to her was so proud of having done the milking himself, Janice hadn't the heart to refuse it. It never occurred to either of us to question its safety.'

'We mustn't jump to conclusions,' McWorter warned him, 'and self-recrimination at this stage is counter-productive. However, it can't do any harm to get her started on a course of sulphonamides right away . . . you know the dosage?'

'Twelve tablets of 0.2 grams to be taken each day until the fever recedes?' Alan suddenly felt like a student doing ward rounds with his old boss.

'Protein shock therapy might help . . . TAB vaccine . . . what do you think?' McWorter left the ball firmly in his young colleague's court.

Alan agreed. 'I'll get on to it right away,' he said, getting to his feet.

'Was that your only reason for coming?' Dr Mac was clearly disappointed that he was not going to stay longer.

'Oh, no, I meant to tell you,' Alan was struggling into his overcoat as he spoke, 'Flora has found someone to keep house for you . . . Mornings only, Monday to Friday. The lady is willing to start on Monday. What do you say?'

Remembering the uncomfortable atmosphere at dinner that evening, Ewan jumped at the suggestion.

'Marvellous! Do I know her?'

'I couldn't say. She's fairly new to the district . . . lives on Eisdalsa . . . a Mrs Bartlet – Molly Bartlet. She has a couple of kids and her husband's a computer buff. He's also working part-time in the Post Office while Jeanie Clark's in hospital.'

'How is Jeanie?'

'Had her operation last week and by all accounts she's doing fine. I've only been able to speak to the surgeon over the phone, but Willie was at the door a couple of days ago and seemed very much happier about her. She'll be sent back to Oban for a day or two's rest before she is discharged.'

'That's good news. I was sure she needed heroic surgery, you know, but I couldn't persuade her of the urgency of her case. You're obviously more persuasive than I am.'

'I told her you were worrying about her and that if she didn't go to the hospital it might affect your recovery,' he confessed.

The old man nodded. 'You were probably right,' he agreed. Then, as though their earlier conversation had never been interrupted, 'Bartlet, you say? Can't say I recall the family. That can only mean that they're pretty healthy specimens.'

'So, what shall I tell Flora?' Alan demanded, conscious that time was slipping by and it was getting rather late. 'That you'll be home next week?'

'The sooner the better,' the old man confessed. 'Some days you can cut the atmosphere here with a knife. I really don't know what's got into the Monteiths. They never used to be so tetchy with each other.'

Alan Beaton, who knew little of either the Marquis or Lady Christina, was unwilling to voice any opinion.

'I'll call in and collect you on Tuesday after morning surgery,' he suggested.

'I can't wait,' replied Ewan, and felt as excited as a schoolboy, looking forward to the holidays. 'It will be good to get into my own place again, after all this time.'

'Don't think this means you're going back to work,'

Alan warned. One of the reasons for persuading the Monteiths to take Dr Mac as a house guest had been to keep him away from the practice for as long as possible. Alan had seen how the old doctor's eyes had lit up when they'd discussed Janice's fever. He knew it was going to be difficult to keep Ewan out of the surgery once he was back in his own home.

'We'll see how it goes,' Ewan replied, and Alan suspected that he had just added further to his own problems. Flora would never forgive him if, as a result of returning to work too soon, Ewan McWorter were to have a relapse.

'I'll see you on Tuesday, then.' He went to the door.

'I shall want to hear all about this planning proposal when you have time to discuss it,' Ewan called after him.

'The planning application is to be discussed by the Committee in Oban on Wednesday. Flora has asked for leave to be there. I'm sure she will be the better person to fill you in . . . Goodnight.'

Flora was still in the surgery when Alan returned.

'What on earth are you doing here at this hour?' he demanded.

'I had a lot of records to catch up with.' Her explanation convinced neither of them. 'Besides which, I wondered if you might need me for . . . Janice's prescription?'

'I suppose you thought, He's going to ask Dr Mac's advice. Perhaps now we shall be getting somewhere!'

She blushed, unwilling to admit that he was not mistaken.

'Well, as it happens, you were right.'

Alan took down the pharmacopoeia and shuffled through the pages. He found what he was looking for and rapidly wrote out the prescription.

'There, that ought to do it. Since you're here, I can get her started on that tonight. . . the sooner the better.'

She glanced at what he had put down and frowned.

'What's up? Can't you read it?'

'I'm not sure if we have any Rubiazol.' She got up, rooted around amongst the products stacked neatly along the shelves and grabbed hold of a white plastic container with some relief.

'Dr Mac tends to hang on to samples even when there's little chance of their ever being used,' she explained. 'This is the latest sulphonamide compound from these people.' She showed him the bottle. He checked the description against the entry in the pharmacopoeia and nodded.

'That should do the trick.'

Flora too glanced at the entry.

'But it says "useful in cases of Brucellosis". That's rather unusual isn't it? Here in the UK?'

'Not as rare as you might think, in agricultural communities,' Alan replied. 'Anyway, there's a good chance we're right.'

When she gave him a knowing glance, he modified it to, 'Dr Mac was the first to hit on undulant fever, but I was able to confirm that Janice has had some goat's milk recently and it's highly likely it wasn't pasteurised.'

She counted out the correct number of tablets and watched him pack them away into his bag.

'TAB vaccine available?'

She found the necessary phials.

'There's ten in a pack.'

'I'll not need anything like that number, but put it in the box . . . I might think about giving the rest of the family a shot too.' He swayed a little as he fastened the medical case.

'Look at you, you're dead beat,' she observed. 'Why don't I drive you to Janice's and then we'll go back to my house and I'll make us a meal? By the time you've finished, it'll be far too late to get anything at the pub.'

It was a tempting offer. He accepted willingly.

'Shall we go in the Jag?' When she hesitated, he said, 'It's OK, you can still do the driving.'

Alan astonished even himself with this pronouncement. Until now no one else had ever been allowed to drive his precious vehicle. He gained considerable satisfaction from the look of astonishment on Flora's face as he tossed her the keys. By the time they reached the car, she had recovered her composure and climbed into the driving seat as though it was something she did every day of the week. As they set off along the unlit road, with only the occasional lay-by to allow two vehicles to pass, he closed his eyes, although whether this was because he was tired or just too anxious to dare to look where they were going, Flora neither knew nor cared!

'That was delicious.' Alan pushed his plate away, although at least half of what she had cooked remained uneaten. 'I'm only sorry I couldn't do justice to your culinary skills.' His speech was slurred, partly because he was over tired, but, credit must also be given to the half bottle of Australian Merlot he had had no difficulty in consuming as an accompaniment to her steak.

He yawned. 'I'm sorry, I'm afraid I'm not very good company.'

As Flora reached across to collect his plate, their fingers touched lightly. It seemed only natural that he should take her hand and brush the back with his lips.

She withdrew it as though she had touched a hot stove.

'I'm sorry, I only wanted to thank you . . . you've been very kind . . .' his explanation fell upon the empty air. She had made a rapid departure into the tiny kitchenette next door.

'It's very late, perhaps you should be going now.' She made a clatter with the pans and dishes but stopped abruptly when he leaned both hands on the door frame at her back and protested, 'You must let me do the drying up.'

'Oh, no,' she said hurriedly. 'I can manage these few bits and pieces. Please go . . . you need your sleep.'

'I never told you, did I?' he went on, ignoring her protest and picking up a dish towel from the hanging rail. 'Dr Mac is moving back into his own house on Tuesday.' He leaned across her in the narrow space and grabbed a glass which he polished vigorously, then looked about him for somewhere to put it down.

Flora took it from him as their eyes met and placed it on a shelf behind his head. It seemed the most natural thing in the world for him to take her in his arms and for a moment she relaxed against him as though willing him to kiss her. Then, suddenly, she thrust him away, turned to the sink and began fishing in the soapy water for cutlery.

'Please go,' she said. 'This wasn't why I asked you back here tonight. It wouldn't work, can't you see that?'

Her father's warning came back to her. She recalled the stupid rumour he had related to her and went cold suddenly. Was it true after all that Alan was a philanderer, happy to make a pass at any female he happened to encounter?

He let his arms drop to his side, replaced the dish towel carefully on the rail and left.

She listened for the rattle of the latch and heard him close the front door. For some moments she studied her own reflection in the mirror above the sink. It seemed to take a very long time for the single tear to leave the corner of her eye and travel slowly down her scarlet cheek. With a sudden flick of a soapy finger she wiped it away.

Outside, the air was clear and crisp with the first chill of winter. Alan shrugged himself into his warm coat. Not wanting to disturb the neighbours at this late hour, he left the Jaguar parked outside her door and set off at a brisk pace for the other end of the village. There would be no frost, he had been told, because of the proximity of the sea, but the light north-easterly wind made the air feel several degrees below freezing. The heavens, free of cloud, were deepest blue. Bright stars, like lights on a Christmas tree, hung suspended against the velvet vaults of heaven. He turned his back on the harbour, pausing to pick out familiar planets in the sky, and in so doing, saw the light from Flora's cottage reflected in the windows of the café opposite.

He took a step or two back towards her door, wondering if there was something he should have said to put things right between them. He had meant nothing more than to thank her for taking care of him, and now, inexplicably, it had all gone wrong.

'You moved too soon, Beaton, you silly ass,' he told himself.

Tomorrow he would have to find a way to make her understand. He let himself into the little house beside the Post Office, and closed the door.

Flora, having parked her little blue Clio in the supermarket car park, turned into Argyll Square, battling against the north-westerly wind which was blowing up from the harbour.

She was still feeling the embarrassment of having to ask Desmond Bartlet to give her a lift as far as the surgery.

'I drove back with the doctor last night,' she explained, and saw him raise an eyebrow at the sight of the E-type Jaguar still standing at her door. 'I quite forgot I would need to be in early this morning. I'm taking a few hours off later, to go to the Planning Meeting.'

'That's where I'm going now,' said Desmond. 'I'll take you all the way, if you like?'

'Oh, no, thanks all the same,' she had replied. 'I shall have to do an hour or so before the surgery opens. I can leave just in time for the meeting.'

No doubt Alan would be wondering by now how it was she had managed to retrieve her car. Well, let him worry for a bit. The uncertainty would do him good. Things had almost got out of hand last night.

Flora had no intention of once again falling in love with a man she couldn't trust. The first time she had taken that road, it had cost her her job. She had made the mistake of falling for the son-in-law of the company's Chief Executive. Had his wife insisted upon a divorce, he would have been ruined. Once she understood that his marriage and his job were more important to her lover than she was, Flora had the sense to get out . . . fast. Having once burnt her fingers in the fires of passion, however, she was not going to make the same mistake again. She was too comfortable working for Dr Mac to let a casual affair with Alan Beaton threaten her position.

With her head down against the bitingly cold wind and her face wrapped round in a soft, mohair scarf, she hardly noticed the man approaching her until she walked into him full tilt and exclaimed, 'Oh, I beg your pardon!'

'Well, Flora, this is a surprise!'

'Jack?'

'Just arrived yesterday,' he explained, genuinely delighted to see her again.

'What are you doing back here so soon? Where are you staying?'

'Here in town, this time. This is strictly a business call.'

' Nevertheless, you should have let us know you were coming. You could have stayed in the village. Any one of us would have run you in to town if you had asked . . .'

She knew she was rambling unnecessarily. It was the shock of meeting the Australian so unexpectedly.

'Look, I've a meeting to attend this morning,' he told

her, 'but it should be over by about twelve. How about lunch? We could meet at my hotel, it's just along the Promenade. The Gateway . . . do you know it?'

'Well . . . yes,' she answered doubtfully, remembering that she was only here on sufferance and should get back to work as soon as possible. 'But I won't have to be too long, I'm sneaking time off as it is.'

'Shall we say twelve-thirty in the bar?' He glanced at his watch. 'Good Lord, I'm late for my appointment with the solicitor. Sorry, I'll have to go!' He scurried away and she saw him pause before the red sandstone façade of the nineteenth-century building which housed the Bank Chambers. He entered a side door giving access to the upper floors which housed a collection of legal and actuarial companies.

Giving not a moment's thought to what Jack's business might be, Flora turned into Argyll Street and made her way up the hill towards the Council Offices.

The Council Chamber was not the imposing room she had expected. Shrouded in November gloom, which was compounded by the dark wooden panelling on the walls and the inadequate lighting provided by a pair of ugly chandeliers in need of dusting, it was a relic of a bygone age.

Approximately half the space was occupied by a series of huge mahogany tables set around three sides of an open square. Facing these, several rows of cheap, canvas-bottomed stackable chairs were quickly filling up with the members of the public who had come to exercise their democratic right to witness the deliberations of their elected Councillors. Flora spotted her father seated beneath a window, close to one of a number of clumsy old radiators set about the walls, and edged past several of her neighbours to reach him.

'You must have been up early for a change,' she observed, teasing the old man who rarely emerged from his cottage before the post round.

'Don't you have any work to do?' he retaliated good-humouredly.

'Dr Beaton thought that one of us should be here,' she explained. 'Dr Mac is very anxious to know what happens.'

It was an impressive gathering; most encouraging to realise that so many of their neighbours were concerned to hear the planning application discussed.

A seedy-looking official poked his head around the door, made a rapid head count and withdrew hurriedly. Clearly the Councillors had not anticipated such a strong public reaction. Soon more chairs were being man-handled through the door at the back and there was a general closing of the ranks to make way for newcomers. Flora waved to Marty Crane who had just arrived with Willie Clark. While she watched the broad-beamed Celia Robertson attempting rather unsuccessfully to squeeze herself into a space suitable for someone half her size, Flora did not notice the arrival of the town's most senior solicitor, nor did she catch a glimpse of his companion before he sat down and was shielded from her view. Beside her, Bill, deep in argument with Desmond Bartlet, also missed the entry of the principal players in the game which was about to begin.

There was a lot of boring stuff first about some minute

from a previous meeting being incorrect. Flora allowed her attention to be distracted by the collection of old photographs on the walls. Amongst the views of the town dating back to the early 1900s, there was a number of large sepia prints of former Councillors, from the time when Argyll had had its own County Council. Now ruled centrally from Glasgow, the entire Strathclyde region was divided up only for some matters, one of which being local planning concerns. Such things were considered to be better managed at local level, which was all very well except for the fact that most of the finances were in the hands of the Regional Council and there was little money to spare to cover the cost of staff in the local Planning Department. Good, bad or indifferent, the officers had insufficient time to carry out their work effectively. It was all right the elected Councillors demanding explanations as to why this or that had not been done. Colin Campbell, Senior Planning Officer, would have liked to tell Councillor Fergus Montgomery that, try as he might, he could not fit eight days' work a week into five.

The wrangling ceased at last with a sharp reminder to the officers that their efficiency would have to improve.

There followed a list of planning applications for house extensions, provision of access and change of use of premises, until the Chairman came to the last item on the agenda.

'Outline Planning Application for various developments in the villages of Seileach and Eisdalsa. The applicants are Humbert Development Corporation of America.'

There was a general buzz of conversation in the public

gallery. So Marty Crane had been right after all. It had been the landlord of the Tigh na Broch who had first suggested that the person behind the plan might be the garrulous American, Milton Humbert, who had been a guest at the castle for the best part of the month of August. Milton had spent a lot of time interrogating the locals in Marty's bar and it was this which had aroused his suspicions.

'In respect of the public notice published on the eighth of October last, have any objections been received?'

A pale-faced, scared individual, clearly a junior member of the planning team, had been allocated the task of reporting on the sackful of correspondence received, concerning this particular matter. He rose to his feet and in a strangled voice began, 'One hundred and twenty-seven letters have been received, Mr Chairman, thirteen of which are largely in favour of the proposals.'

There was a disturbance amongst the rear seats.

'What's that?' demanded Angus Dewar, indignantly. 'What's that he says about being in favour? Who's in favour?' He looked about him wildly, hoping to catch a guilty look on one of the nearby faces.

'Kindly raise your voice, Mr Pendlebury,' said the Chairman. 'People at the back can't hear you.'

'There are thirteen letters in support of the proposal and one hundred and fourteen opposed for a variety of reasons. Do you wish me to itemize the concerns expressed?'

Clearly shaken by the size of the written response, coupled with the public interest exhibited by the well-filled public gallery, the Chairman felt obliged to give all the views a fair and proper hearing.

'No, I will allow HDC to outline their plans first. I will then accept a statement from the Eisdalsa Island Residents' Action Committee, to be given by their nominated spokesperson, Miss Margaret McColl. After that, I will hear from any public bodies represented and finally a summary of the written objections. I would remind members of the public that their views may be expressed only through their representative. I will, however, allow time, for questions only before a final decision is taken. Now, I believe that HDC is represented by Beresford & McKie, Solicitors?'

Murdoch McKie was a prominent figure in the town, recognised by all those present as the man who, in full Highland dress, each year led the local pipe band through the streets to the Highland Gathering. Today his dress was less flamboyant, the drabness of his dark suit, shiny at pants and elbows relieved only somewhat by a brightly coloured kipper tie which seemed to date from the '60s.

'Mr Chairman, I have the honour to represent the interests of the applicant, Humbert Development Corporation of America . . .'

'Yes, yes,' interrupted the Chairman, impatiently. At this rate they would be having to adjourn the meeting before the business was half completed. 'Please get on with it!'

An injured look spread over McKie's face. He had ambitions to become a Euro MP and did not often get an opportunity to speak before such an active gathering of prospective constituents. He hoped the proceedings would find space in the *Oban Recorder* and searched the room for any sign of a press desk. Satisfied that all was well in that quarter, he proceeded.

'The exact extent of the area under discussion can be illustrated by the map which my client's representative, Mr McDougal, has brought along with him. I will ask him to display this and also show you a series of slides which will illustrate the need for urgent action to preserve particular aspects of the villages which are in imminent danger of total destruction by the forces of nature. I should explain that while it is my client's intention to make substantial changes to the area, there is also concern to retain the historical and natural ambience which make these two villages attractive to tourists. Nothing is planned that would have any major impact upon the unique environment of the slate islands.'

Flora had heard only the first sentence. She strained now to get a look at the lawyer's companion and knew at once that the head and shoulders she was looking at were, indeed, those of Jack McDougal. Her immediate reaction was one of anger and contempt. How dare he inveigle himself into her confidence and that of her father, while all the time plotting to disrupt their lives? She stared angrily at him as he rose to unveil the map attached to a large easel standing in the corner of the room.

Jack pointed out the boundaries of the territory that Milton had leased, albeit on a provisional basis, from George Monteith. It amounted to all the land along the shore which was not already the private property of the householders, from the foot of Smiddy Brae to the base of Caisteal an Spuilleadair and the whole of Eisdalsa

Island, together with the glen which ran up from behind the Tigh na Broch Hotel right to the boundary with Johnstone's famous gardens.

'We feel that a golf course would be an appropriate development in the glen and would want to encourage the local people to use it as well as the anticipated influx of visitors. Additional housing is indicated here and here . . .' He showed two areas of waste ground which were recognised as a local eyesore, one, the site of the skips for collecting waste from the villages and the other a piece of rough ground where caravans often parked, free of charge, during the summer months.

'On the island of Eisdalsa, the plan shows a small hotel to augment the existing holiday accommodation, a marina at the northern end, making use of one of the flooded quarries, and restoration of the harbour for the casual use of passing vessels and for use by the island's permanent residents.' As Jack spoke he pointed out each area under discussion, adding finally, 'As you can see, the design for the hotel has been somewhat modified from the original plan.'

There was no longer any indication of a bridge or any suggestion of a car park on the island. A car ferry, which had been indicated on the earlier plan, seemed to have been removed. On the Seileach side, an area of ground was marked out rather vaguely, as a possible site for caravans and a section of the shore had been allocated for small boats, with a floating jetty as before. There was, however, no longer any suggestion of power boats for water skiing.

It was just as though someone had eavesdropped on

their protest meetings and adjusted the scheme accordingly.

The plan had become innocuous. In some cases the proposals were exactly those which the local people had been demanding for many years. Many of those in the public gallery were clearly relieved at what they had just seen and heard. The sceptics among them, however, suspected that the modifications had been made as a first step towards gaining acceptance. Once the plan was under way, it would be far easier for the developers to persuade the authorities to allow further changes to take place. Bill Douglas listened to the comments of those around him with a sinking heart. His neighbours were suggesting that the plan was much better than they had feared, forgetting that there was no requirement at all for any kind of change to take place, even one. It was the oldest trick in the book to suggest something outrageous was about to happen and then modify it to seemingly reasonable proportions. Those making the decisions were so relieved they were not to be faced with the worst scenario that they readily accepted the lesser of two evils!

Jack spent a few moments flipping through a set of slides depicting the various ruined buildings on the island and outwith Seileach village which had once been associated with the slate industry.

'We feel that these sites are worthy of preservation. They are part of the local heritage and should be restored so that visitors can see them as they were a hundred years ago.'

It sounded good, Bill thought, until you began to wonder what lay behind the notion that old engine sheds and quarry reinforcements were worth rebuilding. What might they be used for? Ice cream parlours? Burger bars? God forbid they should become part of a theme park with women sitting outside the cottages spinning, while their menfolk chipped away at the roofing slates in their reconstructed shelters below the hill!

Jack's explanation came to an end. He thanked the Councillors for attending to his dissertation and resumed his seat. Not once had he shown any sign of recognition of those villagers present in the public gallery.

Murdo McKie was on his feet again.

'As Mr McDougal has explained, the developers wish to exploit the natural advantages of the site for the purpose of encouraging tourism. They make no bones about their financial interest in the enterprise. Their motive is profit. They are however prepared to invest hugely in the area, thereby improving the condition of the present population as well as providing accommodation and jobs for a small army of additional workers. The increased population will bring renewed prosperity to local businesses. We understand, for example, that in present circumstances, the village shop is under threat of closure and that Post Office services may be withdrawn. The school may well be closed within a few years unless there is an influx of younger families. My clients are prepared to assist the Authority in improving roads and services, particularly the means of access to Eisdalsa Island, which has long been a thorn in the Regional Council's side. I feel sure, gentlemen, that when you have studied the proposals at your leisure you will see what a tremendous advantage there will be to the area if my client's proposals are accepted.' He sat down, clearly pleased with what he had accomplished.

'Miss McColl?'

Margaret rose to her feet. She had positioned herself quite deliberately so that she had a good view of both the Councillors around the table and of her adversary. She wanted to gauge the reactions of both to what she had to say.

The anxious expectancy amongst the spectators was quite tangible. The speech she had prepared had been based upon the original plan, not this revised version. How would their spokeswoman cope with so many amendments?

Long years in the courtroom had prepared Margaret McColl for this sort of emergency. As Jack spoke, she had amended her own notes, crossing through whole paragraphs at a time, scribbling alternative arguments as she went. This would not be the careful statement she had laboured over every evening for the past week, but she remained undaunted by the challenge set by the Australian.

'Mr Chairman, we have heard the statement from Mr McKie that this proposal of the Humbert Development Corporation aims to make a profit. Gentlemen, I submit that that is all it is intended to do. We have heard some vague suggestions that this benevolent corporation wishes to invest money in our infrastructure. Of course it does. How else will your building regulators or the Clyde River Authority be satisfied that additional building can take place? There is no sewage treatment works in this area and it is clear that the present method of septic tank drainage will not be adequate to support the additional accommodation proposed. Where is this treatment works to be situated? At any point along the shore line it would be visible and unsightly. On Eisdalsa itself, it would be impossible to find a site which was a sufficient distance from a domestic dwelling.' She quoted the regulations regarding the siting of sewage treatment works.

'Proposals to open the northernmost quarry and turn it into a marina have been sketched in so lightly that it is still unclear how this work is to be carried out. It is the contention of civil engineers who have advised us, that any scheme to open this quarry would require the removal of such large quantities of rock and an opening of such magnitude, facing directly into the teeth of the worst winter gales, that the causeway separating two of the quarries would be under threat. Destruction of that causeway would prevent access to one-third of the total area of the island and in particular that part which, being uninhabited, presents the greatest attraction to tourists. In other words, it is our concern that once the island has been opened up in this way ostensibly for tourism, there will be nothing left for the visitors to admire.

'The section of the island designated for building an hotel, contains relics of the slate industry . . . our unique heritage. Far from preserving these structures, by building over the land on which they stand, the plan threatens to destroy them completely.

'We look at the siting of boat parks, caravan sites, a new hotel, and even the golf course, with concern. What will the first-time visitor see when he reaches the top of Smiddy Brae? It will be a very different landscape from today's. Why should anyone travel great distances to reach this particular place, if it is to look like every other modern sea-side resort anywhere in the world?

'Those who have chosen to live on Eisdalsa or in Seileach, those retired folks who have put their life's savings into their modest properties and younger people who have accepted a lower standard of living quite deliberately so that they might bring up their families within a very special environment, will see all their hopes of a future uncluttered by the trivialities of modern urban environments, shattered. Yes, it is true that village businesses could do with a little more trade. They do, indeed, need better roads, a more frequent bus service, something for the young people to do in the evening . . . but do we see any hope of the village children gaining any benefit from this scheme? Is it not a fact that the plan provides for what can loosely be described as an up-market holiday facility aimed at the very rich? Where do our children fit into that scenario? Will they be invited to swim in the pool or play on the tennis courts? Are they going to have the money to water ski or dive in the bay? Certainly the local fishermen's children will not, because their fathers will be out of work. No mention is made in these proposals of any survey having been taken to measure the impact of all this boating activity upon wildlife in the area. Yet it is for a view of this very wildlife that so many of today's visitors come to our villages. Jobs have been mentioned. What work will there be for local people, unskilled and untrained in today's hospitality industry. We are not talking bed and breakfast and pub lunches here, gentlemen. I challenge Mr McDougal to say just how many local jobs will be created by this development, and what will they be? Cutting grass? Sweeping the streets? Cleaning out the swimming pool? We beg you, gentlemen, to look very closely at every aspect of this plan and to see beyond the immediate temptation offered by the promise of a large injection of money.'

When she came to an end, Margaret sat down quite suddenly, to a round of applause from her colleagues. This display was quickly quashed by the Chairman.

'I would have you know, ladies and gentlemen, that you are here on sufferance and I am empowered to clear the room if such an outburst occurs a second time.'

Margaret was on her feet again in an instant.

'I must correct you, sir,' she protested. 'These people are here of right. That they were carried away in this manner is merely an indication of the strength of feelings in the community. I trust that you will take that into account during your deliberations.'

Bill Douglas nudged his daughter and nodded enthusiastically. 'Let us not forget we are all voters!' he said, in a stage whisper.

Margaret turned to the public seated behind her, willing them to make no further disturbance. She might have been the conductor of an orchestra so meekly did they respond to her commanding look.

The Chairman turned to the young man from the Planning Department.

'We will now hear comment from the interested public bodies . . . Crown Commissioners; Historic Scotland;

Scottish Natural Heritage. Mr Pendlebury?'

'Each of these bodies was contacted, sir. None of them was prepared to offer any opinion one way or the other. The representative from the Clyde River Board is here, Mr Charles Meadows.'

The man was obviously well known to the Chairman for he leaned across to where the River Authority representative sat and asked, 'Anything to add, Charles?'

A trifle flustered, Mr Meadows stood up, cleared his throat nervously and said, 'I have been given no details of proposals for waste disposal in this scheme. My Authority will submit a report when we have seen what is intended.'

The Chairman found this most unsatisfactory. 'My committee will be unable to make a decision on this matter until we have it. Perhaps you will make arrangements to discuss this aspect of the plan with Mr McDougal at the earliest possible date? I can allow only ten days for the submission of your report . . .'

'Really fancies himself does that little sod,' observed Marty Crane to his next-door neighbour. 'Who does he think he is – Hitler?'

'Fact is,' whispered Willie Clark, 'they should have got their act together before this. Ian Campbell's gone quite red.'

'Serves him right,' said Marty, who had no sympathy to spare for Council officials.

'Very well,' said the Chairman. 'We will now hear the points raised by those objecting to the scheme in writing.'

The Planning Officer got to his feet once again. He

shuffled his papers in an irritating fashion and the Chairman began to tap on the desk with his pen. 'Come along, man, we don't have all day.'

'I'm sorry, sir,' mumbled the other. 'I was just trying to get the points into order.'

'Is there anything there which has not been said already?' came the demand.

'No, not really,' was the reply.

'Very well, let the minutes record that one hundred and . . .'

'Thirteen.'

'One hundred and thirteen letters of protest were received. My committee will read them all,' he added for the benefit of the public gallery. Islanders exchanged triumphant looks. Bill Douglas had been right on that score at least.

'I shall adjourn the meeting to be reconvened two weeks from today.' There was some discussion about the actual date. 'At that time I hope it will be possible to announce our decision on this matter.'

The Chairman formally closed the meeting.

Jack hurried out with his solicitor in tow and the man from the Clyde River Board following close behind. As Flora and her father passed by the tight little group outside in the corridor, she paused at Jack's elbow.

'I find I have to return to the surgery right away, Mr McDougal,' she said coolly. Jack, more concerned than he would have them know about his failure to bring the Water Authority on board, was too engrossed to do more than nod an acknowledgement of her snub.

Chapter Fourteen

The flimsy airmail letter bore a Canadian post mark. Cissy slit open the envelope, anticipating an early booking for next season. Christmas was not over yet . . . lucky people, to be able to think about next year's holidays already!

The handwriting was vaguely familiar although, cramped into the limited space allowed, she found it quite hard to read. Her correspondent had been obliged to finish off by writing in the margin and she had to search for the signature.

She had found great difficulty focusing her eyes of late and had given up all but the most essential reading. Promising herself, not for the first time, a visit to the optician, she groped in the desk drawer and finally drew out a large magnifying glass. The signature leapt into focus . . . Pierre d'Orsay! She felt a frisson of excitement at the sight of his name. Try as she might to be professional about their association, she had been aware from the very first moment he had introduced himself of a strong attraction between them. Maybe it was because of the sharp contrast between this gentle, self-effacing man and those others . . . the Swiss, the Germans, and above all that ghastly American. Now, at the sight of his letter, all those earlier feelings returned.

She moved closer to the window and, still using the magnifying glass, read:

My Dear Lady Christina,

I understand that there is a move afoot to develop your beautiful islands into some kind of holiday resort along the American pattern. If true, then this action must be stopped. I have been forced to spend a lifetime living and working in the great conurbations of the world and from time to time have sought an escape in the watering places which trip most readily off the tongue. I can tell you that I found your islands more relaxing and more beneficial to a weary soul than any of those other places. I cannot sit back while anything or anybody threatens to destroy the unique atmosphere of Eisdalsa.

According to the account which I have read, there is likely to be a legal wrangle over proposals to develop the villages. I know only too well that such battles can prove very costly. Should it prove to be necessary to raise money, it would give me great satisfaction to contribute to the defence fund.

Not knowing who is behind the move to oppose the development, I approach the one person from whom I can be sure to obtain an

*objective and unbiased opinion. Please keep
me in touch with events, so that I may be ready
to make my contribution should the need
arise.*

*It is my fondest wish to return to Seileach
Castle at the earliest opportunity. Perhaps you
would be kind enough to pencil in my booking
for August of next year.*

*With all good wishes, I remain, my lady,
your very obedient
    servant,
    Pierre d'Orsay*

Cissy put the letter aside and went to the refrigerator. She
poured herself a glass of ice-cold water and gulped it
down in one draught. She looked at the empty jug in
astonishment. She felt sure she had filled it once already
this morning. Had she really drunk so much? She refilled
the jug from the tap and replaced it. George always preferred iced water in his whisky these days . . . a nasty
habit, Dr Mac called it, caught from their American
guests.

Reminded instantly of Milton Humbert, she picked up
Pierre's letter and read it again.

Who, she wondered, had broadcast the news about the
developers? There were a great many people in the
village who had computers these days. Several did all
their business from home, she knew. With all this talk
about access through the Internet, she supposed someone
must have spread the news that way. Unaware of her
involvement in the deal, Pierre was asking her to co-

operate in a campaign directed against her own husband. Much as she hated the idea of Humbert's taking over large parts of George's estate, she could hardly be seen to be actively working to defeat his interests.

She put the letter aside, tucking it into a section in the bureau where she kept her personal correspondence. There was no call to reply just at the moment. Better to wait until the outcome of the planning meeting was known. She knew that half the village and most of those on the island had attended a meeting a day or two before. Through her daily help, she had learned that the Planning Committee's decision had been postponed for a couple of weeks. Mary had also told her, wide-eyed and conspiratorial, that the spokesman for the developers had been none other than that nice Mr McDougal from Australia. The one who had been staying at Miss Douglas's house.

Cissy had hoped to discuss the plans with someone who knew what was going on but she had spoken to no one in recent days. Even her regular callers seemed to have been avoiding her. Was it possible that their absence was a criticism of George's collaboration with the developers? Had he become an ogre in the eyes of the villagers, as a result of his dealings with Humbert? Flora Douglas must have known what Jack McDougal was up to. If not, she must have been very put out to find that she had been harbouring this schemer. Poor Flora, was she too being ostracised? Maybe Cissy should try to talk to her . . .

She had been feeling rather seedy of late. Perhaps she might make a visit to the surgery, get to know this new doctor a little better and have a chat with Flora at the same time. She lifted the telephone and dialled.

'Cissy Monteith, Flora. How is the waiting room looking this morning?'

'Well, there's just the one patient waiting, but if you are thinking of coming down, don't be too long. Dr Beaton has a heavy list of home visits today.'

By the time Cissy arrived at the surgery that morning, the last patient was just pulling out of the car park. She pushed open the swing doors and approached the glassed-in reception counter. Alan Beaton was sitting at Flora's desk, punching something into the computer.

Flora came to the counter to greet her.

'If you would like to go in, Cissy, Doctor will join you directly.'

Cissy opened the door to the familiar consulting room. Despite its new occupant, it had not changed since her last visit. That must have been two or more years ago. She had scalded her arm lifting heavy cooking pots and Dr Mac had bundled her off to the hospital. It was her dismay at seeing the condition of the tired old Victorian building, looking more like a mental institution than a modern accident unit, that had first got her involved in raising money in a big way. Since then she had enthusiastically put her time and energy, together with the facilities offered by the castle, to very good effect. Now she contemplated her annual fund-raising party with dismay. She thought wearily of the preparations she ought to be making for the event which, last year, had raised over five thousand pounds towards the new hospital. What if, despite all her hard work, the villagers were to shun her party? Maybe, because of George's part in the development plan, all her efforts would be in vain.

If people refused to come along and spend their money, she would never forgive him!

Her angry imaginings had caused her to perspire freely so that when Alan came in and sat down, the first thing he asked was, 'Do you find the room hot?' He was reluctant to address her as 'my lady' again, yet lacked the confidence to call her by her Christian name.

'Pardon? Oh, no . . . thank you. I was just having some rather angry thoughts.'

'Not about us, I hope? I've been as quick as I can.'

He gave her a glance which reminded her of a scolded dog.

'Oh, no, of course not,' she said, and then, seeing his broad smile, she laughed.

'I'm afraid all this trouble about the future of the villages is getting me down. I feel like piggy in the middle.'

'What can I do for you, my . . .?'

'Please, call me Cissy,' she interrupted. 'Everybody does. These outmoded titles are so pompous, don't you think? Cissy or Mrs Monteith will do just as well.'

'Cissy it is then.' Alan smiled, relieved to have got that out of the way. 'What can I do for you?' He reached for her file. It was a very slim one.

'I have been feeling generally under the weather lately,' she told him. 'I'm troubled with my sight . . . can't manage to read anything more than a newspaper article these days.'

'Well,' he commented, shuffling through her notes, 'you don't appear to have caused Dr McWorter much grief over the years.' He cast a glance over the list of visits she had made. There was reference once or twice to infertility problems and menstrual difficulties. She had never managed to conceive and this problem had been the subject of the majority of visits made over recent years.

'I see you have been a patient of Dr Mac's since you were a girl,' Alan observed. 'Were you born in these parts?'

'As good as. My parents came to farm on Lunga when I was just a wee tot. I went to the village school until I was eleven but then I was sent to England to school . . . St George's, Ascot, do you know it?'

He shook his head. 'I was at school in Surrey, myself. A college which provided education for the sons of doctors. One of these self-perpetuating situations, I'm afraid.'

'You sound as though you might have wanted to do something else?'

'There was never any question of it,' he replied. 'Male members of my family have been doctors for generations.'

It was true. It had never occurred to him that he would become anything other than a doctor.

'It's probably what we do best,' he decided. 'My great-grandfather was the medical officer in the quarries here, during the late 1800s.'

'Was that why you came here to work?'

'Oh, no! That was sheer chance. I knew nothing of Eisdalsa, other than a few vague family references to the place. It wasn't until I arrived here that I discovered the

Tigh na Broch was once my grandfather's home. I took this post while looking for a move back into the Health Service. I've been abroad, you see, and if you once leave the confines of the NHS, it's not all that easy to get back in.'

'Like having a black mark against your name?'

'Something like that.'

While they spoke, Alan had been observing her closely and his practised eye had registered a number of indications about his distinguished patient's health. She peered at him as though having difficulty focusing. Her eyes were slightly bloodshot and, something which had struck him at their previous encounter, despite the carefully applied make-up, her skin was dry and almost grey in colour.

Without further ado, he popped a thermometer into her mouth and took her wrist lightly between his fingers.

Unable to speak, she followed his actions with her eyes. Having measured her pulse carefully, he read the thermometer and grunted in a manner she found alarming. Fearful now that he might actually be finding something wrong, she said nothing while he measured her blood pressure and then asked to listen to her heart and lungs.

'How long have you had this trouble with your eyesight?' he asked.

'I don't know. It's gradually got worse over the last few weeks.'

'Do you find that you are drinking more than usual?'

She thought about the jug of iced water and realised that she had indeed been drinking large quantities of water daily, for some considerable time.

'Anything else unusual happening?' he asked, casually.

'I seem to lose my temper rather more readily than I used to and often feel tired and depressed.' She found herself confessing to weeping at the least provocation, something she clearly found very embarrassing.

'I'm going to take a sample of blood, but I shall need it first thing in the morning after you've starved for a bit. Do you think you could come in tomorrow before the surgery opens?'

'What is it you suspect?' she asked him, anxiously. With all their other worries this was hardly the time for her to be ill.

'You may have a touch of diabetes.'

'Diabetes!' Now she was thoroughly alarmed.

'It's a possibility. How old are you?' He studied her notes. 'Forty-nine!' He sounded surprised. Despite the fact that she was a little rundown at present, she was a remarkably fine-looking woman for her age.

'Look, there's nothing to get too worried about,' he tried to reassure her. 'It's not the dread disease it's so often painted. Once identified, it is normally a simple process to get things under control.'

'But don't you have to have injections?' she demanded. 'And isn't there a tremendous fuss about food and so on?'

'Not necessarily,' he assured her. 'A sensible diet and oral medication is usually sufficient these days. The tests take only a day or two so if we can get the blood sample off right away, I can probably begin treatment in a day or two.'

'Thank you, Dr Beaton.' Cissy adjusted her clothes and rose to leave. At the door she hesitated, then turned back to him.

'I'm afraid I was rather short with you the other night. I do apologise.'

He shrugged off her apology.

'It was an inconvenient time to call,' he replied. 'I had been rather taken up with Dr Pullson's case, and of course her absence from the practice has given me extra work.'

'How is Janice?'

'Getting better . . . now we have confirmed the cause of her illness.'

'Did Dr Mac came up with the solution then?' Cissy asked, suddenly smiling for the first time that morning. The effect was electrifying.

He grinned in response. Everyone had this unfailing faith in McWorter. He wondered if there would ever come a time when patients viewed his capabilities in the same way.

'Let's say two heads were better than one!' he told her. 'Now, if you will excuse me, I have patients waiting.'

She went out into the reception area where she found Flora hard at work at her computer.

'Did you go to the meeting at the Council Offices?'

Flora sighed. Turning away from the screen, she resigned herself to the interruption. Cissy Monteith was a dear friend but just at the moment, Flora had no desire to give Alan Beaton any reason to reprimand her. As she saw him emerge from his consulting room, she said, rather more loudly than was necessary, 'Yes,

I've given Dr McWorter all the details. Perhaps you would like to ask him about it? I'm sure he would welcome a visit.'

They both watched Alan pass through to the main door.

As he opened it he called back to Flora, 'You know the order of visits. If there are any emergency calls, you can reach me on Dr Pullson's number, about twelve o'clock.'

He was gone. Flora found herself gazing at the door through which he had just left.

'Flora, do you think George was wrong to lease that ground to Milton Humbert?' Cissy demanded, ignoring the obvious tension between Flora and the doctor.

'I'm sure he had his reasons,' Flora, muttered forcing herself to attend to Cissy. She had no wish to be drawn further into this argument which had already caused her so much grief

'They're clear enough,' Cissy confessed. 'We need the money. If we don't raise some cash soon, the roof to the main hall is going to collapse.'

'Aren't there grants for that sort of thing?' Flora had little sympathy to spare for the aristocracy when they cried poverty. What they usually meant was that all their assets were frozen ones. They had no idea what it was to have so little cash it was a toss up between paying the rent or giving the kids their school dinner money.

'One might think so,' said Cissy. 'George has made enquiries, but it seems that that sort of money is given only to charitable organisations. Ours is a profit-making concern and therefore not eligible for help.'

'What, not even as a listed building?'

'Oh, I'm sure Historic Scotland would help if they could, but they don't have that kind of money to spend. Anyway, not everyone admires Seileach Castle. It's not the most attractive building, you must admit.'

'No, but it has such important historical connections and it is central to the history of the slate industry.'

'Anyway, the roof won't wait while the powers that be deliberate. We need big money and we need it now.'

'And forget the village,' Flora observed, unconvinced.

'You know it's the last thing I would wish, to see the village damaged in any way,' Cissy protested. 'I've tried to reason with George but he is determined to proceed with the deal. HDC has already taken an option on the land they want.'

'To be honest, Cissy, I can't see a lot to complain of in the plan . . . not the one put forward at Wednesday's meeting anyway,' Flora confessed. 'I've seen how people are forced to scrape a living here and I can't fault any move that offers them better prospects of employment. The initial plans have been modified considerably, as a matter of fact. They are now talking about a twenty-bed-roomed hotel on the island, a golf course and marina. There are certainly suggestions for other developments at a later date but no doubt they can be fought over, one by one. There was so little to argue about on Wednesday that I can't see the Council turning them down.'

'What did the protesters have to say? Were they even allowed to say anything?' Cissy asked.

'One person was allowed to represent the residents and the Eisdalsa lot chose their retired lawyer, Margaret McColl. She made an eloquent speech about the environment and the effect upon the value of privately owned properties but one could see from the Councillors' faces that they were not convinced of the argument. The promise of investment and jobs is what buys votes here, as anywhere else.'

'So what happens next?'

'The verdict will be given in a fortnight's time. If it goes against the villagers they'll probably call another meeting. They are determined to fight to the bitter end over this.'

Cissy didn't know whether to be pleased or not. She didn't want the coastline spoiled but she didn't wish to perpetuate her feud with George. If the Council would only turn down the proposal, everything would be all right.

A smaller number of islanders was present when the Planning Committee met again, two weeks later. On this occasion, the representative of the water and sewage disposal authority came well prepared. He described the necessity of improving water supplies to meet the increased demands and explained the need for a much improved waste-disposal system. 'My Authority has no budget available for a major overhaul of these proportions,' he concluded, 'and I am therefore instructed to refuse support for the development as it stands. My principals are willing to look at a modified scheme, in keeping with the present provision.'

'There goes the hotel on Eisdalsa,' Marty whispered to Kirsty Brown. They were both uncertain of their response to the introduction of competition with their own small enterprises. Humbert's development would bring greater numbers of visitors to the district, but would they patronise the existing businesses? Neither Marty nor Kirsty believed that they could sustain a battle with a giant corporation undercutting prices at every level and offering much better facilities.

'There is the argument that visitors might wish to experience a village pub, rather than use some swish ultra-modern bar,' Marty had suggested hopefully, but they both knew that they were clutching at straws.

'If the enterprise doesn't get underway as a rousing success within two years, we shall all go to the wall,' Kirsty had assured him. 'Who do you imagine will want to come here with all the building works going on? That's going to put paid to the first year. After that, we re going to have to rely on Humbert's being a success because by then we shall have lost all our regular clients.'

The Chairman was now summing up the Committee's decision.

'We are not averse to change,' he began, 'everyone knows that things cannot stand still for ever and we would wish to encourage any proposal which offers the prospect of new employment in this area. We are, however, constrained by two matters. There is a great weight of public opinion against the extent of the proposed changes and, as you have just heard, the Clyde River Board cannot allow any development which strains their resources beyond the limits of public health and safety. We are, however, satisfied that two of the proposals may go ahead as enhancements to the tourist facilities offered in the area. The first is the golf course which we can see as being of benefit to the local residents as well as an attraction for visitors. Included in this is the provision of a club house as described in a detailed plan supplied retrospectively by the developers. The second proposition, to open up one of the quarries on Eisdalsa for the provision of a marina, together with a small utility building for the use of visiting yachtsmen, is agreed.'

There was a moment's complete silence while these words sank in. The islanders looked at each other in bewilderment. Their most decisive argument against the development had been the preservation of this particular quarry, their fears for the local wildlife and for the access to that part of the island that was most appreciated by visitors.

Most disturbing to Flora Douglas was the inscrutable look on Jack McDougal's face. His scheme had fallen at the first hurdle and yet he did not seem unduly put out. There was more to this decision than met the eye. What were they up to? As the meeting broke up, she turned around to hear her father voicing her own suspicions.

'One foot in the door is all they need,' he said. 'Now they can get started on these two projects, while they go to appeal over the rest. Mark my words, we haven't heard the last of this. What they can't achieve in one fell swoop, they will accomplish by stealth. I know how these big boys work. We've got to see to it that they get no further with their artful scheming.'

Since midday, Rob Fullerton's children had been running around the island carrying hurriedly constructed banners reading 'No invasion'; 'No hotels for us Mr Humbert'; and 'Yanks go home!' Their parents made no attempt to fetch them in when Jack McDougal arrived with a second gentleman.

Both were inappropriately dressed for the island, in dark lounge suits and smart shirts and ties. At first sight of them, Desmond Bartlet's son, Andy, rushed inside, slamming the door behind him and shouting, 'Look out, Mummy, Mormons!'

Jack carried in one hand an expensive leather brief case while in the other he held what appeared to be a solid wooden box. The second man bore on his shoulder a number of lengths of timber. Their passage was marked by small knots of islanders who gathered together to stare after them in silence as they passed by.

The two men walked to the far side of the island. There they spent a long time measuring up the ground around the quarry and erecting their posts with the aid of a theodolite.

Bill Douglas and Rob Fullerton, who had climbed to the top of the hill to observe their activities, were reminded of the way in which a wild animal marks his territory by spraying points on the boundary with his own urine. By establishing the levels for the initial work to be done on the rim of the quarry, Jack Douglas was quite deliberately laying claim to Humbert Development Corporation's right to that part of the island.

The sight aroused extraordinary passions in both men. Captain Billy spoke for them both when he uttered a very seaman-like oath and declared, 'If those bastards get away with this, it will be over my dead body!'

Jack and his companion were unaccustomed to such heavy work. Inappropriately dressed on a warm afternoon, they returned to the harbour tea room, alongside the Tacksman's Bar, literally gasping for a cup of tea. In normal circumstances, the tea room closed shortly before dusk every day throughout the visitor season. The sun was still high in the heavens when Jack and his companion arrived to find one last group of tourists seated outside in the sunshine, lingering over their tea and scones. The two men pushed past a scattering of empty chairs and tables, clearing their passage to the door, but as Jack reached out for the handle, the cardboard sign which hung in the window was abruptly turned from OPEN to CLOSED.

The message was quite clear. Jack McDougal was no longer welcome here on Eisdalsa.

Chapter Fifteen

Coming up to Christmas there was a general air of euphoria in both villages. On Eisdalsa Island the party roster went up as usual. Because each household wanted to throw a party and hoped that everyone else would attend, it was normal to book the date, thereby ensuring there would be no clashes. From Christmas Eve until New Year's Day, there would be a function of one kind or another every night.

The Tacksman's Bar was full most evenings now, and in the absence of police supervision after the last ferry had run, Kirsty allowed the merrymaking to go on well into the early hours. Marty Crane, obliged to observe the licensing rules more rigidly, concentrated on making his Christmas bonus through his restaurant which did a roaring trade right up until Christmas Eve.

If the threatened developments were mentioned by the revellers at all, it was to make some derisory joke about foreign interlopers or to congratulate themselves upon their stand against bureaucracy and the powerful barons of industry.

Jack McDougal remained in town during this period,

not wishing to antagonise the locals at the Tigh na Broch any more than he had to. Now that he was no longer obliged to wear the disguise of an impecunious traveller, he was at least able to enjoy the comforts of the one five-star hotel in the area.

On a day when Flora had taken leave to do her own and her father's weekly shopping, he chanced to see her on the South Quay where the fishing boats landed their catch. Flora would have preferred to do all her shopping in the supermarket, but Bill insisted that his fish come straight off the local boats, unfrozen, and she was obliged to make this unwanted and time-consuming detour to buy it.

Jack hung about while she completed her transaction at the market stall and then approached her.

'Flora, I waited for you after the meeting. I thought we had a date.'

'That was before I discovered I had been harbouring a super spy in my loft!' she told him bluntly. 'Anyway, I cancelled the appointment. I felt sure you understood my message.'

'I hung around for a while anyway, in the hope that you might change your mind.'

'You could hardly expect me to carry on as though nothing had happened. As it was I found myself the subject of some pretty unpleasant comments on account of you and your activities.'

'Yes, I suppose you would be suspected of being involved. I hadn't thought of that.'

'I'm afraid there were a lot of things you never thought about,' she told him, sharply.

'Look, it's too cold to hang about out here,' he insisted. 'Won't you come and have a cup of tea in the hotel? There's something I have to explain.'

She was cold and the idea of a warming drink in the comfort of the Gateway's superior lounge appealed greatly.

'Oh, very well,' she said. 'I can't stay long. It's getting late and I hate driving down that narrow road in the dark.'

They seated themselves in a corner of the lounge and while Jack ordered tea and scones, they talked about trivial matters. While Flora poured the tea, he apologised again for deceiving her about the purpose of his stay in Seileach.

'I was sent here by my employers,' he explained, 'to do a feasibility study. My boss had come across the place during the summer and my assignment was to assess the chances of obtaining planning consents to build a holiday complex. So far as I was concerned it was just another project of the kind we carry out all the time around the globe.'

'But you must have known there would be opposition to this type of development . . . after all, your own people were islanders. Or was that just another lie?' she wondered, still angry.

'Oh, no! That's absolutely true, although it was only when I began my researches that I discovered my family originated right there on Eisdalsa. I gave your father the description passed down to me by my family and he identified my great-grandfather's croft.

'I promise you, I had no intention of deceiving you, Flora. The nature of my work means I'm often obliged to do it rather secretively, so as not to distort the evidence I'm collecting. I hope you can understand . . .'

'Did you, for one moment, consider the effect that your plans might have on those of us already living in the villages?' she asked. 'People bought their houses at Seileach and on Eisdalsa because they liked the place as it was. They don't want to live in the middle of a theme park! Not everyone gets a kick out of seeing the peace of the countryside sacrificed to the whims of mindless fun seekers and those who are ready to make a fast buck out of the common man's insatiable craving for novelty.'

He winced at the harshness of her words but before he could counter her somewhat exaggerated picture of his proposal, she went on. Her pent-up anger at his betrayal, left to fester in her mind since the day of the meeting, now burst forth in a flurry of accusations.

'You have picked on one of the most beautiful bays in Scotland, which in any one year is visited by no more than a few fishing boats and the occasional cruising yacht. The reefs around the islands, which are teeming with life, are disturbed by nothing more than the odd group of divers who visit once or twice a year on their holidays and the occasional lone individual who is probably a local photographer. The quarrymen's cottages have changed little outwardly since the day they were built and their very compactness ensures the overall population will never overwhelm the resources available. Now you come along, with your scheme to increase the number of visitors tenfold. You plan a hotel on Eisdalsa which will demand more water than the total consumed by the two villages put together; you intend to increase traffic on our single road, sufficient to justify a motorway and promptly decide your hotel patrons will need a car ferry so they can keep an eye on their expensive vehicles while they roam the two square miles of wilderness which will be left outwith Eisdalsa village and the harbour. No doubt your city-bred clients will be looking for well-lit paved walkways instead of rough pathways, trimmed lawns and carefully tended flower beds where harebells, angelica and coltsfoot now grow. Sea birds nesting on the cliffs, otters and other wild creatures whose safe haven Eisdalsa has been for nearly a century, will be endangered by their ill-behaved pets, allowed to roam the hill, unfettered, while seals will be driven away and the reefs destroyed by high powered speed boats tearing around the bay from morn 'til night!'

'Hold on!' He stopped her flow of words in full spate. 'The Council has turned down the proposal for a hotel,' he reminded her. 'In fact, they have left so little of the scheme unaltered, I doubt if my company will want to proceed at all. The most expensive item was always going to be the conversion of the quarry into a marina. The idea was to lure the yachtsmen in with the promise of a night or two's comfort and entertainment in the hotel, particularly during spells of bad weather. Without the hotel, the marina will have no more to offer than cheaper moorings anywhere along the coast.'

Flora still regarded him with suspicion.

'If you're expecting them to give up on the idea, why are you still hanging around?'

'I'm working on a simplified plan, in close co-operation with the Building Control Officer,' he told her. 'When the costings have been completed and our ideas modified to the satisfaction of the Planning Committee, I shall take the whole thing back to my Board of Directors. I'm certain they'll turn it down as uneconomic.'

'But you've already spent a lot of money. Surely HDC will want to see something in return for its investment?'

'A drop in the ocean . . . nothing more than a tax-deductible blip in the Corporation's finances,' Jack assured her in such a way that she believed him.

She poured more tea into both their cups and stirred her own thoughtfully for a few moments.

'The kind of development you envisage might just as easily have been carried out somewhere where there would be no public to raise objections. Perhaps you should take over a deserted township somewhere . . . Lord knows there are enough of those up in the north.'

He appeared to take her suggestion seriously. 'Do you know of anywhere with natural attributes similar to those of Eisdalsa?'

'Not off hand . . . but I'll be only too happy to act as a guide if you want to take a look.' Flora smiled and he suspected she was only joking.

'That's a date!' he exclaimed, taking up her challenge.

Flora coloured, hoping fervently that he was not being serious.

'Will you still be here for New Year?' she asked now, hurriedly changing the subject.

'I'm not sure,' he told her. 'I may have to go south to meet Mr Humbert in London . . . I believe he'll be passing through on his way to Australia for the holiday period.'

'Lucky man.' She glanced out of the great bay window and shivered at the sight of a bleak December sky from which the light was already fading.

'I intend to try to persuade him to give up the idea of any appeal against the Council's decision,' Jack confessed.

'I wonder why he picked on Eisdalsa for his project?' she mused. 'He must have known people would be against it.'

'I don't think you can have met my boss when he was here,' Jack laughed cynically. 'Milton Humbert's rather like a spoilt child. He only ever wants something which is dear to the heart of someone else. At the first hint of opposition he'll dig in his heels and fight to get it away from them.'

'He sounds like a monster,' Flora said, laughing for the first time. How different she looked when her eyes sparkled with merriment like that. He noticed her cheeks colouring under his admiring gaze and quickly looked away.

Convinced at last that he was being absolutely honest with her, Flora nodded, glanced at her watch and exclaimed, 'Oh, dear, I hadn't realised it was getting so late. I shall have to go, or I shall miss the last ferry to Eisdalsa. I have to deliver Dad's groceries . . . he'll be waiting for his supper!'

When she stood up and began struggling into her coat, Jack leaped to her assistance. In that brief moment of contact, she was aware of a curious frisson of excitement.

Quickly drawing away from him, she thanked him for the tea.

'If you *are* going to be around at New Year,' she suggested, 'maybe we should see it in together? I don't suppose you have ever experienced a real Hogmanay?'

'No, I'd like that . . . very much. As soon as I've seen Milton, I'll let you know what's happening.'

He escorted her to the door and gazed thoughtfully after her receding figure. He followed her progress as she darted between late-afternoon shoppers, until at last she rounded the corner and was out of sight.

'Oh, Flora,' he sighed. 'I just hope I'm right about Milt giving up!' Despite his promise to speak to Milton, he could not as yet, forgo any opportunity to further his cause. He must tackle the doctor, the first chance he had.

Alan had remained neutral during Jack's dispute with the villagers so that when, on a particularly bleak December day, he and the Australian met by chance in the High Street, he readily agreed to accompany Jack to the nearest bar for a pint of beer and a sandwich.

Over their simple lunch, the Australian enquired after the old doctor whose dramatic heart attack had been responsible for Alan's arrival at Seileach.

'Dr McWorter's quite well,' Alan told him, 'raring to get back to work as a matter of fact. I myself don't think he's ready yet, and with his part-time assistant still recovering from illness, I can't contemplate leaving him on his own now. He'll do some consultations after the holiday, but I shall continue to make the house calls for a while yet.'

'What of the future?' asked Jack. 'Is there any chance of you taking over the practice if the old man decides to retire?'

'No chance whatsoever. I don't have that sort of money to invest and I'm unlikely to make enough out of the work here to be able to pay off a loan.'

'I suppose it would be a very different story if there was an influx of additional residents and an increase in the number of tourists?'

'No doubt about it,' Alan agreed, 'but in that case there would be a queue of doctors wanting to take it on and I would come way down in the pecking order.'

'Oh, I don't know. It's possible Humbert's would consider buying out the practice from the NHS and putting in its own private medical service with a properly equipped clinic. Would you be interested then?'

Alan regarded him curiously. Already familiar with the idea of private medicine arranged by large corporations for their own staff, he did not find the suggestion extraordinary.

'Is this some kind of an offer?'

'Might be,' Jack told him. 'It all depends.'

'On what?' Alan demanded.

'The outcome of the Public Enquiry . . . if there should be one,' he added hastily, realising that Flora might already have assured the villagers there was to be no further action on the main proposals.

He slanted the discussion away from ownership of the practice.

'I suppose there are times when a doctor is called out in stormy weather or at night?' he asked, casually.

'Yes, although generally people situated in remote places, particularly the small islands where there are perhaps only one or two families, are in direct contact with the coastguard and are more likely to call out the lifeboat or a helicopter to bring them in to the hospital. I've been lucky so far.'

'But if you did have to go, say, to Eisdalsa or Lunga, how would you get there in the middle of the night?'

'Using the ordinary ferry boat, of course. The men are expected to be on call for emergencies.'

'What! An open motor boat? You can't be serious! Surely you wouldn't take sick and injured people off in that?' Jack thought of the little boat in which he had crossed to Eisdalsa on a choppy sea in October. He shuddered to think what the crossing might be like in January.

'If necessary, yes. There's a stretcher and an invalid chair in both ferry waiting rooms for that purpose. They are used occasionally, particularly in the winter months. Of course, if I should consider it necessary, I would call out the helicopter or the lifeboat, even to Eisdalsa.'

Jack made a mental note of what the doctor had told him but not wishing to alert Alan to the fact that his enquiry was anything more than idle curiosity, he rapidly changed the subject.

'I'm hoping to be around to experience your Scottish New Year,' he said. 'Since I was a little nipper I've always heard about Hogmanay from the old folks. They tried to make an occasion of it at home always, but a barbecue in midsummer in the middle of a searing hot desert is not quite the same, I suspect. It seems a great pity to be here alone, and unable to join in the fun.'

'I'm told that the Monteiths are throwing a charity "do" at the castle,' Alan told him. 'Flora was talking about it only yesterday. She seems to think it's our duty to go . . . it's in support of the new hospital. Why don't you join us?'

'Oh, I wouldn't want to play gooseberry, mate!' Jack laughed, but he was pleased with the invitation.

'Actually, you'd be doing me a favour,' Alan assured him. 'The lady is a great believer in safety in numbers, if you see what I mean.'

Jack knew exactly what he meant. From the start he had been attracted to Flora Douglas and, given half the chance, would have taken full advantage of his position as her lodger. Not once during the time he had spent in her house had she given the slightest indication that she was similarly disposed towards him.

'Well then, provided I'm back from London in time, I'll be glad to join you,' he agreed. 'Thanks very much.'

'I'll ask Flora to get our tickets. I believe they're on sale at the Post Office in Seileach.'

'No, don't do that,' said Jack. 'Let me pick them up. I could do with an excuse to make a visit to the village . . . mend a few fences . . . you know how it is. I'm afraid I upset some of the people down there.'

'I think you did give them a bit of a shock,' Alan agreed, 'but no one's particularly concerned about the project as it stands now . . . except perhaps the real stalwarts, like Bill Douglas and Miss McColl. The small business owners seem to be quite keen on the idea of a golf course. There's even talk of an annual event, something to bring in the really class players.'

Jack grinned, delighted to learn that his strategy was paying off.

'Trouble with that kind of thing,' he suggested disarmingly, 'is that there are not enough places for people to stay. During an event lasting several days, they're not going to want to drive twenty or thirty miles a day in order to reach the course.'

'Maybe not,' said Alan, laughing. 'Just as well, really. It will leave all the more time for the rest of us to play!'

'You coming along to the Tigh na Broch this evening?' George asked. 'We don't seem to have been anywhere together for ages.'

Cissy popped a pill into her mouth and washed it down with the last of her coffee. She had been careful to stick to her new regime ever since Alan had confirmed she did indeed have a mild form of diabetes. She adjusted the glasses she was still not properly accustomed to wearing, and smiled at him.

After the initial shock of learning that she suffered from a disease which was commonly considered to make dramatic changes to one's lifestyle, she had been agreeably surprised at how easily she had slipped into the routine Alan had prescribed for her. What was more, after only a week or two she felt infinitely better in herself and now that she had been to collect her spectacles, actually read comfortably again, while the television was no longer an irritating jumble of half-seen images.

George had been alarmed to hear of her condition and had, without her knowledge, made an appointment to see

Alan himself to get the facts of her case. The thought that his wife might be a permanent invalid had stopped him in his tracks. He realised, quite suddenly, how he'd been wasting precious time they should have been enjoying together. Even when Alan assured the Marquis that his wife was in no danger, he was still solicitous for her health and enquired several times a day how she was feeling.

Cissy, enjoying this return to something like normality in their relationship, did not like to tell him that his constant enquiries irritated her. It was better than being ignored, as she had been for weeks past. Perhaps if she went out with him tonight, he would see that her condition was indeed under control.

'Do you know, I think I will come with you,' she decided. 'I won't be able to take any alcohol, of course, but it will be a change to see a few people and it'll be an opportunity to sell some tickets for the New Year's party.'

Jack arrived at the Post Office just before the mail van. Desmond was obliged to deal with the driver before he could turn his attention to the Australian.

'Well, Mr McDougal?' he asked in a rather unfriendly manner, indicating that Jack was not a welcome customer.

'Good morning,' he replied pleasantly, ignoring the rebuff. 'I understand I can get tickets for the New Year's Eve party at the castle here?'

Tickets had been slow to sell. People were still smarting from the manner in which George Monteith had put them all under threat a few weeks before. Nevertheless, they were aware that it was Cissy and her committee who were trying to raise money for the hospital, not George Monteith, and were beginning to come around, slowly. Desmond wished he could tell this pariah that the tickets were all sold out, but it wasn't true and Cissy Monteith would be annoyed if word got back to her that he had refused to supply someone. Desmond liked to air his opinions rather volubly, but he was always careful not to antagonise people of influence.

'I wouldn't have thought a charity ball was quite your kind of thing,' he grumbled, hoping to put Jack off. Cissy's other patrons would surely resent the Australian's presence at their party.

Jack, sensing the man's reluctance to serve him, did not press his request just for the moment. Instead, he took a different tack.

'Can a small business like this give a young guy like yourself, a satisfactory income?' he asked, in that direct and slightly offensive manner of his.

Desmond immediately leaped to his own defence.

'In no way!' he declared. 'I'm only doing this on a temporary basis . . . helping out while the postmistress is on sick leave. I happen to be in the happy position of being able to adjust my working hours to fit this in as well.'

'Oh, what do you do for a day job then?'

'You probably wouldn't be aware of the business I'm in . . . I design web sites for the Internet.'

'Really?' Jack feigned ignorance of the up and coming world of computer technology.

'Don't suppose there's too many people using the

Internet, Down Under?' Desmond suggested.

Jack bristled at that. Who did this Pommy think he was? Talking about Jack's fellow countrymen as though they were a bunch of hayseeds.

'Oh, I think you'll find there are one or two folks down there who surf something other than Bondi Beach,' he suggested. 'As a matter of fact, I spotted the Eisdalsa web site when I was back home. It was well done, but full of irregularities, of course. Whoever did it should have got his facts right first. You don't happen to know who it was, do you?'

Desmond wasn't too sure how to take the question. Was McDougal fishing around because he intended to take legal action?

'Might have been any of a number of folks,' he answered, vaguely. 'Loads of people are on line in these parts.'

'It's just that my company will be looking for a decent web site . . . for the golf course and the marina,' Jack added, hastily. 'Since we are promising more jobs for local people, this seemed a good place to start.'

Desmond was instantly on the alert. If there was real work to be had, his idealistic condemnation of Humbert's development plans could always be reversed.

'I might be able to help you there,' he suggested. 'If you'd like to come over to my place, I live on Eisdalsa, I can show you a few of the things I've done.'

'I might just do that.' Jack did not want to show too much enthusiasm at this stage. Like playing a game fish, he thought to himself. Just a tickle at first then a gentle pull or two before the final strike!

'I'm home every afternoon after two o'clock,' Desmond told him. 'I close the Post Office at twelve-thirty during the winter season.'

'Don't let me forget what I came for.' Jack pulled him up abruptly. 'Three tickets for the Charity Ball.'

Desmond, without further hesitation, delved into the recesses of the counter cupboard and came up with a wad of tickets. He peeled off three. 'Sure you can't stretch to a fourth?' he asked only half humorously. 'Someone will be without a partner.'

'Quite sure, thank you,' Jack replied, sharply. If Desmond was fishing to know who was going with him, let him buy a ticket and come and see for himself.

There had been few words spoken as they drove between high banks and around blind bends in the pitch blackness. It was as though their entire world was encompassed by the pool of bright light created by the headlamps of their four by four.

George turned off the road, swung across the cattle grid and up the steep slope to park in front of the hotel. He leaped smartly down from the Discovery's lofty seat and turned up the collar of his storm proof jacket, bowing his head to the wind blowing straight in from the Atlantic. By the time he had reached Cissy's door, she had it open and was already struggling to reach down from the high step.

'These vehicles were never made for decorous descent,' she laughed, shivering as the gale struck her in the face. He caught her in his arms, holding her gently as though she were fragile enough to break in his grasp.

Standing there together in the dark, with the wind howling in the sycamore branches overhead, he kissed her as fervently as he had ever done, hard on the mouth, making her gasp for breath.

'I'm sorry, love,' he said, 'I've been such a fool. I should have talked to you first before I committed us to all this hassle.'

She smiled up into his wide-set, clear grey eyes in which sparkled reflections of the mellow lighting from above the hotel entrance. Suddenly warmed by the flood of affection which overwhelmed her, she returned his kiss, nuzzling into the bristly red beard. 'No harm done,' she assured him. 'Now that we know there won't be any Sky Rail or water skis and certainly no cars on Eisdalsa, I don't suppose there'll be any further opposition to the plans. People will probably thank you for making it all possible.'

'Let's hope so.'

He bent towards her again but just at that moment they heard the tramp of feet on the road below, the sound of laughter and the shouts of happy, young voices.

'Best go inside,' she said, 'or people will begin to talk!'

As one familiar with the effects of salt air upon mortice locks, George lent his shoulder to the glass panel and pushed open the door.

The Badger Bar was as full as they had ever known it. The sudden change of temperature misted Cissy's new spectacles, blinding her for a moment. As heads turned to see who had arrived, there was a sudden hush. No one knew quite how to behave. Should they greet the newcomers as though nothing had happened? Or should they shun them, as a week or two before, they most certainly would have done?

Marty Crane, the perfect landlord, solved the problem.

'Good evening, sir, madam,' he greeted them with exaggerated respect. 'What can I do you for?'

'A pint of heavy and a whisky chaser for me,' George replied in time-honoured form. He glanced swiftly at his wife. 'Tonic water?' She nodded. 'Tonic, with ice and lemon for the lady!'

Immediately the silence was broken as first one then another of those gathered around the bar acknowledged their presence.

'Good evening, George, bagged any rabbits yet?' The clear starlit evenings were ideal for going after the pesky animals and Cissy had certainly noticed one or two shots quite close to the castle grounds these past two or three nights.

'No,' replied the Marquis, 'but I imagine you have.' He grinned broadly at his interrogator, knowing full well that Archie McGillivray would have been out on the moors just as soon as the evenings began to draw in.

'Rabbits are the thing,' observed Tam McGreggor, His Lordship's gillie, 'just so long as it is not a brace of pheasants that you are taking.'

'Well spoken, Tam!' cried George, calling for a refill of his gamekeeper's glass. It was well known that quite a number of the local lads favoured pheasant over turkey for their Christmas dinner.

'Will there be a stag cull this season?' Giles Scott enquired. 'If so it would be as well to inform the press of the numbers and get the whole thing straight with the animal rights activists. They'll usually listen to reason if they are given the numbers.'

'After all,' Duncan McLeod chipped in, 'they have already said that shooting is better than hunting with dogs. Will there be venison on the table at New Year's then, Mrs Monteith?'

'I should jolly well think so,' Cissy assured him. 'I shall be calling on Mrs McLeod to come and help with the game pies.'

The ice having been broken for them by their stalwart friends, the Monteiths settled down to a pleasant evening full of goodwill, in which the beer and the whisky flowed freely. As the till rang out its merry tune for the umpteenth time, Marty Crane nodded cheerily to his wife. These little local disagreements never lasted long. It looked as though it was going to be a friendly holiday after all.

George launched into an account of how Jack McDougal had first approached him. By the time he got around to his reasons for giving HDC an option on a lease, the alcoholic euphoria was such that they were happy to accept his explanation without further question. Some went so far as to congratulate him on his good business sense! Scarcely anyone noticed Alan and Flora entering the bar a few minutes before normal closing time.

'Sorry it's such a quick one, Marty,' Alan explained. 'We've been burning the midnight oil in order to be able to close down the surgery for the holiday.' He glanced around at the red faces and listened to the noise level.

Only slightly raising his voice so that those nearby would be warned, he announced, 'We saw Sergeant McNab parked just along the road, so those of you who don't want to spend Christmas day in clink had best walk home.'

He turned to Cissy, noting the tonic water with some suspicion.

'No gin, I promise,' she told him cheerfully, 'just ask Marty.'

She looked remarkably fit after such a short time.

'You look stunning in those glasses,' Flora told her. 'Dorothy Parker didn't know what she was talking about.'

'Who's she?' asked one of the young fishermen who had come to the bar to replenish the glasses of Jamie McPhee and his three-man crew.

'An American woman,' laughed Cissy. 'She was famous for her sharp wit and one of her famous sayings was "Men seldom make passes at girls who wear glasses".'

'Load of nonsense,' said George, 'my girl looks great, doesn't she, Beaton?'

'They certainly do suit you, Cissy,' Alan agreed. 'These days there are so many attractive styles, I think most women look good in them.'

Flora, who had worn glasses since her student days, felt two inches taller. He had actually been looking at her when he said it.

'I rather thought McDougal might have been in here tonight,' observed Giles Scott. 'I understand he's still around.'

'Even he doesn't have the brass neck to come in here, not on a night like this anyhow.' This from Marty Crane.

'He's gone to London,' Flora informed them, 'but I believe he'll be back for New Year's.'

Marty raised his eyebrows but said nothing. She was surprisingly well informed about their common adversary.

'I think we could be a little more tolerant towards Jack,' she continued. 'After all, he has to all intents and purposes lost his case and I can't see anything wrong with the idea of a golf course.'

'All the same, the marina can go ahead now without any consideration having been given to our doubts about opening up that quarry at the north end,' said McPhee quietly. 'I reckon it'll cost half a million, that job, and there's no guarantee that the first big storm won't tear down the remainder of the quarry wall and destroy the whole set-up. Even if they get away without causing serious damage due to blasting, it'll be years before the company can even begin to recoup their outlay.'

Giles Scott was thoughtful.

'You know, Jamie is right. If they're prepared to spend that amount of money, they must have additional plans for making a profit.'

'If you want my opinion,' intervened Bill Douglas, one of a group of pensioners who had tucked themselves away in the corner to indulge in a welter of reminiscences, 'we haven't seen the last of these scheming bastards yet. They'll go for an appeal, I'm certain of it. Just you mark my words, they'll get on with that part of the work for which they've had permission, obeying all the rules and keeping in everyone's good books, until the appeal. And they'll win! So don't be so certain we've waved goodbye to the Eisdalsa bridge and ski boats and that Sky Rail thing.'

As the old man was speaking, Marty had rung for time and the momentary lull in conversation which fell throughout the bar left Bill's words echoing in everyone's ears.

Some laughed and others jeered good-naturedly, but there were one or two who were more circumspect. Old Bill might be a bit garrulous at times but he was no fool and what he had suggested carried the uncomfortable ring of truth.

Chapter Sixteen

Milton T. Humbert read again the two closely typed sheets he held in his hand, his colour mounting as rage and frustration took hold. He screwed the paper into a tight ball and hurled it across the room so that, miraculously, it landed in the waste paper basket.

He stood by the window of his sumptuously furnished Edwardian suite and gazed across the red brick wall opposite, right into the mews of Buckingham Palace. Although it was his aim to erect his steel and concrete bedroom factories in every major city and holiday Mecca around the world, when he came to Europe, it was elegance and a taste of history that he demanded for his own comfort.

He glanced impatiently at his watch.

The boy was late.

He poured himself another whisky and swore gently as he replaced the glass stopper in the empty decanter. Moving to the bedside console he lifted the telephone and pressed for Room Service. At that instant there was a sharp tap on the door.

'Room Service? This is 503. Send me up a bottle of

Islay malt and plenty of ice . . . right away.'

He strode across the softly yielding carpet and flung open the door.

'What kept you?'

''Plane was late taking off and at Heathrow there must have been half a dozen international flights arriving at about the same time. There wasn't a taxi to be had . . . in the end I decided that rather than wait in line, it was quicker to take the tube.'

Jack removed his overcoat and threw it, together with his bulging briefcase, on to the nearest chair. Milton stood centre floor, feet slightly apart, hands clenched tightly behind his back. It was a sure sign that a lecture was about to be delivered.

'What happened up there?' he demanded. 'I sent you on a simple mission, to sweeten the locals, find out what made the authorities tick and sketch me a plan which would satisfy everyone. You go in there, all guns blazing, and start up a major conflict. What the hell were you thinking of?'

'It wasn't like that, Mr Humbert.' Jack dared not use a more familiar address when his boss was in this mood. 'I kept a really low profile. I'm absolutely sure that no one had any idea I was involved, until the moment I walked into that Planning meeting.'

'Who was there to recognise you?'

'People I had been seeing every day for several weeks, including my own landlady!'

'Are you telling me that members of the public were admitted?' demanded the American.

'Half the population of the slate islands was exercising

its democratic right to witness the proceedings.'

Jack's tone was sour.

For years he had been forced to listen to Milton pontificating upon the virtues of that great democratic institution which was the United States Government. Other nations' democracies, however, were merely a hindrance to his activities and something to be combated relentlessly, with every weapon at his disposal.

'You must have done something to upset them,' he insisted. 'It's such a sleepy little place . . . nothing ever happens there. The residents are on their beam ends, desperate for work. The land is worthless save for the kind of development I'm proposing – and yet they turn me down. Who else is to blame for that but the man who set it all up?'

'There's a very strong heritage lobby,' Jack insisted. 'It seems they love all those ruined buildings and rusty pieces of ironwork . . . they're even talking now of having them preserved, making overtures to the Scottish National Trust to take over the area as a site of special historic interest. Another very forceful group are concerned about damage to wildlife in the area. Did you know that the Sound of Lorn has been nominated for special protection by the European Commission for Conservation?'

'These organisations only put on the pressure in order to get the guys with real drive and initiative, like ourselves, to hand over a few extra dollars. Offer them a substantial donation to their funds and they'll soon back down.'

'It doesn't work like that over here,' the Australian

argued. 'Just because the mighty dollar moves mountains in the Third World, doesn't mean that you can get away with bribery in the UK.'

'Every man, and every institution, has its price. That's probably the mistake you made. Not free enough with the handouts.'

Jack's angry retort remained unspoken. At that moment there was a rap on the door. Milton's whisky had arrived.

They remained silent while the waiter poured the contents of the bottle into the fine crystal decanter and polished a pair of cut-glass tumblers before setting them on the table.

'Will that be all, sir?' the man enquired.

Milton had made his point. The truth was, he couldn't do without McDougal . . . best trouble shooter he'd ever had. The boy appeared sufficiently cowed by his onslaught. He could now afford to be magnanimous.

'You must be ravenous,' he suggested. 'Get anything to eat on the plane?'

In no way mollified by his employer's sudden change of mood, Jack replied, sullenly. 'Nothing since breakfast. There's not enough time to serve a meal on that flight.'

'Not worth eating anyway.' Milton's opinion of airline catering arrangements were well known. He had at one time considered buying up one of the major airline food suppliers in order to improve standards on his own charter flights. Once he looked into the economics of the operation, however, he had very quickly changed his mind!

Milton gave his order to the waiter. 'A plate of smoked

salmon and cucumber sandwiches,' he demanded. 'Oh, and you'd better bring some coffee as well.'

As the man departed, carrying his tray, Jack opened the door for him and slipped him a few coins.

'Thanks,' he mouthed silently, and smiled, ashamed of his employer's behaviour.

'When you've eaten, we'll set about drawing up our plan of action.'

Jack's heart sank. He had hoped the Council's decision would allow them to bow out gracefully from the entire project, but Milton was obviously not prepared to give up the fight after only one round.

'It says here,' his boss searched through the crumpled letter retrieved from the waste paper basket, 'that we can go to appeal. You'd better prepare the necessary paperwork.'

'You want me to engage a Scottish lawyer?'

'Whatever for? It's only a planning consent we're fighting over, not a petition for divorce. We've handled countless appeals of this nature in England.'

'You might find yourself in difficulties without a proper legal adviser. They do things rather differently in Scotland.'

'Nonsense! What is there to know? This initial decision is simply a sop to the voters. Next time around good sense is sure to prevail. No Government official is going to turn down the promise of investment on this scale, not to mention the possibility of jobs in an area of high unemployment.'

'But it's not quite like that, is it?' Jack protested.

'What d'you mean?'

'What sort of jobs will you be offering the local people? You always go for the best-trained staff at the cheapest rate. Where do you think you're going to get people of that calibre on the west coast of Scotland? If they had the skills you're looking for, they wouldn't be unemployed and hanging around there in the first place.'

'The locals will find plenty to do.'

'Menial tasks for which most of them are unfitted . . . is that what you mean? There are plenty of those already. No one is prepared to take them on for the wages you are prepared to pay. They receive more on welfare than they take home from a forty-hour week at your usual rates. I don't know if you've heard, but there's a strong possibility of the introduction of a minimum wage agreement should Labour win the next election. That could add millions to our wages bill throughout the UK.'

'There are ways of getting around that, as well you know.' Milton already had his accountants working on it. 'You're just splitting hairs.' He brushed aside Jack's argument.

They both knew that once the scheme was under way, they would be bringing in well-qualified workers from all over Europe and from the Far East. People who would be willing to work for a pittance, just for the opportunity to come to Britain for as long as their work permits allowed. It was the way the company operated all around the globe.

'I tell you, Milton, I'm not prepared to go to an appeal without legal assistance,' Jack insisted.

'You won't have to, boy,' came the reply. Milton knew just how much this manner of address offended his subordinate and noted with satisfaction how Jack's cheeks coloured under the riposte.

'I shall be conducting our part in this inquiry myself!'

'If you want to get off early this afternoon, Flora, I can hold the fort,' Alan said. He glanced into the nearly empty waiting room. 'Mrs Clark?' He smiled at Jeanie and held the door for her to pass through into the consulting room. 'Take a seat. I'll be with you in just one minute.' He nodded to Willie Clark who had driven his wife down to the surgery. 'You coming in too, Willie?'

The storekeeper coloured a little and shook his head. He found everything to do with doctors and hospitals alarming.

'I'll just wait here the now,' he answered, and continued to sort through the magazines on the rack.

'Are you sure you can manage?' Flora would welcome some time off. She still had a few things to do to prepare for the party this evening and she really ought to pop across to see her dad before the ferry shut down for the holiday . . . apart from a late special at one o'clock in the morning, there would be no more ferries running to the island until 2 January.

'I can manage,' Alan reassured her. 'You get off right away. Oh, and by the way,' he delved into his top pocket, 'here's your ticket . . . just in case. I'd hate you to miss the ball because I was called out at the last minute. I'll pick you up at eight-thirty, all being well. If I don't turn up by nine, go along without me. I'll catch up with you there.'

'What about Jack?'

With their friends and neighbours so ready to gossip, Flora had been reluctant to be seen partnering either one of the two men. By turning up as a threesome, though, they signalled no particular commitment . . . and that was the way she wanted to keep it.

'Nothing from him as yet,' Alan told her. 'He hung on to his own ticket. Said he might have to arrive at the last minute and that he'd see us at the castle.'

'But the last train gets in at three o'clock, he can't get here at all after that.'

'You don't know our friend as well as you think,' Alan laughed. 'He'll find a way, believe me.'

'I'll see you later on then.' She began to shut down the computer while Alan returned to his consulting room.

'Now then, Jeanie.' He closed the door behind him and sat down opposite his patient. 'My, but you look a sight better than the last time I saw you.'

The high colour had gone and she had lost a lot of weight. At a guess she was down to a reasonable ten stone or so. He had never known Jeanie Clark when she was well. It would take Dr McWorter to tell him just how much she had improved as a result of her heart bypass.

He took her wrist, making the usual tests, and found nothing abnormal.

'May I take a look at the wound?' he asked, and noted how painfully she moved as she struggled to remove her blouse.

'Here, let me help you. You're bound to be sore for quite a while after.'

'They never said it would be this painful,' she grumbled, speaking for the first time.

She flinched as he moved his fingers gently across the huge scar which stretched right across her rib cage.

'Sorry.' He smiled at her. 'Are my hands cold?' He rubbed them vigorously together before resuming the examination. It was a tidy job and as far as he could see there was no sign yet of extraneous scar tissue. That was always the problem after this kind of surgery. A bit of a cobble in the suturing might leave a patient with uncomfortable lumps and bumps which could only be removed by further surgery.

'Well, they seem to have done a pretty good job here,' he said, folding his stethoscope and dropping it on the pile of papers on his desk. 'Now, tell me about yourself. How are you feeling?'

'Tired and sore,' she said, showing no emotion at all.

'You know that when they cut your rib cage like that, they have to wire it up, don't you? They told you all that?'

'Oh, yes, they tell you all about what's going to happen to you, but when you're feeling as ill as I was, you don't take it all in properly.'

'It's going to be three months before your ribs will feel anything like normal,' he explained, 'and in fact, after any major surgery, where nervous tissue has to be cut, there will always be a certain amount of discomfort. You have to keep telling yourself, if it wasn't for the operation I wouldn't be here.'

'Some mornings when I wake up, so stiff and sore I can hardly get out of bed, I think I might have been better off dead,' she replied, startling him.

'Come, on Jeanie, you don't really mean that? What

would poor old Willie do without you?'

'He'd have to get on with his life, that's what.'

This did not sound like the caring, selfless woman Ewan McWorter had described. Alan wondered if the personality change was simply a result of her weakness, or a permanent legacy from the operation.

'He has been very worried about you, you know.'

'Has he? He managed to disguise it pretty well.' Jeanie sounded extraordinarily bitter.

'Whenever I've seen him he has been very anxious – enquiring about your treatment, calling at the house in the evenings to find out if I have heard anything.' It was a slight exaggeration but there had been evenings during those first weeks, while she was still in the local hospital, when Alan had spent hours talking to Willie Clark about his wife's operation.

'He came to see me once . . . *once* . . . during all my time in Glasgow!' She sounded petulant, almost childlike in her accusations.

'He had the shop to run,' Alan reminded her gently. 'He told me himself how anxious he was that everything should be shipshape for your return. Mr Bartlet was brought in immediately to manage the Post Office side of things, but I think Willie felt it was his responsibility to keep an eye on what was going on, for your sake.'

'Nonsense, 'she replied sharply. 'The reason he didn't come is because he doesn't like hospitals . . . selfish brute!'

'Oh, well, that's between the two of you,' Alan told her gently. 'But at least let me give you a word of warning. It is common knowledge that heart surgery can leave a person depressed and with startling mood changes. The trauma of the operation and the massive consumption of drugs over a relatively short period can have an overwhelming effect upon the personality. You will have to take things easy for a few months yet, and most important of all you should try not to make any important decisions during that period. In fact, you'd be best advised not to make any major changes in your life for the present. Just carry on as normally as possible and hopefully, one day in the not too distant future, you will suddenly discover you feel just like your old self again.'

It was a cheering prospect but Jeanie seemed unmoved by his words. She was only half concentrating upon what he was saying. She stood up and shrugged herself painfully into her coat. Casting him an accusatory glance, she gathered up her handbag and made for the door. Alan had quite deliberately made no effort to assist her. It was time she stopped relying on other people and started doing things for herself once again. He pulled her up short when she had her hand on the door knob.

'They told you in the hospital about the importance of regular exercise?'

'Och, I was never one to take walks, doctor. Just delivering the mail is exercise enough for me.' She cast the words over her shoulder, still grasping the handle. 'I never had the time.'

'Well, you have all the time in the world now,' he told her. 'Take a walk every day. Not too far at first. Make a challenge of it . . . plan to go just a little further each time, even if it's only a few yards. When you can get to the surgery on foot, I shall tell you it's time to start work again.'

Mary Withall

'I'll never be able to walk all the way here,' she protested.

'Then you'll not get back to your work,' he told her decisively. 'Because I won't sign the medical certificate!'

She stared at him long and hard. He stared back. If it was to be a battle of wills, Alan suspected she might well be the winner. Suddenly her expression changed. She pulled the lapels of her warm winter coat into line, patted down the front, obviously appreciating the straight fall where once a huge stomach had bulged and said surprisingly cheerfully, 'I suppose there are some compensations. I had to buy a whole new wardrobe . . . everything was far too large.'

'That's the way,' Alan congratulated her. 'Try looking on the bright side and you'll soon have this thing licked!'

She was about to close the door behind her when he called out once again.

'Since he's here with you, might I have a word with Willie? There's something I wanted to ask him . . . about the house.'

'All right, is it. You're not going to give it up just yet?'

'Oh, no, although I can't tell you yet how long I shall be staying on. It all depends upon Dr McWorter and Dr Pullson . . . she's been ill too, you see.'

'Stay as long as you like, doctor,' Jeanie told him. 'We've no bookings for the coming season . . . Willie's done nothing about it. Anyway, the way I feel at present, I couldn't cope with the comings and goings . . . letting by the week makes for a hard Saturday, changeover day.'

'That's very good of you, Jeanie,' he told her, appreciating that she could make twice as much every week by

406

letting her cottage to holiday makers.

'To tell the truth, doctor, I canna be botherin' about anything just now,' she told him. 'I'm too tired . . . just too tired.' Her voice had lapsed once again into that monotonous whine.

She seemed to have forgotten already what had been said only minutes before. He made a brief note and looked up to see her still holding the door ajar, hovering uncertainly.

'Mrs Clark!' he called.

'Aye?'

'You were going to fetch Willie.'

'Oh, aye.'

He heard her exchange a few words with her husband and then Willie Clark was at the door. He was obviously a worried man.

'Sit down, Mr Clark,' Alan said.

'What is it, doctor?' Jeanie's husband asked. 'If it's something wrong with the house, you'll need to get in a workman. I've nae time at all to be fixing things just now.'

'It's nothing to do with the house, Willie. It's your wife I want to talk about.'

'Oh, aye. She's slow to pick up, is she no', doctor?'

'It'll take time.'

'I just want m'old Jeanie back again.' There were tears in the man's eyes.

'Look, Willie. . .' Alan hesitated for a moment only. 'You have to understand that your wife has undergone a very traumatic experience. It may have changed her nature completely, possibly permanently. My best advice to you is to accept her as she is, not to keep harping back to what you have lost. At the moment Jeanie is very depressed. Try to interest her in what's going on around her. She may not be able to help much physically, but that doesn't mean that she can't be involved . . . be included in everything that's going on. Don't shield her and don't prevent her from doing anything she feels capable of doing. I've told her she must walk . . . every day, rain or shine. That's important. It will make the difference between a complete recovery and her remaining a semi-invalid for life. If you can find time to accompany her sometimes, that will help her a lot. She feels very alone in all this.'

Willie made to protest.

'Oh, I know how much you care,' Alan assured him, 'but Jeanie doesn't see it. You will have to forgive her. At the moment she sees only the darkest side of everything. She can't help it. You do understand that, don't you? Don't, under any circumstances, dissuade her from going out every day,' he repeated. 'If you have to be firm, then be firm. If she accuses you of being uncaring . . . well, so be it. It's something which you will have to put up with for the time being.'

Willie nodded gloomily.

Alan continued, 'Her short-term memory is poor?'

'She forgets what's been said only minutes before-hand,' Willie confirmed.

'Encourage her to try to remember,' Alan urged him. 'Don't be too ready to help her. It will take time and a great deal of patience.'

'Oh, aye.' The man still seemed utterly bewildered.

Alan believed the operation had been as much of a shock to the husband as it had been to the patient herself.

A lot of trouble was taken these days to inform patients of what was going on, but many surgeons still didn't do enough about counselling the relatives.

'Was that Jeanie Clark I saw leaving just now?'

Ewan McWorter had taken to wandering into the surgery about this time every day. Normally Alan welcomed the old man's presence. They would have a wee dram and go over the day's events. It was a help to Alan to hear something of his patients' past histories and it gave Ewan the feeling that he was getting a grasp of things again. Today, however, Alan would gladly have forgone the exchange. He had to dash into town to retrieve his dinner jacket from the cleaner's. Had he thought, he might have asked Flora to collect it for him. He had left himself with barely half an hour to spare before the shop closed down for the whole of the holiday.

'What will you be doing with yourself this evening?' he asked Ewan.

'Och, I'll watch the television until the "bells", I suppose,' the older man replied, rather wistfully Alan thought. 'Then I'll take m'sel' off to my lonely wee bed.'

'I'm not sure I wouldn't rather be you than me,' Alan told him. He was already worn out, and a night of drinking and dancing was the last thing he fancied just now.

'You'll be off to the castle, I suppose?'

'Yes, Flora has promised Jack McDougal and myself a real Hogmanay to remember!'

'All three of you going then?' the old man probed. 'I'm

surprised Flora gives that Australian fella the time of day. Her father considers her to be something of a traitor. Fraternising with the enemy, he calls it.'

'I don't believe that other people have such strong opinions on the matter as Bill Douglas,' Alan assured him, 'not now the development plan has been modified.'

'I'm glad you're going to be with them nevertheless,' observed Ewan. 'I've nothing against the lad myself, but I'd hate to see our Flora flitting to Australia with him. It isn't only Bill Douglas who can't do without her.

'I'll let you get away, laddie,' he concluded, seeing Alan glance anxiously at his watch. 'Have a good time . . . if they'll let you!'

The chances of his getting through the whole of the New Year's break without a single call-out were minimal. He would have to take what came and make the most of any free time his patients allowed him.

Left alone to finish clearing up before closing the surgery for the night, Ewan McWorter's words came back, hitting Alan like a cold shower. Not for a moment had he considered the possibility that Flora might go off with Jack McDougal. While he had at one time wondered at the propriety of McDougal's staying as a lodger in Flora's house, her subsequent behaviour had allayed the suspicion there had been anything of a more personal nature in the arrangement. Since Jack's departure and reappearance, their meetings had all been in public and, so far as he was aware, in Alan's presence. For a while Flora had been quite scathing about McDougal's part in the development scheme although he had noticed that her attitude in that quarter had changed of late.

As he packed up his instruments and returned patients' files to their proper place, he questioned his own response to the suggestion that Flora and Jack might be more than friends. How would he react should the pair of them take off together?

He enjoyed working with Flora. She was very good at her job and handled the patients well. It would be difficult to replace her, but was that all? What of himself? Would he find her absence disturbing? Would he miss their comfortable repartee? The answer was, yes. He would find her absence unbearable. In fact, he went so far as to tell himself that he would be unlikely to want to stay here if Flora were to go away . . .

He closed the lid of the Edwardian roll-top desk and locked it automatically, tucking the key into its hiding place above the door lintel and smiling as he did so at the naïvety of this concession towards security regulations. Nothing had gone missing from these premises in the eighty years since the first doctor had screwed his brass plate on the outer door. Why would anyone want to break in now?

He carried the patients' files into the reception area and replaced them in the filing cabinet. As he reached for his coat, the telephone began to ring.

Flora wallowed in a hot bath, unable to see any water for the blanket of creamy foam which covered her whole body as far as her chin. This was sheer luxury . . . a bath at four o'clock, on a Friday afternoon.

It had been a tiring week, catching up on the backlog of patients, mostly suffering from a catalogue of

Christmas indulgences. She hoped that Alan got away in time to collect his suit. She might have offered to fetch it for him herself, but she had not relished the idea of a dash into town and back again in the dark. Besides he should have got himself organised for the party days ago. Just like a man, to leave everything until the last minute.

I'll bet Jack McDougal will turn up fresh as a daisy, immaculate in evening dress, she thought. When they were discussing arrangements, she had jokingly suggested he might hire full Highland dress for the occasion. She wondered how he would look in the kilt!

There was a loud hammering on the front door.

Should she lie doggo and pretend she wasn't there? Maybe it was something important. Alan would have rung from the surgery if so. It might be her father coming to pay his customary New Year's Eve visit. If it was, it would save her a trip over to the island.

She grabbed a towelling robe which was draped over the stool, rubbed her hair to stop it dripping all over her face, and went to open the door.

'Jack!' She grabbed at the neck of the robe, wondering what he must think of her, answering a caller so scantily clad.

'Oh, sorry,' he said, breezily. 'I seem to have caught you at an awkward moment.'

'I was in the bath,' she explained, quite unnecessarily. 'Are you coming in?'

'I wanted to ask a favour,' he said, as she led the way into the cramped little living room.

'I'll just put the kettle on,' she called over her shoulder.

'I'm dying for a cup of tea.'

'I'll make it, if you want to get dressed?'

'Oh, that'll take me ages this evening,' she told him. 'Have you never witnessed a woman getting ready for a ball?'

More times than he liked to admit, he thought, but smiled and shrugged his shoulders, not trusting himself to give an honest answer.

This woman was such a curious mixture of wanton hussy and prim virgin. He wondered, not for the first time, about her background. What age was it she had admitted to? Twenty-eight? She must be all of that. He doubted if she had managed to live so long without some romantic involvement.

She clattered about in the kitchen for a few moments before emerging with two steaming cups and a biscuit tin held precariously under one arm.

'Here, catch.' She dropped the tin on to his knees and he caught it deftly, just before it slipped to the floor.

'Rugby football?' she asked.

'In my youth.'

'Any good?'

'I played wing three-quarter at Uni. Even had a try-out for the State team.'

'There was a chap here in the 1930s played for Scotland . . . the doctor's son. Come to think of it, he was probably a Beaton, too.'

Now why is it that name comes up in every conversation? Jack asked himself, regretting that they were to be a threesome this evening.

'When is Alan picking you up?' he asked aloud.

'Half-eight.' Then, remembering, 'What was it you wanted to ask me?'

'Oh . . . it's rather a cheek really, only I didn't fancy the idea of driving down that narrow road back to town. Not after I've had a few drinks. Would you mind if I took the room upstairs again?'

'Just for the one night?'

'I'm willing to pay the going rate.'

She looked delicious when she blushed. Without make-up her skin glowed in the firelight.

For a moment only she was going to refuse. Then she saw something in the way he regarded her that suggested a challenge. He thinks I wouldn't dare defy convention, she told herself. She tossed the damp, dark locks away from her face, and pushed a stray strand of hair behind her ear. 'I suppose it would be all right,' she said. 'I haven't been up in the loft since you left. The bed's not aired, but I could put an electric fire on right away. It should be all right by the time you want to use it.'

There she was, blushing again. He loved it!

'My bag's in the car.'

'There's just one thing I have to say.' She motioned him to a chair. 'About the development . . . Nothing's happened as yet and people are beginning to ask questions. Is any of it going ahead?'

'Not until the spring, if at all,' he answered honestly.

'And there's not going to be any more controversial stuff?'

He placed one hand on his heart and crossed his fingers on the other, which he held behind his back. 'I swear.'

The truth was he had spent hours during the past two

days going over the likely objections which would be
raised by the islanders if they were to go to appeal. He
had laid each of them on the line for Milton. If the local
people engaged a decent advocate to speak for them, they
should have a better than evens chance of winning their
case. He had done some research since the preliminary
hearing, and had discovered that the odds were usually in
favour of the locals when it came to an appeal in matters
of this kind. At first Milton had been reluctant to accept
his assessment, but in the end Jack felt he had won the
argument. They had just six weeks in which to lodge an
appeal. Milton had decided that he would talk it over with
the lawyers while he was in Queensland and he would let
Jack know the outcome of his deliberations, some time in
January.

Watching Jack's expression change as each of these
thoughts passed through his mind, Flora suspected he
was still not being completely open with her.

'All right,' she answered, 'but only for the one night! I
shall have to spend tomorrow with my father and I will
probably stay on the island for the night.'

'Dr Beaton?'

'Yes, speaking.'

'Oban Coastguard. We have had a distress call from a
fishing boat in trouble off Scarba. There appear to be two
casualties, one requiring more than first aid.'

'What's the nature of the injuries?'

'Severe burns . . . a gas cylinder exploded . . . some
damage to limbs.'

'Who called for assistance? Is there someone on the

spot able to carry out instructions?'

'Only the ship's apprentice . . . just a young laddie.'

'Where are the casualties? Still aboard the vessel?'

'Yes. They managed to get the fire under control. She's dropped a sea anchor, but the one uninjured crew member isn't sure she will hold . . . they're drifting near rocks, just offshore.'

'OK.' Alan thought rapidly. 'How long before you can pick me up at the ferry landing for Lunga?'

'Twenty minutes to half an hour.'

'Are you still in contact with the boy?'

'Yes.'

'Will you relay a message?'

'Of course. Fire away, doctor.'

'The biggest problem will be shock. Tell him to see they are well covered and kept as warm as possible.'

Alan waited, hearing a jumble of voices in the background.

'Right, doctor. Anything more?'

'The burned areas ought to be covered with the cleanest thing that comes to hand, sheets or towels are best . . . Tell him not to try to move either of the men and not to administer anything in the way of drink. Is that clear?'

'My man is relaying your words as you speak.'

'OK, I'll see you in half an hour.'

Alan replaced the 'phone and reached for his medical case. It took him a few moments to gather together what equipment he felt he might need. He slammed the surgery door behind him and threw his case on to the back seat of the Jaguar. Before opening the driver's door, he checked himself and went first to hammer on Ewan McWorter's front door.

Alan waited impatiently; it took a few moments for the old man to shuffle into his hall and open up.

'What's up?' he demanded, noting Alan's anxiety.

'Accident at sea. I could be away for some time. If anyone should ring in with an emergency, you'll have to ask them to call for an ambulance . . . I've switched the line through to you.' He hesitated, looking Ewan straight in the eye. 'No going out yourself, d'you hear? I've enough problems on my hands without you throwing a wobbly.'

Ewan nodded. 'My advice might be old-fashioned, but my patients will still listen to it.'

Alan grinned, realising he was being unnecessarily overbearing. Ewan could cope perfectly well on the end of a telephone.

'Should you need Flora . . . remember, she'll be at the castle. Oh, there's a favour you could do for us both. Would you give her a ring and tell her to go along without me. I was supposed to pick her up half-eight and this could take hours.'

'Leave it to me, Alan. Now, you take good care of yourself, Don't you go worrying about what's happening here!'

As he stepped from the Jaguar on to the quay, Alan was surprised at the force of the wind which, further inland, had seemed little more than a gusty breeze. Here, beside the sea, it blew from the north-west carrying icy air from the snow-covered mountains of Mull. He shivered, pulled

417

his oilskin jacket together at the throat and stared into the darkness in hopes of seeing the approach of the lifeboat. After a while he heard the soft chug-chugging of a vessel approaching from the other side of the sound. The ferry crossing from the island of Seileach to Lunga was a considerably greater distance and less sheltered than that between Eisdalsa and the village where he lived. It was some moments before the outlines of Jamie McPhee's boat, the *Lass of Lunga*, hove into view.

'Is that you, doctor?' He heard the familiar voice and went closer to the harbour wall to get a clearer view.

'Jamie? Jamie McPhee?'

'Aye . . . will you hop aboard, Dr Beaton?'

'I was told to wait for the lifeboat,' he explained.

'Oh, aye . . . so they said,' Jamie held out a hand to steady Alan as he stepped down over the thwarts and picked his way between coils of rope and piled lobster cages.

'I heard the distress call and offered my services,' the fisherman explained. 'The seas are getting up and the wee boat is lying into danger. The coxswain asked that I come for you while he makes straight for the scene. Every second counts in conditions such as these.'

'Of course.'

Clutching his medical bag to his chest, Alan squatted on an upturned fish box and turned his back on the wintry blast.

By the time they had rounded the northernmost point of Lunga and had started down channel towards the forbidding black mass of the island of Scarba, his fingers were frozen and he was beginning to wonder what possible use he was going to be when they did eventually arrive at the scene of the accident.

Ahead of them, thrown into sharp silhouette by lights from the far side, a scattering of rocks fanned outwards from the land, barring their way. Alan watched in trepidation as Jamie, with the skill of one born to the area and who had spent his whole life at sea, manoeuvred his craft between the jagged outcrop and emerged effortlessly on the far side.

Bathed in the dazzling beam of the lifeboat's searchlight, the stricken vessel dragged at its anchor chain, moving relentlessly towards the boiling surf which lay no more than fifty yards away, on its starboard side.

The lifeboat already had a line on board and Alan could see the slim figure of a young boy, the only ablebodied man remaining, heaving on the tow rope and trying desperately to attach it to a stanchion aft of the wheelhouse.

To encouraging shouts which were loud enough to be heard above the screaming of the gale in the rigging and the roaring of the surf along the beach, the lifeboat at last took the doomed ship in tow. As it took up the strain on the wildly careering vessel, the boy was seen groping with the winch, in an attempt to haul in the anchor. Time seemed to stand still while the lifeboat's crew and the men aboard the *Lass of Lunga* looked on, unable to go to his aid.

At last the anchor came free and was wound in with such a rush that the boy stumbled backwards and was in danger of falling over the side.

The lifeboat was now in total control and began, agonisingly slowly, to haul the stricken vessel away from the nearest rocks.

Lunging helplessly from one wave top to the next, the wrecked boat was towed around the headland and into a more sheltered cove. Jamie McPhee guided his own vessel in the wake of the other boats and was at last able to bring the *Lass of Lunga* alongside, so that the doctor could climb aboard the wreck. Until this moment Alan had been an interested bystander. Now he was faced with the problem of leaping from one deck to another in these heavy seas which tossed both vessels so frantically he felt he was negotiating a cake-walk at the fair. His confidence was further diminished when, despite the life jacket he was already wearing, Jamie insisted upon tying a rope around his waist and making it fast to a stanchion.

'I shall need that,' Alan shouted into the wind, as Jamie relieved him of his medical bag.

'You'll want both hands to steady yourself,' came the reply. 'We'll pass it across to you later.'

He was relieved to find that two of the lifeboat's crew had already swung aboard the fishing boat and were now waiting to receive him as he prepared to jump the narrow gap between the heaving vessels.

For an instant Alan allowed himself to look down into the inky black waters which separated them. With a shudder, he raised his eyes to those of the waiting men and listened for their instructions.

'All right, doctor, on the count of three!'

Alan braced himself against the wheelhouse.

'One . . . two . . .' He never heard the last word. With

a superhuman effort he launched himself into the air and felt himself caught by the upper arms. His feet, scrabbling wildly for the rail, slipped on the wet wood and suddenly he was dangling in the narrow gap between the two hulls, up to his waist in freezing water. He was grateful then that Jamie had tied the rope around him for it was by this alone that the men were able to grasp hold and haul him on board before the two hulls smashed together with his body sandwiched between them.

They steadied him as he landed on the slippery deck of the fishing smack. The rush of adrenaline warmed him, so that when he was shown the first of the injured men, despite the wet and the cold, he felt ready to attend him at once. His bag was passed across but in the noise of the gale he did not hear Jamie McPhee telling the lifeboatmen that he would stand off until they had further need of him.

In a moment of panic, Alan watched the *Lass of Lunga* draw away, and wondered if he would ever see Jamie again. Then one of the seamen was at his side urging him to take a look at the first of the two casualties.

The man was huddled in the well of the after deck, covered in blankets only partially protected from the wet by a set of waterproofs which their owner might have been expected to be wearing, in these conditions.

'Can I have some more light down here?' Alan asked. Each of the men produced a powerful torch, one of which Alan had them lash to a post behind his head so that the light moved only in unison with the movements of the boat.

Carefully he removed the minimum amount of cover

from the unconscious seaman, exposing horrific wounds. The right side of his face was a mass of blackened flesh on which huge blisters had already formed. His nose and lips had disappeared completely and his hair was a frizzled mass which crumbled in Alan's hands as he felt for a pulse below the left ear.

'Hallo, old man, I'm Alan Beaton.' He spoke clearly, attempting to illicit a response, any response, from the silent figure under his hands. 'What's your name?'

He bent forward to catch any small sound which might be emitted from the scorched lips.

'Malcolm Mc . . .' came the feeble reply. Alan did not catch the surname.

'All right, Malcolm, we'll soon have you feeling more comfortable,' he told him. 'Now, tell me. . . are you burned anywhere other than your face?'

Malcolm made an attempt at moving an arm and Alan peeled back the blanket further, to reveal a pair of blackened hands scorched no doubt, in his attempts to put out the fire.

The man appeared agitated, his eyes rolling from side to side. He was trying to say something. Alan leaned forward once again.

'Tom . . . is Tom all right?'

Alan turned to the lifeboatmen. 'Where's the other?'

'In here.'

Alan could do little for the burns. He prepared an injection of morphine and replaced the covers. 'As soon as you can, get him into a cradle and across to the lifeboat. The sooner we get him to hospital, the better.'

In the wheelhouse he found the boy who had so gallantly taken command of the vessel after the accident. He knelt beside his comrade, cradling the man's head in his arms. His face was chalk white, eyes unblinking. His grip on the injured man was so fierce that Alan was forced to loosen his fingers before he could persuade him to move aside.

He glanced over his shoulder at the lifeboatman who had accompanied him into the wheelhouse.

'Give the boy your torch, will you?'

The man seemed surprised but handed over the powerful light, just the same. In the boy's hands it wavered giddily until Alan reached behind him and closed his own fingers over the boy's. 'Just about here, son.' He guided the light on to the injured man and when he released his grip, the boy held steady.

'What's your name?' asked the lifeboatman.

'Sam. Sam Clunie,' he answered automatically, concentrating now on keeping the light steady.

'Can you tell us what happened, Sam?' asked Alan as he unwrapped the collection of coats and towels . . . everything the boy had managed to find to keep the man warm. As he drew back the last of these covers the full extent of the damage was revealed, and the boy looked as though he might be sick.

'Breathe deeply,' Alan advised, unrelenting in his insistence that the boy remained at his side. 'You'll get used to it in a few minutes.'

Tom had caught the full force of the explosion in his face and chest so that his skin was blackened and bloody like his companion on deck. In addition he had been lifted off his feet and slammed against the wall so that there appeared to be superficial abrasions and bruises all over his body.

Alan gave Sam a short while to regain his composure and then urged him to answer the other man's question.

'Tommy came in here to brew up,' Sam began weakly. 'There must have been a build up of gas . . . the tap's a bit stiff and it sometimes gets left turned on . . . just a bit . . . not enough to cause more than a loud plop when you light it . . .'

He gagged again as Alan cut away Tommy's sleeve to reveal a severe compound fracture of the forearm. The shattered bone had pierced the skin, and caused it to stick out at an unnatural angle.

The artery was pierced and there had been severe bleeding, but the tightly wrapped coverings had soaked up the blood which, in congealing, had prevented further bleeding. Now, as Alan removed the sodden cloths, the flow resumed, with blood spurting high into the air. He placed his fingers firmly on the pressure point and the flow stopped. Without turning around, he spoke calmly to the other man.

'In my case you'll find a rubber tourniquet. Get it out for me, will you?' He reached behind him and took the green strap, fixing it firmly in place above the elbow and shifting slightly to allow the other man to come closer.

'I want you to mind the tourniquet. Do you have a watch you can see clearly?' The seaman raised his wrist to reveal a good quality waterproof watch.

'Release the pressure every four minutes, allow the blood to start flowing again and then tighten it. OK?'

The man crouched down. Now all three had their

various responsibilities and Alan could get on with the job.

His examination had revealed further wounds to Tom's legs . . . mainly abrasions and bruising it was true but it would be a while before he would be able to walk easily. The degree of burn damage to his face and hands was less than his companion's. Alan wondered about this until he heard Sam, half sobbing now that the initial shock was beginning to wear off, say to the other man, 'I thought Tommy was dead . . . he was thrown against the wall by the explosion. Then the flames shot up and I just stood there . . . looking . . . not knowing what to do. It was Malcolm who got a coat and started beating at the flames. That's how he got so badly burnt . . . trying to pull Tommy out of reach. His clothes were burning too by the time I got the extinguisher to work.'

At this stage of his confession, the boy dissolved in tears and his hand dropped to his side.

'Steady with the light,' said Alan, ignoring the outburst. 'Can you reach into my bag and pull out that pack of dressings?'

The sterile packs were produced while he set to work to reduce the distortion in the fractured arm. He administered morphine and then, with the help of the lifeboatman, applied extension to the limb until the shattered bones slipped into a more natural position. Holding this area of the wound tightly in one hand, Alan waited while his assistant stripped off the plastic sleeve so that he could apply the sterile dressings, first one at the point at which bone had pierced skin, then a second and a third. He bound crêpe bandage over the lot, in order to hold them secure. It was time to relax and take stock.

'OK,' he said to the lifeboatman, 'undo the tourniquet and let's see how bad the bleeding is . . . now.'

He had avoided any attempt to suture the torn artery. He might do more harm than good under these conditions. That was a job best left for the operating theatre, if possible.

The tourniquet was loosened and then removed. A spot of blood appeared through the crêpe bandaging and all three of them watched as it grew to the size of a tenpence coin before ceasing to grow any further. If the arm was held steady during the journey to hospital, the dressings should suffice.

'Do you have inflatable splints aboard the lifeboat?' Alan asked.

His assistant nodded. He got to his feet and went outside.

Alan worked away steadily, doing what he could to cover the worst of the abrasions on Tommy's legs. As he worked he chatted to the boy whose colour had by now returned to normal. Concentrating on holding the torch had helped him to regain his composure and his answers to Alan's questions were made without hesitation.

'Do you often go to sea like this?'

'It's my first time . . . as a proper apprentice, that is.'

'Is it now? Well, you've had quite an initiation then, haven't you? Learned a few things tonight, I'd say.'

'I'll never use a gas stove that is nae working right, tha's for sure. an' . . .' He hesitated now.

'What?' Alan looked up to see what was troubling the lad.

'An' I'm goin' to take a First Aid course like Tommy said I should. I was so frightened when it happened . . . not knowin'.'

'You had the sense to get on the radio,' Alan reassured him. 'We wouldn't be here now if you hadn't done that. How did you know how to work it?'

'I'd watched Tommy. He let me stand by while he spoke to the Coastguard. It's easy.'

'You're a good lad. Tommy should be really grateful to you for what you've done.'

The boy looked relieved.

In a few moments, the lifeboatman returned with his companion, carrying a lightweight folding stretcher. It took a matter of minutes only to have Tommy comfortably splinted and strapped into the cradle ready to be passed across to the lifeboat. In the meantime, the first of the two casualties had already been lifted off. For a moment Alan believed that only the boy, Sam and himself remained on board the fishing boat. It was with considerable relief that he heard a voice from the wheelhouse.

'It's your choice, doctor, you can either come back to port with young Sam here and me, or we'll transfer you to the lifeboat and you can go back to Oban with the casualties?'

'What about Jamie McPhee?' he sked.

'He's coming back to Seileach with us,' said the pilot. 'Just in case we have any trouble.'

Remembering that earlier transfer from one ship to

another, Alan elected to stay where he was.

The clouds had parted and the stars were shining brightly in the heavens. The wind had dropped a little but the air was still cold and despite their being at sea, there was a touch of frost in it. A white rime was forming on the rigging of the mast and coating the wet timbers of the deck.

'Those two will be well taken care of in the West Highland.' Alan joined Sam and the pilot in the wheel-house. 'There's no medical cover at all on the islands at the moment. I think I'd better go back with you.'

He sent a message to the lifeboat to be passed on to the hospital staff and settled down to watch Jamie McPhee take up his position in the little convoy that sailed towards the northern end of Lunga. At that point the lifeboat took off at high speed, bound for Oban, while the damaged fishing boat and the *Lass of Lunga* made for the ferry landing where Alan had parked his car.

'I'm surprised you didn't want to go to the hospital with your friends,' Alan remarked to the boy who was chatting away quite comfortably to the boatman. 'Oh, I'm OK now, doctor,' the lad replied. 'Besides, as long as one member of the crew remains on board and is at the wheel when she runs into harbour, there'll be no question of Tommy having to pay salvage money.'

Sam looked to his companion for confirmation. The seaman nodded his head solemnly, then gave Alan a meaningful wink.

Not for the first time since he had arrived in this remote corner of the British Isles, Alan wondered at the bravery and generosity of his fellow human beings.

As they tied up at the quay so that the doctor could clamber ashore, Alan was filled with admiration for the brotherhood of the sea.

Jamie McPhee, giving him a steadying hand, was anxious to avoid seeing the doctor get a second wetting that evening. He had been surprised at the way Alan Beaton, clearly a novice when it came to boats and the sea, had handled himself this evening. What sort of a man is it, he wondered, who risks his life in this way for complete strangers? It did not occur to him to question the fact that neither he, nor the crew of the lifeboat had hesitated to turn out when the call came but then, the ways of the sea were second nature to *them*.

Chapter Seventeen

Flora glanced in the full-length mirror on the back of her wardrobe door, and declared herself satisfied.

Her mother's double row of pearls sat well at her creamy throat. The green velvet gown exposed narrow shoulders which had long since lost their summer tan and emphasised the rich brown of her eyes, enhanced tonight with carefully applied make-up. Her short-cut, immaculately groomed dark hair gleamed in the lamplight, while a pair of drop earrings made of pearls in a diamond setting, drew attention to her neat, well-shaped ears.

Touching her lips one last time with the brush, she stood back from the mirror, satisfied at last with the overall effect.

She had heard Jack descend from his loft room ten minutes before. It was nearly nine o'clock and Alan had not yet returned. Her plan to arrive at the ball with both men and so stop tongues from wagging had failed dismally. Reluctant as she was to appear at the ball alone with Jack, she knew from what Dr Mac had told her that Alan was going to be a long time yet. In fairness to the Australian, she could not keep him waiting any longer.

Jack turned to face her as she lifted the latch. His admiring whistle was completely drowned out by her own delighted exclamation.

She studied his outfit carefully from the snowy white ruff at his throat to the real badger fur of his sporran which sat perfectly upon the brightly coloured McDougal tartan kilt. His black dancing pumps bore silver buckles, carrying the same pattern as the buttons on his dark velvet jacket. His tartan plaid was secured at the shoulder by a splendid cairngorm brooch. The outfit suited him so well . . . there was no doubting his Highland origins now!

'What d'you think?' He did a little twirl and the kilt flared, perfectly.

'Moss Bros have done you proud,' she said.

'What d'you mean, Moss Bros?' he demanded. 'I'll have you know that this was made by the finest Scottish tailor in Oxford Street!'

'I didn't know there was one . . . in Oxford Street.'

'As you can see, I didn't entirely waste my time while I was down in London.'

'I hope not, indeed,' she told him. 'Has Mr Humbert decided to give up the fight?'

'I'd like to be able to say yes, but I'm sorry to tell you, Milt is still very determined.'

Her obvious disappointment made Jack wish he hadn't mentioned his trip to London.

Reminded of his recent mission, all Flora's doubts about the wisdom of appearing in company with Jack McDougal returned. Not so long ago he had been public enemy number one. Dare she expose herself to gossip by arriving with him this evening?

He saw the look of doubt which had suddenly clouded her face.

'You look so solemn. I thought we were supposed to be going to a party?'

He held her gently, one hand on either shoulder, and gazed at her with a quizzical expression which made her laugh.

'That's better,' he said, and kissed her lightly on the tip of her nose.

Suddenly she was in his arms, his mouth pressed firmly against her own. Their lips parted and she found his moist tongue exploring hers. With a little sob of excitement she felt his fingers brush her breasts as he nibbled at her ear and allowed his lips to travel in butter-fly touches down her neck, across her bare shoulders and downwards until he kissed her in her rather immodest cleavage. Aware, quite suddenly, of the pressure of his arousal in her groin, she found herself wet with desire. She could feel that she was slipping out of control, and she didn't care. They sank on to the couch . . . his hands were everywhere. He had slipped his fingers under her bra strap and carefully eased down her dress so that now her breasts were completely exposed. She gave herself up to his searching tongue and cried out ecstatically when he teased one erect nipple with his fingers before taking it into his mouth and suckling like a baby.

Suddenly, she pushed him away.

'We have to go,' she told him. 'People are expecting us. How could we explain our absence?'

'We could tell them we had better fucking things to

do,' he said lightly. With great reluctance he began to reposition her shoulder straps and pull her bodice into shape.

She caught hold of his hands and kissed them.

'There'll be time . . . later,' she said softly.

He gazed at her, unbelieving. Then, seeing the invitation in her eyes, he gathered her into his arms once more and kissed her with such passion she feared she would faint.

Somehow they released themselves and sat primly, side by side on the couch. She dabbed at her hot cheeks with a ridiculously small lace handkerchief. He removed a man-sized square of cambric from his jacket pocket and began to remove the smudged lipstick around her mouth.

'I'll have to do it all again,' she declared, jumping up to stare at the wreckage of her face in the mirror above the mantelshelf. 'Pour us a dram, will you? Then we'll get going.'

'No point in waiting any longer for Alan, I suppose?' Jack regretted his question the moment it passed his lips when he saw her face cloud over.

Silently, Flora went back into her bedroom and closed the door.

As she scrubbed furiously at the ruined make-up and began to replace it, she recalled the passionate moments which had just passed. Supposing Alan had walked in on them? What would he have thought?

Don't be ridiculous, Flora Douglas, she told herself. It was obvious what he would have thought . . . and what of it? She was a grown woman, wasn't she? Free to take any man she wanted?

Nevertheless, she blushed as she remembered the touch of Jack's fingers and the musky smell of him.

'Later,' she had promised him.

The evening could not pass swiftly enough for her.

When she opened the door, she found him sipping his whisky and gazing thoughtfully into the fire. He turned at the sound of the latch. Flora's flushed skin and those bright, expectant eyes made her more beautiful than ever.

'Not again,' she laughed as he took hold of her hands and gazed at her with admiration.

'I've been thinking . . .' he said. 'When I get back to Queensland I'll have another go at Milton. The company doesn't need all this hassle. Milton has plenty of other fish to fry . . . the whole of China is just sitting there, begging to be developed into the kind of places he provides.'

'Do you mean it?' she asked, gazing up at him with those beautiful, liquid eyes. With great fortitude, he resisted spoiling her make-up again.

'Here, take your dram,' he said, handing her a glass of the Bruichladdich he had brought with him.

As she lifted her glass, there was a knock on the outer door. Without waiting for an answer, Bill Douglas blundered in. If he was surprised to find her in company with Jack McDougal, he made no comment.

'Oh, Dad, I'm glad you're here,' she cried. 'I was going to come over this afternoon, to wish you all the best, but time simply flew by. I shall be cooking your Ne'er day dinner tomorrow, as usual.'

'I thought you might be busy,' he said,' so I decided to call in m'sel'. I've had a dram or two up at the Badger Bar.'

He need not have said. His nose was red with a touch of purple and he staggered slightly as she led him to a chair beside the fire.

He gave Jack the briefest nod of recognition, making it obvious that he was disturbed to find the Australian in his daughter's living room.

'We've been waiting for Dr Beaton to arrive,' she explained, hoping that her father would not suspect he had interrupted a romantic moment. 'Once he comes, we shall all be away to the castle.'

'Ah, I thought you might be going to the dance. Dr Beaton, you say? Is he no' out with the lifeboat just now? I thought Jamie McPhee was away to pick him up.'

News travelled fast in the islands.

'Aye, but he's expected back here just as soon as the casualties are away to the hospital.'

'You'll take a drink with us, sir?' Jack poured a glass and handed it over without waiting for a reply.

Bill Douglas took it, because he would never refuse a glass of good malt whisky, but he showed no sign of softening his attitude towards Jack. The man was an enemy. He had betrayed their trust and infiltrated their community with the intention of disrupting their lives. Bill Douglas, for one, was not about to forgive him that easily.

Flora, hating the atmosphere created by her father's antagonism, decided she wanted out of this situation. She glanced at her watch and said, 'We've waited long enough, Jack. I doubt if Alan will even think to come here at this hour. When he does get back, he'll go straight to the castle.'

Acting spontaneously, Jack searched for his car keys, realised he had no pockets in which to keep them and started up the ladder to the loft. 'I'll just fetch my keys,' he said, by way of explanation.

Quite unknowingly, he left behind him an atmosphere heavily charged with anger, dismay and distrust.

In the ensuing silence, father and daughter heard the ladder creaking as he reached the top.

'He's staying here?' Bill was outraged.

'Only for the one night. He had to have somewhere to change.' Flora was defiant.

'Well, girl, it's your reputation you'll be sacrificing.' He spat out the words in his distress. 'I only hope he's worth it!'

Without another word, the old man hauled himself painfully out of his chair, crammed his tweed deerstalker on his head, and reached for his walking stick. She watched while he stumbled towards the door, moving only when she heard it slam behind him. Suddenly goaded into action, she followed him, flinging it open again and calling after him as he shuffled away down the street towards the pier. 'I'll see you tomorrow, Dad . . . about twelve.'

There was no indication he had heard her.

Sorrowfully, she withdrew and closed the door. Bill had had a lot to drink this evening. Maybe he would feel better about things in the morning. When they were alone, she would be able to explain about Jack . . . tell her father how the Australian had promised to persuade his boss to withdraw from the fight.

*

For the Hogmanay party, the main hall of the castle was as festive a setting as anyone might wish. Tonight, the usually sombre dark oak panelling was relieved by holly branches and fir, tastefully decorated with tinsel and red ribbons. Beneath the splendid oriel window, on a raised dais at the far end of the room, a thirty-foot Christmas tree had been set up, and alongside it the flashing lights and all the paraphernalia of a state-of-the-art disco.

In the main dining room, its winter shrouds removed from the furniture for this one occasion, the banqueting table creaked under the weight of food, much of it taken directly from the estate. Haunches of venison sat side by side with colourfully garnished dishes of roast pheasant, grouse and quail, while a rack of lamb, each rib decorated with a little white chef's cap, formed the centrepiece. At either end of the table upon huge dishes of the finest porcelain were suckling pigs, each with an orange stuffed in its mouth. Colourful salads, delicately decorated desserts and huge silver bowls filled with fresh fruit, completed the bountiful fare.

Young people thronged the floor, moving in time to the music of the disco, while the ancient stone walls vibrated to the monotonous beat of the 1990s.

Every form of dress was acceptable on this the most important night of the Scottish year. The Marquis was resplendent in the predominantly green and black tartan of his clan, while Campbells, McAllans and McBeaths, Douglases, McLeods and McLeans, all added their own bright colours to the scene. Others of the menfolk were in formal evening dress, making a fitting background not only to the tartans but to the rich colours of the ladies' dresses.

Cissy, looking regal in a close-fitting gown of cream satin, wore her husband's tartan in the form of a silk plaid flung over her left shoulder and fastened with a diamond-studded clasp. In her hair she wore a discreet tiara, a family heirloom which seldom left the vaults of the Edinburgh bank in which it was stored.

Not all the men wore dinner jackets and not all the ladies were so splendidly adorned as their hostess, for this was a party to which everyone was invited, from occupants of the lowliest cottage to those of the grandest house in the district, and apart from celebrating the ending of the old year and the commencement of the new, the sole object of the exercise was to raise money for the hospital.

As the wine and spirits flowed, the sound levels rose and a spirit of goodwill prevailed. In such an atmosphere, old scores were put aside and Cissy noted with relief that George was tonight surrounded by life-long friends who, a week or two before, would have passed him by on the other side of the street.

There had been no formality in greeting the guests on arrival, but Cissy made it her business to speak with everyone at some time during the evening. Towards mid-night she came upon Janice Pullson and her husband, taking a breather in the orangery which led off from the dining room.

'Why, Janice, how good to see you out and about again!' she greeted her. 'Are you quite recovered?'

Janice, who had taken rather too much out of herself

while dancing, was fanning herself and sipping at a tall glass of mineral water, half-filled with ice cubes. She had had a battle with Gordon to get him to bring her at all this evening and nothing was going to make her admit he had been right to try to dissuade her.

'I'm one hundred per cent fit,' she declared. 'It's only the men who are trying to make an invalid of me still.'

'I hear you have not been too well yourself, Mrs Monteith,' Gordon Pullson interrupted, steering the conversation away from his wife. He knew how she hated to be asked about her health. In truth, Janice was looking very flushed. She was so eager to get back to work that any attempt on his part to get her to slow down met with enormous resistance. If he tried to prevent her from doing anything, she got so worked up that he feared she might have another relapse, so he considered it best not to argue.

'Oh, I'm fine now', Cissy assured him. 'Thanks to that new broom down at the surgery. I must have had diabetes for some time, but Dr Mac never spotted it.'

'We can only act on what our patients tell us about themselves.' Janice was quick to come to her colleague's defence. 'You certainly never told me you had any problems. Come to think of it, I can't remember you paying a visit to the surgery in the last couple of years.'

'I confess!' Cissy was laughing. 'It wasn't until I caught a glimpse of our dishy new doctor that I finally decided to go along. I must say I'm glad I did. I can read now as much as I like and I'm feeling so much better. When one reaches middle age one expects to feel less energetic, so I never thought twice about the fact that I was slowing down . . . it happened so gradually you see.'

'Unlike my own problem which manifested itself quite suddenly,' Janice told her.

'It sounds as if you both owe a lot to Alan Beaton.' George had joined them and overheard the conversation. 'It's a pity he has such a bad name in other respects.'

'What on earth are you talking about?' demanded Janice. 'What is the poor young man accused of?'

'Bit of a ladies' man by all accounts,' George told her. 'Pity, really, not the best reputation for a GP, is it?'

'First I've heard of it,' said Gordon Pullson. 'Tell me more . . .' The two men sidled off.

'And they accuse women of being gossips!' said Cissy.

Janice was very troubled. She had got to know Alan Beaton well during the past weeks. The very last accusation she would make against him was that of philanderer. She knew only too well what such talk could do to a doctor's career.

Flora glanced anxiously at the splendid long-case clock which stood beside the door into the dining room. She was wondering if it was as accurate as George Monteith had claimed.

'Always go by it . . . especially on occasions like this,' she had heard him boast. Well, at this moment it indicated there were only fifteen minutes of the old year left.

Jack noticed her looking towards the great oak outer doors and read her thoughts.

'I doubt he's going to turn up now,' he said, trying not

to sound too relieved. It had been a good evening so far. They had danced a lot, and drunk more of His Lordship's excellent wine than was good for them. Flora had scarcely touched the food which he had brought her. Her plate still lay between them on the hard wooden bench, the only seating they had managed to find.

They had exchanged few words with any other revellers. Jack had seen surprise on the faces of those who recognised Flora's partner as their arch enemy of a few weeks previously, and was conscious of the fact that by his very presence he was preventing her from having a good time. It might, after all, have been better if Beaton had been here with them.

He, too, looked towards the main door and saw a small knot of men gathered around the latest arrival. After a few moments the group broke up and the man moved further into the ballroom. Jack barely recognised the fisherman, Jamie McPhee, freshly groomed and wearing a collar and tie for the occasion. Earlier in the evening, McWorter had telephoned Flora with news of the accident at sea. Maybe McPhee had some more up-to-date information.

'Excuse me,' he said to Flora, 'I won't be a minute.' He moved across the floor to join those gathered about the fisherman.

'Are they badly hurt?' someone asked.

Jack was close enough to hear McPhee's reply.

'Aye . . . they looked bad enough to me. They'll be thankful it was yon Dr Beaton who was there, the night. I canna see old man McWorter doin' what that laddie did.'

Jack noticed an exchange of uncomfortable glances. There had been more than a few jokes passing between the menfolk that evening concerning the advantages of being a young doctor in a country practice. Even Jack, excluded though he was from the general banter, had heard something of what was being said when he visited the men's room, down in the basement below the hall.

'It was no night for a landlubber to be leaping from deck to deck, I can tell you.' With the first large whisky sitting comfortably in his stomach, Jamie was getting into his stride.

'Where were you?' asked one young, admiring voice.

'As close to the Corrievreckan as I'd ever want to be on a dark stormy night, I can tell ye.'

Heads were nodding. There followed a number of tales, both true and apocryphal, of other shipwrecks. A man did not live on this coast for long without accepting such disasters as a part of everyday life.

The music had stopped.

In the momentary silence which followed, the door flew open and there stood Alan Beaton, with Ewan McWorter close behind.

Heedless of the eyes upon her, Flora ran across the polished boards to greet them.

'I had quite given you up,' she told Alan. And to Ewan added, 'How nice to see you here after all, doctor. Does Cissy know you are coming?'

'I'm afraid it all took rather longer than I'd expected,' Alan replied, apologetically. 'Where's McDougal? I hope he's been looking after you properly?'

He stood back, taking in every detail of Flora's appearance. She was flushed from the dancing. The long green velvet gown was a trifle dusty at the hem and a tiny sliver of white shoulder strap had crept into view from beneath the tight-fitting bodice. One or two strands of her sleek, black hair were just a little out of place.

Seeing the direction of his stare, she reached up self-consciously, and touched the wayward locks.

'I'm afraid I haven't had time to change,' he said, indicating that he was still wearing his working suit. 'It was close to midnight by the time I got back to the surgery so I persuaded Dr Mac to come along and join us.'

Meanwhile George Monteith had mounted the platform and was calling for silence. When they were quiet, he began to speak.

'As you know, for the last few years it has been our custom to hold this function here at the castle, in support of the fund for building a new hospital. This venture is my wife's particular interest and she has asked that she might have a few words with you all before the main events of the evening begin.'

Cissy stood beside him, looking rather nervous. As he left the platform, she stepped forward to speak.

'Ladies and gentlemen, I just wanted to thank you all for coming along this evening and helping us to celebrate another new year in time-honoured fashion. Last year, you will know, that three thousand pounds was raised by this one function alone and the hospital fund received a total of seventy thousand pounds from all sources. I am happy to tell you that a quick calculation suggests that tonight's event, despite all the difficulties we have had recently . . .' she caught sight of Jack McDougal and had the satisfaction of seeing him redden and glance down at the floor '. . . may exceed last year's takings. Thank you so much for your generosity.'

There was some polite clapping until a disembodied voice called out, 'What the hell! Any publicity is good publicity,' and there followed a great burst of laughter.

Suddenly everyone was cheering, and the congratulations that Cissy received from those gathered closest to the platform were entirely sincere.

The old clock began to strike.

Everyone fell silent . . . Boom . . . boom . . . boom . . . On the twelfth stroke, from high up on the castle's battlements they heard the strains of a familiar pibroch. As the piper descended the winding staircase that led upwards from the main hall, the sound grew louder and was soon joined by a further three pipes, the musicians forming up beside the door to the turret in order to greet their leader. Now the pipers circled the ballroom and as the initial pibroch to welcome the New Year came to a close, glasses were raised and flushed faces lifted for a husband's or a lover's kiss.

Alan felt Flora's lips fasten upon his own. His action in drawing her to him was quite spontaneous. As they parted, he was relieved to see she was smiling happily. She passed on to Ewan McWorter who whirled her around with a force more appropriate to a man twenty years his junior before kissing her firmly on the lips and stepping back to regain his breath.

Cissy had arrived amongst them, exchanging greetings. She too moved along from Alan to Ewan.

The pipers were tuning up for the first reel of the

evening, and as the familiar notes fell upon well-accustomed ears, partners formed themselves into sets and the real dancing began. Alan found himself being led into the throng by Cissy Monteith who began by gathering up the Pullsons and the McPhees. She searched around for another pair. Flora stood uncertainly on the sidelines, with Ewan. She turned to find Jack on her other side.

'I used to be able to do this,' he said. 'My old grandpa always made us dance reels on Burns Night and at New Year. I'm not sure if I remember all the moves . . .'

'Come on, I'll show you!' she said, and grabbing his hand she led him over to join Cissy's set.

As the dance progressed and partners were exchanged all down the line, Alan complimented Janice on her appearance. 'You look great,' he told her. 'I'm glad to see you up and about again.'

She laughed. 'A testament to your skill, Alan,' she managed to gasp, as he passed her back to her husband and found Flora in his arms.

'Who's taking you home tonight?' he asked.

'Whichever one of you is still standing upright when dawn breaks,' she laughed.

'That could be me,' he said. 'Jack's had more than enough already.'

They parted and stood facing one another, clapping, as an excited, overheated Jack McDougal stumbled through the intricate steps before finally waltzing Cissy Monteith to the end of the row and returning her to her partner.

On the far side of the room, Desmond Bartlet sat beside his wife, looking less than delighted with this turn of events. Since his discussion with Jack McDougal about the kind of web site HDC might want, should their scheme go ahead after all, he had put in many hours on a design. True, Jack had made no promises. He had been careful to explain that his company might find the restraints put upon their proposal too inhibiting and decide not to proceed. He had, however, indicated that there was a good chance the company would proceed with the initial stages, those which had gained the approval of the authorities and ultimately the villagers themselves. With this in mind, Desmond had concentrated on the golf course and on promoting existing features in the village. Though he said it himself, he had done a splendid job and could not wait to get the site up and running.

Earlier on, he had gained a certain satisfaction from watching McDougal being shunned by many of the villagers. People must believe that the scheme was going to go ahead, if the Australian was still so unpopular. Now, however, here he was dancing with the Marquis's wife and the McPhees of all people. It hardly seemed fair. After months in their midst, he and Molly were still trying to become accepted as part of the community, and here was this stranger, an apparent threat to everyone's existence, cavorting with the people of influence and, to all appearances, having the time of his life.

Enviously, he watched the dancers enjoying themselves. He and Molly would have to join a club and learn, he decided. He wondered what he would look like in full Highland dress and made up his mind to go into town and order an outfit as soon as possible. He wondered what tartan he should choose. Monteith's was quite a decent combination of colours. Surely anybody living on the Marquis's land must be entitled to wear it?

The Jaguar drew up outside Flora's house, just as the sun began to peek above Caisteal an Spuilleadair. They had left Jack's hired car at the castle, to be collected when its owner recovered from his excesses.

With Flora's assistance, Alan hauled the Australian out of the car and, supporting him with one heavy arm hung loosely across his own shoulders, heaved him in through the narrow front door. By pushing from behind he finally persuaded a protesting Jack up the ladder and into the loft. A struggle ensued while Alan relieved him of his jacket and shirt before rolling him away from his kilt and on to the bed.

'He is OK?' Flora asked, looking up from the refrigerator where she was sorting out some breakfast for them both.

Alan rubbed his aching arms and took the chair closest to the fire, which had been coaxed into flame and was now roaring comfortingly up the chimney.

'Bacon and eggs all right?' she asked.

'Marvellous,' he replied. 'I don't know when I've been so hungry.'

'You can't have eaten much last night.'

She laid the rashers side by side in the pan and placed it on the hob. 'Mushrooms? Tomatoes?'

'Fried bread?' His eyes were sparkling.

'Doctor!'

'Forget the cholesterol for once – there's nothing to beat fried bread, all crisp and brown.'

They ate silently, enjoying the food and the intimacy of their situation.

'I'm glad I made it in the end,' he said, wiping a crumb of toast from the corner of his mouth and swallowing the remains of his coffee.

'Another cup?' she asked. 'I can easily brew some more.'

'Please.'

Any excuse to remain in her presence . . . but there were other, more pressing matters to be considered.

'Do you mind if I use your phone?' he asked. 'I'd like to know how those two chaps are doing.'

'Help yourself. I'll put the kettle on again.'

In the little kitchenette Flora filled the kettle and looked at herself in the glass, shaking her head at her reflection. What a sight! She wondered what he must think of her, so dishevelled, with not a scrap of make-up . . . It had been an interesting evening. Jack had been all attention until Alan's arrival but after that, he seemed to have bowed out. Had he felt intimidated by the attention which had been showered on the doctor? Of course, he had drunk rather a lot by then. She supposed it was to give him some Dutch courage. Instead of paying attention to her he had partnered several of the village women, some of whom, a week or two before, would have declined his offer. His thoughtful gesture, if that was what it was, had left Alan a free hand to partner Flora for the remainder of the night.

Her father was going to ask her about her evening. What was she to say? She had had a good time with Jack, certainly, and there was something of the rebel in her which tempted her to tell her father just that. But then, she had to admit to herself, once Alan arrived on the scene, she had had eyes for no one else.

She smiled at her own reflection. A while back she had resigned herself to becoming an old maid. Now here she was, choosing between a pair of suitors either one of whom would more than satisfy most of the women of her acquaintance. She ought to be beside herself with joy.

In her little living room, Alan was still discussing the two injured seamen with his colleague at the hospital. At last he put down the phone and accepted a steaming cup of coffee.

'How are they?' Flora asked.

'Not so good. The serious burns case has been airlifted to Glasgow to the special unit. The other fellow, the one with the broken arm, is still there. At the time, you know, it was touch and go whether he would lose it. Fortunately my original alignment was satisfactory so they managed to repair the torn artery and otherwise leave it alone. Providing we've managed to avoid infection, all should be well.'

'He's a lucky man,' she said. 'Last night they were saying that there was no way Dr Mac could have managed, clambering from one boat to another and then dealing with the casualties while the ship was tossing about like that.'

'They love to exaggerate,' Alan laughed. 'It was cold and wet, right enough, but I was too busy to notice any discomfort. Luckily I don't get seasick.'

'Jamie McPhee thinks you're a hero!'

She privately wondered if his actions last night would

be enough to allay the suspicions of those patients who still had not come to accept Alan as their doctor.

'When it comes to accidents at sea, I suppose it *is* a young man's calling,' he agreed. 'The only trouble is that for the most part a country practice is merely a sinecure for those about to retire. I can't see a young man, perhaps with a family to support, being able to afford to take over here. Even with the special supplement, it still doesn't bring in a living wage. It's a fine situation for gaining experience of general practice, but it's no prospect for anyone with ambition.'

Flora's heart sank. She had known he was unlikely to stay forever but that had not prevented her from hoping . . . dreaming of just such a possibility. In her mind she had begun to picture the two of them, growing old together, caring for the community in this idyllic setting.

'I'd better get along to the surgery,' Alan said. 'I'd like to check on Dr Mac and there might be other calls to attend to. By the way, Janice feels well enough to return to working on Thursdays, but I've drawn the line at her taking any house calls or emergency duties for the time being.'

'You've been working so hard lately,' Flora told him, 'it's time you had a day or two off. When is Dr Mac going to do a bit?'

'He seemed to enjoy being in charge last night,' Alan grinned. 'I don't doubt he'll be demanding to get back into harness any day now. We'll have to break him in gently at first, but it shouldn't be too long before things get back to normal.'

Flora tried to seem pleased, but could not help feeling

disappointed that he showed no sign of dismay at the prospect of moving on.

' You never did get to be a real Associate Practitioner,' she said. 'Will you take that up, once Dr Mac is fully operational?'

'I hardly think so. My original appointment was only for three months. They're unlikely to renew it. In any case, I've languished here far too long.'

'Like the poor chap in "La Belle Dame sans Merci",' she said.

> 'And I awoke and found me here,
> On the cold hill's side.
> La Belle Dame sans Merci,
> Had me enthralled.'

Alan quoted the poem, eyes shining in the light from the fire. He gazed intently at her for a few seconds. Flora held her breath, wondering what he could be thinking.

Suddenly he pulled her into his arms and kissed her.

'It was a marvellous evening,' he murmured, 'and that breakfast was the best I ever tasted.'

'I aim to please,' she retorted, lightly.

'Well, I must be off,' he sighed at last. 'I'll call in on Dr Mac and make sure there are no calls to answer at the surgery. I shouldn't worry too much about Jack. He may have a bit of a headache when he wakes up.'

'He'll have to take care of that himself,' she declared. 'I've promised to go over and spend the day with my father.'

Alan could not disguise his jubilation at her apparent indifference to Jack's discomfort. Impulsively he clasped her shoulders and drew her towards him for a parting kiss.

'Happy New Year,' he said, by way of an excuse.

How could she protest?

'Happy New Year, Alan.'

Last night Jamie McPhee had offered to give her a ride across to the island in his boat. Flora rang him now, to say she was ready.

'How you can continue to associate yourself with either of those two young men is more than I can fathom.'

Flora had been prattling away for some time, telling her father everything that had occurred at the castle the previous evening. Now he pushed aside his plate and placed both hands on the table, leaning forward to emphasise his point. 'Don't you understand what a spectacle you are making of yourself?'

'No, I don't understand.' Flora gaped at him, not understanding the vehemence of her father's words.

'What can anyone possibly have against Dr Beaton? He is one of the kindest men I know and a really good doctor. Ask Jamie McPhee how he performed yesterday after that boat accident. Ask Janice Pullson, if you don't believe me. If it hadn't been for Alan she could easily be away in a fever hospital, still fighting for her life!'

'I can only tell you what I've heard,' said Bill.

'All right then, tell me. All you do is keep pussyfooting around the subject, telling me to be careful. Careful of what, I'd like to know?'

Bill looked down at his hands which were busily engaged in filling his pipe. 'I'm given to understand that he was seen in company with a woman a short time after he arrived here. They were apparently – having sex – in the heather, out on Caisteal an Spuilleadair. The younger men around here think it a big joke, but the married ones are fearful for their wives' reputations. It's hardly the way for a doctor to behave.'

Flora was staring at him as though he were speaking in some foreign language. After a moment's silence, she said in a quiet voice, vibrant with anger, 'If it was true, and I'm sure it's not, what business is it of anyone else? It's not as if he were performing on the public highway!'

'He was spotted out on the hill above the village, with a woman who was quite plainly stripping off her clothes.'

'How could anyone possibly know it was Alan, away up there?'

'It was Giles Scott who saw him. He was viewing the mountainside through his binoculars . . . searching for birds . . . spotted a courting pair.'

'That's disgusting!' Flora slammed down her cutlery and began to clear the table.

Bill watched her without speaking.

'Anyway, it's too cold for that sort of thing at this time of year,' she protested.

'It wasn't recently. Some time in August, I believe.'

'And this stupid story is still going the rounds?' she demanded angrily. 'People can have very little to occupy their minds if that's all they can find to talk about!'

She stamped out into the kitchen and began washing dishes.

'Hey, leave me a few unbroken plates in there, will you!' her father called after her, hoping to lighten the atmosphere. He had known this would be her reaction, but could not let her continue to make a fool of herself in this way.

'I don't know how you can talk to people with minds like that,' Flora called out to him.

She came back into the room with a pile of clean plates and began replacing them in her mother's mahogany display cabinet. They only ever used these plates on high days and holidays, but the way she felt at the moment she could quite easily have thrown them all at her father.

'There has to be some perfectly simple explanation for all this,' she decided. 'Giles Scott is blind as a bat . . . look at the thickness of the lenses in his spectacles.'

'All I'm saying to you is this,' her father reasoned, 'just because you work with the fellow, doesn't mean you have to associate with him in your private life.'

He really did not wish to antagonise her. After all, she had been kind enough to come across and cook his dinner for him. He ought to be trying to cheer her up.

Flora slammed a saucepan on to the draining board and began to scrub it vigorously with steel wool.

'When was the last time you cleaned these properly?' she demanded by way of retaliation. She certainly knew how to goad him.

'I never trusted that McDougal fellow from the first,' her father now changed tack. 'I know your opinion of his fancy scheme, but believe me, there's nothing in it for any of us. Marty and Kirsty's enterprises are under threat and even the Post Office could be taken over. With that business gone, Jeanie and Willie wouldn't be able to keep the village store open.'

'What makes you think Jack has designs on the Post Office, for goodness' sake?' The whole thing was beyond reason.

'Post Office Counters have been quizzing Desmond Bartlet about the amount of trade and suggesting that if there are not substantial rises in the level of sales next season, they will have to close the counter down in the village store. There's a hint that there might be an alternative venue for a Post Office in the future. Where else but somewhere in McDougal's scheme of things?'

Flora didn't believe a word of any of this. Why did her father always have to spoil things in this way? She wished she had stayed in her own house today . . . perhaps invited Alan back to tea or gone for a walk over the mountain.

She had heard some wild village gossip in her time, but never anything to equal this vicious little tale. The very idea of Alan having a tumble in the heather in full view of the local twitcher! It would be hilarious if it was not so mean and spiteful.

Well, she had no intention of allowing this to go on festering in people's minds. She would tell him outright what they were saying about him. She was sure he must have a perfectly simple explanation.

Chapter Eighteen

'It's just as I feared.' Margaret McColl burst in upon Celia just as she was putting the final touches to a new display. Startled, she dropped her tack hammer and cursed in a most unladylike manner.

Most of the museum exhibits were still shrouded in their winter coverings, and in the absence of the customary spot lighting, switched off to conserve electricity, the chill gloom gave the building the atmosphere of a morgue.

Margaret shivered. 'Don't you have any heating on in here?'

'The temperature is kept constant,' Celia reminded her. 'It just seems colder in here at this time of the year. Anyway, what's just as you feared?'

'Eh? Oh . . . they're going to appeal after all!'

'Oh, no!'

' 'Fraid so. I was sure we hadn't heard the last of it when that Australian fellow turned up again at Christmas. There were the Monteiths and that Flora Douglas, wining and dining him . . . we should have guessed, then.'

'How d'you know they're appealing?' Celia was too busy getting ready for the new season to be worrying about all this now.

'This letter is from the Chief Planning Officer,' Margaret spread the paper on the reception desk. 'They're notifying all objectors to the original application that there's to be a Public Inquiry. If we want to make a submission to the Reporter, we have to put our arguments in writing within six weeks.'

'Reporter? Who's he?'

'He's a sort of impartial chairman or ombudsman . . . chosen by the Scottish Office to hear the arguments in cases of this kind. He listens to what all the parties have to say. It's upon his recommendation that the outcome of the appeal is decided.'

'I would have thought that we'd already said everything we can on the matter,' Celia protested. 'Won't our original letters of objection do?'

'It doesn't work like that,' her friend assured her. 'I'm no expert on these things, but I do know that objectors must present their arguments both in writing and, if required to do so, in person, at the public enquiry.'

'Can't you speak for us, as you did before?'

'It won't be sufficient . . . we really need an advocate with experience of the procedure. Someone who can assemble the witnesses and put the evidence in the best possible light.'

'Won't that be terribly expensive?'

'Yes, I'm sure it will.'

'I can't see people being prepared to put their hands that deeply into their pockets.' Celia picked up another tack and hammered it fiercely into the display board.

'I'm not so sure you're right.' Margaret was inclined to believe that her neighbours were as far-sighted as she was herself. 'If we manage to fight off this one group of developers, it will make others think twice about trying to take us over. I can't be alone in thinking this way.'

'You're not!' her friend assured her. 'But I can't answer for the others. You'll have to ask them yourself.'

When the Chairman of the Community Council was first approached to call a public meeting, he was sceptical about the amount of interest there would be. At first, he suggested that since the greatest impact of the development would be upon the island of Eisdalsa, they should fight their own battle. Not satisfied with this response, Margaret went around both villages informing key members of the community of the need for a strong local response to the appeal. By her efforts she was able to raise a powerful lobby in support of the meeting she wanted. Together, Dr Ewan McWorter, Marty Crane and Willie Clark from the village store approached Giles Scott on behalf of the villagers and finally persuaded him where his duty lay.

The meeting was called for eight o'clock on Thursday, 5 February. The local Councillor, Fergus Montgomery, was invited to attend and permission sought from the Roads and Ferries Department to supply an additional late ferry for the Eisdalsa contingent.

They had begun by laying out chairs for the meeting in the small room, used mainly for the toddlers' group and the meetings of the Churchwomen's Guild. By seven-thirty, all the seats were filled and more cars were pulling into the car park by the minute.

'We'll have to use the main hall,' Giles conceded at last, and orchestrated the removal by the simple process of asking each person already seated to carry his or her chair through into the larger room. While the village matrons then proceeded to struggle with the additional chairs stacked at the side and place them ready for those who were still arriving, their menfolk stood around in small groups, nodding sagely at the profound observations of their more garrulous companions. Only when it was quite clear that there was no more space available for further chairs to be placed, did these little groups break up and the men take their seats.

Alan Beaton, watching this activity with interest, responded to Flora's acid observations upon the men's behaviour by remarking, 'It's the way of things in Africa and most places east of Suez, so why not here?'

Had they been anywhere else, she might have thumped him for this remark. As it was she said, 'Oh, you!' and left it at that.

Their relationship had progressed easily since the departure of Jack McDougal on the day following the ball. When she had returned that evening from visiting her father, Flora found that Jack had already left. There was a note on the kitchen table and the money for his room.

'Sorry to have missed you,' was all he had written. 'Hope this will cover the cost of a night's stay.' Nothing more. No word of what he was proposing to do next, nor yet where he was going. Embarrassed, no doubt, by the fact that she and Alan had been obliged to carry him home and put him to bed, he had departed rather than face the music! Now that he and his wretched Milton T. Humbert had decided to go ahead with their scheming after all, she was glad to have seen the last of him.

As for the matter of Alan and the rumours about him . . . his actions on the night of the shipwreck seemed to have modified people's opinion. The nasty tales surrounding him seemed to have stopped circulating and the number of female patients presenting themselves at the surgery on days when Alan was consulting, had begun to increase. In view of this, she decided not to bother him with her father's tale.

At the front of the hall, Margaret McColl was on her feet, explaining the process by which a Public Inquiry would be conducted. She urged the meeting to accept the principle of engaging an advocate to speak for them.

All the old arguments about the development's threat to village life and the environment had been revisited, while Fergus Montgomery raised issues concerning over-burdening of public services – water, roads, electrical supplies and waste disposal. Although HDC had made certain proposals concerning the provision of access roads and additional water supplies, the Planning Department's subsequent investigation had revealed that the cost of linking the services to the new development would be theirs and there were insufficient funds to cover it.

Giles Scott, leaning forward in order to hear exactly what the Councillor was saying, observed dryly, 'Of course, it doesn't help that your lot agreed to the first part of the scheme. There are going to be questions asked such as why, if a golf course and a marina are in order, a hotel and all the other innovations HDC are proposing are not.'

'At the time,' the Councillor answered him defensively, 'the Planning Committee could find no argument against the construction of a golf course, nor a marina for that matter. Neither would be unsightly or cause any pollution so far as we could see, and both projects promised employment for local people.'

'Mark my words . . . once these monsters gain a foothold amongst us, they will infiltrate little by little into every aspect of village life.' This from a tiny, ancient lady, dressed from head to toe in rusty black. Her sharp tongue and wizened countenance made Martha McLean an object of fear amongst the village children who were convinced she was a witch. Her words tonight did indeed resound around the hall like some kind of incantation.

Ewan McWorter took up this refrain.

'What Martha says is right. If the golf club becomes popular and encourages greater numbers of visitors, and if the visiting yachts demand improved services, before you know it we will have further applications for all those other things which we are objecting to now. If we don't put a foot down at this stage, I can see the entire plan being forced upon us by stealth.'

Celia Robertson was on her feet. 'Mr Chairman, that has to be the strongest argument we have heard yet for pulling out all the stops, engaging a proper advocate and seeing these people off once and for all. If they get the message that the first two items are not going to lead to other developments, there is every chance they will pull out altogether. No organisation is going to go to such levels of expenditure with no prospect of making a profit, and there are limits to the money to be made from a golf course and a marina without supporting facilities.'

She sat down to applause, albeit mainly from the contingent from Eisdalsa.

'An advocate will cost a great deal of money. Are we prepared to pay for it?' demanded Giles Scott.

'If everyone in this hall tonight were to donate a fiver, we would be well on the way to raising a decent fighting fund,' suggested Bill Douglas.

'We could appeal for help on the Internet,' Desmond Bartlet called out. 'There are people all around the world who are familiar with Eisdalsa and the slate workings. Surely they will give their support?'

Bill Douglas was on his feet. There were several audible groans, but as always the Chairman gave their oldest inhabitant his moment.

'Mr Chairman, we can go on all night talking like this and making no decisions. There are six weeks in which to make any representations to the Reporter and we have already squandered the best part of one of them, deciding whether or not to hold this meeting.' Giles Scott shuffled uncomfortably while Captain Billy continued. 'I suggest we take a vote on whether to proceed along the lines put to us by Miss McColl, and then, if we are agreed, I suggest a small steering committee be set up to engage a suitable advocate and carry out whatever he requires by way of collecting information, witnesses and so on.'

For Bill Douglas it was a short speech and, as was

usually the case, to the point. It was clear that the meeting was in general agreement with what he had said.

'Very well,' Giles Scott decided. 'The proposal is that the community shall petition the Scottish Office Reporter, to uphold the decision of the Strathclyde Regional Council in refusing planning consent for certain aspects of the HDC scheme. To this end we agree to appoint an advocate, experienced in these matters, to put our case for us. All those agreed?'

A forest of hands went up. It was impossible to make an accurate count.

'Those against?'

This time only a scattering of hands were raised in some parts of the hall. Looking around, Flora decided that for the most part these were the parishioners most noted for keeping a very tight hold on their wallets while the remainder consisted of the few people who firmly believed they stood to make a killing out of the development.

'That motion is carried overwhelmingly,' declared Giles Scott.

He sat down, mopping his brow, apparently finished.

'What about the steering committee?' shouted someone from the back of the hall.

Momentarily startled and then embarrassed by his oversight, Scott called for nominations. A group consisting of Margaret McColl, Celia Robertson, Marty Crane, Jeanie Clark and Jamie McPhee was quickly nominated, and the remainder of the population were able to sit back, fully satisfied that their interests would be safeguarded.

Celia Robertson was on her feet.

'Mr Chairman, the amount of five pounds per head of those present has been suggested. May I propose that this be the minimum contribution of each household, but that those who are so disposed, may wish to pledge a larger sum? This additional money could be collected as and when necessary.'

It was agreed. As they filed out of the hall many people were willing to press their contributions upon Celia there and then. When only the steering committee and the Chairman of the Community Council remained, Celia was able to announce that she had already received the sum of nine hundred pounds.

'That will just about cover the cost of postage,' suggested Margaret McColl, rather cynically. 'I just hope we can find an advocate who is lenient with his charges, as well as experienced in these matters.'

Despite the rapid recovery of both his colleagues, Alan was still unable to heap the full burden of responsibility for the practice on Ewan McWorter's shoulders. He was also reluctant to allow Janice to turn out on a winter's night when it was her turn for emergency duty. Despite his determination to give greater consideration to his own career and to move on as soon as possible, he found himself, at the beginning of February, still carrying the major responsibility for the Seileach practice upon his own shoulders.

The Health Authorities, convinced by hospital reports that Ewan would soon be back to normal, had proposed that Alan remain for a further three months and begin to give a certain amount of time to the other practice in the

Associate Partnership. This involved him in travelling a considerable distance twice each week, and familiarising himself with a whole new group of patients. The second practice at Kilglashan, was run on very different principles from Ewan McWorter's. Many of the patients were town dwellers, albeit a very small country town, but their attitudes and expectations differed considerably from those of the slate islanders. The surgery operated on an appointments only basis and while this helped the GP in arranging his time to the best advantage, Alan was aware that people who were really ill and nervous about their condition were more reluctant to visit the doctor when they were obliged to think about it several days in advance. He had never subscribed to the idea of feeling ill to order. Perhaps more important than these considerations was the lack of community spirit he found in Kilglashan. There was a far greater interest in making money too. People seemed to be judged for what they had, or claimed to have, rather than what they were. He found their incipient greed and disregard for the interests of their neighbours anathema to him. If his experience in this other practice taught him anything, it was to look very closely at any situation he was offered in the future, before agreeing to take it on.

With these additional responsibilities, Alan seldom found time to glance at the papers. His only contact with the day-to-day news of what was happening in the outside world came to him via nightly news bulletins on the television.

On Friday evening, after a fairly relaxed day in which he had taken a few house calls while Janice took the morning and evening surgeries, he settled down to watch the news.

He sipped at the last of the malt whisky Ewan had given him as a New Year's present, and allowed his eyes to close. On screen, they had reached that part of the bulletin devoted to Scottish news. He came to with a start at the mention of one Alexander Thornton-Mowbray. It was not a name to forget. Paying greater attention now to the item under discussion, he turned up the sound.

'You represent the local population in this dispute over the installation of a windmill, Mr Thornton-Mowbray,' the interviewer was saying. 'We understand that the company in question is prepared to offer the villagers a considerable number of concessions should they withdraw their objections. Is it right that by pursuing your case, people may be denied the benefits associated with this development?'

The imposing figure on the screen, apparently captured leaving the Law Courts, was still wearing his wig and gown. He looked quite unlike the overweight gentleman Alan remembered, in tweed jacket and corduroys, struggling up Caisteal an Spuilleadair on a hot August day, seeking help for his wife.

'Let's get it straight,' Thornton-Mowbray interrupted the interviewer, 'these are not *my* objections. I have been briefed to represent the interests of the villagers . . . the very people you claim are being misled.'

'I didn't mean to imply you were misleading them, Mr Mowbray . . .'

'Thornton-Mowbray!'

'I beg your pardon, Mr Thornton-Mowbray.'

'My clients are fully conversant with the consequences of their decision.'

It was clear that the Advocate was challenging the presenter to intimate that the villagers must be out of their minds. The interviewer, however, checked himself just in time and there was a slight pause before the next question.

'That's telling 'em,' said Alan, who disliked the haranguing which these TV presenters often gave their interviewees. It wasn't as if they themselves cared, one way or the other, about the subject under discussion, just so long as the outcome was confrontational. If the interviewee lost his cool and caused sparks to fly . . . so much the better.

Alexander Thornton-Mowbray was not going to be led down that path.

'That's the kind of chap our people need for their inquiry,' Alan said to himself, remembering the discussion in the hall last night. 'Come to think of it, that's not a bad idea . . . He was here last summer and seemed to enjoy staying in the place. Maybe he would feel as strongly as the villagers about McDougal's proposals.'

He returned to the living room and thumbed through the local telephone directory. Margaret McColl was a healthy sixty-five year old. He had never had occasion to meet her in the surgery and had seen her only once – at last night's meeting.

'Good evening, Miss McColl. This is Dr Beaton, Ewan McWorter's locum . . .

'No, it's nothing to do with the surgery. I wonder, have you been watching the evening news on TV? You have? So you saw the item on the objections to a wind-powered generator? You did. Then perhaps you already know the Advocate who was being interviewed . . . I understand he was staying in a rented cottage on Eisdalsa last summer and wondered if perhaps you had come across him? Yes, that's right, the name's Thornton-Mowbray . . . Alexander Thornton-Mowbray. I believe he has quite a name for this particular line of work. Well, the fact is, I have his address . . . No, not a friend exactly, I just helped him out in a medical capacity while he was here. . . Owes me a favour? . . . I suppose you could say that, yes . . . So you'd like to get in touch with him? Well, this is the address . . .'

Desmond Bartlet was annoyed. There had been no word at all from Jack McDougal since their discussion about his part in HDC's plans. He had long ago completed the web site Jack had requested and, hearing nothing, had begun to assume that his work had been wasted. Now here they were, still pursuing the plan but without contacting him. Well, world-wide corporation or not, people did not treat Desmond Bartlet in that way and hope to get away with it!

He sat down at his computer, brought up the file he had worked on so assiduously before Christmas and began to revise the text. Taking each aspect of the plan in turn and using the arguments he had heard the evening before, he explained the islanders' viewpoint in every case. It was a clear and concise condemnation of the proposals. With an appeal to all those people around the world who had any connections with Eisdalsa to place their objections on record and support the fight by sending in donations, he completed the page and saved his work.

By rights he supposed he should show Celia or Margaret McColl what he had done, but there seemed to be nothing for them to object to. The sooner the message went out, the sooner the support would come flooding in.

On impulse he called up the site he had reserved for HDC, applied his new attachment and pressed OK.

'Dr Beaton? This is Margaret McColl. I thought you would like to know that we have made contact with Mr Thornton-Mowbray and he is willing to take our case.'

'I'm very pleased to hear it, Miss McColl. Thank you for letting me know.'

'In view of your previous involvement with Mr Thornton-Mowbray, I wondered if you might care to join our small working party, doctor?'

'Oh, I don't think that would be appropriate.' Alan was flattered but could see no way in which he could be of assistance. 'I've been here such a short while. . .'

'Celia Robertson tells me that Beaton doctors have served this community on and off for the best part of a hundred years. Surely that gives you some right to express your feelings in this matter?'

'Any claims I made would be viewed with some scepticism by the other side. Mr McDougal knows only too well that my personal association with Argyll is very recent.'

'Oh, well . . . if you insist.'

'If there is anything the practice can offer by way of evidence . . . the pressure which a seasonal influx of visitors might put upon the medical cover for the area, for instance . . . I'll be happy to lend a hand with that.'

'Thank you, Dr Beaton. That is a good idea. I may be in touch with you again.'

'Naturally, any matters relating to the practice should be addressed to Dr McWorter.'

'Of course.' She did not need Alan Beaton to remind her that Ewan was already a member of her working party. What she really hoped was to be able to provide their advocate with a group of witnesses who would represent the younger elements of the community. People who had plans for the future, which were unrelated to those of Milton T. Humbert and his wretched corporation. Ewan was a dear man, but he hardly presented the image of a progressive and forward-looking society.

The small contingent of islanders which travelled to Edinburgh to brief their Advocate returned confident that he was indeed the right man. What was more, understanding the difficulties often experienced by a group attempting to raise money for their cause, he had promised to put a ceiling on the charges they would have to meet.

'I've worked with community groups on many occasions,' he explained, 'and I've usually found that there is somebody willing to take on the burden of secretarial duties on behalf of the others. There are certain costs which cannot be avoided, unfortunately. My office staff must be paid for their time and there are practical necessities such as post and printing, then the witness state-ments have to be edited and published in book form . . . it all costs money. Charges can, however, be kept to a minimum by appointing one of yourselves to act as my clerk, as it were, a go-between with my office. Someone who can collect all the data, brief the witnesses and chivvy them up if they're slow in coming forward with their statements.'

'The witnesses don't actually have to stand up and give their evidence?' This was from Bill Douglas. Thornton-Mowbray seemed surprised.

'You said the statements had to be printed . . .'

'Oh, yes. Each witness reads out his statement in full and then makes himself or herself,' he smiled broadly at Celia and Margaret, 'available for cross questioning by the other side.'

'Will all the witnesses be local people?' asked Margaret, thinking of the likely additional expense of bringing in outsiders.

'Scottish Natural Heritage are often interested in these matters. In your case,' he addressed Celia, 'there is likely to be some input from the Scottish Museums Council. As I see it, a major part of your case is related to the effect the development might have on those who visit the area to experience its natural beauty or delve into its histori-cal associations.'

'How will we get in touch with these organisations?' Margaret asked. She knew Celia had certain contacts through the museum but had no idea where to find Scottish Natural Heritage.

'Leave that to me,' he suggested. 'I work all the time

with these and other bodies concerned with the environment. You'd be surprised how many groups will creep out of the woodwork once they hear about an inquiry of this kind.'

'None of them was interested when we attended the initial meeting,' grumbled Bill Douglas. 'It would have saved us all a lot of time and trouble if they had made objections then.'

'A determined Planning Department has its ways of clouding the issue when it is basically in support of a project,' he explained. 'Nothing that could be used against them, you understand,' he added hastily, 'but there are ways of *not* saying certain things which can make the proposals seem innocuous. The good thing about involvement by public bodies,' he added, 'is that they won't make any charge for their time. It might, however, be a nice gesture if you could manage to accommodate them yourselves? Apart from helping their organisations with expenses, it's a good opportunity to get to know the representatives and put over your point of view. Remember, they will be representing their own interests at the inquiry, not yours. It's as well if both coincide!'

They chose Jamie McPhee to put the case for the local fishermen and Celia to explain how the development might disrupt or even destroy the many sites of historical interest in the area.

'Someone has to talk about the danger to the north quarry . . . the one they're going to open for a marina,' said Bill. 'The rim of the quarry is already breaking down. I can remember when that retaining wall continued around three sides. Now two are already exposed to the waves at high tide.'

Dr McWorter could see that his old friend was anxious to take part as a witness but felt he must nip the idea in the bud. Margaret was quite right to suggest that it was younger voices that should be heard. 'There are two aspects to the marina proposal,' he said. 'One is an engineering consideration and it seems to me that Mr Wilson is the obvious choice there – the other is the navigational argument. We all know how treacherous these waters can be. In bad weather, yachts in the hands of amateur sailors would stand little chance of reaching a safe harbour at that end of the island.'

Bill was going to take up the point and give them an anecdote or two about the navigating of problem harbour entrances when Ewan interrupted him once again.

'The man to talk on that subject is undoubtedly Robbie Fullerton.'

As master of the puffer, he knew every small island, every submerged rock and every treacherous current in the sound. His word, on matters of safety at sea, was beyond dispute.

'I was going to suggest Barbara Fullerton to speak on behalf of the parents and the village school,' Celia put in. 'Could husband and wife both be witnesses?'

'I can't see why not,' said Margaret.

'We must involve some people from the other side,' said Bill, still smarting from Ewan's rebuff. 'What about Jeanie? After all, she might be expected to welcome the influx of trade. If she were to speak out against the scheme, it might have some weight with the Reporter.'

Celia agreed that what he said was absolutely true.

'We certainly don't want our wee village shop changed into some modern minimarket that looks just like all the others,' Jeanie Clark agreed. 'We like our village store as it is, warm and friendly, a place where you can have a chat and exchange gossip . . . not some chrome and glass affair which you can find almost anywhere in the country.'

'Save it for the inquiry,' said Margaret, bluntly. 'We don't need to spend time now deciding what our witnesses ought to be saying. The statements need to be personal, fresh, the work of one mind . . . not a committee. Until someone comes and asks for help in writing down what they want to say, let's leave it to the witnesses themselves.'

She turned now to Ewan McWorter.

'Dr Mac, have you thought what would be the effect on your practice of a large number of additional people arriving in the district for perhaps six or nine months of the year?'

'Young Beaton and I were discussing this point only yesterday,' he answered.

So, thought Margaret, he did continue to give it some thought after all.

'It could be rather tricky,' the old doctor explained. 'There's no provision made in this practice for the additional patients who may or may not present themselves during holiday periods. At present the extra bodies we deal with are offset by the fact that some of the regulars absent themselves from time to time and the whole thing balances itself out. Now if you're asking me what would be the case if, added to our present commitment, we were to have a big hotel, a caravan park or chalet complex, and a marina full of visiting yachts, I can tell you we could not cope, certainly not with the staff we have at present. Whether the Health Board would be prepared to fund an additional GP and perhaps a couple of nursing staff, I can't say, but I think it's very unlikely.'

'A medical service which is spread too thinly would endanger the whole population?' verified Margaret.

'Precisely.'

'Will you stand up and say that?' she demanded.

'No. If I do, they will simply think that this old buffer is too set in his ways and doesn't want to change. They'd blame me for wanting to continue as a one-man band, when in fact nothing is farther from the truth. I am enjoying working with my two young colleagues at the present time, but the Board has made it quite clear that as soon as I'm able to work full-time, one of the others has to go!'

'Would you allow Dr Beaton to speak for the practice?'

'Of course, if he were willing, but he's not. He is very conscious of being the new boy around here. Last night we decided Janice should be the one to speak on our behalf.'

'That's good,' said Margaret. 'It will give us a nice balance of the sexes. Now, who else?'

'I thought Marty Crane for the hotel trade, and perhaps one of the people who has a letting cottage . . . oh, and we must certainly have one of the B&B ladies.'

'What about my Flora? She'd give a good account of herself and she's been running her B&B business for at least five years.'

Conscious that they had deliberately prevented Bill Douglas from being one of the witnesses, Margaret did not have the heart to deny him this second opportunity to be involved.

'Flora it is then . . . always provided she's willing to do it.'

Chapter Nineteen

'Alex, Alex! It's gone eight o'clock. You said you wanted to be up and away by now!'

Alicia Thornton-Mowbray carried crockery to the table and began arranging it.

She had been delighted when her husband had agreed to take on the Eisdalsa case. They had stayed in the district on a number of occasions, enjoying the anonymity it gave them. Alex's frequent appearances on television, together with newspaper reports of planning disputes in which he was involved, had given him a very high profile in recent years. By booking in as plain Mr and Mrs Mowbray they had managed to blend in with the locals without being recognised. Or, if they were, people were too polite to mention it.

Last summer they had decided upon a holiday cottage in preference to the hotels in the locality, and had relished the freedom which this had given them.

Understanding her husband's need for a quiet place in which to relax after the stresses of the working day, Alicia had chosen for the period of the Inquiry the cottage they had occupied last summer.

Alex stumbled down the stairs and cursed loudly as he hit his head on the lintel of the low doorway.

'These places must have been built for midgets,' he complained, not for the first time since his arrival. Last time it had taken him the best part of a week to remember to duck his head.

'Not as idyllic as we remembered,' he told his wife now. 'I'd forgotten about the low ceilings.'

'Have you hurt yourself?' she asked, giving him a careful appraisal as he took his seat at the table. His iron-grey hair was carefully cut, left just long enough to give him an air of flamboyance while retaining the degree of dignity which his appearances in a Court of Law demanded. By the man in the street, she considered he might be taken for a writer, perhaps, or an actor . . . a well-groomed actor, of course. Alicia kissed the injured spot on the crown of his head and rubbed her fingers through the tight curls which had so embarrassed him in his youth.

'Come on, eat your cornflakes,' she urged him. 'I've cooked bacon and eggs for a special treat.'

He was not normally allowed so much cholesterol at breakfast – doctor's orders – but they both agreed that the sea air made them ravenously hungry and she knew he would get nothing to eat between now and this evening. Alex never ate in the middle of the day while he was working.

'You coming along this morning?' he asked.

'Who's speaking?'

'Well, there'll be the opening remarks by the Reporter. It's your friend Miles McQuarry, by the way. Then the representative from Humbert Developments will give his reasons for appealing against the Council's decision. I have no idea what he's going to say . . .'

'I thought the evidence had to be given in writing, weeks before the Inquiry?'

'Yes . . . well . . . all the other side have produced is their original plan with a few alterations. It's a proper mess. The Reporter could have something to say about their lack of preparation but Miles is a fairly reasonable character. He won't spend time nit-picking over the rules . . . he'll be more interested in everyone getting a fair hearing.'

'But suppose they come up with something quite new? You won't have been able to prepare a rebuttal,' his wife complained.

'Oh, I don't anticipate any surprises.' He sipped at his coffee while he flipped through the pages of the neatly bound submission which his own side had managed to produce.

'I think I'll give it a miss today,' Alicia replied in answer to his question. 'I'll just potter about here . . . take a walk round the island and speak to a few of the natives. You never know, I might pick up something useful to the cause. Anyway, I've heard Miles speaking before and I've read the proposals put forward in the planning application. It's the local people I'm looking forward to hearing. How do you think they'll stand up under questioning?'

'Who can say? So much depends on HDC's representative. We have no idea who they've briefed. All the documentation I've seen so far has been signed by Milton T. Humbert himself.'

*

Celia was terrified. She hadn't stood up in front of a group of her peers since the day she'd received her retirement presents and burst into tears before the end of her reply. She had taken early retirement, worn out by the continuous haranguing of successive governments and the relentless progress towards student and parent power.

She shuffled through the notes for her presentation, gulped down her third cup of coffee that morning, this one laced with a drop of whisky, and hoped someone had remembered to unlock the loos at the hall!

Bill Douglas might have wished he had some more important role to perform but, ever practical, he had been the one to offer to get in early and supervise setting up the hall. Alex Thornton-Mowbray had explained to him how the hall should be laid out and now, in company with Tony Squires, the caretaker, he arrived promptly at nine o'clock to start work. The two men began by erecting a trestle table.

'Can't you get those legs down your end?' grumbled the caretaker.

Captain Billy struggled to no avail.

'It'll take half a can of WD40 to loosen this rust,' he grumbled.

'It's a knack,' the other told him, unhelpfully. He pulled down his own end of the trestle table and waited for Bill to do the same.

'Here, let me lend a hand.'

The newcomer was a stranger to them both, but in the

urgency of the moment they accepted his help and soon the table was in position with the required number of chairs set behind it.

Soon two further tables were set up, one facing the first and the other the front of the hall. Tony began to put out the seating for the general public while Bill and the stranger erected one further, smaller table, facing the room

'Top table,' said Bill, who had in his hand the sketch plan hastily drawn for him by Alex in the bar the night before.

'How many chairs needed there?' asked Tony.

'One,' said the stranger. 'That's mine.'

To Tony, the announcement meant nothing. His job was to open up the hall on request and keep the place clean. The former he accomplished with West Highland alacrity, the latter with a degree of indifference which was illustrated by the clouds of dust which arose as each pile of chairs was separated and placed in position.

Captain Billy's response was immediate.

'You'll be the Reporter, sir.' If he had been wearing his service cap he would have saluted.

'Yes, indeed . . . Miles McQuarry. How do you do?' As they shook hands, he looked about him, searching for a men's room.

'Is there somewhere where I may wash my hands?' he asked. The sleeves and front of his jacket were dusty and his tie had slipped round beneath his ear. 'I wouldn't like your people to think I didn't care!'

Janice Pullson hoped they would get to her sometime

during the afternoon. Alan had promised to cover for her tomorrow, if it was really necessary, but she had already imposed too much on his generosity, ever since he'd arrived. Ewan's return to work, far from reducing Alan's burden, seemed to have increased it. He really needed his day off.

The three of them had sat around in Ewan's living room, debating for hours how they were going to put their case. She had gone away at last to write her own statement. Mr Mowbray had said it must be brief and to the point if they hoped to hold the attention of the Recorder. Much of what they wanted to say would have to be left, in the hope that the other side's questions would give Janice an opportunity for expanding on the balder statements.

'I find it very difficult to think on my feet,' she told them, apprehensively. 'I can always remember what I *should* have said when it's too late.'

'We're all like that,' Alan tried to reassure her. 'Just do your best. It's not a trial, you know, and after all, what we doctors have to say may not carry any weight at all with the Recorder.'

'Either Alan or I will try to be in the hall when it's your turn,' said Ewan. 'We'll sit close enough to pass you a note if it's really necessary.'

Flora had taken leave to attend the whole of the hearing. Still not totally convinced that HDC's plan was going to be all that bad for the economy of the district, she had determined to listen to all the arguments before making up her own mind. Nothing could possibly be as black and white as her father had painted it. Certainly the golf course would be welcomed by the locals and she could not see much to complain about in the idea of a marina on the island, although she understood there might be problems with the entrance to the old flooded quarry. She herself would be pointing out that those who stayed in her bed and breakfast accommodation were people who enjoyed the peace and quiet of the countryside. They were not fanatical divers, did not sail dinghies or water ski . . . they preferred to roam the hills in search of wild flowers, to fish in the quarries or out in the bay on calm days and, when the opportunity arose, to explore the smaller islands in the sound. They came hoping to see wildlife, the large variety of sea birds which the slate islands boasted, the wild animals. Others might be searching for information about their ancestors amongst the records Celia kept in her museum. What was certain was that no one came here looking for holiday night life, unless it was to sample the unusual atmosphere of the Tacksman's Bar, the friendly reception afforded by Marty Crane or Ruth's magnificent cooking.

Whether she found herself siding with HDC or not, these were undeniable facts.

The helicopter left the launch pad at Connel at ten o'clock, precisely. Jack would have chosen a less spectacular means of arrival but Milton was determined to impress his adversaries. They needed to be shown exactly who they were dealing with!

'Are you sure you know where we're headed?' he demanded of the pilot as they circled above the village and descended towards the car park at the rear of the village hall. He didn't remember any building which he would consider suitable for an official inquiry. Jack had assured him that the proceedings would be in the hands of a top official from the Scottish Office. Milton recognised the hotel and the school . . . surely they wouldn't hold the meeting there?

'Come on, this is the place,' said Jack, leaping down on to the ground and holding the door open for his boss to clamber out. He turned to dismiss the pilot. 'Be back at four o'clock. There's no point in you hanging about here all day.'

He watched the machine thrust into the air and hover for a few moments above the flooded quarry behind Seileach village before soaring up and over Caisteal an Spuilleadair. As the sound of the engines faded, he found Milton at his elbow.

'I thought you said this was to be conducted like a court of law?' he said.

'So it is,' Jack told him. 'In the village hall. I don't know what you're beefing about. This is what they mean, here in Scotland, by "bringing democracy to the people".'

Milton sighed, relieved he had not taken Jack's advice about engaging a Scottish Advocate. He wouldn't have had the nerve to expect a high-class lawyer to conduct his case in a place like this.

Jack looked about him, recognising a few of the people who were lining up to take their place in the hall. It seemed as though there might be quite a crowd. He had hoped that with the inquiry taking place mid-week, most of them would be obliged to stay away. No doubt it would be regarded by many as the best entertainment offered in the village for many months. He wondered if Flora would be there. He hoped she would give him a chance to explain why the appeal was still going ahead despite his promise to dissuade Milton. He knew she would be thinking badly of him for clearing off without saying goodbye . . .

Milton had ignored all his warnings about the opposition he was likely to meet. He had convinced himself that the demonstration against his project was being whipped up by a minority in the community, just a few people with a grudge against foreign interference. He put his faith in support from the castle and those English people who had invested their pensions in the place. Some of them were going to make a handsome profit when he eventually bought them out.

Inside the hall, there was a flurry of anticipation at their appearance. The helicopter's arrival had not gone unnoticed and a rumour quickly spread that a national television crew had arrived. When the doors swung open to admit Milton T. Humbert and Jack McDougal, the wave of disappointment which passed through the public was recognised even by Milton himself.

The chairs carefully allocated to the principals in the Inquiry had long ago been removed by those in the body of the hall and it was the Reporter himself who finally found one for Milton.

'P'raps that'll teach 'em to get here in good time tomorrow,' observed Bill, as he slid into the seat beside his daughter.

Flora did not answer.

Right up to the last moment, she had hoped Jack would stand by his promise to dissuade Milton from going ahead with the appeal. She firmly believed she had shown him how pointless it was for HDC to continue the fight. Having failed in that, the least he could have done was to stay away from the hearing himself. She saw him scanning the faces of the crowd and purposely looked away, not wishing him to see her.

Margaret McColl, seated alone at the table allocated to their Advocate and herself, watched Milton Humbert arrange documents on the table in front of him. She recognised the set of HDC plans, now so familiar to them all, and their own submission, neatly bound between blue covers with a distinctive black plastic spine. There were also one or two letters. Otherwise the table was bare.

By contrast, the table set out in front of her was laden with boxes of files, all neatly numbered. Two clean note pads and a jam jar of well-sharpened pencils completed their layout.

In the last few moments the Reporter had disappeared only to re-emerge on the stroke of nine-thirty, preceded by Alexander Thornton-Mowbray.

There was a buzz of excitement as many in the body of the hall, caught sight of their Advocate for the first time.

He was an impressive figure, well over six foot in height with a leonine head set between broad shoulders. A well-cut, fine mohair suit in charcoal grey gave his figure a rather more trim appearance than it deserved. He cast a broad smile in the direction of his audience, acknowledging one or two of those he had met the previous evening.

One cynic was heard to murmur to his neighbour, 'Well, if looks are anything to go by, he might just be worth the money he's charging us.'

' Wait 'til you hear him speak! 'The remark came from Jamie McPhee, seated in the row behind. In order to miss nothing of the debate, he had thought it worth giving up three days' fishing. He would make up his quota next week.

The Reporter exchanged a few words with Councillor Fergus Montgomery, who had taken up his position on the table set aside for witnesses. Solemnly, he moved across to shake hands with Alex and exchange a few pleasantries. It was clear to everyone that they knew one another, but they must not appear to be too familiar. Lastly, he introduced himself to Milton T. Humbert.

'I am your Reporter for the purpose of this exercise,' he explained to the American.

'What's that . . . like a judge?' Milton found the whole thing quite bewildering. Jack had tried to enlighten him on the procedure, but at that time he had not been prepared to concentrate. In his opinion it was time some of these European countries scrapped their muddled medieval ways and got themselves tuned in to the twentieth century.

'I will explain the procedure in a few moments,' said Miles McQuarry. 'You are not represented legally?'

'No, I intend to conduct my case myself!' Milton replied, rather too confidently.

McQuarry raised his eyebrows, ever so slightly, and as he passed in front of Alex and returned to his seat, murmured 'Pity!'

'Now then, ladies and gentlemen . . .'

McQuarry might not carry the title of Judge, but it was not difficult to see him in that role. In that bare, poorly furnished place, sadly in need of a coat of paint and a lick of polish, his presence was such that one could easily be deceived into thinking this was indeed a court of law. The audience fell silent, listening intently to what he had to say.

'This is not a court of law, but it is a Public Inquiry held on behalf of the Secretary of State for Scotland and, consequently, of Parliament itself. It is my task to listen to all of the submissions in the case, and based upon what I hear in the course of the next three days I shall make my recommendations to the Secretary of State. These will be published within six weeks.

'Witness statements have already been submitted in full and circulated to all interested parties. I shall ask each witness to make only a brief statement outlining his or her main points and then allow time for questions to be asked on any part of the full statement.' At this point he paused and addressed Milton's table.

'Despite repeated requests for a statement, I have received nothing from the appellants in this case, other than the original plan submitted to the Local Planning Department. Do I take it that this is your submission?'

This had been a subject of heated debate between Jack and his employer. Jack had read the instructions they had received most carefully.

'You have to prepare something in addition to the plans,' he'd insisted. 'They will want reasons as well as intentions.'

To this Milton had replied airily, 'When have you ever heard Milton T. Humbert give reasons for anything he does? Our plan is a good one . . . good enough to speak for itself!'

'What if some of the points are questioned? You'll have to give an explanation then.'

'If that happens I shall just bring in the little extras we've considered – like a new medical centre and the bridge which I'm prepared to fund out of my own pocket!'

The Reporter was continuing with his introductory remarks.

'Additional material, not already submitted in writing, will not be allowed.' His glance travelled from Thornton-Mowbray to Councillor Montgomery and then across to Milton. While the two former nodded their agreement, Milton appeared thoroughly confused. He looked angrily at his companion, shuffled the little pile of paper in front of him and was about to get to his feet to make a protest when Jack pulled him down and whispered a few words into his ear.

'Now,' the Reporter continued, ignoring the slight disturbance, 'during the proceedings I shall be taking notes and as I cannot write in shorthand, I fear this may take a little time. You will forgive me if I have to ask you to pause occasionally while I catch up.'

There was a ripple of laughter around the hall. It was

probably a set speech which he used on all such occasions, but it helped to relieve the tension. He turned towards Milton.

'The appellant in this case is the Humbert Development Corporation of the United States of America, represented by its President, Mr Milton T. Humbert. Speaking on behalf of the Argyll and Bute District of the Strathclyde Regional Council we have Councillor Fergus Montgomery, and for the residents of the islands of Seileach and Eisdalsa, Mr Alexander Thornton-Mowbray, QC. Two other bodies have submitted evidence. These are the Scottish Natural Heritage Trust and the Scottish Museums Council whose witnesses will be Mr Martin McLure and Miss Isobel Shankey. These two witnesses have asked to be allowed to give their evidence on Friday and I shall see to it that we time their submissions for eleven o'clock, just after the morning break. Councillor Montgomery has asked to be allowed to speak this afternoon, directly after the appellant has made his case. Are any of your witnesses tied to a particular timetable, Mr Thornton-Mowbray?'

'Only Dr Pullson, sir. She too would be obliged if she may give her evidence today.'

'Very well . . . let's to it then. Mr Humbert, you have the floor!'

Milton rose to his feet and lifted the bulky folder containing his company's detailed plan.

He cleared his throat and began to read straight from the document. When he had completed the first paragraph, the Reporter stopped him.

'Mr Humbert, I had overlooked the fact that your company has failed to comply with the requirements, as laid down in my letter to you of the fifth of February. When dealing with someone from overseas, it is customary to be somewhat lenient in these matters. I am therefore prepared to accept your original plan in place of the submission which was asked for, but I must insist you do not take up the time of this hearing by reading the entire contents of this lengthy document. Please deliver a short résumé . . . I can allow you ten minutes only before I call for questions from the other parties.'

Angrily, Milton stumbled through the document from one page to the next. There were frequent pauses while he read whole paragraphs to himself first and then attempted to paraphrase what was there. Finally he threw down the document in disgust and leaned across the table, supporting himself on his hands and addressing McQuarry directly.

'This is a development designed to bring prosperity to a rundown backwater. It is my company's intention to invest large sums of money to turn the area into a tourist paradise, and by so doing provide jobs for the unemployed while improving business for those enterprises already in operation. The people opposed to my plan are a small and selfish minority . . . big fish in a little pond, in which they control everything that goes on. All the rest have either been bribed or threatened into objecting to my scheme. The poor people, those without decent housing and proper jobs, welcome what we are intending to do here.'

He sat down to a swelling murmur of protest from the body of the hall.

'Thank you.' The Reporter prevented him from standing again to defend his accusations. 'Councillor Montgomery?'

The Local Authority's position had been made all the more difficult by the fact that the Planning Department initially supported the scheme, and had indeed encouraged the developers to believe there would be no problem in obtaining full planning consent. When the Planning Committee subsequently turned down a major part of the plan it was on the grounds of lack of money alone. Although Humbert Developments had agreed to finance improvements to the infrastructure of the two villages, the increased traffic anticipated would require major improvements to the single road linking the islands with the nearest trunk road. This constituted a level of investment which the Council could not afford. Permission had, however, been given to go ahead with the golf course and the marina, neither of which were thought to put pressure on the roads.

At the start, the Planning Officers had either deliberately, or by an oversight, given insufficient information to water and electricity suppliers, who had raised no objections at the time. Now they were saying that the estimated increase in population would necessitate the upgrading of the electricity supply and a major investment to improve water and sewerage provision. Neither body could support such expenditure.

Fergus Montgomery, Chairman of the Area Planning Committee, had first been elected to office twenty-five years before. His family farm and the small group of caravans and holiday chalets he owned were insufficient to maintain his comfortable lifestyle without the additional income from his activities as a local representative. While he had come to regard his elected office as his due, he was nevertheless well aware of his reliance upon the continued support of the voters. The strength of opposition to this plan, as witnessed by the sackful of letters of protest as well as the unprecedented numbers of people turning up for the Council meetings, had woken him up to the fact that if he did not show solidarity with his neighbours, his seat might be in danger at the next election.

The slap-happy manner in which the Planning Officers had treated the proposal initially had left the Chairman of the Planning Committee in a very difficult position. Fergus had been obliged to spend long hours in consultation with the authority's legal department in order to find a convincing defence for their decision to refuse the application.

He rose to question Milton.

'May I ask Mr Humbert what correspondence he has entered into with the various bodies concerned with the environment? I have in mind the RSPB, SERA, Scottish Wildlife Trust and others.'

Milton looked at Jack who almost imperceptibly shook his head.

'I relied upon my staff to carry out researches on my behalf,' he answered, arrogantly. 'They were given to understand that such enquiries would be the responsibility of the Planning Department.'

'Oh, I see. Then you may not have learned of the by-laws relating to safe access to those places to which members of the public are invited for their enjoyment?'

'Sorry?'

'I refer, sir,' addressing the Reporter, 'to that section of the local by-laws referring to dangerous structures visited by members of the general public, such as the quarry mentioned in Mr Humbert's proposals for a marina.'

'Just hold on there, fella!' Milton forgot for a moment where he was. 'I beg your pardon, sir,' he apologised to the Reporter, 'but I already have consent for the conversion of the north quarry into a marina.'

'So I believe. Mr Montgomery?'

'Consent for that part of the plan *was* given, sir, provided the developers complied with certain unspecified conditions. If I may refer to the Argyll and Bute District by-laws Section eight, sub-section C . . .' Fergus Montgomery lifted three sheets of paper from the file which lay open in front of him and distributed one to each of the tables '. . . you will note that this requires owners of property representing a danger to members of the public to have it suitably fenced. A structure such as a quarry would require a fence at least two metres in height.'

'That's not a problem.' Milton breathed a sigh of relief. 'My company will be happy to provide such a fence.'

'Another condition of granting this application,' Fergus pressed on, disregarding the interruption, 'is that the proposal shall in no way detract from the natural amenity of the area.'

'Sailing boats are as common as seagulls around here,' declared Milton, exasperated by the Councillor's pedantic manner. 'How could you claim they would detract from the view?'

'We have nothing against the boats,' Fergus Montgomery told him patiently, 'it is the fence which would contravene the by-laws.'

Milton sat back, a wide grin on his face, and tucked his thumbs under a pair of extremely colourful braces.

'If this fence is so important . . . why isn't there one in place, already?'

'When the by-laws were passed in 1975, the quarry was already in existence.'

'So?'

'We can only impose these by-laws when granting a new planning consent. Until now, no one has asked to alter the quarry in any way, therefore the Council had no jurisdiction in the matter.'

'Supposing someone had fallen into it and drowned?'

'Ah, then we could have made an order had we been so directed by the Procurator Fiscal investigating the death.'

Milton was pale and beginning to shake with rage. Jack leaned forward and tapped him on the arm, telling him to sit down, let the matter go.

His point made to his satisfaction, Councillor Montgomery resumed his seat, while the audience, who until now had been straining to hear the exchange and experiencing some difficulty in following the argument, suddenly burst into applause. Old Fergus was actually earning his money for a change!

The Recorder called for silence and cautioned the public about making such spontaneous outbursts.

Alex Thornton-Mowbray now took over the questioning.

'Your defence of this proposal is based very largely

upon your ability to provide employment, Mr Humbert. Would you agree?'

Was he being sarcastic? Margaret wondered. She was goaded into action when Alex whispered, 'find document C3.' She searched the files for the paper while he continued.

'You state that there is a high proportion of unemployed people in the district, and it is this situation which you aim to put to rights with your development.'

Milton agreed.

'A very worthy aim, I am sure. Can you tell us what proportion of the community was registered as unemployed at the time when your research was conducted?'

Milton turned to Jack, who wrote down a figure and passed it to him.

'In September, the figure was around five per cent,' he answered. Then, grasping his opportunity to show how well-informed he was about local conditions, 'Naturally, at that time of the year there is bound to be a higher level of employment.'

'Because of the tourist trade, you mean?'

'Of course.'

'Of the five per cent, those remaining unemployed at that time of the year, how many do you believe would be suitable for work in your own organisation?'

'I don't know . . . it would depend on what skills and experience they could offer.'

'But, Mr Humbert, there is well-documented evidence to show that the hotel and catering industry in Argyll is lamentably short of skilled personnel to cover the summer season.'

He addressed the Reporter. 'If you will refer to item C3 of my supporting material you will find a recent report on the employment situation in the Argyll and Bute District. I put it to you, Mr Humbert, that far from providing jobs for the unemployed, you will be drawing on the limited staffing resources currently available during the summer season, and by attracting newcomers into the area, to live and work, will only be adding to the unemployment figures during the off-peak season.'

Jack had known all along that this was a weak point in Milton's argument. He remembered discussing employment with Desmond Bartlet, when they had been planning the web site. That was another thing he ought to have followed up . . .

The truth was that since Christmas he had become less and less enthusiastic about Milton's proposals for Eisdalsa. His employer's determination to go ahead with the appeal was born more of pride than any real commitment to improving the situation of the islanders.

'There will be no off-peak season, as you describe it,' protested Milton. 'My guests will be able to enjoy the benefit of a covered garden area where they will be protected from the weather at all times.'

'It is difficult to imagine a large number of holiday makers paying a great deal of money to remain beneath your glass dome, which from October to March will, for the most part, be obscured by continuous rain and lashed by Atlantic gales,' observed Thornton-Mowbray. 'Thank you, Mr Humbert. I have no further questions for the present.'

*

Janice Pullson spoke of the problems likely to arise from a seasonal increase in temporary patients, within a practice which covered a hundred square miles of mountainous terrain, with its patients scattered for the most part in small isolated communities.

'My colleagues and I suggest that the concentration of a large number of people in this one area will deprive others in our practice of their fair share of the medical cover available,' she concluded.

When it came to questioning her, Councillor Montgomery emphasised the problem by asking, 'Dr Pullson, am I to understand that the Health Board will be unable to provide additional cover to accommodate these increased numbers of temporary patients?'

'Our enquiries have shown that additional staffing would only be considered if, after a number of years, it could be shown that the increase in workload was constant.'

Thornton-Mowbray was on his feet in an instant.

'Item D1, sir,' he called out. 'A letter from the Regional Health Board confirming what Dr Pullson has just told you.'

The Reporter seemed to be having some difficulty finding the particular document. Margaret crossed the floor to give him a second copy.

Janice, grateful for Alex's support, continued a little more confidently. 'Since the practice is already compensated for the additional miles to be travelled, the only justification for additional staff would be a figure well above the current patient list.'

'But you already have a tourist influx during the

summer months,' protested Milton. 'How do you cope with that?'

'The numbers of visitors are, at present, in reasonable proportion to the permanent population, and time given to their care can be offset by the occasional absence of regular patients who are themselves away on holiday. There is pressure on the facilities during the months of July and August but at a time when minor ailments such as colds and 'flu are at a minimum. The figures quoted in HDC's plan far outweigh the number of permanent patients.'

Milton leaped into the fray with both feet. 'These temporary patients would of course be expecting to pay for your services,' he decided. 'You would not treat them under the National Health Service. The extra money could pay for additional staff.'

'Anyone who normally receives treatment under the National Health Service is entitled to the same services as he would receive from his own doctor, that includes free drugs if that is his usual situation. Most European countries have reciprocal arrangements and their nationals would not expect to pay for treatment, either. There is little possibility of funding an additional doctor on the basis of a limited number of visitors coming from countries outwith NHS reciprocal arrangements.'

'What if my organisation were to set up a private clinic?' Milton demanded.

'That would be subject to the restrictions placed upon all private health care,' she insisted. In view of a discussion Alan recalled having with Jack McDougal, she had been warned that such a proposition might be put to her.

The Recorder interrupted at that point.

'Mr Humbert, I have studied your submission very carefully and can find no reference to the provision of a private clinic. This would be subject to a different set of planning regulations and, in any case, I have already made it plain that we are not here to discuss matters which arise as an afterthought. If you have not already mentioned it in your written submission, we cannot discuss the provision of a health clinic. Next question.'

'No further questions.'

During the next two days, Thornton-Mowbray shepherded his impressive collection of witnesses with consummate skill, allowing each of them to speak freely on their subject whilst being ready at all times to step in to clarify a point or to soften the impact of Milton's questioning on those rare occasions when the answers might jeopardise their case. By the time they reached Flora on the final afternoon, he was beginning to feel they were home and dry.

Chapter Twenty

The hall was packed for the final session.

That morning they had heard the representative from the Wildlife Trust explain how excessive use of highly powered boats for such activities as paragliding and water skiing presented a very real threat to life on those reefs, which were popular with the diving fraternity.

The fragile eco-system in the area was already under threat from overfishing by transitory vessels, often flying under foreign flags. This had been emphasised by Jamie McPhee, who had described the decline of the fish population brought about by salmon netting and by a method of hoovering up the sea life on the ocean bed.

'Oh, come now, Mr McPhee,' said Milton, 'you're not suggesting that the tourists visiting Eisdalsa for their summer holidays are going to engage in hoovering up the life from the ocean floor?'

'No,' Jamie replied, 'they're already too late for that, the seabed is like a ploughed field. Regulations are now in place to prevent further fishing of that kind, and there's every chance the seabed can regenerate so that the shellfish stocks should eventually return to normal. With the type and level of activity you are proposing, however, life out there in the bay will never get a chance to recover. . .'

Alex Thornton-Mowbray interjected, 'Do you see harm coming to animals other than the fish, Mr McPhee?'

'Fast motor boats disturb the birds, the seals, and the sea otters in the area. In recent years there have been more and more schools of porpoises and basking sharks around the islands to the south. This year they have been seen close to the shores of Eisdalsa itself. One small firm has made a healthy profit these past two seasons by taking boating expeditions to view these animals.'

'What's so different from them taking motor boat trips around the bay and what I am proposing?' Milton demanded.

'You don't expect to see too many seals when you are travelling at thirty-five knots,' Jamie retorted sharply. His reply was accompanied by hearty agreement from those in the body of the hall.

'What do you believe will happen to this small firm and its wildlife expeditions should Mr Humbert's development go ahead?' asked Alex.

'It will undoubtedly be put out of business.'

A shocked silence accompanied McPhee's bald statement.

The Reporter looked towards Milton. 'Mr Humbert?'

'No further questions,' replied the disgruntled American.

He had long since ceased to look to Jack to haul him out of the various ditches he seemed to be digging for himself. Two days ago his assistant had decided to sit back and take no further part in the debate. It happened when Flora took the stand and gave her short speech in defence of the bed and breakfast trade in the area.

Some weeks before, in an unguarded moment, Jack had been careless enough to suggest that she might be more sympathetic than some to their scheme. At the time he had been defending his association with the daughter of one of their chief antagonists. William Douglas had taken it upon himself to write personally to Milton Humbert care of his Bermuda address, suggesting in richly nautical language that he should up anchor and take his ill-conceived scheme somewhere it would be better appreciated.

Forced to listen to Milton's tirade upon the subject of those ungrateful Limeys, Jack had said, 'Look, the old boy means well enough. He's only defending what he sees as his own territory. It's an instinct we all have. His daughter is a good friend of mine and she doesn't see a lot wrong with what we're trying to do. Why don't we take on board some of her modifications, and perhaps we would be more acceptable in the eyes of the rest?'

Milton had been unwilling to give ground at the time but he had not forgotten what Jack had said about Flora's attitude. When it came to questioning her, he determined to pull no punches.

Flora cut a neat little figure. She spoke up well and smiled delightfully at the Recorder, making him feel a good ten years younger.

She read out the short résumé of her evidence and put down her notes, surprised herself that she felt so calm and confident.

'Miss Douglas, you would like to have your available accommodation filled throughout the season, no doubt?' Milton smiled, disarmingly.

'Of course.'

'And you can understand the need to find more jobs for local people?'

'Yes, there are always some people looking for a few hours' work.'

'I don't mean casual labour, I mean full-time employment.'

'Yes, I believe that there are many people in the area who would appreciate more stability in their employment.'

'Then why are you so opposed to what my company is trying to do? Can't you see that a place where there are outstanding facilities for their entertainment and enjoyment, cannot fail to attract tourists of every kind, including those who would normally take accommodation in your . . . er . . . house.' He found it difficult to accept that anyone would wish to be so accommodated when on holiday. He himself would never contemplate staying in one of those miserable little cottages.

'You mean my bed and breakfast facility?' She could use their exaggerated language as well as he.

'Yes, indeed.'

'I would like to see both of my rooms let, throughout the season, of course I would. The additional money I earn in this way helps me to live a little more comfortably than I could on my wages.'

'Your wages? You have other employment then?'

'Of course. You don't imagine I can live on the fifty

pounds or so I can make from letting rooms?'

He feigned interest. If she was employed part-time as a house cleaner or shop assistant, he would compare her wage with what he was prepared to pay her as a chambermaid.

'May I ask what you do?'

'I am a pharmacist. I work at the doctor's surgery, doubling up as the receptionist.'

He hesitated. So, she was a professional woman, someone with academic qualifications. What on earth was she doing buried in a place like this? He could not resist asking.

'You could get work anywhere, Miss Douglas. Why choose to live here?'

'Because, Mr Humbert, I was born here and like many of my neighbours I can think of nowhere else where I would prefer to live.'

'Then why do you wish to prevent others from doing the same?'

'I don't. We are always pleased to find newcomers living amongst us, enjoying the enormous benefits of our simple lifestyle. Someone who is willing to put something of himself into the running of the community as well as taking out all that is on offer will always be welcome. Neither are we are opposed to change. Remarkable though it may seem, this village has changed beyond all recognition during my lifetime, but those changes have evolved slowly in accordance with the changing pattern of society as a whole. They have not been imposed upon us by outsiders who have never troubled to stay here long enough to understand the way we live.'

'But think what the village could be like with a decently paved road, a reconstructed harbour, the old buildings all rebuilt and turned into useful premises for shops and craft studios. We are willing to keep the theme of the old slate quarries, you know.'

'You mean, like Disney World. A showplace for people to gawp at? Perhaps you would like some of us to sit outside splitting slates or spinning and weaving and making our own tackety boots?' Flora could feel the strength of the support emerging from the body of the hall as she went on, 'Contrary to the image you might wish to portray, you are no philanthropist, Mr Milton T. Humbert. You are a chancer. Didn't they call people like you carpet baggers once upon a time, back in the good ol' US of A? You and those like you prey on the unwary and don't care how you disrupt other people's lives in the process of making a fast buck.'

She finally sat down, flushed and shaking, suddenly aware of the enormity of what she had done.

'One moment, Miss Douglas.' She was aware that the Reporter was addressing her. 'It may be that Mr Humbert has other questions for you. Mr Humbert?'

'No . . . nothing else . . . thank you.' Milton was crushed. She had been his one hope of support. Jack regarded her proudly and watched while she gathered her notes and handbag and returned to her seat.

Alan had arrived in the course of her ordeal in the witness box. He greeted her with a beaming smile. 'That's telling 'em,' he murmured as he took hold of her hand and continued to hold it while the Reporter called upon the next witness.

*

Delivered late on Friday afternoon, Milton's concluding speech, a jumble of statements which he had already made, emphasised the increased value which his enterprise would put upon property in the district and repeated the promise of jobs and business opportunities which his scheme would create.

As the American continued, stumbling through his notes, searching for one last detail which would swing the case in his direction, the public became restive. Jack, embarrassed by Milton's performance and sensing that anything that was said now would do more harm than good, urged him to sit down.

'In conclusion, Mr Reporter, sir,' Milton continued, and Jack cringed as he watched a cloud pass briefly across the face of Miles McQuarry, 'I would like to thank you for your kind attention to my appeal and I would urge you to consider the best interests of the real people who matter in this case, those who have had no voice at this hearing. I refer to the unemployed, the homeless and those who suffer the most primitive of living conditions – fellow human beings whose promise of future comfort and security is threatened by the selfishness of a few individuals.'

'Thank you Mr Humbert. Mr Thornton-Mowbray?'

Alex took his time arranging his papers before addressing the Reporter. By the time he was ready to speak, the atmosphere was electric.

'It is clear from the explanations given by the appellant in this case, that it is the intention of Humbert Development Corporation to take over this village in its entirety and remould it into something which is quite alien. When the slate quarries ceased working at the beginning of the First World War the villages were deserted, only a few elderly men and women remaining. There were in addition a number of cottages maintained by absentee tenants, forced to go elsewhere to work. Today sixty people inhabit Eisdalsa Island on a permanent basis while rather more than that number live in the village here. In the past twenty years there has been a steady influx of people seeking a different kind of life from that which they left behind in the cities and industrial towns of our country. These newcomers were willing to forgo the benefits of having a Marks & Spencer and an Asda around every corner and can manage very well without a weekly visit to the bingo hall or the cinema. In short, they came here to enjoy the silence and the scenery and that intangible something called fellowship . . . the companionship to be gained by being amongst people of like mind, who are willing to live and let live; who are not constantly trying to make others conform to their own way of thinking.

'An important part of this regeneration has been the need to attract casual visitors to the area who will spend time, in particular during the summer months, enjoying the environment and bringing much-needed capital into this fragile economy. So attractive do many of them find it that they return over and over again, becoming familiar faces to be made welcome by the residents for a few weeks in every year. Despite what you have heard, there is employment here for those who conscientiously seek it.

'Modern technology has allowed many people to work

from their own homes and commuting into the nearest conurbations takes no longer than from many suburbs into the city centre. It has to be accepted that this is a dormitory area with a small industry depending upon tourism. To change it into a vast holiday complex attracting the numbers necessary to justify the cost of putting it here, would be to alter entirely the quality of this beautiful area, which we have been told is one of particular historical and natural interest. It is likely to drive out those who have worked so hard to restore the villages to their present situation and make them less appealing to those who have supported the economy by their visits over many years. I urge you, sir, to uphold the decision of the Argyll and Bute District Council and deny planning consent for this proposal.'

Alex Thornton-Mowbray sat down to tumultuous applause. The villagers had contained themselves well over the past three days but now all their pent-up frustration and anger at some of the things which had been said, and their pride in the performance of their own people, came bubbling out in the form of loud laughter and friendly exchanges even between old enemies.

Ewan McWorter, sitting quietly at the back of the hall throughout the afternoon, thought how proud his Annie would have been to have seen them for once united, all petty squabbles forgotten in this fight against a common enemy.

Alan and Flora were moving in silence towards the doors at the back of the hall when Jack approached them.

'I thought you were very impressive on Wednesday,' he told her.

She flushed but remained silent, unable to forgive his betrayal.

'Your lawyer was quite outstanding,' Jack commented as Bill Douglas sidled up to join his daughter.

'He's the best, there is,' agreed the old man. 'You could have done with one like him. I'm surprised an organisation the size of Humbert Developments couldn't afford a decent legal representative.'

'Yes . . . well, Mr Humbert wanted to represent himself.'

'Oh, I think he did that,' said Flora, suddenly. 'More than adequately.' She released Alan's hand and left all three of them staring after her as she hurried away.

'Was it something I said?' asked Jack.

'More likely something you didn't say,' said Bill Douglas, and hurried after his daughter.

'She thought you were going to stop Milton going to appeal,' said Alan. 'It's cost them a great deal of money, you know.'

'How much?'

'Nearly five thousand . . . that's fifty pounds a household on average. A lot of money for some of these people to find.'

'They cared that much?' Jack felt somehow dirty and ashamed. 'They were good . . . the witnesses,' he continued. 'There's an amazing amount of knowledge and ability locked up in this tiny place.'

'Perhaps they know something you and I don't,' suggested Alan. 'Will you be going back to Queensland now?'

'I suppose so, until Milton gets some other great idea

. . . then I shall be off again, setting his stamp on some unsuspecting beauty spot.'

'Why do you do it?'

'It's a job. One day when I've given it all up, I'll be back. Will I find you here?'

'I doubt it. I'll be moving on quite soon.'

They shook hands.

'Good day, mate!' Jack grinned. 'Take care of our little Flora for me.'

'Oh, I think she can take care of herself, don't you?'

'Yes, she certainly can!' They heard the chatter of its rotor blades as the helicopter hovered above the hall and came in to land.

'Look me up if you come across to Oz.'

Jack was gone.

Alan turned away, and seeing Ewan struggling to his feet, went to help the old doctor to his car. They had to pause at the door for Ewan to catch his breath.

'It was hot in there,' he murmured.

Alan looked closely at him.

'You feeling OK?'

'Just a bit tired.'

'You've been doing too much lately. You should have stayed away today.'

'Annie would have wanted me to be here,' he said. 'She wouldn't have missed it for the world.'

Cissy sat down in front of her bureau and searched in the drawer where she kept unanswered correspondence. She had hoped she would not have to do this. Five thousand pounds was the sum   being talked of in the village. How could they possibly raise that amount?

'Lost something?' she was startled to find George at her elbow.

'A letter . . . from that Canadian who was here for the shooting. He was asking about a booking this year . . .'

'This one, you mean?' Her husband was holding out the letter from Pierre d'Orsay.

'Yes, that's it!' She attempted to snatch it from him but he continued to hold it just out of reach.

'I wish you wouldn't read my private letters,' she grumbled.

'Oh, I didn't realise it was *private*,' he teased. 'I'm not sure I like you to receive letters of that nature. A man could get quite jealous!'

'Oh, what nonsense, George. He's just being polite – probably because it will give him an edge over other prospective clients. You did hammer home the fact that rooms in the shooting season are limited and much sought after!'

'Well, it's true . . . about their being limited anyway. How many bookings do we have for next season?'

'This is the only one.'

'Pity.'

'Don't be like that, George. I know he was a bit . . . well . . . French in his attitude towards me, but you must admit it was a pleasant change from the way those Germans behaved. As for Milton Humbert. . . .!'

'How did it go today?' he asked. She had been down in the village hall all week.

'Well, your American made a complete hash of it. He was so sure that he was going to walk away with the whole thing at the beginning he'd made hardly any preparation, you know. It was good to see someone like that being put in his place for a change.'

'So you don't think he's going to win the appeal?'

'I heard their advocate say the villagers had a good chance of success. I daresay it helped a bit that Alex Thornton-Mowbray and the Reporter are buddies.'

'Thornton-Mowbray? Was he there?'

'He was the advocate briefed by the villagers. Do you know him?'

'I should, he was the old man's QC in that big fight they had over building the dam to supply electricity to the villages in the glen.'

'At Lochan Dubh?'

'Yes.'

'But that was years ago.'

'He was a very young man at the time . . . one of the youngest QCs at the bar. Anyway, he spoke up for the need for progress like a good 'un. Won the day for my old dad, anyway.'

'So, he's not always against progress?' Cissy considered. 'In which case he must really have believed the villagers were right to object.'

'You must have a pretty cynical view of lawyers to suspect otherwise,' George laughed. 'Anyway, I hope they think he was worth the money.'

'I'm sure they do. I haven't heard anyone complain about paying up.'

'It's a lot of money to raise. Will they do it, do you think?'

'They might need a little bit of help. You don't really

mind, do you, if I write to Pierre . . . tell him his contribution would be welcome?'

'No, why not? He did make the offer after all.'

'I just thought . . . well . . . if Humbert is turned down, it'll be our loss as well as his.'

'I told you right from the beginning that I was in this game for the price of the option on the lease. Humbert loses that anyway. If you ask me, he should be glad he lost his appeal . . . if he *has* lost it. Maybe I should have shown him before but he was so bloody cocksure about that quarry business . . .'

'Shown him what?'

'Some time before he died, my father had a survey done of that quarry. The marine engineers assessed the cost of opening it up to the sea, so that Dad could use it as a marina. Exactly what these guys are proposing, in fact. Fifteen years ago it was going to cost seventy thousand. Goodness knows what it would have cost today.'

'Why didn't you say something?'

'It was for me to know and for them to find out.' He winked at her.

'You're an old rogue,' she told him.

'Well, people like him need to catch a cold now and again. I had to have that money and there was no way he was going to make a donation to the restoration fund by any other means.'

'I feel badly about the villagers having to pay out near enough five thousand pounds, though,' she told him.

'Well, we need every penny we can lay hands on ourselves. I'll tell you what, though. I still think the plan for a golf course in the glen is a brilliant idea. I've half a mind to donate the land to this Residents' Action Group and see if they can get something going on their own.'

She put her arms around him and hugged him.

'What's that for?'

'For being a great big cuddly old bear . . . that's what!'

'Not so much of the old, if you don't mind!' He gave her a kiss before handing back Pierre's note. 'If it's money you're after, you'd better start writing that letter to your boyfriend.'

The Tacksman's Bar was packed that night. It seemed as though the entire population of Seileach village wanted to come across to the island to celebrate the ending of the Inquiry and Angus Dewar made no complaint about the fact that it was going to take an extra three or four ferry crossings to get them all home.

Alexander Thornton-Mowbray, nearly a head taller than anyone else, formed the focus of much of the attention, but each of the day's other heroes commanded a small knot of admirers. All tension gone now that the ordeal was over, their relief was evidenced by their loud conversation and raucous laughter.

'Without Alex, we couldn't have done it,' declared Celia, squashed tight into a corner between Flora Douglas and Alexander's wife, Alicia. 'Did you go to the hearing every day, Mrs Thornton-Mowbray?'

'Not every day, no,' she answered. 'I have to say, I was very impressed by what I heard of your evidence. As a

517

casual visitor, one sees only the picture-postcard image of the place. I feel now as though I have seen right into the hearts of people here and I'm very envious of you all.'

'There's nothing to stop you coming to join us,' suggested Flora.

'We've thought seriously about it this week, believe me. The only problem would be to find a house with a high enough ceiling.'

The colourful bruise on Alexander's forehead bore witness to his forgetfulness. He had hit it again coming down to supper and the mark still showed. They watched him conversing with a group of men standing against the bar. Alicia noticed how he delicately fingered the lump from time to time, examining the damage.

'He's not the only tall person to have lived in one of these cottages,' Flora laughed. 'I'm sure he would learn to duck if he spent enough time here.'

'Perhaps you should buy the old coalrea and have it converted?' suggested Celia. 'It's like a small warehouse in there – plenty of headroom . . . enough for an upper floor. It could be made into a marvellous house. Actually, the building is in dire need of conservation, and change of use to a dwelling house would be an ideal way of maintaining it. You'd have to keep it as it is externally, of course, because it's a Listed Building, but at least the ceilings would be high enough to preserve Alex's brains intact.'

'It's certainly worth thinking about,' Alicia agreed, looking up into the face of Captain Billy who wore a permanent smile this evening, delighted as he was with the outcome of the week's activities.

'Thank you, that's very kind.' She accepted the drink he had bought her most graciously. It was her third whisky of the evening and she determined to sip it slowly. One of them had to be in a fit state to find their way back to the cottage afterwards. She watched Alexander polish off yet another beer and was thankful they did not have to think about driving home afterwards. He looked so relaxed amongst these people. Perhaps Celia's was not such a bad idea after all . . .

'Have you met my father, Bill Douglas?' Flora introduced them.

'How do you do, Mr Douglas? Are you just over here for the evening too?'

'Oh, no,' Flora answered for him. 'Dad lives over here. I have my own place on the other side. He stays in a cottage quite near where you are. I'm surprised you haven't met him before. Things have been a bit topsy-turvy this past week.'

'Wait a minute,' Alicia said, 'you'll be the gentleman who goes out every day with a sextant . . . I've watched you from the top of the hill. Do you take readings every day?' She was intrigued. The only other time she had seen one used was on her grandfather's yacht, when she was a girl.

'Just a habit,' Captain Billy told her, 'I like to keep my hand in.'

'The only trouble is, the position of the island varies considerably, depending upon how much he's had to drink the night before,' Flora said, laughing.

'Ah, here comes your handsome young doctor,' said

Alicia suddenly. 'Now there's a good enough reason for buying a house here, I must say!'

Flora was surprised that the Thornton-Mowbrays should know Alan when they hadn't even met long-standing islanders such as her father.

He spotted Flora and came across. Before he could exchange a greeting with her, Alicia broke in with, 'Well, look who's here . . . my knight in shining armour.' The whisky had gone to her head and her remark was louder than she had intended.

Several heads turned and more than one spectator overheard the exchange which followed.

'You do remember me, don't you?' Alicia shuffled along the bench so that there was a space between Flora and herself. She patted the place, inviting him to sit down.

'Alicia Thornton-Mowbray. You know . . . we thought I'd broken my ankle that day on the hill?'

'Of course!' Alan had been wondering all the way across, how he was going to tell Flora his news. He was so relieved to have found her here he had scarcely registered Alicia's greeting. Taking a harder look at her, he recalled that hot August afternoon they had met. What he remembered most clearly about the event was the struggle he and Jack McDougal had had, carrying her down to the road.

'Your husband wrote to say the ankle wasn't broken. I presume it's fully recovered by now?'

'Oh, yes. Mind you, it turned every colour under the sun during that first week and the surgeon did say that had I attempted to walk on it after I fell, I would probably have been in plaster for weeks.'

'Torn ligament?'

'Something of that sort. Anyway, it's all better now, thanks to you.'

'Can I get you ladies a drink?' he asked, anxious to abandon the topic. It was Flora he'd come to see. Clearly this was not a good moment for what he had to say.

'A small whisky for me,' said Alicia.

'Tonic water, please.' Flora was conscious of the need to stay sober enough to escort her father across the green. Since Angus would have a great many passengers to get across later, she had decided to sleep, for what was left of the night, on Bill's old Z-bed.

'Yes,' Alicia was carrying on with her story despite the fact that Alan was away, at the bar, 'he saved my life that day. Had he not bandaged my foot and not allowed me to put it to the ground, I would probably have been lame for life. The surgeon told me that.'

Flora smiled at the exaggeration but was nevertheless intrigued enough to ask, 'When was this? I didn't realise that you and Alex had been here before.'

'It was last August. We were staying in the cottage we're renting now. I was wearing these ridiculous high-heeled shoes and quite inappropriately dressed, but it was such a warm afternoon we decided on impulse to climb up that hill over the way . . .'

'Caisteal an Spuilleadair?'

'Is that what they call it? Well, anyway, I caught my foot in a clump of heather and nearly went over the cliff. Poor old Alex thought I was a goner. So did I for a moment. Then when I tried to get up there was this terrible pain. I yelled, I can tell you!'

'What about Alan?' Flora could not contain her curiosity.

'Alex left me and went to get help and a few moments later this glorious creature appeared. "I'm the local GP," he said, "I've sent your husband to get some assistance." Well, painful as my foot was, I hoped old Alex would be away a good long time! It's not often these days that I have a handsome young man all to myself. He felt my ankle, which by that time had swelled up like a balloon, and decided there was no way I was going to be able to walk on it. Then he wanted something to bandage it up. So, there we were, in the middle of nowhere, with nothing to make into a bandage but my cotton underslip. Well, what was I to do?' Her voice had risen and she was laughing and talking at the same time, attracting attention from everyone in the vicinity. Flora was beginning to wish Alan would come back.

'I just stripped off my dress . . . a really tight-fitting little number it was, as I remember. And there I was, sitting in the heather in my bra and panties, tearing my slip into bandages. You should have seen the doctor's face! Still, all credit to him. He recovered very quickly and as soon as I'd made myself respectable again he got down to the business of bandaging me up. By that time Alex came back with that Australian chap . . . Yes, of course, that's who it was. I thought I remembered him from somewhere when I saw him sitting in the hall this week, next to the American. Anyway, the two younger men carried me all the way down to the hotel and Alex went off to get our car from the pier. He drove me to hospital and we went home the next day.'

Had Flora been looking in the right direction she would have seen Giles Scott exchange embarrassed glances with his wife. Flora wasn't in the least bothered that others may have overheard this story which would, without doubt, be all around the village by morning. So all that stuff about the new doctor bonking in the heather was quite unfounded. She had always known it was nonsense!

Alan returned with the drinks at that moment, bringing Alex with him.

'You didn't tell me you knew Mr Thornton-Mowbray,' said Flora as they all shifted along to make room for the lawyer and Alan drew up a stool beside them.

'It was Dr Beaton who first put us in touch with Alex,' Margaret McColl chipped in. 'We shall be forever in your debt, Dr Beaton.' She stood up and rapped on a table to gain everyone's attention.

'We know that it's not over yet,' she began. 'To paraphrase a great statesman whom some of us are old enough to remember, "This may not be the end, but it's certainly the end of the beginning and we all pray that it's the beginning of the end." We are sorry about the reason for your having to be here, Alex, but we have Milton T. Humbert to thank for introducing two very good friends to the island. We hope you will return often and if this week's exercise is as successful as we all hope, we shall expect you and Alicia to join us in a proper celebration when the time comes!'

Alex was on his feet already. He had only to lift his head to command their undivided attention.

'Thank you, Margaret.' He beamed at his colleague. 'My work was made simple by yourself and all of you good people here. I wish other experiences of a similar nature always worked out so satisfactorily. Alicia and I will certainly return to join in your celebrations, but as Margaret says, the battle won't be won until it's lost.'

'What chance do we have?' asked Jamie McPhee.

'When I took up this fight I would have assessed your chances as sixty per cent to Mr Humbert and forty to yourselves.' This created a few worried faces, but the frowns quickly dispersed when he continued. 'When I learned that Miles McQuarry was to be the Reporter, my estimate shifted slightly in your favour. Miles happens to enjoy cruising around these islands in his yacht. I don't think he takes too kindly to speed boats.' There was general laughter. 'Then, once I'd heard our own witnesses perform,' he was looking directly at Flora as he spoke, 'I believed the odds were reversed. I'd say sixty-forty in your favour is nearer the mark now.' Everyone cheered at this. He raised his hand to silence them. 'There is, however, the unpredictable political factor. Much depends upon the present climate in the Foreign Office. If American investment is the flavour of the month, we have . . . to put it quite bluntly . . . had it.'

'But I thought the result depended entirely on the verdict of the Reporter?' Bill Douglas was a great believer in the integrity of those in command.

Alex's response placed a sudden damper on their high spirits. 'That is what you might be forgiven for believing, Captain Billy,' he replied, pleasing the old man with the use of his nickname. 'We can but hope.'

'You did very well today, kid.' Jamie McPhee leaned across Alan to plant a kiss on Flora's cheek. 'My privilege,' he explained, noting Alan's frown. 'She's a sort of cousin of mine!'

'I don't know where you cooked up that idea,' gasped Flora. 'We went to school together, is all . . . and I used to call his mother "Auntie". We're not related.'

Alan felt pleased that the fisherman had considered he was owed any explanation. Were they beginning to regard Flora and himself as a couple? Well, he was happy enough with the notion. He wondered whether she felt the same? He would know soon enough.

After the speeches things became rather more subdued. Some of the less regular patrons, those older folk who reserved their visits to the bar for high days and holidays, departed and were quickly followed by Alex and his wife.

Alan found himself standing at the bar beside Desmond Bartlet.

'I was glad Mrs Pullson put in her two-penn'orth about the health clinic,' Desmond told him. 'McQuarry nearly had an apoplexy when Humbert brought it up.'

'McDougal questioned me quite closely on my attitude to private health care, so I was half expecting something of the kind,' Alan told him. 'Why were you so sure he was going to raise it?'

'Jack McDougal gave me what amounted to the company's manifesto . . . just after Christmas,' Desmond explained. 'If they won the appeal, I was to design their web site. There were several other items Margaret knew of and had briefed Thornton-Mowbray on in case they were raised at the last minute. Didn't you notice the thunderous look Humbert gave the Recorder when he announced no new evidence could be produced?'

'I'm afraid I wasn't there all the time,' Alan replied. 'What sort of proposals were they?'

'A bridge across from Seileach, a car park on the far side of the new hotel, and a Sky Rail from Caisteal an Spuilleadair.'

'You mean, all those items were fact, not just wild speculation born of some Highlander's colourful imagination?'

'Every one genuine, I guarantee it. When I saw what they were proposing for later on I made sure Margaret McColl had a list. We couldn't do anything about it unless Humbert brought up one of the items himself. Fortunately, that's exactly what he tried to do.'

Alan considered what Desmond had said.

'You stood to make a lot of money, had they gone ahead with their web site?'

Desmond cast an anxious glance to either side.

'Yes. I don't think I would have been too popular with the others, though. In a way it's a relief to know that none of it will be going ahead.'

'You might have kept quiet . . . Humbert would have stood a better chance if you had. I think Janice's response when he raised the issue of a private clinic made a deep impression on the Recorder.'

'I could have . . . but I decided not to.'

'May I ask why?'

Desmond hesitated for a moment only before replying:

'Ever since I arrived here with my family, I have been trying to force my ideas on everyone else. It was sheer impertinence on my part . . . I can see that now. People have devised their own ways of coping with this particular situation and I should have sat back and observed what was going on before I jumped in with all my up-to-the-minute solutions.' He remained silent for a few minutes. The beer had loosened his tongue but Alan felt that he had a need to talk to someone. In Desmond's estimation, the doctor represented a neutral opinion. He allowed himself to be used as a sounding board.

'I suppose it was my experience in the Post Office that began my conversion,' Desmond continued, 'listening to the way the locals talked, noticing how genuine their concern was for other people's welfare. Not a day went by when someone didn't ask after a neighbour who hadn't been about for a bit. You hear horror stories of old people dying in their city apartments and being there for weeks before anyone finds out. That couldn't happen here, you know. If someone collapsed alone at home, everyone would know about it before the day was out.'

'Yes, I've noticed that,' Alan agreed. 'When I first came here, I used to think that old people living alone were greatly at risk. Now I know just how well they would be cared for, I have no hesitation in recommending that my elderly patients continue to live in their own homes for as long as possible.'

'I knew this was a great place to live the first time I set eyes on it,' Desmond continued. He might have been talking to himself. 'I had the advantage of being able to work from home so the usual constraints about access to employment didn't apply and it's a wonderful place to bring up kids.'

'So you think you'll stay?' Alan was grinning now.

'Not even Milton T. Humbert could keep me away!'

Alan could see that sentiment becoming a part of the local language.

'How about you then?'

'Sorry? How do you mean?'

'Well, are you stopping or just passing through?'

'Sadly, I shall be leaving at the end of the month.'

He hadn't meant to say anything until he'd told Flora, but the conversation had become so relaxed and the drink had caused him to drop his professional reserve.

'I'd better see how the others are getting on,' he said, hurriedly. It was all the more important now that he find an opportunity to speak to Flora alone, before Bartlet broadcast his news.

Alan shouldered his way across the room. On the way he bumped into Bill Douglas who began to tell him a convoluted story about the seal he had found trapped by the low tide in the north quarry.

'It must have been a youngster, the old fellows are usually too fly to get caught,' he said. 'They come in for the big fish, you know. The fry swim into the quarry at the springs and then find they can't get out. They're obliged to remain in there for good. It's not such a terrible ordeal for them, though. They get fat on the abundance of food brought in by the tides.'

'I've often seen people fishing there,' said Alan. 'What do they catch?'

He could see the women around Flora all talking excitedly together, among them Bartlet's wife, Molly. He turned back to hear Bill saying, 'You'd think a seal could clamber out of that quarry even at low tide, wouldn't you? But they can't, you know. The walls are too sheer. I don't know what that fellow Humbert was thinking of, trying to turn it into a marina. Anyone could have told him that the spot he had chosen as a quay is composed of drystone walling built to retain the edge of the quarry. It would never hold a boat in the kind of gales we get, especially there where it's exposed to the north-westerlies.'

Alan turned back to where the women had been seated and to his dismay found that Flora had gone. He looked around wildly, caught sight of Celia Robertson and asked her, 'Has Flora left?'

'Yes . . . she said something about going to fetch Bill a coat. It's turned rather windy out there.'

Angus Dewar appeared.

'Last ferry in five minute, folks,' he announced. He accepted the large whisky someone had left for him on the bar and downed it in a single swallow. Catching sight of Alan he came over.

'I don't know whether it's anything to worry about, doctor,' he said, 'but Giles Scott has just driven past Dr Mac's place. The house was in darkness but the front door stood wide open. Giles says he stepped inside and gave a shout but there was no response so he came on home and telephoned the house, thinking Dr Mac might have gone to bed and left it open by mistake. The doctor didn't answer, so then Giles phoned the police.'

'You're going over right away?' Alan demanded.

'Just collecting up the last of my passengers.' Angus

would have turned back to the bar in expectation of one last glass of whisky before they left, but Alan was by now thoroughly alarmed.

'Come on, man, this could be an emergency . . . I have to get across to Seileach now!'

Others in the bar had sensed the doctor's urgency and quickly assembled for the trip across the water.

Flora, returning with her father's coat, calmer now that she had got over her initial annoyance at hearing Alan's news second hand, was just in time to see him leap aboard the ferry.

Chapter Twenty-one

Bill Douglas had been burning the midnight oil for more than a week. Those living nearby could hear him tapping away at his old Underwood at all hours. Rumour had it that he was writing his memoirs.

He scanned the typewritten sheets before him one last time, anxiously checking for any mistakes. He had no wish to have his reputation tarnished by some careless slip.

He glanced at the brass ship's clock screwed to the wall above his writing table. It was just after noon, nearly time for the post. He returned his masterpiece to its envelope and went to put on the kettle.

The swelling of excited voices, in chorus with the familiar barking of the island dogs, brought him hurrying to his door. Impatiently he followed Jeanie Clark's slow progress as she made her way from house to house around the harbour. Whatever the news she was carrying, it was enough to have caused small groups of islanders to gather in her wake. He could see Des Bartlet hurrying across the green towards Jamie McPhee's, and even Celia Robertson seemed to have left the museum visitors to their own devices, while she went to join them.

As the dogs came bounding around the corner, old Red well in advance of his team of Labradors, Bill made the tea and got out the biscuits.

Since the Public Inquiry, his morning routine had changed considerably. It had begun one morning very soon after the Inquiry, when his own post had exceeded the total number of letters received by all the other islanders together. There was such a pile that Jeanie Clark had offered to help him by slitting open the envelopes while he made a note of the contents of each. As the donations began to pour in, it had become accepted she would spend half an hour each day assisting him in this way.

While the real work had been going on, Jeanie had been lying in her hospital bed, unable to help. Now, although Bill could have managed perfectly well on his own, he was able to appreciate Jeanie's need to be involved and so accepted her help. As the weeks went by, he had come to look forward to their daily sessions.

The cheques had begun to flow in by post, most of them in response to Desmond's appeal via the Internet. It wasn't that the locals objected to paying up. When approached, they did so without complaint and often very generously. It was just that the older generation in partic- ular expected a more personal approach. Jeanie had orig- inally volunteered to undertake a door-to-door collection of donations while she was still on the sick list, unable to resume her work as Postie.

Dr Beaton's instruction to walk a little further every day meant that she needed to plan a schedule which would, in due course, take her to each of the houses on Seileach, within a three-mile radius. By the time she had visited them all, she was fit enough to reach the doctor's surgery on foot.

What a day for celebration it had been when she accomplished this feat for the first time! Flora had made her a cup of tea and the doctor himself had come out to join them. He had presented her with a fancy certificate. You could easily do that sort of thing on the computer, she knew, but all the same it was a nice gesture. The citation read:

Mrs Jeanie Clark, Postmistress, having completed the required number of miles on foot for a sufficient period of time is deemed fit to return to her duties.

Signed by the doctor and witnessed by Flora Douglas, this document, lovingly framed by Willie Clark, now hung behind the counter in the Post Office for everyone to read. Strangers might wonder what it was doing there but the villagers, aware of the agonies Jeanie had gone through to attain this objective and having followed her progress every step of the way, shared in the pride with which she displayed her certificate

Ruff, the Collie, arrived first at Bill's door and had his choice of the mutton chops which the Captain had prepared. The Labradors arrived in a group and polished off the remainder. Only the little Jack Russell, Dodger, stuck close to his beloved friend, running around her in tight circles and barking excitedly as they approached each of the houses.

To Dodger, post duty took priority over lunch. Besides which, his preference was for a nice juicy slice of liver and a rasher of bacon and he had every confidence that Bill would have saved *his* portion on a separate plate.

'What's all the excitement?' Bill demanded as Jeanie stepped over the threshold and left her blue and red canvas bag to share the floor of the lobby with the rest of his clutter.

Without waiting for an invitation, she sat down heavily in the best armchair and began fanning herself with his post, a collection of envelopes held together by a thick elastic band.

'I'm getting too old for this sort of thing,' she declared happily, and accepted the proffered cup with a sigh of contentment. 'It's so good to be the bearer of good tidings for once!'

'Don't keep me in suspense,' he commanded.

'We've won!'

He put down his cup and stared at her in disbelief.

'Margaret has received the official verdict. When I saw the envelope with the Scottish Office stamp on the flap, I knew it had to be the result, so I went to her house first.'

They had all been so sure at the beginning. Everyone was convinced that they were going to win. As the weeks had gone by, little by little, doubt had crept into their conversations. Like the scab which forms over an open wound, a crust of explanations and rationalisations had been built to ward off the disappointment of defeat. The islanders had lived with this growing tension for weeks past. Many had become short-tempered, relationships between neighbours becoming more strained as the days went by without any news . . .

Now all their worries were over. He could hardly believe it. With the realisation came the reaction. Bill suddenly felt physically sick.

'That's been brewing so long the spoon will stand up by itself in the cup,' Jeanie observed as she watched him, with trembling hands, attempting to pour more tea into the saucer than the cup. 'In any case, I would have thought a dram would be more appropriate. After all, it *is* a celebration!'

Bill certainly agreed with that. He reached for the Famous Grouse and half-filled a couple of tumblers.

'Hey! I've work to do,' she complained, but the protest was half-hearted.

Bill raised his glass. '"Here's t' us and those like us. They're no money and the're a' deid"!'

'*Slainte!*'

'I've this to show you,' he declared, setting down his glass before sliding his work out of the brown envelope.

'What is it?'

'The accounts as of yesterday.'

'How much?'

'Three thousand, one hundred and fifty-six pounds,' he announced, proudly.

'Will it be enough?'

'We haven't had Thornton-Mowbray's invoice yet. I suppose he's been waiting for the outcome of the Inquiry.'

'What if it's more ? Someone was talking of five thousand at one time.'

'We'll raise it somehow. Another appeal on the Internet perhaps. However much it turns out to be, it will have been worth every penny.'

Jeanie recalled seeing something in that morning's post. 'I'm sure I remember a letter with a Canadian postmark,' she said, sorting through the little pile she had brought him.

As well as the air letter from Canada, she extracted a couple of bills, two letters from Holland and another from Australia. She examined the flap of this last, looking for some indication of its origin but found nothing but a logo, a picture of a small blue kingfisher.

The Dutch contributions, both from recent visitors to the island's museum, represented the equivalent of ten pounds in sterling. The Canadian envelope contained a letter as well as a cheque.

Bill let out a low whistle and handed the flimsy slip of paper to Jeanie. 'That's the largest single contribution yet,' he observed.

'How much is it?' she asked, having difficulty in deciphering the spidery writing. The sum was quoted in Canadian dollars.

'Almost five hundred pounds!' he replied and waited impatiently while she scanned the contents of the accompanying letter.'

'Who's this Pierre d' Orsay?' she demanded. 'Sounds French to me.'

Bill thought hard for a few minutes. 'There was a French Canadian staying at the castle last summer. He got on well with the old Doc, I remember. They did a bit of fishing together. He was over here visiting the island on a couple of occasions. He didn't think much of that chap Humbert, that I *do* remember.'

'It's a very generous donation.'

'Probably spite,' said Bill, rather more cynically than he perhaps intended. 'He'll be only too pleased to see the Yank sent off.'

Jeanie slit open the Australian letter.

The envelope contained nothing but a couple of one-hundred dollar bills. There was no letter, not even a compliments slip . . . nothing to say where the contribution had come from.

She re-examined the envelope. The postmark was blurred. There was nothing to identify the donor, only the kingfisher logo.

Bill took the envelope from her and attached it to the Australian bank notes. 'I'll keep this one out for now. Flora might have some ideas.'

People were entitled to remain anonymous, he supposed, but he would have liked to have a name. His donations list would look untidy with nothing written down beside the amount.

'What are two hundred dollars Australian worth?' asked Jeanie.

'About a hundred pounds, give or take a few pennies.'

'Not a bad haul today then, considering we thought we were ready to wind it all up.'

They were all there this evening. Spontaneous parties were always the best, Flora thought, as she stood shoulder to shoulder with Kirsty, filling the glasses as fast as the orders were barked at her. She placed a brimming pint pot in front of Robbie Fullerton and waited as he counted out the necessary coins.

She had arrived home from the surgery at lunchtime to find her father's message on her answerphone.

Thankfully, it had been an unusually short surgery this morning considering that Wednesday was their half day. Her boss had taken the opportunity to get off early for his appointment at the Regional Health Board Offices and it was unlikely there would be anyone answering the phone in the surgery at this hour. Nevertheless, she dialled the number and left a message.

'. . . I expect there'll be something going on on the island this evening,' she concluded. 'Come over and join us, if you don't feel too tired.'

She had bathed and washed her hair, taking particular care over her preparations. A new summer dress hung in the wardrobe which she hadn't worn before. On impulse, she decided to put it on. It was full-skirted and pretty long. Ankle-length seemed to be the fashion this spring, according to the flashy magazines Cissy Monteith passed on to them for the patients' waiting room.

Her sensible brown brogues looked weird beneath the flowing skirts. Flora slipped them off and exchanged them for a pair of stiletto-heeled sandals, knowing she would regret it the moment she set foot on the rough island pathways.

The thought reminded her of that story Alicia had told her on that last night following the Inquiry. Suppose *she* were to injure her ankle wearing these silly shoes?

Hopefully Kirsty would be able to find her a bit of crêpe bandage and she wouldn't be required to tear up the one and only decent slip she possessed!

Although it was still early in the afternoon, she could be quite sure that her father was hammering the whisky bottle already. She could well imagine that on a day like this, they would be having a midsummer 'first footing' over on Eisdalsa. The least she could do was go over and cook him a decent meal to soak up the alcohol.

She closed her front door and ran down to the harbour, shouting to Angus to wait when she saw the ferry just pulling away from the quay. The boat was pretty full already. The tourist season was well under way and so far the numbers of visitors had been very promising. She herself had received bookings right up until the end of September. Of course, there *had* been a lot of coverage in the Scottish press and even a snippet about their case on ITV's lunchtime broadcast. As a consequence, Eisdalsa had become an important addition to every tourist's itinerary.

'It's a grand day, right enough,' Angus greeted her. Acknowledging an attempt by one of the passengers to make room for her on the seat, Flora smiled and refused. 'I'll just stand here beside Angus,' she explained, and proceeded to impress the strangers with her ability to remain on her feet despite a rather choppy crossing.

'They'll be pretty excited over there?' she asked.

'Oh, aye. There'll no' be any work done the day, I'm thinking.'

'Once all the excitement dies down, things are going to seem pretty flat.'

'I shouldna' worry, missie,' he told her. 'In a day or two someone will think of something to row about, and everything will be back to normal.'

Although she wished it were otherwise, Flora was forced to agree with him. In the course of their dispute with Milton Humbert, long-standing island feuds had been put aside and even the Seileachans had begun to make friendly overtures towards the Eisdalsas.

'Maybe we should try to find other ways of getting together and co-operating a little more,' she suggested.

'Och, what's the point?' Angus replied. 'If there's nae wars there wouldnae be anythin' t' talk about!'

'That's a pretty cynical viewpoint,' she answered, but in her heart she knew he was speaking the truth. At least the squabbles were petty ones and the differences were usually patched up in the end. The Humbert business had shown how determined these people could become when threatened. It really didn't matter if they had their differences, as long as they all worked together when the chips were down.

'See, that's the envelope, there.'

At her request, Bill had handed Flora the file containing the most recent contributions.

'That one's a bit of a mystery. The only thing we know about it is that it comes from Australia.'

'Have you had any other contributions from there?' she asked.

'I should say we have . . . There were a lot of quarry workers who went off to the gold fields to make their fortunes, you know. I suppose a good many of them decided to stay on. There seem to be people of Eisdalsa descent in just about every state of Australia and in New Zealand, too. We must have had twenty letters from there, mostly from the South Island around a place called Dunedin.'

Flora examined the envelope which had contained the anonymous donation.

'Postmark's Queensland,' she said.

She turned up the flap and exposed the tiny blue king-fisher.

The logo confirmed her suspicion. Jack had mentioned something about his Kookuburra Resort being on one of the Whitsunday Islands . . . that was Queensland wasn't it? She took out the two one-hundred dollar bills and smiled to herself. What would Milton say if he realised that his minion was sending donations to his opponent's fighting fund?

Reminded of Jack, she again experienced a wave of remorse about her own behaviour at their last encounter. She had been very hard on him. After all, he was only doing his job. She wondered what he was doing now. Where had he been when he heard the result of the Appeal?

'There's this other one which is also a bit of a mystery,' Bill broke into her thoughts. 'Do you know a Canadian called Pierre something or other?'

'Pierre d'Orsay? Of course. He was Dr Mac's friend. It was Pierre who looked after him when he had his first heart attack.'

They both fell silent for a few moments.

Bill, sharing her sadness, touched her gently on the shoulder and she turned into his arms as she had done when she was a child.

'I still miss him terribly,' she murmured, tears flowing down her hot cheeks. 'I can't help wondering what might have happened had we been there . . . Alan might have been able to do something. I know he still feels guilty for the way poor Ewan died.'

'That's nonsense,' Bill protested, gently. 'Neither of you has any reason to blame yourselves. Ewan died in his own home with his beloved Annie's photograph in his hands. He must have known he was going. I expect if he had wanted to, he could have called for help. The telephone was right beside his chair.'

What he said was absolutely true.

Alan had arrived at the doctor's house at the same time as the police car from Oban. Together, he and Sergeant McNab had entered the house, but it was Alan who had found Ewan . . . in the little study which opened out of the living room.

Bill was probably correct in his assessment of the old doctor's state of mind. Alan had assured the sergeant that the door was normally kept locked. Ewan must have left it open deliberately, to save them having to break it down.

'Considerate to the last,' Bill murmured, and wiped the tears from his daughter's face with a rather grubby tea towel. 'Look what you're doing to your make-up, lass,' he said. 'You go and repair the damage and I'll make us a nice cup of tea.'

'What's the state of the fighting fund now?' Jamie McPhee demanded of Margaret McColl. 'Are we going to have enough, do you think?'

I'm still waiting for Alex Thornton-Mowbray's bill,'

she said, 'but when I was talking with him on the phone, earlier, he assured me it won't be more than three thousand.'

'We've got that already, I know,' said Jamie. 'Captain Billy was saying that we'd topped the three thousand mark two days ago.'

'There are other expenses . . . there's accommodation for Alex and his wife . . . . I think we must offer to pay the rental for their cottage, and then there's travelling expenses and accommodation for the outside witnesses. Alex did suggest we ought to make a gesture towards the charitable organisations . . .'

She spotted Bill Douglas and called him over. 'Jamie's asking about the fund, Billy. Any more contributions today?'

'Yes, some of them rather generous.'

He went on to tell her about the morning's post. 'I don't anticipate very much more coming in now. Most of the householders have paid up and even the holiday cottage people have sent in their donations. The total is going to be nearer four thousand than three, that I can promise.'

There was a sigh of relief all round.

'What are we going to do with the remainder?' asked Celia. 'We can hardly hand it back.'

'Oh, I'm sure we'll think of something,' laughed Margaret.

'I wonder if I might make a suggestion?'

They had all been so deeply engrossed in their conversation that none in the group had noticed the arrival of George Monteith and his wife. George only occasionally visited the island, preferring the Tigh na Broch as his regular watering place. Even before the Humbert incident, he had never felt entirely comfortable with the islanders. Here on Eisdalsa, around every corner one was confronted with reminders of the old slate quarriers. Some even believed the island to be haunted by them. It was as though the attitudes of those men and their families had lingered on, long after they'd departed. The deference which they had shown towards their Laird, and the distance it had created between them, seemed still to exist, even amongst the incomers from across the border.

'Good evening, sir.' Bill was the first on his feet. 'Can I get you something to drink?' There was a general shuffling-up as room was found for the newcomers to be seated.

George gave their order and turned to Margaret.

'Many congratulations, Miss McColl, you must be very relieved at the outcome of the appeal.'

'Very,' answered Margaret. She still found it difficult to warm to the man who had caused all their problems in the first place. Had he refused a lease on the land, none of this would have been necessary. He knew that as well as she. There was no point in dwelling on it now.

'I overheard what you said, that there was some surplus cash in your fighting fund,' George went on. 'I wonder if I might make an impertinent suggestion?'

A few hackles began to rise. Margaret bristled with indignation. How dare he try to interfere in what they did with the money? Even now, in the face of his defeat, he was still trying to influence their lives.

His remark was received in stony silence.

George, apparently unaware of the atmosphere he had created, carried on.

'I gather from what has been said that there was one part of the Humbert plan to which there were no objections. I refer to the construction of a golf course in the glen.'

Hearing the Marquis speaking, one or two others joined the group around him, hoping he was not about to spring any more unpleasant surprises on them.

Desmond it was who broke the silence.

'I believe there are a few of us who would have made good use of such a facility had it been available.'

Despite their resentment towards George Monteith, the others had to agree. Several added a cautious affirmation.

'Suppose I provided the land. Would you people be prepared to build the course?' George was amused to see the stunned look on all their faces.

'Personally, I'd welcome the idea but I'm afraid the cost would amount to far more than we've been able to raise,' Celia protested.

'If a Charitable Trust was formed, it could gain access to certain grants,' Margaret intervened. She had been a keen golfer during her working days in Edinburgh. When she came here to live it had been one of the activities she had missed most. Despite her resentment at the Marquis's interference, she found herself warming to the idea.

'What site do you have in mind exactly?' asked Desmond.

'The same as shown on the development plan, the glen that runs up behind the Tigh na Broch,' George told them. 'Duncan McLeod is finding the farm a bit too much for him to cope with these days. I have already suggested that he give up that section of the grazing. The area will just be left lying fallow if you don't make use of it.'

Margaret drew in a deep breath and managed a smile as she spoke in her special, professional voice. 'It's a very generous offer, my lord. If you will put your agreement donating the land in writing, I'll call a meeting of interested parties and we'll talk about it.'

'Done!' said George and called for drinks all round.

Kirsty watched George return to stand beside his wife. She noted how casually he placed his arm around Cissy's shoulders and joined in with the general laughter at some casual remark of his wife's. She sighed, resigned to the fact that the couple's differences had been resolved. She should be pleased for them, after all they were friends . . . both of them. Thoughtfully, she pulled another pint.

It was gone ten o'clock when the door flew open to admit Angus Dewar, who seemed to be running an out-of-the-ordinary ferry service this evening. Flora looked up expectantly and was not disappointed.

As Alan fought his way to the bar, she pulled a pint for him. 'I was beginning to think you weren't going to come,' she told him, placing the brimming glass on the mat in front of him.

'The traffic was terrible until I got as far as the Rest and Be Thankful. After that it thinned out bit. It's further to Dunoon than I imagined.'

'What did they say?'

'Look, can you leave this?' he urged her. 'It's still quite warm outside . . . I fancy a walk up the hill.'

Flora glanced down at her flimsy shoes and debated whether she should risk them on the rough pathway. There was urgency in Alan's tone. It was obvious that he had something important to talk about. Throwing all caution to the wind, she put down her glass cloth and said to Kirsty, 'That's me for the evening. I'm off now.'

Kirsty glanced from one to the other and nodded.

'OK,' she said. 'Don't do anything I wouldn't do!'

'That gives her plenty of leeway,' observed Rob Fullerton's son Kenny as he took Flora's place at the pumps. There was never any shortage of helpers in the Tacksman's Bar.

They struggled up the steep steps cut into the side of the hill and came out on to a wide meadow.

Thankfully, Flora pulled off her sandals and ran barefoot on turf which, in the absence of cattle, now long gone from the island, grew freely with silky spikes of fescue and wild oat waving in the evening breeze.

Along the well-trodden path, the grass was shorter and here grew small alpine flowers, purple thyme and the pinky-white stonecrop of a variety specific to Eisdalsa. Here and there bright yellow potentilla and the delicate blue of the harebell, shimmered against the darker foliage of heather yet to flower. Along the cliff edge, the thorny whins were thrown into silhouette against the reddening skies of the dying day. The heavy scent of their golden flowers filled the air, blending with the salty tang of the ocean.

They had reached the look-out point where, at some time, long ago, a cairn had been raised. On its flattened top a bronze plaque indicated the position of islands in the sound and named all but the smallest of the rocky outcrops.

Alan flung himself down upon the soft turf and surveyed the wide expanse of ocean. The sea was in a calmer mood now that the evening breeze had changed direction. Each dark rocky islet wore a white frill of gently breaking surf and the water-filled quarries at the foot of the hill mirrored the slowly moving clouds, pink and purple in the rays of the setting sun.

He drew in a deep breath and stretched lazily.

'Well?' Flora asked.

'Well, what?' he teased.

'What did they say?'

'They said, if I felt I could manage with Janice's help alone . . . without additional cover from an Associate Partner . . . they would be pleased to have me stay on permanently.'

'That's wonderful!' she cried. 'I thought you were going to be asked to remain only until they could find a replacement.'

'So did I.' He hesitated, unsure how to proceed. 'I couldn't give them an answer . . . not right away.'

She seemed disappointed. 'Oh?' she asked

'Well, to begin with, there's the small question of a premium . . . I'd have to find some capital from somewhere and the unhappy truth is, my job in the oil fields just about cleared the debts I ran up during my training.'

'Is it a lot of money?'

'Well, let's say it's more than I have managed to save since I came here.'

'There are always bank loans,' she suggested, hopefully.

'Yes, there are several sources of finance that I might be able to call on, but that would mean making a long-term commitment. I'm not sure that I'm ready to do that.'

'It's not the most lucrative practice, I know,' said Flora sadly, 'but I had hoped you might have come to recognise the other advantages of staying on here . . . in addition to the money you might make.'

'Oh, I have. That's why I asked for time to consider the offer.'

Alan sat up, locking his hands around his knees. Continuing to concentrate his gaze upon the distant islands he added, 'It was really a question of giving *you* time to consider the offer.'

'Why? What difference would my opinion make to your choice of a job?' Hardly able to breathe, Flora listened to her own words echoing in her head, unable to believe that the moment she had dreamed of might have arrived.

'It would make *all* the difference. Don't you know that?'

His voice had taken on a deeper tone. There was a catch in his throat as he continued, 'I can't carry on working here . . .'

Panic-stricken, she too sat up and turned to face him.
'No?'

He continued as if she had not spoken. '. . . unless you will promise to remain here with me.'

He turned to study her face.

'How long were you thinking of?' she whispered.

'Oh, about forty or fifty years should be long enough.'
He leaned over her and kissed her gently on the lips.

Suddenly they were in each other's arms, devouring
one another with their kisses. After a few moments,
which might have been hours for all Alan knew, she
pulled away from him and began to laugh.

Her chuckles turned into hysterical laughter. Thinking
that the excitement of the day and an unusually large consumption of alcohol had finally taken their toll, Alan was
on the point of administering the customary slap on the
face, when she stopped as suddenly as she had begun.

'What's so funny?' he asked.

'This isn't the first time you've been known to have
your way with a woman in the heather,' she giggled
again.

'Why? What do you mean?'

She explained.

'Good Lord,' he was quite shocked. 'It just shows you
how careful you have to be in a place like this.'

'It certainly lends a whole new meaning to the idea of
bird watching,' she said, wiping the tears of laughter from
her eyes.

'No wonder they're called twitchers!' He joined in
with her high spirits.

'But,' she answered, kissing him again, 'I don't think
they'd frown so much upon husbands and wives doing it
. . .'

More seriously now, she asked him, 'Did Dad tell you
about the donation which came from Queensland?'

'I gather there were two rather generous cheques
today.'

'The Australian one was from Jack McDougal. He must have decided to send it before the result of the enquiry was known.'

'A bit like an American Presidential candidate conceding defeat would you say?'

'Maybe . . .'

'What are you thinking?'

'I was wondering if we should make some gesture . . . ask him back for a proper holiday, perhaps. He really wasn't such a bad sort . . . doing his job, that's all.'

Alan looked up sharply, studying her face intently. Did he have a rival still?

'I've no objection to you asking him to our wedding,' he said at last. 'I might even invite him to be my best man!'

She kissed him quickly on the forehead and he gathered her into his arms once again.

The sun had almost disappeared behind Ben More as, hand in hand, Flora still in her stockinged feet, they negotiated the steep slope to the head of the cliff path. While she replaced her shoes, Alan peered down into the northernmost quarry, that which had been destined to become a marina.

Jack's marker posts were still in position just as he had fixed them three months before. The one nearest the sea had been tipped over by the gales and looked ready to pull right out of the ground. The others provided convenient perches for a group of black-backed gulls, resting from their day's labours. From somewhere to the south he heard the unmistakable chattering of a flock of oyster-catchers and then, just as the sun dipped below the mountains to the north, a pair of cormorants skimmed across the waves, following the western shore and travelling northwards towards their roost on the cliffs of Caisteal an Spuilleadair. The two dark shadows rose slightly to clear the outlying rocks and dipped again towards the water. It seemed as though they were saluting the lovers as they passed.

'Your father was right, you know . . . nothing ever really changes,' Alan murmured as she slipped her arm through his. 'All of this . . . it's been here forever. Nothing can make it go away.'

'Make no mistake about it,' she assured him, 'things are changing all the time . . . but with any luck, it will be so slowly you'll never notice it.'